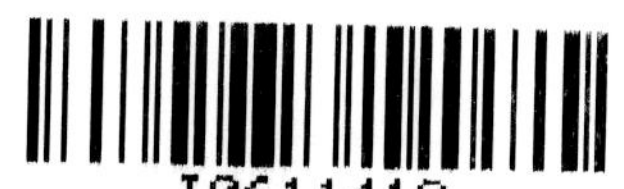
I0611412

ALSO BY ADAM SYDNEY

My Heart Is a Drummer

Yolanda Polanski and the Bus to Sheboygan

Adam Sydney

Newcraft Press ✚ Tucson, Arizona

YOLANDA POLANSKI AND THE BUS TO SHEBOYGAN

Published by Newcraft Press, Tucson, Arizona.

ISBN: 978-0-9851636-3-1

newcraftpress.com
facebook.com/NewcraftPress
adamsydney.wordpress.com
twitter.com/adamsydney1

Acknowledgements

I would like to thank a few people who have been instrumental in the creation of this novel. Their generous support has made all the difference: Tre Cox, Ginia Desmond, Joséphine Dubois, Allen Gibson, Eric Kaldahl, Tim Keene, Gail Sydney, Cassandra Walsh Rohland, and Simon Woodham.

1

You scared me.

Mr. Krimm's left nipple was noticeably larger than his right, surprised and staring, the eye of a belligerent rainbow trout. In contrast, the other nipple looked down, disappointed with itself, which I supposed it had a right to be.

I'd seen them both on his "home page." Mr. Krimm had been a boy wrestler, and his imbalance was clear in an especially sweaty shot. In it, he gritted his teeth, straining at his opponent, while his nipples went about their day behind their Lycra, imperious and affronting, mild and downcast. I wondered if they were ever to meet, would they wrestle? Or perhaps they would be glad to finally get a good look at each other and embrace, two long lost brothers, rubbing noses like two Eskimo.

As I sat across from him, I couldn't help but wonder what else was out of balance with Mr. Krimm. His face was regular and flat as the prairies it had sprung from—and as flat as the accent those prairies had spawned. He had two, similar hands and, presumably, two regular feet, because he'd walked with a steady gait. But I'd observed that his step over-controlled the natural sway of the rear. I had a feeling that his left nipple wouldn't approve of this and his right nipple wouldn't say anything but would secretly resent Mr. Krimm for the weakness.

Did our physical appearance betray our souls? My left ear was quite a bit higher than my right. It caused my glasses to be always crooked, and I felt certain that this made me look delightfully unaware, unselfconscious and a little disheveled—none of which was true in the slightest. In fact, it was such an uncommon physical trait that I wondered if crooked ears were a sign of a preternatural empathy in those who always seemed to have one ear cocked, listening for the subtle signs of the human heart. My fellow travelers.

"But I don't understand, Miss Polanski."

I sensed Mr. Krimm didn't like me, possibly because he could see that I embraced disharmony. I didn't hide it under layers of cotton and lapels.

Perhaps our personal relationship with our deformities betrayed even more than just our souls? I instantly detected Mr. Krimm's philosophy of life: a duality in which there could only ever be one dominant partner, one submissive.

Pushing my glasses into an even more brazen angle, I moved to knock my opponent off balance. "Tits pretty straightforward, Mr. Krimm. I'm completely different from any other teacher you'll ever meet for the nipple fact that I treat my students as peers, and they act like them."

It had the desired effect. His face crumpled, unsure, for a moment. He was pinned.

He went on, more hesitantly. "But they're six."

"I know."

"They're not your peers."

I smiled, pushing the left side of my glasses so high that I saw two Mr. Krimms, blinking and helpless. Time for the sleeper hold.

"Ahh, but I don't believe they *are* my peers. I just teat them as if they're my peers."

In my head, I slowly counted: one… two… three. And then I slammed the mat. Mr. Krimm had been an interesting opponent, but far too easy to overcome. In my mind, I began to rearrange the little chairs in my new classroom into groupings of seven students each, which naturally would form perfect quadrilaterals: the shape of success.

But I was a bit too hasty: "Well, thank you, Miss Polanski. We'll be in touch."

He'd squirmed out of my grasp just before the bell! I had to get him prone again, against the ropes.

"*Ms.*"

"Sorry. *Ms.*"

"But my resume, you haven't even looked at tit—"

"I'm sorry, but you seem to be using terms for nipples quite a bit. Why is that?"

"Why do you think you've noticed them?"

"They've been fairly obvious."

"Well, the left one, anyway."

"I'm sorry?"

"There's nothing wrong with inequality, Mr. Krimm. Nothing is truly equal in this world. Inequality doesn't always lead to a winner and a loser; it's often a challenge that encourages us to personally excel. For instance, I excelled at guano farming in Tlaxcalacingo, yet I never looked down on the natives—even when I was looking down *toward* them. You'd like to excel, wouldn't you, Mr. Krimm?"

At this, he stopped short and suppressed a grin. I felt as if it were my turn on the mat.

The grin expelled an "Oh."

And I actually began to perspire! For a moment, I believed that he'd realized the true extent of my advantage—my natural empathic powers—but I remained calm, my hands folded serenely in my lap. I sensed this behavior would calm him.

"'Oh,' Mr. Krimm?"

"We'll be in touch."

"But I think it's all just been a nipple misunderstanding—"

"No. No, don't do that."

"But you and I both know that I'm the perfect candidate to teat at this school—"

"You can stop that now, Miss Polanski." He now seemed awfully good-humored. "But why me?"

I instinctively knew when to keep quiet.

"I never actually *said* you didn't have the job! John knows I'm more careful than that."

I shrugged; it was the right thing to do in the circumstance. It also gave me time to reformulate my attack, although I still perceived that Mr. Krimm's physical irregularity was his most sensitive spot. Or *spots*, so to speak.

He'd now grown almost conspiratorial toward me: "Actually, you were pretty good."

"But not good enough for the job."

Mr. Krimm's smile faltered a bit at the gravity of my voice. "I'm sorry?"

"You just said I wouldn't be hired."

Then I saw the unmistakable glint of fear in his eyes, and I focused my attention on the dusty, tropical houseplant in the window behind him. Just like Mr. Krimm, it struggled to survive against its very own nature and would eventually pay for its mistake. I almost pitied it for a moment.

"But this is not the Amazon, Mr. Krimm."

"What?!"

"I'm worried about you. You're going to regret turning me down, and regret can be so..."

The smile was gone now. "And if this had been an actual interview—"

"...so regretful."

Down for the count. Game, set and match. The surrender in his eyes was so clear, so abject, that even an ordinary person would have felt it. I just had to hope that my god-given sensitivity would ensure as swift a victory with my larger mission, too. After all, this town cried out for help to me, desperate for my gift, perhaps even my leadership. I couldn't let it down.

"I'm terribly sorry, Miss Polanski. I misunderstood what was going on here. But no, I'm not hiring you."

I rose, having always lived by the maxim that one should part from a position of advantage.

"Oh, and Mr. Krimm—" I leaned into him, my glasses so crooked now that I found it difficult to focus. He stared up at me, his mouth in the shape of a certain poplar in Sandusky, Ohio. The memory was a pleasant one, and I found myself wanting to wrestle the leafy, Erie summer off his lips.

"—nipple."

* * *

Arby's.

Her weakness was mediocrity, but her strength was an unerring ability to dismiss this fact—to rise above. A Midwest titan!

I paused at the edge of Mrs. Stefano's table, finally setting things in motion. "Oh, what a coincidence!"

She looked up from her wrinkled foil and caloric mess—a fawn, a kitten—and I knew. I knew.

I continued. "We met at Darby Hills Elementary? I was in last week. For an interview with Mr. Krimm."

She put down the fry. Not the most promising reaction (I knew the importance of this fry to Mrs. Stefano, and to deny herself—!), but I'd dealt with and succeeded in spite of much sharper reactions. In fact, my interview with Mr. Krimm had been sharper, but his sharpness was just what I'd needed to slice through the fallacy of my far too humble self-worth in regards to my natural talents. The last month had been crammed full of epiphanies; it groaned with revelations.

As far back as I could remember, I'd always just accepted my uncanny ability to read people as a gift I'd been born with—something on which I really couldn't improve and for which I really couldn't take credit. So in a sense, it was my ability to see right into the soul of others that had provided significance to recent signs and directed me to the place where I was most needed: Two Rivers, Wisconsin. I'd been merely passive, a vessel, a slave to my powers.

But now, as I inspected Mrs. Stefano's shirt, I suddenly realized that I'd always been much more active in the process. I wasn't just some sort of slack-jawed psychic-vibration receptor; I was an active interpreter, applying a keen understanding of psychological currents to the millions of indicators human beings offered each other on a daily basis, from which I carefully strung together a cohesive narrative of their behavior—their life! It had never been an innate gift at all! It was a skill I'd been consistently sharpening for years, honed against the lethal barbs that people turned out toward the world in their desire for an imagined safety that was, frankly, available to none of us.

Mrs. Stefano was wearing a shirt that sported a pattern of repeating teddy bears. Black, brown, beige, black, brown, beige. In the past, I'd seen her in dresses, shirts, and even a kind of jumpsuit, all of which featured cartoon animals as a theme. (The jumpsuit had been covered with kangaroos, and only later did I notice that it included a large "pouch" of its own over Mrs. Stefano's well-rounded middle.) (She appeared to keep Stella D'Oro breadsticks within.)

Although these fashion decisions lent her an air of juvenility that was profoundly unwarranted, at last I'd come to realize that I'd been drawn to her for more than just a "feeling" that she was the right person for the job I was about to give her. Unaware of my own perceptiveness, I'd not only connected the subconscious dots presented to me—I'd reconstructed her dominant, personal psychodrama!

I recognized now that this was the *true* reason I'd chosen her.

And the psychodrama was all so clear to me now. Mrs. Stefano's father had loved his dog more than his daughter—probably a miniature Schnauzer or Corgi/Lab mix—and she'd always been painfully aware of the fact. When she was thirteen, or possibly as late as thirteen and a half, she'd attempted to poison the dog with chocolate cupcakes but succeeded only in causing massive diarrhea in the animal, which she was forced to clean up. The guilt, coupled with the smell of her rival's b.m., had forged a lifelong wound in her heart that she'd never been able to heal.

But Mrs. Stefano was a resourceful woman, psychologically speaking. Instead of collapsing under the pressure of such trauma, she was *strengthened* by it! Now, in her fifties, she finally felt comfortable embracing the truth that had nearly crushed her as a child. In fact, she almost *flew* this wound, a flag across her large chest. And the animals, who'd once received the love she'd so desperately craved, were tiny now, under her direct control. They reminded her—every time she looked in the mirror—how strong she really was. After all, wearing such unfortunate clothing could only ever be attempted by a person with a profoundly healthy self-confidence.

I was in the presence of an extraordinary victor.

Feeling the need to praise her, instead I simply glanced at her espadrilles, which played peek-a-boo with toes pointed in a surprising variety of directions.

"Oh, I remember now. *Ms.* Polanski." Clearly, Mr. Krimm had mentioned my fighting spirit to her, because Mrs. Stefano suddenly averted her gaze. Step one: De-fuse.

I instinctively softened my voice: "It seemed the perfect position for me—I'm new to Two Rivers—but, I don't know. I usually use cartoons quite a bit with my students. You know, fairy tales and such. Stuffed animals. I love anthropomorphic whimsy. Skinks, kangaroos, that sort of thing. But I just got the feeling that Mr. Krimm doesn't appreciate the beauty of, well," and here, I couldn't help swallowing back some discomfort at the colloquialism, "cute critters'. His eyes reflect merely competence. Does that make sense? A tepid PTA meeting followed by a potluck with Wal-Mart tablecloths and 'lite' dressings? In that vein."

Mrs. Stefano considered her "meal" intensely, clearly debating whether she could live with herself if she were to leave it half-eaten. But food had always been one of her weapons against the injustice of life, from the poison chocolate cupcake to her present, and also doubtlessly poisonous, "All-American Roastburger." I knew she'd remain in her booth.

That was because after a week of surveillance, I'd determined that lunchtime at Arby's was the perfect occasion to approach her. It was Mrs. Stefano's moment of weakness; her soul would be as open as her mouth. She always sat in the corner, surveying the dining room as if it were her kingdom, as if her fondest dream had come true and it were here, before her, processed, sticky, and underwhelming.

My second choice to approach her had been the post office—she was constantly at the post office—but there, she seemed much more guarded, somehow, clutching her large parcels to her chest and peeking around them at the people in line behind her. As there could be no logical reason on earth to be guilty about sending large parcels through the United States Postal Service, I realized that my next step would be to determine the cause of this particular flaw.

But Mrs. Stefano surprised me: she rose. "I have to go."

This was my only chance for success; I couldn't let go. "After all, what's wrong with some light-hearted play in class? Look at your beautiful blouse! You see, that's what I mean: teddy bears! How… how merry."

She glanced at me sharply, her pug nose crinkling. "I really have to get back to work."

"And Mr. Krimm said—right to my face—that he wouldn't hire me."

"I don't know anything about that."

"I was so hurt that when I got home, I wished I'd had something just like a teddy bear to comfort me. Soft and plush—"

"Bye." At this, she turned and practically ran out of the restaurant, her "cankles" jiggling, full of varicose veins vying for prominence beneath her denim skirt.

But what Mrs. Stefano did not yet understand was that Ms. Yolanda Jean Polanski had once removed a roofing staple from the center of her right hand with the edge of an American Express Titanium card—without anesthesia and without slowing down on the west gable. (Claude apologized later for the ensuing infection, but we never roofed together again.) Did she really think that I would give up this easily?

I followed her out to her white Hyundai Accent with its tell-tale dent in the rear fender. Sometimes, this was the only thing that could help me identify it in a parking lot full of white Asian cars. In fact, the dent was almost a friend now, and I smiled to myself upon finally approaching it so closely. Of course there were other ways of identifying cars and people, but I hadn't the patience for license plates. They were simply nonsense words and numbers that never added up to anything significant. If police officers could just learn to be a bit more observant, they wouldn't even need them.

"Did you make that blouse yourself? You must be so handy—"

She stopped at the door of her Hyundai and whirled around at me, her shirred skirt flaring momentarily into the shape of disappointment. Mrs. Stefano was crying! Somehow, I'd managed to be even more effective than I'd hoped—I'd zeroed in on the pain of her childhood, and she was now thrashing with these memories. I imagined her battling with a beast of a sewing machine at her kitchen table, sweat on her upper lip and the fire of a righteous woman in her heart. She was a fighter! And Mrs. Stefano wore her victorious, regrettable creations proudly; in this case, I noticed for the first time that her blouse featured a Peter Pan collar, and I shuddered.

But then I felt pride in her work—in her—too, surer than ever that she'd be the perfect partner. Members of Team Polanski never flinched at reality. We overcame it.

"Look. Please. Please! Just leave me alone." She fumbled for her keys, her pudgy hands stabbing into her purse.

But it was more than her father's dog-love that was upsetting Mrs. Stefano; I'd touched on a subject that absolutely terrified her, an immediate threat that had been borne of her craving for paternal love.

And then it became crystal clear.

"I know, Mrs. Stefano. About Mr. Krimm."

This increased her frenzy. "I can call 911!"

"Of course, you can. But who would they believe? You or him?"

"What?!"

"And what would your 'furry friends' think?"

She screwed up her face at this. "But that's not illegal!"

"Isn't it?" Perhaps the laws on sexual harassment were different in Wisconsin? I made a mental image-note of Mrs. Stefano wearing the two O's in Google like a pair of glasses.

"I'll have to 'web search' it."

Was Mr. Krimm taking advantage of her need because of some secret he held over her? "I feel you should know that a goat herder in Tajikstan kept me more or less prisoner in a cave for a month after he'd discovered that I was an accidentally illegal alien. Apparently, he liked to watch me rinse out my underclothes."

"What do you want?"

"Extra sausage."

It took a moment for Mrs. Stefano's entire body to freeze.

"We both know you're not vegetarian, Mrs. Stefano."

"Pizza?"

Waiting for her to blink, I studied her closely and found that here was actually something majestic about her bulk, colossal. Even though I'd quickly uncovered her darkest secrets and laid them bare before the both of us, she still stood tall, buxom.

"'I lift my lamp beside the golden door!'"

It was barely audible: "What?"

My heart warmed: I sorely needed an ally who could pull off "innocent" like this, and I knew Mrs. Stefano understood me perfectly. (After the fire at the bakery, Claude had always insisted on one thing: "innocence," his pencil moustache confirming it, demanding it. I could never be sure.)

She and I were two whirlpools joining, widening, deepening.

"What we could draw down into the frigid depths of the ocean together, eh, Mrs. Stefano! Joey's Pizzeria, tonight, seven p.m."

I turned away, chuckling when I heard her last murmur.

"But I'm lactose-intolerant."

2

You don't scare me.

Two Rivers, Wisconsin. Bethlehem, Judea. (The locals referred to their town as "Trivvers," an unfortunate contraction that bore no reason to acknowledge it ever, ever again.)

If it weren't for the lake... How often had I spoken these words to myself in the last few weeks? The lake stopped the Midwest in its tracks; it would never itself *be* the Midwest. The flat lands to my west harbored "I Can't Believe It's Not Butter" and corners in the spare bedrooms of ranch houses featuring photo shrines to the high-school athletic careers of people now laboring away as breezy receptionists or bartenders. The flat lands harbored cows.

But Lake Michigan held only its secrets below; secrets I didn't wish ever to know.

Of course, I already understood every secret in Two Rivers, and its ultimate secret was that Two Rivers' deepest, darkest mysteries involved nothing more scandalous than a niece's dislike of homemade teapot cozies willed by ancient aunts now sitting at the back of cupboards, forgotten. And stolen Milky Ways. But only the short kind.

"The house is haunted."

"Haunted?"

Samuel Ziewick stepped across my threshold, penetrating my privacy. We both felt it.

"It was a joke, Sam."

"Oh!"

"Why aren't you laughing?"

"Why aren't you?"

"Let me get you some cranberry juice, Sam."

"Sammy. Please, everybody calls me Sammy."

I gestured toward my couch, immediately intuiting his strategy for the day, and therefore, mine. Today, his was feigned innocence; mine, playful resourcefulness.

"Well, I'm not everyone. Am I, Sam."

He eyed the couch, eager to give me the impression that he didn't want to sit there, but he did. Naturally.

"So how are you settling in, Yolanda?"

I was in the kitchen, preparing his drink. The kitchen still smelled of the dumplings of previous residents (does every kitchen in Wisconsin smell of dumplings?), but I'd conquer that, too. All in good time.

"Everybody calls me Yolanda."

"But that's what I just called you."

"But you're not everyone. Not to me."

The living room smelled of dumplings, too. In fact, the whole house did. I swallowed a wave of nausea when I momentarily imagined the previous tenants. There was Boggle involved. Boggle, Velveeta nachos and DVDs of America's Funniest Videos. I was certain of it. The place really was haunted.

He giggled, of all things. "You always get me going."

"Do I? Here's your drink."

"Thanks. So what's the problem?" He took a sip and choked on it before laughing outright. "Is there booze in this?"

"We're both adults, Sam."

Now he was howling. "You get me every time!"

Cat and mouse. And Samuel Ziewick was most definitely the mouse.

"The shower's dripping."

The house had been built in 1947, perhaps a brief moment in which the residents of Two Rivers believed there was such a thing as an ever-expanding, open-sky future. So perhaps in contrast, the structure was anemic—rooms that furiously denied space, mean windows that squinted at the street, a ceiling whose true purpose was to crush its hated victims below out of existence. The toilet seat was always so, so cold. (My new residence brought to mind a certain nuclear shelter in South Korea. Claude had called its atmosphere "nut-crushing.")

"Do you remember what I told you?" Sam had sobered a bit, pushing a lock of hair out of his face.

"Samuel. I remember everything you've ever told me."

Sam Ziewick was by far the best Two Rivers had ever seen. He had hands that sculpted air, distinguished features that drew you back to them and clothing that perfectly caressed the body beneath. The most furious rumor in Two Rivers was that he'd actually lived in Milwaukee for a whole year. Which almost touched Chicago. Which almost touched the big, wide world.

So how had Sam managed to grow up and live most of his life smarter and better-looking than his fellow townspeople? What was his personal psychodrama, the moment that had defined the man who stood before me now? I had to shift my empathic forensics into high gear.

It took merely an instant for the relevant evidence to become clear: he drove a late model Cadillac; he wore Brut cologne; he retreated into deliberately sophomoric humor; his middle name was Irwin.

"Is that right?"

"Yes, Sam. I must remind you of Brenda."

"Excuse me?"

"Bryn, then."

Obviously, when Sam had been in first grade, a young girl, headstrong, perceptive, had enrolled in his school, and he'd become immediately smitten with her, an equal. She'd moved from Detroit, probably, or some other Cadillac-producing city where street smarts were necessary for survival. And she'd immediately recognized a worthy ally. Unfortunately, when little Brenda or Bryn (I was almost certain it was Brenda, but whatever it was, it had to have sounded like "Brut" had publicly returned his interest in the middle of the crowded cafeteria, Sam had panicked, worried that all his classmates from Two Rivers would think he believed he was better than they. So, instead, he called her a "doo-doo head" ("poo-poo face?"), cementing his position forever in the minds of the townspeople as the jokester, "just one of the guys." And ever since, he'd giggled in the face of sophistication—although it took a moderately sophisticated person to identify sophistication in the first place! So in fact, the giggles had the unintended, converse effect of indicating his latent erudition to those who were sufficiently erudite to recognize it.

And I was. The details of the defining moment of his life were as plain as day to me.

Disappointingly, Sam was laughing again. I couldn't imagine how this awkward sense of humor could actually disrupt my plans per se, but it was disquieting, nonetheless.

So I laughed, louder, harder, longer. I laughed to compete, to equalize. I laughed as Marie Antoinette did before the guillotine, the sunshine on her teeth chilling all in attendance, mirthless, pitiless.

"Stop! I'm going to wet myself!"

I allowed his Two Rivers comment to pass out of existence as I allowed so much of unenlightened Two Rivers to do—simply raindrops running down my coat, joining under my feet, coming together down, down into the sewers that collected all that the town presently had to offer.

It hadn't had much to offer Sam, so far. And now, clinging unrelentingly to the ghost of little Brenda and everything she would have offered him, he was bereft, driving a car her father could have built, wearing a cologne that reminded him of her and the fall of 1975, defending himself with a wall of childish laughter against minds who could never understand. And his middle name was Irwin.

"You do know, Sam, that *Coupe de Ville* is French for 'the wound of the town.'"

"The wound of the—"

"Tell me something. If I wanted to break my lease, what would I need to do?"

He looked much more presentable frowning. "Why would you ask me that?"

"The shower... constant dripping..." I allowed my voice to trail off.

"Do you remember, I told you to be sure to twist the shower head counterclockwise whenever it starts dripping?"

"Was it counterclockwise?"

"Here." He handed me his Seabreeze and passed into the hallway, the scent of vintage grooming products in his wake. And me. Assuredly me.

I moved as if to block the view into my bedroom. "I'm afraid you caught me while I was sorting my... my underthings, Sam."

But he was already in the washroom, desperate to give the impression that he hadn't heard me, that he wouldn't find some excuse to bleed the radiator next to my bed.

I followed him, disturbed and then assured that the only reason he was wearing "Dockers" trousers was for the purpose of Two Rivers stealth.

After all, a landlord had so many transactions, so many interactions. The utter banality of "Dockers" would calm the locals much as his humor did, gradually taming them, a cleverly painted decoy floating in their midst.

And I, suddenly emerging from the rushes, would raise my sight on the gaggle, both barrels soon obscuring the air with the acrid smoke of renaissance—a gun-toting missionary!

"They must positively flock to you, by now."

"Pardon?"

"The 'Dockers.'" He looked down, as if he had no idea what I meant. "Well, they're stain-resistant."

"You don't miss a trick, do you, Sam."

"I don't?"

I hesitated in the doorway, my eyes firmly on the vinyl flooring. "It's just that I'm not used to joining a man in a situation that's so—intimate."

"Oh, that's okay; just stay there. You see, you just twist the shower head like this, and the drip will stop. See?"

"Yes."

"Is the toilet giving you any problems? The last folks who lived here said that when the bowl was really full it would—"

"Sam, Sam, Sam! Please. You don't have to impress me."

"Impress you?"

"I stand in awe."

"You do." He studied me for a moment, lifting, opening, unbuttoning from across the lavatory. I felt my face flush, suddenly unsure if my attraction were an act any longer, or something else, something real not only for him, but finally for me, too.

Because if there was one thing to which I responded—almost a reflex, animal, biological—it was a reckless man. Clearly, he'd sublimated his desire for little Brenda all these years with a yearning to break free from his existence and run wild through the world, aching to dare, to play, to win!

I was prepared to sacrifice everything for my plan, but my body? The idea was absurd, and yet exquisite: what could be more effective than physical honesty? Sam was too clever for anything less; he'd recognize insincerity as quickly as I'd recognized the true motive behind the "Dockers" and the comments in poor taste formulated merely to put Two Rivers at ease.

Astonished, I realized that truly, it had been inevitable all along. In targeting the most urbane, perceptive man in town to help me in my mission, how could I expect any other outcome? Perhaps it had been an obscure motivation for the plan in the first place! Dizzying, I considered the tapestry of the unconscious: seemingly disparate colors and textures that met up, crossing in the most unexpected angles, repeating far, far down the length in patterns that only could be seen—that only could be grasped!—with a cool perspective on the whole. The relentless grinding of life's eventuality, of its undeniable meaning gripped me. I felt certain he saw this in my blush, too—or perhaps he'd recognized it much sooner than I: that first moment we met in the driveway, the curtains of Two Rivers twitching at an event the likes of which its population would someday stand in utter awe.

As I did now. Finally, I understood that I'd known all along Sam would be a partner in my plan—the daredevil, the adventurer—hence my incarceration at 618 Frick Street.

"Raw sewage can be a real bitch."

It was my turn to chuckle.

Clearly I would have to make the first move—*our* first move. It wasn't quite time.

"All right, Sam. 'Raw sewage can be a real bitch.'"

* * *

With my back to the town, I gazed past the breakwater, knowing that I at least shared the steadying horizon with San Franciscans, with Habaneros, with Shanghainese. The waters of Lake Michigan eventually flowed into Oceania; I had to remain focused on that.

"Reow."

But even the stray cats of Two Rivers, Wisconsin were eager to draw me back, draw me down into the bake sales and snow mobile jamborees and J.C. Penney culottes that flapped in the wind like flags of surrender. Even the stray cats wanted me to discuss the weather primarily as it pertained to farming conditions. I pitied them for it. Even the stray cats were jejune.

"Rooww."

And this one couldn't have been more predictable: beige tabby, medium sized, medium-beige behavior. It twisted around my ankles, the clichéd purring boring the both of us even before it left its whiskered lips.

"You know, you can rise above this."

"I'm sorry?"

Mrs. Stefano had come up behind me. She wore beige culottes, much wider than they were long, and I shuddered at my finely honed powers of perception.

"I said, 'You can rise above this,' Mrs. Stefano. Everyone here can. J.C. Penney's. Ten-cents-off coupons. Pink ice milk that drools out of a machine."

"Well, I'm lactose-intolerant, so—"

"Correct answer. There are some things that deserve nothing less than intolerance."

"I see you've met Tabby III."

I sighed. "Don't tell me this town has named all of its strays, too? Has the Midwest squeezed every form of iconoclasm out of Two Rivers?"

"The guys at the marina name them. My favorite was Tabby II."

"Would I be expected to ask what happened to it? And Tabby I?"

"Tabby I got run over, but they didn't call him Tabby I. They just called him Tabby."

"Did they."

"And no one knows whatever happened to Tabby II. He was orange."

"Not beige? I'm sorry. Let's go."

I was distressed to note that the cat followed me, running ahead into the humid evening, stopping to rub against a street sign, speaking up to me from the long, shadowed grass as I passed it. The drone of a small plane above (Piper J-3? Cessna 172?) reminded me of the breezes and eddies and gales that blew across the plains, indifferent to the troubles of the inhabitants of Wisconsin. And here I was, flanked by two such inhabitants: a cat whose instincts were so deficient that I expected it to end up like "Tabby II" within the week—possibly at my own hands—and a woman who insisted on wearing cartoon-themed clothing in spite of the fact that she was being sexually harassed by her boss. Today, it was a homemade, yellow blouse sporting stylized sparrows that had somehow thwarted nature and gotten their beaks to smile.

But once again, I realized that there was a commendable bravery in Mrs. Stefano's manner—in the face of brutal oppression and salacious cruelty: cartoon sparrows! Perhaps she looked down at them scattered across her blouse while cowering near the water cooler or in a restroom stall, attuned to the slightest sign that Mr. Krimm was closing in. Perhaps her roiling heart was pacified, then, her perspective on the situation broadened. After all, what was hate, what was fear in a world that could celebrate cartoon sparrows whose open beaks produced perhaps the most apt appraisal of the futility of mankind that has ever been uttered: "Tweeeet!!!!"?

Mrs. Stefano squealed like a school girl when the cat ran between my legs, only to stop and look back at me, curious at its effect. I was careful to communicate that there was none.

"He likes you!"

"Don't change the subject."

"Then why are you doing this to me?" I didn't like the idea of a partner who whined at quite this pitch, but a few weeks in my company would lower her register. I had that effect.

"*For* you, not *to* you. *With* you. Surely, you don't expect me to stand aside and allow it to continue?"

"But there's nothing really wrong with it."

"You don't really believe that."

Mrs. Stefano looked close to tears again. No, she really didn't believe that. "What do you want?"

"I'd like to look forward now—to potentialities. To the cherries; I have a feeling we've both had enough of the pits."

"Roww-oww."

The cat was at least intelligent enough not to follow us into Joey's Pizzeria. Perhaps there were lines of propriety that even the stray souls of Two Rivers didn't cross. I hoped so. And if not, my plan would soon be providing the poor townspeople with much more challenging lines to cross, lines that were so far from their present lines that they almost blended with the distant horizon, like Lake Michigan and its silent, watery secrets. Soon, I would be drawing a line in the sand, and it would mean an endless, spreading universe to any Two Riverian brave enough to cross it.

But for now, I had to contend merely with "cheesy buffalo wings" and "deep-fried pizza balls." Mrs. Stefano and I studied the "laminated" menu; I struggled inwardly to keep my distaste under control. The restaurant touted neither quality nor price in its bill of fare; the value of its food was measured in ounces, and in two cases, pounds. I denied myself a recollection of Paris, of respect and love for the table, of *boeuf en croute* that was proof of the existence of god.

"—and a quarter pound of stuffed cheesy sticks with Ranch."

"Okay. And for you, ma'am?"

"Parlez-vous Francais?"

"Huh?"

"Small pizza. Sausage."

"The Pounder, or—"

"Yes! Yes. The 'Pounder.' Thank you."

Mrs. Stefano sucked her Mountain Dew as the server bounced off. "Pounder I hardly know her. I always say that."

"Mrs. Stefano. I want to help you."

"Help me?"

"Obviously, I know what's going on."

"Only help me?"

"Is there something else?"

"You said Mr. Krimm."

"Exactly."

"How is that helping *me*?"

"But you don't want it to continue, do you?"

Mrs. Stefano bit her straw, tears coming to her eyes. "What if I said yes? There's nothing wrong with it! What if I said I didn't care, because I'm providing a kind of a service!"

Normally, I was attuned to such psychological subtleties! How could I have made such a miscalculation? Mrs. Stefano was in love with her paternal substitute, Mr. Krimm!

Did I really expect to execute such a delicate, intricate mission if I were to make such fundamental blunders? Damage control was in order. (Claude had once crowned me the Queen of Damage Control, although they still came for him the next day, his tattoos rippling and glistening in the sun, his fencing mask retired forever. I could still smell his heady musk.)

"All right. But I assumed that as you're married—"

"My husband died last year."

"I'm sorry." Damage control. "I *am* sorry. I am." I took a deep breath, neurons flashing in pairs, in groups, stretching across empty space in a flurry of discrete goals. "I'll admit that Mr. Krimm has a certain—" I halted, visualizing the larger of the nipples. "But surely since you know what he did to me—I know your integrity, your strength runs deeper than that."

She squinted, and if I hadn't known very much better, I would have believed that she was "confused." Although my tactics had been proven slightly off-target, I had chosen my lieutenant wisely.

Finally: "Oh. I get it." Mrs. Stefano shook her head vigorously, twisting her straw in her fingers. Her voice concentrated itself into a stage whisper that was louder than her normal voice. "If I tell you, then you won't say anything. I shouldn't, but you're kind of forcing me to: Mr. Krimm wasn't supposed to tell you that he wouldn't hire you while he was interviewing you. He's supposed to send you a letter. He got into big trouble a few years ago, because the lady said, you know, 'How could he know that he didn't want to hire me until he'd interviewed everyone?' It was sort of discrimination. She still works at Darby Hills. Connie Jackson."

I sat back against the soiled vinyl and absorbed this piece of intelligence. Mrs. Stefano became more intriguing, more delightful by the minute. Not only did she have the chutzpah to fly in the face of her provincially innocent community and conduct a brazen affair with her superior (perhaps a dog-hating, surrogate father? I would have to do a little research into Mr. Krimm's pet ownership record), but she had a perverse pleasure in betraying him, too, therefore keeping his power over her in check.

"Your sparrows are merely camouflage, Mrs. Stefano."

"Excuse me?"

"Touché. But you're right, of course. So I suppose he's allergic? Or he's more of a cat person?"

"Excuse me?!"

"I won't blow your cover—if you don't blow mine!"

"So you promise you won't say anything to anybody? About you-know-what?"

"Please! I have more sense than that."

"Wait a minute. *Your* cover?"

"'Excuse me?'"

"You said *your* cover?"

"'Excuse me?'"

"I don't really understand."

"And that's exactly how we'll play it."

Mrs. Stefano sighed, staring too strongly at the mangled straw in her hand. It appeared that her hair style involved hot rollers. It wasn't something I normally offered as a component of my relationship with team members, but I found myself testing different cuts, styles that would narrow, perhaps even wizen, rather than accentuate the dimples that erupted across her face.

"Obviously long layers are in order, but why do I consistently find myself doing this?"

"Doing what?"

"Shaping acolytes into a facsimile of me. Or perhaps not of me, but of what I strive to become. But you are amazing as you are, Mrs. Stefano! And you don't know what's going on here because I have haven't bothered to tell you the plan. Don't you see?"

"No."

"Of course not! When I was eight years old, my Uncle Clarence promised me that he'd take me fishing if I spelled 'angular' correctly. Now it was during hurricane season, I'll grant him that, but after I immediately spelled it correctly, his excuses extended right up until his death twenty-four years later. I never even saw the inside of his boat."

At least Mrs. Stefano had stopped torturing her straw.

"You're wondering why it's taken me forty years to learn a lesson that's probably immediately obvious to you, and I'll tell you why: idealism. But you're ideal *as you are*, Mrs. Stefano. Truly. You're the perfect Mrs. Stefano. Your hair—your clothes—that wonderful straw—the entire façade and its cracks, which perhaps only I have ever truly appreciated—*you* have the formula for Mrs. Stefano, not I. Everything is as it should be."

She actually seemed heartened by my revelation. "So you're saying *everything* is really okay? Even *you-know-what*? I thought you just said I should stop."

I continued. "Don't you see? I was wrong. I still believe to this day that I would've made the best damned fisherwoman in Islamorada. But I suppose Uncle Clarence saw a Farah Fawcett, and I saw a Dorothy Hamill. And I was right! I was right. And I will no longer allow Uncle Clarence's presumptions to be mine. With you as my witness, Mrs. Stefano, I hereby disinherit misgivings of every kind."

It was a personal revelation! Mrs. Stefano would be my first team member with latitude, the first with autonomy. I vowed to no longer "shape," but rather to "empower." Instead of giving her the game plan, I'd give her only the goals; she would craft the best *Mrs. Stefano* tactic for attaining them. It was an exciting moment for me, and I could tell that it was an exciting moment for Mrs. Stefano, too, as some of her dimples had deepened.

"So what do you say? Are you up for it?"

"You really think it's okay?"

"More than okay—I think you're absolutely *perfect.*"

She made a high-pitched noise. "Well, okay then! And I should totally be 'myself?'"

"I wouldn't have it any other way. We are going to make a team the likes of which Two Rivers has never seen. And when we're finished, this town will be utterly transformed."

"And I'll do all the sewing?!"

I was about to ask her to clarify that last statement, but the cat was just outside the window, staring at me as it relaxed behind some shrubbery, daring me along with the rest of Two Rivers to wholeheartedly live up to my word. Challenging me to knock the town off its plodding course to utter obscurity.

I folded my hands over the napkin in my lap, refusing to be the first to break eye contact with the interloper outside. I had, in fact, accepted this challenge a month earlier on my fateful Greyhound bus trip to Sheboygan, and accepting it had been as absolute as my acceptance of Mrs. Stefano. Now, with her—and Sam Ziewick—by my side, I would not be stared down, and I would not be broken.

"Do you want one of my stuffed cheesy sticks with ranch?"

"I would love one, Mrs. Stefano. Thank you very much." The thing had the heft and shape of a flaccid penis. "It's going to take more than a few 'cheesy sticks' to keep us down, I can tell you that!"

"Oh, well, they're better with ranch."

"Please don't say 'ranch' again."

3

Where's my mommy?

"You have got to be kidding me." Del let out a hearty, hearty laugh—distinctly unnerving for me.

"No, I'm perfectly serious." Why were the ladies at home improvement stores always so incredulous when I needed to discuss my little projects?

Another guffaw erupted, which allowed me to see right down into her generous mouth and count her many silver fillings. "I'm sorry, but that's the craziest thing I've ever heard in my life! You're putting me on!"

I hadn't driven all the way to Two Rivers' sister city, Manitowoc, universally considered the slower of the siblings, to be laughed at like this. (Claude would have pointed out that I'd come to a store whose name sounded like a cross between "manure" and "retard.") (Of course, Claude would have then attempted to convince Del to join him in some sort of garden-tool theft ring, effectively destroying my plan before it had been executed.)

I smothered my ire. "Are you able to help me?"

"I don't even think that's legal!"

I had to gain the upper hand. I inspected her blunt nails, her worn blue jeans, her short, very coarse chestnut hair. Del's features brought to mind the grizzled face of a plains-burned Indian chief, one who hung on tenaciously to a freedom that everyone else in the tribe had long ago accepted as about to be trampled by the U.S. Cavalry. In a way, her utter disregard for the world's even most basic standards of beauty was admirable, but the thing of it was, she'd been "rode hard and put away wet," and it had clearly been she who had done the riding and the putting away.

I smiled politely. "Is Del short for Delilah?"

Almost too quickly to believe, Del's dismissive grin turned into a snarl. "Why would you say that?"

I was right! I'd revisit this revelation in a moment. "Just a guess. So my project—"

"Look, I don't know who the hell you're trying to kid with this Miss Priss act, and I don't know what you're trying to pull with me, but obviously, you're up to something illegal here, and I do not have to put up with this. *A secret room?!*"

"But I can assure you that—"

"You can *assure* me? You can *assure* me! What the hell is this, Masterpiece fucking Theatre? Honey, I've got half a mind to call the cops right now."

Damage control! (Claude, in his coarse, accurate way, would've given me three options at this point: flee, fuck or fight.) (He invariably chose the second.)

I stalled for a moment to think. "I'm terribly sorry if I've upset you—"

"I've worked here for ten years, and I've never had somebody walk in here and try to pull this kind of crap, asking me to build some James Bond bullshit secret room and talking like you're Queen Victoria and how many scarves are you wearing?! Are you, like, undercover or something? Is that what's going on here? Because if you are, you're going to have to act more like a real human being. This shit is not believable. Or is this some reality show?!" She looked around.

"But I can assu—I *am* a real human being. I am!"

Where was my psychoanalytical acuity when I needed it most? I scanned her quickly for clues, for insight into past experiences that had shaped who stood before me now—and quite menacingly, as a matter of fact. There were no immediate signs: the plaid shirt, the can of chewing tobacco, the large belt buckle of an American eagle, none of it seemed to provide any foothold for her personality, her needs, her desires. I was dry, and now, because of my instinct to trust her, I'd managed to put my entire plan for Two Rivers into jeopardy. I had to figure her out, and quickly.

And as always, it suddenly struck me: Delilah. Her name was the key to her personality!

Delilah, the girlfriend with the scissors. Clearly, she had a very passive relationship with her overbearing, possibly abusive and long-haired husband, hence her desire to hide her real name with a powerless diminutive. But she denied this weakness in other areas of her life, this inner, shorn Samson, by presenting a threatening demeanor, an act in which she pretended to demand dominance, yet secretly ached for guidance, for control by a stronger personality.

No wonder her hair was so short!

"Your husband wouldn't like the way you're speaking to me at all—"

"*Husband?!*" She screamed out a laugh, a futile attempt to erase the truth from my lips. "Are you hitting on me? Is that what's going on here? Because your skinny, crazy ass is about as far off the fucking mark as it could be."

Fluidly, I changed tack. "I'm just, I suppose, a little different than most of the folks around here. I can't help it! My clothes, I suppose my hair. The scarves. I mean, are you going to attack me for being different, too?" I held my breath, praying that she'd recognize the mistreatment we apparently had in common and hoping that the part of her heart damaged by all the taunts, all the cruelties over the years would open up to our similarities.

But Del only regarded me coolly, her ravaged skin screaming out for moisturizer.

"Is it for pot? Are you growing pot?"

I wasn't sure if a confirmation of her suspicion would be a good thing or a bad thing. I remained neutral. "Growing pot *is* illegal."

She hitched up her pants and inspected the floor as if looking for a place to spit. I had spent many hours over the course of a week evaluating each of the store's "associates" in the lumber department and had finally chosen Del simply because I had a good feeling about her. This had always been the core reason I chose everyone with whom I "associated," and I had never been proven wrong before. During my observations, I'd determined that her strength and attitude would be a definite asset to my team, but now I realized that I'd failed to formulate my recruitment strategy as carefully as I always had in the past. This time, I'd simply assumed my immediate psychological assessment during our conversation would be enough, but I found this tactic to be vastly misguided.

Although I knew her name was at the heart of it all, I simply couldn't decode the secret while under her towering menace. So I began desperately to consider alternative schemes to convince Del to join up—schemes that I knew could prove violently dangerous if misguided.

She leveled me with a blinkless stare, the veins in her eyes pronounced, angry. "Okay. If this is some test from corporate, I've already failed it, so why stop now. But I don't think it is. And for whatever reason, lady, you really rub me the wrong way, so I'd love to see you rotting away in jail. I'd also love to knock that smarmy, innocent look right off your face with a hammer. Now, I'm pretty sure that building a secret room in your house is illegal—especially since you're only renting it—and I really, *really* want to call the cops on you. But I don't want to go through all the paperwork and trial and shit, for a variety of reasons, so I'm going to do you a huge favor. I never, *ever* want to deal with you again, okay? There's the door. If you just walk out of it and make sure I never, *ever* lay eyes on you in Menard's again, you'll actually get away with it—*this time.*"

"Well, it wouldn't actually be a secret *room*, per se, more of a secret *closet*—"

"Lady—" I could actually hear her teeth gnash, the sound of an ancient, cursed door fighting the entrance of treasure seekers into the tomb it had guarded for millennia. "I'm about ready to go to jail myself for what I'm about to do to your face. Get the fuck out of here. *Now.*"

"But don't you want to 'stick it to the man' with me, as it were? After all, we've both been rejected by a patriarchal society that can't—"

She actually raised her fist.

"Two-thousand dollars."

My offer was immediately swallowed up by the beep of something backing up nearby, and Del's hand merely continued to the nametag perched atop her generous bosom. She flicked the edge of it with her thumb, keeping time to some hard-rock song in her mind all about irritation and murder. *Centurion,* my mind called out, *hear the trumpet call of your destiny!*

"For *me* to build—"

"Three-thousand dollars. Just a bookshelf in front of the closet."

"Mother fucker."

Del knew a minor element of my plan, now. I couldn't afford to have her acting against me with the intelligence she'd acquired, and I wasn't yet prepared to take more drastic measures to keep her silent. I'd simply have to knock down her resistance to me brick-by-brick as she built up the false closet in my home. Eventually, once I'd determined the key to her psychodrama, I would succeed.

"Please tell me you live in Manitowoc."

"Oh, is that how you pronounce it?"

"Shit."

"Two Rivers, actually."

"Shit!"

"Four-thousand."

Del looked around the lumber section again, perhaps seeking out the hidden camera of a reality show. But this really was reality—her new reality.

Someday, she'd thank me.

"But I want to kill you."

* * *

Two Rivers, Two Rivers, Two Rivers.

During the summer I spent in Brazil, I'd come to believe that the mud cart tracks and rocky footpaths of the old village had become the very arteries of my soul made somehow external by an unknowable force of nature. (Claude pointed out the many instances and types of feces on my "arteries;" I disregarded his humor.) It had always fascinated me how our surroundings could somehow become a part of us: an actual, physical manifestation of how we felt toward a particular time in our lives. And even the weather played a part, a percussion section, under and around the symphony, mutating in different, yet complementary rhythms.

But if Sao Domingo had spread out before me as the course of my very lifeblood, its thunderstorms revealing sunshine at the most unexpected moments just as my own hopes and inspirations would emerge as suddenly and as blessedly, today Two Rivers closed around my throat like a goiter. Its flat, grey sky was a steady constriction on the lungs that made it increasingly difficult to breathe—that made it increasingly difficult to *want* to breathe!

And that cat had insisted on following me home.

As I lay on my couch, fruitlessly wishing that my nearest neighbors would turn down their "classic rock" station (how could the experience of hearing "Sweet Home Alabama" for the ten-thousandth time be in any way "classic?") and warily watching the cat on my front porch as he warily watched me through the screen door, I forced my respiration into an easy, regular rhythm. The summer evenings in Two Rivers weren't completely insufferable, and its people had endless redeeming qualities, too, buried, perhaps unlearned. After all, they were the reason I was here at 618 Frick Street, to begin with. A missionary was nothing without her gentle savages.

My campaign was coming along nicely, too. Mrs. Stefano was onboard, Del would be soon, and Sam and I were communicating in such an intimate, charged way that I knew he would have no choice but to do anything I asked of him within the week. But could I, in turn, bridle his raw impetuousness? It was a challenge I was only too glad to wrestle. In oil, if necessary.

And of course, I had a meeting scheduled with Mr. Krimm for the following morning, so that important facet of my mission would once again be back on track.

Sheboygan, Sheboygan, Sheboygan.

My mind passed back again for the thousandth time to that fateful bus trip, to the night that changed the course of my life so utterly. Why did all my most profound events claw their way to the surface of my life at the oddest moments? My mind passed over a few: that urine-soaked restroom in Kiev where I saw the amazing work of a woman named Galina blooming across the wall of my stall and realized that I could never paint again. That urine-soaked adult daycare center in Palo Alto, where a Mr. Francis Solomon had tossed off the simplest of comments, "Food tastes better when you're younger," and I'd vowed to develop a hybrid of the russet potato and sweet yam. That urine-soaked street in Dublin, where I'd lost a sapphire ring, but found an answer to the place in my heart that had never learned to sing before that night (Claude).

And now, that Greyhound to Sheboygan, which I would have doubtlessly found urine-soaked if I'd dared enter the illicit lavatory at the back of the aisle.

Danny had said then, "For fun." For fun. The phrase was at the heart of my mission now; in more ways than one, it *was* the mission. I could almost imagine the crest of our army: a glorious, cartoon sparrow in the upper-left quadrant, a pair of stealth Dockers in the upper-right, a tin of "chaw" in the lower-left, and an ice-cream sundae beside it. And, running beneath it all, our motto, in gold, in capital letters, invincible: *Pro Fructus.*

But of course, it had since become so much more than just "for fun," and in a way Danny would've never imagined when he and I had shared those few, rushed seconds together on the bus to Sheboygan. It had become *pro* so much more than *fructus*, now.

"Tabby III" had approached the screen door, and he considered me now with golden eyes, his tail swishing out subconscious motives and desires unbidden. Clearly, he sensed that I was no "Two Rivers girl," that I had something to offer him that he'd never get from the sleep-walking denizens of the lakeshore. And I supposed that he wasn't alone; each Two Riverian whose life I'd entered since arriving must now have been feeling the same subconscious tug toward enlightenment, toward providence. Toward me.

I had a deep, deep distaste for cats, but I opened my door. Who was I to deny an individual whose most fervent desire was to become a recruit in the cause, to be close to my energy, my purpose? I even managed to be philosophical when he proceeded immediately to spray the corner of my living room and run back outside, his genitals almost winking at me under his upright tail.

Urine-soakings and profundity: two points apparently linked forever in the many-starred constellation that was my life. I closed the door behind "Tabby III," eager to remove the funk that was already wafting up out of the corner and glad to be moving ahead with the next step of my plan the following morning at ten a.m. It was such a vital step, too, because when it was finally accomplished, only then would I have the blueprint—the gospel!—for the rest of my mission: the missing information.

I couldn't help chuckling to myself. When would the residents of Two Rivers learn that it would take much more than a territorial squirt to halt my inexorable progress toward victory in the name of fun?

Answer: very, very soon.

* * *

"Miss Polanski—"

"*Ms.*"

"*Ms.* I'm really kind of busy right now, and I'm not really sure what this has to do with anything." Mr. Krimm wasn't wearing a T-shirt today, and from the moment I'd entered his office, I'd found myself intensely intrigued to see if his nipple disparity was still as extreme as it had been in his youth. You see, it was white, his shirt, and only a thin, poly blend.

Perhaps Mr. Krimm had "grown into" his left one. Perhaps the right one had been just a late bloomer. I stretched my arms over and behind my head, groaning with satisfaction.

"Ahh. Stretching is such an underappreciated stress-reliever, don't you think? You should try it. Go ahead, arms up over your head—"

He remained still.

"Mr. Krimm, I bring up our last meeting only to illustrate my point. With only two pieces, a pawn and a king, it's very difficult to win the match, but it's not impossible. Anything can be done, if we just put our minds to it."

"So you came here to talk about chess."

"Ahh, so you play!"

"No, I—"

"So you know, then, that even a lowly pawn," I gestured in a general way toward the right side of his body, "can take a king." I indicated his left. "Power might not always be as lopsided as it feels."

Mr. Krimm sniffed his Germanic nose, rolling his watery eyes slowly across the ceiling of his office. I imagined him at home, at the kitchen table carving tiny toy soldiers out of yellow maple while his wife cooked sauerbraten. He would continually push his limp gray hair out of his face as he went about the work, making private, satisfying analogies between the perfect little soldiers lined up before him and his careful efforts with the pupils at Darby Hills Elementary. Mr. Krimm was doing all this in lamplight because, for some reason, I imagined him in 1870's Bavaria.

I continued, in part to prevent the arrival of lederhosen in my fantasy: "But the king doesn't necessarily need to fear the pawn before him. The pawn could possibly be just a messenger from the opposing side with a peace agreement, or perhaps he's a defector—"

"Do *you* know how to play chess?"

"Let's not bog ourselves down in vagaries."

"Well, there's only one vagary: why you're here."

"Why I'm here. Excellent question. Well, I assumed you'd given more thought to my taking the position as instructor—"

"We call them 'teachers' here and no. I haven't."

"But you really would regret—"

"I'm regretting allowing you back into my office."

"I understand. But there is a certain, let's say "rook" that's—"

"That's what?! Moving in a straight line down the chessboard with a pizza for the king?"

"Well, straight into a position here at Darby Hills."

He shook his head, smiling as if mildly disappointed that he'd accidentally taken off the limb of one of his little, wooden soldiers, or perhaps shaved off a face.

"*Ms.* Polanski, I've already explained to the superintendent that I thought you were an actor of some kind, someone sent here to test me. He understands perfectly."

Mrs. Stefano had prepared me for this: "And Mr. Dumbriskie said that I *hadn't* been sent to test you."

"Are you suggesting that the superintendent would lie to me?"

"I merely ask, 'if the king controls the board, who controls the king?"

"Please don't make any more chess references—"

"So you'd rather I not say 'checkmate.'"

"I'd rather you leave my office."

"A lawsuit could be very costly, Mr. Krimm. For you and for the school district."

"Ms. Polanski, I'm going to be honest with you. No jury in the world would convict me of absolutely anything, once they'd heard you give testimony. *Anything.* Not that you have any reason to listen to me, but I really think you need professional help."

It was a classic chess move: shifting blame onto the opponent. I'd dealt with it so often that I didn't even need to think about my next counterstrike.

"Well, this 'crazy person' isn't going to give up this fight. I'll use every pawn and every knight and every—"

"We've got a lunch lady position open."

"I'll take it. Now, it's customary where I come from that when a deal is reached, both parties stretch way, way back—"

"Please leave."

* * *

I realized that just as Mr. Krimm's physical inequality had steadily and subconsciously eaten away at his ego over the years until everything he did was calculated to prove his supremacy as an uncompromised, equinippled male, so too did Mrs. Stefano's obsession with cartoon clothing indicate her overwhelming creativity in the face of adversity. Today, it was what—stoats? Weasels?

"Otters! They're my favorite." This was said with more gravity than was at all appropriate for the situation. "I didn't make this one, though. I got it at SeaWorld in Orlando."

"Otters. Oh, I see it now. Very... So I hope your father at least left the dogs at home, rather than insisting on taking them with your family to Florida."

"Why do you keep asking about my father? Remember? He's been dead for twenty years. And this shirt's two years old."

"Well, I'm sure that under it all, he would've really liked your shirt, Mrs. Stefano. He would've respected it, as he did you."

She looked at me unsurely. "Not if he'd known about, you know, *me*. Well, I didn't really understand myself until recently. Not until you made me realize it was okay to, you know, kind of 'let go.' Well, you and then the Internet and stuff."

I couldn't say that I was surprised at how self-aware Mrs. Stefano had become due, at least partially, to my presence. She'd proven herself quite insightful several times over the last two weeks, and I was glad to hear now that she'd broken it off with Mr. Krimm, whom I was absolutely certain did not respect Mrs. Stefano's otter-covered shirt or the strong, increasingly confident woman held rather tightly within it.

And now she had an Internet therapist? I made a mental note to suggest this as an option to my many friends and acquaintances who, for a multitude of reasons, couldn't—or shouldn't—discuss their issues with me or some other live, licensed counselor. I could still do something for them.

"Wonderful." But the word soured in my mouth as I looked down at the mournful mound of food that had just been slid toward me.

"Have a great day."

Food was never meant to be slid.

Nonetheless, I gave the cashier my most winning smile. "Thank you. You know, you would make an excellent artist's model—"

But the young woman had already been absorbed back into the ultimately futile activity behind the counter. If my plan didn't shift into action soon, the poor thing would spend her life in Two Rivers and die with a generous coating of grease and ignorance over her soul.

Of course, we were in Arby's for "lunch."

It was a strange, Wisconsin kind of synchronicity: Mrs. Stefano's corner table was always free for her. We "slid" into the booth and "slid" our lunch down the Formica table, I wishing that some, supreme being heard my prayer and that this time, the food "slid" down my throat.

My prayers were again rejected.

"Mr. Krimm totally hates you, Yolanda."

"It's not *hate*; it's resistance. You'd benefit from recognizing the difference."

"That's not what he says. I heard him talking. He thinks you're going to hate Kryst'l so much that you'll quit. But he's waiting for any reason at all to fire you next week."

"He's resistant to my perceptiveness; he's resistant to my sedition."

"You're not lazy."

"Not lazy—revolutionary! He senses it, and it terrifies him."

Mrs. Stefano remained dubious, her otters stretching to cover her generous bosom as she worked doggedly through the things before her. One particular grouping looked as if it were a nest of egg rolls, and I shuddered.

"So you promise me that you're going to tell me next week. The whole plan."

"Absolutely. I'm just waiting for the final facet to fall into place once classes begin—the facet that will tell us exactly how we are to proceed."

"Well." I wished that Mrs. Stefano wouldn't speak with her mouth still filled with little white wads of bun, but an ally was an ally. "I've got a surprise for you next week, too."

"Oh! How unexpected."

"Well. I bet you're kind of expecting it."

"Am I?"

"You know." She was being coy, now, another grossly inappropriate habit for a fifty-year-old woman that I'd have to break, eventually. Still, I knew that whatever the surprise was, it couldn't affect my mission, so I merely smiled in response.

Nonetheless, I didn't like surprises. (Claude and his vintage toaster oven came to mind: fifteen kinds of melted cheese sandwiches until an unruly Reuben exploded while I happened to be standing nearby, shattering his career as an amateur short-order cook and mine as a deli-foods admirer. As far as I knew, he never touched another hot sandwich again, but the toaster oven remained on the counter, the inoperable centerpiece of his failure.)

I didn't like surprises because they were specifically designed to throw one off balance, to compromise one's ability to react in the most advantageous way. I'd made a career—a life!—of maintaining the advantage. Of course I remained measured in even the most unexpected gales, but it was work! Surprises drew me away from my confrontations, my schemes, my seductions. I resented them.

"So, Mrs. Stefano, you haven't ever wondered what it would feel like to, I don't know, wear a band of leather around your neck?"

"Excuse me?"

"Oh, I suppose like a collar of some sort."

"What, like a dog?"

"Isn't it interesting that you brought up dogs."

"Well, I've never wanted to be a *dog*." This was said slyly, with layers of moist meaning. Perhaps I'd miscalculated, and her father had preferred the company of the family's gerbils to that of his daughter? Or maybe he'd ignored her in preference to a pet otter!

But I didn't want to rush our work untangling Mrs. Stefano's harrowing past and so approached at another, more oblique angle.

"But there must have been some happy, healthy activities from your childhood."

"Polka."

I continued, as if neither one of us had noticed my flinch. "Polka? Your father made you dance?"

"Well, the whole family. But it's kind of died out now."

Undoubtedly by euthanasia, I thought to myself, but I had to soldier on, just as Mrs. Stefano had been soldiering on for me over the past few weeks. I owed her that much.

"Well, then, we're going to *polka*. I'll find out where it's occurring in the area—"

"Occurring! You always talk so funny. 'Occurring polka.'" Her dimples deepened, her titter rang through the restaurant. For a moment, her head was turned in just such a way that there was a marked resemblance to one of the otters on her shirt, playfully cracking an oyster open. My heart felt just like that oyster.

"Mrs. Stefano, *we are going to polka*. You've been on this earth far too long to let your debilitating childhood rob you of any happiness you can gather. I simply won't allow that to happen. We are going to polka: you and I and your wardrobe menagerie!"

"I didn't have a debilitating childhood—"

"Call it what you will. Now, that subject is closed for the day. I'd like to discuss next week."

Shrugging, Mrs. Stefano started in on the "egg rolls." They didn't smell like egg rolls, and I wished, yet once again, that America would respect traditional cuisines, rather than mixing and matching them as if they were tattoos running up its arm: a pair of dice, the Japanese symbol for strength, Satan holding a stick of dynamite in one hand and a boomerang in the other. (Claude had once drugged me and attempted to tattoo a chupacabra on my thigh. But I'd drugged him, too.)

"There is a family that moved to Two Rivers three months ago, and their youngest son is starting first grade at Darby Hills. Danny Kravitz. I've gathered a great deal of information on them—and on him—already, but I need more."

"Is this part of the plan?"

"This is part of the plan. *You* are part of the plan. Do you have access to—"

She dropped her voice and looked around the restaurant. "No, no, no. They don't let me near the files or anything like that. I'd totally get in trouble if I tried. I'll only know more about the student if he comes to Mr. Krimm's office, and I can talk to him and whatnot."

"I see."

"But I know everybody at Darby Hills. Maybe I can do some checking around that way."

"Excellent." I "slid" my food away from me, having barely moved it around in its container.

"So the plan has something to do with this little kid, Yolanda?"

"It has everything to do with 'this little kid.'"

"And you promise that you're not, you know, trying to kidnap him or something. It's really not bad or anything, right?"

I tore my eyes from the egg roll that disappeared into her mouth. No matter what part of the globe from which they originated and what exotic ingredients they contained, the world's cuisines were simply carbon-based matter, were they not? To be immediately broken down by stomach acids into chains of carbohydrates for the purpose of life.

I had to live. Picking up my "Ultimate BLT," I leveled Mrs. Stefano with my most piercing stare.

"Mrs. Stefano, once I can extract the final piece of the puzzle from this young man, our team will be responsible for the best thing that's happened to Two Rivers. Ever."

She nodded sagaciously, the flakes of eggroll skin that covered her chest bound to be consumed by other forms of life down the food chain. It would be the best thing that would ever happen to a certain lucky paramecium, and I silently thanked her for her good deed.

Briefly entertaining the thought of Mrs. Stefano constructing me a kaftan with paramecia all across it, I then simply took a bite of my Arby's carbon matter. Microscopic life clearly wasn't my wardrobe theme.

Suddenly she screeched, and I was worried for a moment that a bun wad had lodged in her throat.

My concern was unnecessary: "Polka I hardly know her!"

4

I sense that something's upset you.

Summer in Two Rivers was like a humid hand placed somewhere very inappropriately on my body. The inhabitants felt that it was necessary to expose larger expanses of their pink, white and lilac bodies to the world, and "flip-flops" became even more acceptable than they normally were—along with a colorful range of toe diseases. Most of those wandering the aisles of the Piggly-Wiggly had designer sunglasses perched on their heads, their cell phones cocked to their ears as they loudly discussed impending "cookouts" and confirmed with the person on the other end how "awesome it was going to be."

But then a young, blond man smiled as he passed me at the mayonnaise, and that smile contained so much more than politeness. It spoke of a race of gentle souls who were always first to see the good in others, who were quick to laugh and chat, and slow to mastermind gun-fueled vendettas or throw a small child out of a moving taxi, even if he had just cheated at a rushed game of craps and handed the ill-gotten pesos out the window to a younger sister emerging from a shadowed alley, a sudden and fleeting goddess of light in her fluorescent t-shirt emblazoned with "Porn Star."

They were nothing like that. In fact, while Two Riverians might have been a bit uncomfortable to behold in their warm-weather gear, it dawned on me that they weren't sun worshippers at all, as I studied their crinkled pedal pushers and faded baseball caps. Rather, it was the Wisconsin sun that worshipped them—and it was my duty to join in. The townspeople were brilliantly pure, protean. It wasn't their fault that the family bar-bque was the closest they'd come in their lives to a truly transcendental, ecstatic event.

At least until Team Polanski's mission was complete.

"Sam!"

As he turned to me, his face underwent the reign of several, subtle emotions: surprise, fear, nervousness, acceptance. (Were these the four stages of grief? I made a mental note to "surf the web" when I returned home.)

"Yolanda."

But of course he'd been grieving: he hadn't seen me for more than two weeks. And it was a kind of little death, to have your first taste of a kindred soul then ripped from you. My heart went out to him.

This decided my tone for our interaction: an outpouring of deserved sympathy.

"How are you, Sam? Really."

"Good. How's the house treating you?" He looked down at a rather large package of toilet paper in his shopping cart, and my compassion expanded even further—if he only knew that I'd already secretly observed him using the stuff!

"It's a challenge."

"A challenge?"

"The American-style light switches—is it down, is it up? I can never remember. That sort of thing."

"American-style?"

"Please, Sam! A man as sophisticated as you? I'm sure you've flicked your share of switches in Sydney, in Tokyo, in Rome!"

"They're the same, aren't they?"

I pushed my cart closer to his, glad that I'd waited through his trip to the drycleaner, waited through his "Supercut," waited as he transacted some executive business in the bank. I'd even waited until he'd turned down the quietest aisle of the supermarket before "bumping into him." (It seemed that even though they entered the summer with their entire bodies and souls, the residents of Two Rivers had little interest in the seasonal promotions aisle. Perhaps if someone invented citronella beer...)

"Okay, Sam."

"Okay?"

"Is it one of your other properties?"

"Is *what* one of my other properties?"

"I know you, Sam. I can sense that something's on your mind. Your dynamism, your *joie de vivre*. They're missing, somehow. I'm so sorry."

"I'm not sure—"

"Look. Come with me." I grabbed his cart and dragged it down the aisle. "We both need a break. We both need to reconnect."

The café that had been recently added to the building was in sight, but Sam stopped his cart forcefully, the usual disarming sense of humor absent. I never dreamt I'd ever miss it, but I did. (Claude had once stopped his Peugeot forcefully in Yemen. The resulting scar on my head followed a path much like a certain hut-to-hut hike up the Hochvernagtspitze.)

"Yolanda, I've got to finish shopping. Could you please let go?"

"You see? As stony as an Austrian Alp. This isn't like you, Sam. Not at all."

"Well, maybe it should be. Maybe this has kind of been my fault."

"I won't mention a certain river in the Sudan."

"You see? I don't understand what that means, either! I'm sorry, Yolanda, but I've basically never understood anything you've ever said to me. I thought you were joking at first, and then—well, I don't know what I thought after that." He took in a tortured breath. "Look, you're my tenant, so I'm more than glad to help you out with anything to do with the house. Honestly. But I'm really busy, and I have to finish shopping. Can you understand that?"

"Yes, Sam. I understand."

He studied me as if he didn't believe this and then turned away, heading back toward the stack of plastic, molded lawn chairs at the head of the aisle.

I understood him better than he understood himself. Soon, he would be alone in his back yard, sitting in one of his own plastic, molded lawn chairs, staring pensively into the stand of pines at the southeast boundary of his property. *I Know Why the Caged Bird Sings* would be open in his lap at the same page as the day before and the day before that: forty-seven.

Suddenly, I imagined all the property he owned across Two Rivers, patches that dotted the landscape, pulling him down, wearing him down, joining him forever to a life that stymied his foreign switch-flicking. No wonder he was so attracted to me. And no wonder he denied what we shared: I simply personified all the adventures he was denying himself; I reminded him that there was a whole world out there, that there was more to life than underwhelming, Midwestern plumbing issues.

It was true on many, many levels: raw sewage *could* be a "real bitch."

I felt a charge run through me as he turned the corner and out of sight. This was precisely why my mission had been born on that Greyhound bus so many weeks prior! This was precisely why I was forcing myself through a summer filled with drug-store sun block and moldy, air-conditioned tire stores, rather than one embellished with parqueted palazzos and Buddhas carved out of remote, seemingly indifferent mountains rising suddenly to embrace the Laotian dusk.

Rather than discourage me, Sam's reaction merely fueled my desire to triumph over the forces that had triumphed over him, the same forces that held Two Rivers' head down under rushing, numbing currents—presumably those of the "two rivers" themselves. I raced toward him, eager to try out a more direct, perhaps more palatable approach. After all, the school year was about to begin; I had no more time for finessing, for gentle urging. It was time to unite and conquer.

"It's the Kravitzes."

He actually jumped at the sound of my voice, the thrill of an electric connection unsuccessfully avoided.

"What? The Kravitzes?! How do you know about the Kravitzes?"

"Please, Sam. This is Two Rivers. I know when Mamie Scherhopf scratches her backside."

"Mamie—?"

I just wished our exchange hadn't been taking place before the "Dorito Collisions of Blazin' Buffalo and Cool Ranch." Their presence alone sucked the supermarket dry of dignity.

"Look, please let me just finish shopping—"

"So it *is* the Kravitzes."

"No, it's not the Kravitzes. It's *you*."

"Of course, it's *me*, Sam. But it's the Kravitzes."

He stopped the cart and swung around at me, his mouth a thin line of peril. I knew it was wrong, but my heart burned for him to strike me in anger, in passion, in surrender.

Instead, he burst out in laughter. It was clearly so cathartic that I allowed the braying to continue for a minute or so. Laughter was clearly Sam's first step toward honesty—with himself, with me. I smiled, although it was cold steel against my teeth.

"Mamie Scherhopf?! Why would you think that I knew someone named Mamie Scherhopf? The thing is, I know I shouldn't laugh at you. I know that!" He laughed harder. "But *you're* following *me!* How can I help it? It's not my fault! I'm not a bad person, I swear!"

I struck him with my most withering look, but this merely fueled his unenlightened, Two Rivers behavior. I'd prepared myself for this eventuality.

"Sam. Can I tell you something?"

"God, no! Why are you doing this to me?"

"I had a dream last night."

This also struck him as funny, for some reason. "In the dream, did you answer any of my questions?"

I continued, undeterred. "Everyone in Two Rivers had a little tag of skin that connected their upper and lower eyelids. It was only a thin strip at childhood, but as the people grew older, it got wider and wider. Eventually, it extended across both eyes. They were blind, Sam. Everyone in Two Rivers eventually had their sight robbed of them, and no one thought to do anything about it."

As I knew it would, this sobered him, and he wiped his eyes. (The first night I'd met Claude, he'd also shared with me a false dream. He'd told the story of an evil, tan rooster that spit at carefully dressed ladies promenading in a square somewhere near Seville in 1905. It had done the trick with me, too; an hour later, I'd permanently misplaced the most expensive panties I would ever own.)

"And in the dream, you came to me, Sam, and begged me to help you, to use my understanding of the sighted world to restore the colors and shapes that you so desperately missed."

Now he winced uncomfortably, the allegory undoubtedly hitting close to home.

"Then you turned into a tangerine with a beard, and I put you in my purse, and we toured with the Supremes as their management team."

I'd miscalculated again. Although I'd carefully concocted my narrative to authentically reflect the subconscious symbols and motivations that infiltrated actual dreams, the last bit reignited his amusement. I was forced to wait, the color rising to my cheeks, as he guffawed at length—surely his least attractive, most Wisconsin character flaw.

"I'm sorry! Honestly! But if you don't want me to laugh at you, all you have to do is just not say anything!"

"It's not as simple as that, Sam. We both know that. And then there are the Kravitzes."

More laughter. "Why do you keep talking about the Kravitzes?!"

I soldiered on in his wake. "There's quite a bit of talk about them around town. Aren't they paying their rent? Or perhaps they've destroyed your property? All those children? And a couple of dogs, I heard—"

I'd managed to rob him of his smile. "They're fine."

"But their youngest, I think they said his name was 'Danny.' You know, I'm starting work at Darby Hills Elementary next week—just a temporary position until an opportunity for an instructor opens up—and everyone is talking about this Danny person. How did you find him to be?"

He looked around at the other shoppers, as if to give me the impression that he wanted to be "rescued."

"What are people saying, Yolanda."

"Oh, you know. This and that. It's really a little tacky to gossip, don't you think?"

"Yeah, but if there's some sort of problem—"

"I couldn't agree more. Anyway, it was a pleasure as always to see you again, Sam. Perhaps next time, we'll meet over Seabreezes and a nice pâté forestier."

"Uh..."

I turned to leave, counting my steps. How many would it be? Twenty? Fifteen before he begged me for more information? Sometimes I felt my advantage really was too unfair.

Forty-four, forty-five steps. I stopped, ostensibly to inspect some sort of product called "Zesty Tuna Helper," and found myself utterly at a loss as to how powder in a box could in any way help anything.

Sam had disappeared down another aisle! I had to be fully briefed about Danny no later than Monday and realized I could wait no longer for Sam's curiosity, his recklessness to send him back to me, which would have inevitably happened.

So I hunted him down in the pickle section.

"We meet again! Of course, you want to know more about this Danny Kravitz person and his potential issues. I just wish I could help. Of course you've doubtlessly sensed, Sam, that I have an extensive background in psychological research, and very often, one can tell a great deal about subjects just by how they express themselves privately."

"Yolanda—"

"Have you been into his room, Sam? Since he moved in?"

"No."

"Never walked past and just got a glimpse or anything?"

"No. Look, what have you heard? He's not a pyromaniac or something, is he?"

I pointedly did not refute this, knowing that often one's deepest fears come to the surface of their own accord. Instead, I tucked deep into the recesses of my mind this nugget: Sam clearly longed to burn down each and every one of his properties, to watch them collapse in on themselves, charred messes, so that he could begin a wild, invigorating life anew—his ancient burden reduced to smoldering cinders at once carried away by the prairie breezes and out onto the white-capped prairie that is Lake Michigan.

Leaving only Yolanda Jean Polanski standing in his life.

"Well, if you happened to get a look at some of the items in his room, perhaps artwork or a dream journal. That sort of thing. I've done studies."

He shook his head and inspected a container of some sort of mustard/relish hybrid. He'd recognized my challenge and was now mulling over how best to accept it.

"Yes, Sam: an escapade! A dare, if you wish. Our first 'adventure together,' I suppose. You're welcome."

The truth of it was that the Kravitz house was three stories, and Danny's room was on the top floor. It was impossible for me to gather intelligence as easily as I could with Sam's single-story ranch.

Frowning, he offered me a look calculated to give the impression that he was too confused to cooperate. "Okay, well, goodbye."

"You're not going to 'run into me' again now, are you, Sam?"

But he'd already turned the corner.

"I await your intelligence!"

My eyes roamed sightlessly over the gherkins. Obviously, the next move in Operation Kravitz was mine. Sam was all too eager to gather the information for me, for his own need of excitement; he and I both knew he just needed some sort of valid excuse to gather it.

And Mrs. Stefano and I would be only too glad to provide that excuse.

* * *

It was always substandard food with Mrs. Stefano. Even though I'd offered to cook some favorite dishes from my time at the Finom Kecske Culinary Institute in Budapest, she'd insisted on "wings" delivered from her favorite grease hole. Graciously, I agreed; ungraciously, I resented.

"Hungary! No, I've never been on a plane in my life! It must be so neat, actually being *in* the clouds."

A summer zephyr toyed with the new gingham café curtains I'd installed in the kitchen. I'd spent more time than was strictly necessary attempting to "fix up" the place—unnecessary because I would never, ever consider the collection of bullying rooms my *home* and because no matter what sophistication I attempted to inject into the shack, it would only ever be a mean-spirited, failed attempt at post-war housing.

But gingham café curtains brought me closer to Geneva. (And Geneva brought me closer to Claude.)

"It's stunning, Mrs. Stefano, being above it all for a moment—a moment to reflect on our significance on earth. To be exposed to the magnificence of our planet and at the same time, our insignificance upon it. It's easy to understand why Judeo-Christian religions believe that 'heaven' is above us, because flying ten miles above the earth undoubtedly brings one closer to the god-spirit."

"Plus you can watch movies in the seat in front of you."

"Mrs. Stefano—"

"That's right, though, isn't it? Tiny little screens and there are buttons on your armrest—"

"Mrs. Stefano, we've got our first task to perform tonight."

She picked up the biggest wing, focused more on getting the maximum amount of sauce in her mouth than anything I had to say. "How come there aren't buttons like that, like when you're at a restaurant so that you can call the waitress if you need her? Or you could just press a button and it blows on you—"

"Please! Tonight's operation is vital. I really need your help."

"Is it part of the 'big plan?'"

"Absolutely."

"Or what if I wanted to recline? How come they don't let me recline at Sizzler?"

"Because they don't want you to choke, Mrs. Stefano. They probably already have enough trouble with that simply due to the taste and consistency of their food."

"You know, you can get kind of a little snotty once in a while. How come? I mean, it doesn't bother me or anything, but it seems like you don't really like living here, sometimes."

Once again, Mrs. Stefano surprised me with her perceptiveness. I reminded myself (for the thousandth time) that I had to rein in my propensity to underestimate Two Riverians, and I sighed. "As usual, you're absolutely right, Mrs. Stefano. You read me like a book."

"Then how come you don't go back to Europe or France or whatever?"

"Because the Seine continues to run, utterly ambivalent to my presence. Because the Pyrenean glaciers thunder down their paths without needing any direction from me. Because the schoolchildren in Calcutta sit on top of their houses at night and bask in the night air, rather than playing 'Xbox 360' and eating 'extreme-flavored snacks' while reclining on their blue leather 'Barcaloungers!'" Mrs. Stefano nodded as she chewed on a grizzled bone, and my heart soared. If I could make her see why my plan was so important for Two Rivers, I could make anyone in the town understand. And if I could do that, my mission would be a resounding success. *Of course* my goal for Two Rivers would make just as much sense to the townsfolk as it did to me! *Of course* they were intelligent and placid and broadminded enough to welcome my mission as their own! The stunting they'd received at the hands of the Midwest was anything but permanent.

For the first time since coming to Wisconsin, I could actually taste victory.

"Barcalounger I hardly know her."

Of course, Mrs. Stefano's response was disappointing, but it was my own fault. If I insisted on making references to people and places of which the residents had no knowledge, how did I expect to make my point understood? There were one or two lessons in life I seemed never able to learn.

While Mrs. Stefano tittered at her own joke, I answered the front door. Of course, I knew who it was.

"Hey."

"Good evening, Del! Won't you come in?"

She spit a rather large wad of purple gum into my yard (I couldn't help wondering how it might impact the workings of a lawn mower) and entered, aggrieved.

Unbeknownst to her, I'd stumbled on the key to her true nature earlier in the week. I'd been studying a watermelon, and instantaneously, all had become clear.

At twelve—or the latest, thirteen—Del had developed a crush on either Scott Baio or G. Gordon Liddy. Her mother, who was normally criminally lenient as to her daughter's behavior, became paradoxically jealous of either Scott or G. Gordon, demanding that "her little watermelon seed" refocus her attentions on a more suitable, local boy. (Watermelon was sweet and pink—a mother—yet watery and bland—an ice sculpture. Del found herself trapped within and frozen in her mother's oblong sphere of influence, joined by countless other victims who were also alternately ignored and criticized by the woman.)

Of course, Del's mother had cruelly named her after an anti-heroine famous for sapping the strength of her lover. Now Delilah faced a choice: she could disobey the woman who'd never seemed to care before and fulfill her role as the shearer of Scott Baio's shaggy locks (merely take a bit off the top for G. Gordon?). Or, she could capitulate to Mother's demands and choose some milquetoast sixth-grader with bad breath and absolutely no background in semi-legal wiretapping. Brilliantly, Del excised herself from this psychosexual quagmire and chose a third option that must have had her mother spinning in her grave.

But the void was still there. Now, although appearing to figuratively and violently shave the head of everyone she met, Del really longed for a maternal figure that would care for her, that would take firm control of her behavior and lead her into greener, more fruitful watermelon patches.

I would be that maternal figure.

"Follow me."

"Oh. Because I was planning on walking into this wall."

"I've got a guest in the kitchen I'd like you to meet."

"Whatever."

Del's heavy footsteps followed me, tinkling my old collection of Delft. I'd recently installed it in an ancient Hoosier cabinet that I'd snatched up at a roadside antiques dealer a week earlier. Of course, the town would think it madness to put a piece of kitchen furniture in my living room, but soon they'd be breathing the air of Bohemia as their own, no longer able to comprehend the murky, stagnant time before.

"Oh, hey, Heather."

"Hi, Del! Wow, this is so weird!"

"You two know each other!" (How could Sam live in Two Rivers and not know Mamie Scherhopf?!)

"We went to high school together. So listen, I want to just take the measurements and split because I've got an early shift tomorrow."

"Oh, you're doing some work for Yolanda?"

Del looked at me, her face flattened into the resentful boredom she must have felt at being put into a position of having to avoid the truth.

"Del's crafting something for me, yes, but it's kind of top-secret right now. I'm sure you can guess why that is, Mrs. Stefano, and I promise to confirm that guess as soon as I can."

Del snorted, reinforcing her original assertion that she didn't have much respect for me, and I realized that this was yet another serendipitous event in my life. *Mrs. Stefano* could help win Del over! I knew I needed Del on my side, but I also realized that the money I'd agreed to pay her would only go so far with her. In order to ensure our success, then, I needed a complete conversion, and the bonds of childhood friendship would provide it.

"All right, then. If you'll just follow me, Del."

"See you, Heather."

"Bye!"

Del had been postponing building the closet for weeks, pleading "extra shifts" and a trip to North Dakota to hunt. Of course, I needed somewhere to secret the private documents that would be piling up soon—documents that, if found, could destroy my operation and possibly everyone associated with it—so I'd upped my offer to five-thousand.

Del had arrived an hour after the call.

"Jesus Christ. You have got to be fucking kidding me."

There was a distinct possibility that for the inevitable battles to come, I would need someone who could be a little rough, who could "talk smack" in tight situations, so I smiled away my distaste at her vulgarity. "No one's kidding anyone, 'fucking' or otherwise."

She gaped at my poky bedroom. With my oversized, antique Amish four-poster dominating the space, she had room to do little else.

"Anyone who comes in here is going to wonder where your closet went. And even if I build some bullshit bookcase over the door, they're going to figure out that there's a closet behind it pretty fucking fast. Frankly."

She was coarse, but she had a point. "Del, it's vital that I have somewhere to store important documents."

"Ummm, safe deposit box?"

"No, it has to be here."

"Why?"

"The establishment is our worst enemy, right now."

"Jesus fucking Christ! Why am I here? Oh, that's right: five-thousand dollars. Focus on the five fucking grand." She was staring at the ceiling, her teeth set in a fierce lock. Her squint narrowed. "How do you get into the attic?"

"The attic?"

She rolled her eyes, tutting but never bothering to actually grace me with her gaze. "The *attic*. Is there a panel in your closet?"

Before waiting for an answer, she threw open the little door and stared up into my most private belongings: clippings of the press coverage, souvenirs ranging far, far back into my girlhood, a vintage peignoir signed by Bridgette Bardot on the inside hem (or so Claude attested when he'd lent it to me). I was surprised at how laid bare I felt before Del, how intimate the experience was for me.

She merely grunted and shut the door, and I found myself wondering if she'd even bothered to notice the accumulation of my life, a testament to the course of my existence—tossed by the four winds, dragged through the shoals, inexorably wrecked in Wisconsin.

"Where's your crapper? Because I am not continuing with this shit until I drop a deuce."

"Did your mother allow you to speak that way to her when she was alive?"

"I had lunch with her yesterday."

"You know what I mean by 'alive.' You both do. You know, I'm afraid I'm going to have to demand that you begin respecting your elders, Del."

"You're like two years older than me, nutbag."

"It's the first door on your left."

Her defensiveness spoke volumes. Clearly, I'd achieved a first step on my way to "mamma."

When I returned to the kitchen, Mrs. Stefano was where I had left her, most of the chicken parts gone at this point.

She looked up, wracked with guilt. "You better grab one before I eat all of them."

"That's all right, Mrs. Stefano. I think I've lost my appetite."

"Oh, I know. Del kind of has a *filthy mouth.*" The last two words were merely mouthed, any whisper behind them lost in the hum of the refrigerator.

I sat next to her. "Mrs. Stefano, I need your help with her. You two are old friends—"

"No, no, no! We were never friends! I just went to high school with her. There were only thirty-two students in our class."

"But we need her, and she now has some vital intelligence that I cannot allow to become common knowledge."

"Oh, I don't know if she's *that* intelligent."

I watched the moths bang against the ancient screen door, feeling their pain and begging the universe to give me patience. "She knows part of our plan." I leaned into Mrs. Stefano, eager to impart the magnitude of my next few sentences. "So what's important to her? What makes her tick? What can we do to get her to join our team?"

"She did auto mechanics in high school."

"Okay." Encouragement was in order. "That's good. That's excellent. What else?"

"In tenth, or maybe eleventh grade, she knocked one of Bobby Smalls' front teeth out. Oh, and she used to wear overalls a lot. Like denim overalls."

This wasn't getting us anywhere. "How do you think we could convince her join our ranks?"

"Gosh, I don't know. You already offered her money..." At least Mrs. Stefano was thinking. "Let's see... You know, it's kind of hard if I don't know what the plan is. Plus, she doesn't seem to *like you too much.*" More silent whispering.

But she had a point. I looked up into the grease-encrusted overhead light. The silhouette of a moth sharpened and softened inside, the insect unknowingly nearing the end of its life above me, because of me.

"Well, Mrs. Stefano, she doesn't dislike you. What if you gave her a reason for empathy? What if you perhaps admitted to a high-school crush all those years ago?"

"With Frankie Bertz?"

"No, not with Frankie Bertz."

I waited silently as she passed through confusion, shock, confusion, shock, confusion.

I could barely hear her response: "You mean—" It was too much to ask of Mrs. Stefano, a suggestion too far, and I withdrew. "Well, we'll continue to think about it. Now, I'd like to go over our mission tonight. We're going to take a drive up Union Street to a particular house there. I'll throw a few pebbles on the roof, and what I'd like you to do is to knock on the door and tell the people who live there that you saw a couple of rats on their roof."

"What?"

"That's all. Just say that you saw a few rats. Pretty simple, eh?"

"But why?"

"Because we need to give the landlord an excuse to inspect the third floor of the house." She needed more: "He's one of us."

"You are completely fucking batshit!"

Mrs. Stefano and I jumped as Del emerged from the shadows of the living room. After briefly wondering why I'd heard neither a flush nor industrial strength boot-fall, I found myself seriously rethinking my decision to include her. Was she a spy? Perhaps a larger bribe would be enough to silence the woman, if not convince her to actually join our cause.

"No, I mean it! I thought you were batshit, but you are *totally* batshit! Dreaming up some Nancy Drew shit—"

Of all things, she was chuckling at us!

"Del—"

"What kind of Mickey Mouse setup are you two running here—secret compartments, lame little tricks that—"

"Del!" I was surprised to find that my bile had boiled over—a very, very infrequent experience. I could sense my ever-faithful conscience urging me to watch my tongue, but for once, it was the weaker impulse. Moreover, I knew that her "Delilah Complex" (I'd coined yet another disorder) meant that the only thing to which she'd truly respond was a masterful leader—a "Samson/mother," if you will. Strength of biblical proportion coursed through my veins.

"What I'm trying to do here may seem 'lame' to you right now; it may seem 'Mickey Mouse.' But it is a step in what may be the most important event to ever happen to this town! I am *not* 'batshit,' my little watermelon seed, I'm perfectly sane and aware of my goal, and I've agreed to pay you a great deal of money to do a simple job. Money which—I'll just come out and say it—is partially to ensure that you will not breathe a rude word of my 'lame,' 'batshit,' 'Mickey Mouse' actions! If you decide that this is something that you cannot do, I'd appreciate it if you'd tell me and Mrs. Stefano right now, so that we can cease our work to transform the future of Two Rivers."

Del had stared at me through this diatribe seemingly without blinking (no wonder her eyes were so bloodshot). Now, crossing her arms over her chest, she shook her head slowly, her dull, hay-like hair failing to catch even the least spark from the overhead light. (Did she wash it with Irish Spring?)

I was without emotion now, cold and as weak as my self-control. I'd said too much; our relationship was too young yet to exploit her need for a dominant mother-figure. Why did passion destroy humankind's hopes just as often as it gave birth to them? The same force that held me in Two Rivers as if a moth to a bulb—and which had inspired such a monumentally brilliant undertaking—had also dashed it in an instant, in a few words rashly spat-out. Why hadn't I realized that Del was still too troubled, too haunted by past traumas to embrace her need for strong leadership?

Because now all she brought to mind was an Easter Island statue, except that the woman before me was infinitely more impassive. Only the moths and the café curtains stirred in the room.

Even Mrs. Stefano had stopped eating.

Finally, Del spoke. "Lady, I don't give a flying fuck what your little 'mission' for Two Rivers is. In fact, I don't know if you've noticed, but so far, we've actually managed to survive pretty well without any of your help. Imagine that."

"That's precisely it, though—"

"Hey! Deaf, are we? I said I don't give two steaming shits what you're doing!"

How would I live the rest of my life, blackened as it would be by this crushing failure?

"And, as you may have noticed, I still want to knock out every fucking tooth in your mouth with my fist." She looked menacingly at Mrs.

Stefano. "Just like Bobby Smalls, only I work out now, so I'll do a better job of it."

Mrs. Stefano smiled apologetically as she blanched. She was wearing her t-shirt with the three cats walking toward viewers on the front side and away from them on the back, a line-up of anuses exposed under their upright tails. It read, simply, "catitude," and I was reminded that Tabby III was probably in the backyard at that moment, urinating on the azaleas I'd recently planted and killing them utterly. But I was glad even of this thought, because it drew me away, if only for an instant, from the massacre in my kitchen, the slaughter of so much planning and work.

"But. But!" Del drew air through her teeth as she shook her head, the sound of pure wrath leaking into my home. "Goddamned number one: what I cannot fucking stand is to see something done half-assed, and any idiot will tell you that you need to convince the people they have rats *first*, and *then* you throw the pebbles! It's like proof, then. Plus, you can't lie to save your fucking life, Heather." Del shifted on her legs, looking down as she groaned with a surprising amount of force. "What the fuck is wrong with me?! And. And! Goddamned number two: fucking with people is fun. So! Don't worry, Heather, you don't have to try and 'convince' me to help out because I'm calling the shots, now. *I'm* knocking on the door, and *you're* throwing the fucking pebbles, and *you*—," her gaze toward me was no less icy than it had ever been, "*You* are going to stay in the car because I'm one-hundred percent fucking certain that if you were in any way involved in this, you'd jack it up so bad that you'd end up landing both you *and* Heather's asses in jail. And I don't fucking hate Heather."

The kitchen's silence screamed in our ears. Del really did have an arresting voice, something that might serve our cause, perhaps on the radio or at a rally.

But both women were turned to me, and I groped around in my mind for a moment, unable to grab hold of a lifeline. Even Tabby III was staring at me through the screen door, merely a hungry cat to anyone who wasn't aware of his maliciousness. My first intelligent thought finally arose: the Midwest had managed to send some very powerful forces to defeat me. But I was stronger, my goal sturdier than this! It would take more than a rather overbearing, earthy woman and a cat whose primary goal in life was to defecate in my dieffenbachia to break my spirit.

And at long last, my reason found its voice, as I knew it would. This was simply another example of the power of the subconscious!

Instinctively recognizing that Del would want to get involved from the first moment I'd laid eyes on her, my intuition had somehow eventually determined that the only way she'd participate was if she believed she were in charge and preventing disasters, delusional though the thought was. The house was microscopic: of course, I would've known on some level that she'd hear the conversation between Mrs. Stefano and me! And I could've postponed my meeting with Mrs. Stefano until after Del went home—but I didn't! Bravissima, subconscious!

It might have been premature to congratulate myself for this brilliant insight, but how could I not? I returned my steeliest gaze to Del. "Well, as Superman says, 'let's do this thing.'"

Del groaned again, and I finally put a face to the sound: sea lion. "Superman does not fucking say that."

Allowing her to think that she was right about this, too, I gathered my things.

"Did you just call me *your little watermelon seed*?!"

* * *

Mrs. Stefano had insisted on bringing the rather pungent box of chicken wings on our drive, but Del surprised me once again. She took one look at my Oldsmobile Regency 98 and forbad the presence of any food in its russet, velour-pillowed interior.

"Fucking A! Where did you get this? It's totally cherry! Some aunt die or something?"

"I only drive Oldsmobiles in the States."(The only promise to Claude I'd never broken: he'd always insisted on wearing berets in Provence, referring to his butler as "mate" in Darwin, and buying used school-girl underwear from vending machines in Tokyo.)

"That makes absolutely no sense, but I don't even care. Fuck me, it's like being in a funeral home!"

I wasn't sure I appreciated the analogy, but the inimitable Mrs. Stefano managed to speak my mind for me. "No, it's not!"

The comment only confirmed that I'd chosen them both wisely, a yin and yang swirling within my circle of influence. When one went too far, the other would nip at her tail.

"It's more like being in a casket!"

Absolutely invigorated to be finally taking action, I managed to ignore Mrs. Stefano's comment and parked under the Union Street oak tree that shaded the car during the day and hid much of it at night from the side windows of the Kravitz house. The light in Danny's third-floor bedroom was on.

Del stared up at the building, calculating. "Do not tell me why we're doing this, because the less I know, the less bullshit charges the cops can throw at me."

I caught Mrs. Stefano's concern in the rear-view mirror. She was peering up at the roof, her mouth open more than it ought to have been in the circumstances.

"I really do appreciate your wry sense of humor, Del, but there are going to be no 'cops.' We've got a very simple, straightforward exercise here. No 'cops.'"

"Whatever." And she got out of the car and marched up to the Kravitz's front door at the precise moment I realized we hadn't strictly synchronized our roles yet.

"When am I supposed to throw the pebbles?"

Mrs. Stefano had a valid question. "When Del gives you the sign. Or maybe when she comes back to the car. All will make itself known."

"Where are my pebbles?"

The yellow porch light came on, and Mrs. Kravitz answered the door, wearing an athletic t-shirt and sweat pants. She stood behind her screen door, the light making both women appear cirrhotic.

"I'm sure there are some by the house."

"I don't think so. Look, it's just grass."

Del seemed to be speaking longer than was absolutely necessary.

"Well, maybe in the street, then. By the curb."

Now Del was laughing, and she glanced toward the Regency.

"I better go and see if I can find some, then."

"No!—"

But Mrs. Stefano had already opened her door. The interior light came on, and my last word echoed down the street.

"Oops. Sorry." She ducked under the seat back an instant before Del and Mrs. Kravitz looked back in our direction. As the interior light was still on and I appeared to be the only person in the car, I released the hood latch, exited the car and peered down into the Oldsmobile's motor compartment, behaving as if I had yelled "No!" because the car wouldn't start. As soon as Del and Mrs. Kravitz turned back to each other, Mrs. Stefano crawled out of her door and hurried into some shrubbery nearby, for some reason.

The evening wasn't necessarily going according to plan.

"Need some help?" Apparently, an older gentleman had been sitting on his porch in the dark, not fifty feet from the car. I cursed myself for not noticing the pipe smoke earlier, for not preparing both women for every eventuality, for allowing Del to stomp off, roughshod, into a role that required more finesse than I was rapidly realizing she was capable of employing.

"Thank you, sir, but it's just… I think it's the distributor cap. It gets loose sometimes." I amazed myself by my quick thinking and the nonchalant timbre of my voice. I'd almost forgotten about this store of ingenuity that had served me so well in the past, that had rescued me from much more dangerous situations than this. I felt my pulse slow; I was destined to salvage the operation.

"Okay. But I was talking to that lady in my bushes."

Mrs. Stefano slowly rose, grimacing at me as she did so. "Oh, I was just looking for the distributor cap."

"You know, I'm the president of our Neighborhood Crime Watch, and you two ladies are looking awfully suspicious." He said this jovially, but there was a sharp probe behind it. Worse, his voice echoed stridently across the neighborhood (I immediately deduced that he was hearing impaired), and my eyes instinctively jumped back to the Kravitz's porch. Surprisingly, no one was there. Del had disappeared, which was both a relief and a concern. I prayed that Mrs. Kravitz hadn't heard her neighbor's last comment.

"Don't worry, Mrs. Stefano. It's here."

"Oh, good." She scuttled back to me and looked down at my car's air-conditioner compressor. "Oh, there it is."

I angled my head slightly away from the man's direction and whispered: "Get back in the car."

"Before you do that though, Miss, I was kind of wondering what brings you to this neck of the woods?" The man was now on the sidewalk. "I thought I heard one of you mentioning something about the police?"

For a reason that neither one of us could determine at the moment, Mrs. Stefano spoke first. "We got lost."

"You got lost in Two Rivers?! Where are you from?"

I had to rectify. "I'm from down south, and I'm so silly, but I wouldn't take my friend's directions. She knows Two Rivers." I turned to Mrs. Stefano, whose eyes had suddenly become very shifty. "You were right about that left!"

"You've got a Wisconsin plate, though."

"Farther south in Wisconsin."

"Oh. Milwaukee, or…"

"Sheboygan."

"And that other lady—"

"Our other friend was asking for directions."

"But I thought you said that this young lady was from Two Rivers." How did he manage to make this interrogation sound so jovial?

Only once realizing that the engine compartment light shed sinister shadows on our faces did I close the hood. The Crime Watch man certainly didn't need help picking us out of a line-up.

"Well, she's just not terribly familiar with this area." I had to gain the upper hand, and quickly. It was time to take a deep breath, open my senses up to psychological clues, and determine the best course of action to deal with the little man.

He was about seventy. His mailbox had been fashioned out of tin to look like a barn. He stood with his hands on his hips, as if spreading a black, satin cape behind him. I had all the information I needed.

While in high school metal shop, a freak accident with a riveting gun had rendered him unconscious. When he'd awakened minutes later in the arms of his burly yet tender instructor, he'd stared up at the pale neck, realizing that his true idol was not the man before him now, but rather Christopher Lee's eponymous role in 1958's "The Horror of Dracula." Ever since, he'd been suffering from "Vampire Disorder," and was determined to suck the life force out of everyone who strayed into his path, one way or another. He'd been powerless to stop the accident that had robbed him of his normality, but he vowed to control his future by sapping those around him of their will to live, and using this energy to his own advantage. Basically, he'd already sucked Mrs. Stefano dry; I could see this in her slumped, defeatist posture. I had to deflect his instincts before he focused his strange malice too strongly on me.

"You know, my neighborhood hasn't managed to organize a Crime Watch, yet, which seems a little ludicrous to me, to be honest! It's such an important aspect of our community. And since you're obviously an expert in the field, I wonder if you might have time to give me a few pointers on how to set one up. My name is Cassandra, and this is—"

It took Mrs. Stefano a millisecond to reply: "Bebe." Perhaps she still had a bit of her vital force left!

"How long have you been president of your organization, Mr. uhh–?"

"What happened to your friend? She seems to have disappeared!" The contrast between the old man's gracious smile and what came out of it was so marked that "Bebe" grabbed at my sleeve as would a desperate infant.

"Oh. I think she *needed to use the restroom.*" À la Mrs. Stefano, I mouthed the last few words, knowing that the man's deafness could be used to frustrate further questioning. "She's battling a *urinary tract infection.*"

Or he could read lips in the dark. "Oh, that's too bad for her. But I thought you said she'd gone to get directions. And I was kind of wondering: since you parked in front of my house, why didn't your friend just ask directions from me, instead of walking all the way down the street like that?"

"Okay, bye." Mrs. Stefano turned and passed immediately into the shadows of the poorly lit street, swiveling her hips so violently that she could have won a "power-walking" competition. I think she sensed that it was best she departed before nothing was left of her.

Of course, the old man and I could only stare after her, her shuffle echoing farther and farther off until it disappeared into the respectably tree-lined darkness.

I was now alone with the rictus of the man's smile boring into me. I could almost feel my power draining toward him, into him.

"That was odd, Cassandra!"

As my mind flailed wildly for another tactic to deflect his control, I feigned exasperation. "And you know, now that I think about it, it was odd that she was in your bushes, too. You know, I'm starting to wonder about her. I really am."

"Oh, but wouldn't you say your behavior's just about as odd as hers? I'm sorry, what did you say your full name was again?"

He'd remembered my first name ten seconds earlier; I'd already forgotten it. Hadn't it begun with a 'k?' "Well, people just call me 'Kiki.'"

"Kiki and Bebe. That's interesting. And your last name?"

The old buzzard had doubtlessly memorized my license plate number. "You know, it's funny. I've just gotten divorced, and the whole last name thing—you know how that is! Are you married?"

"Hey!"

I never thought I'd be so glad to hear Del's voice booming down an unsuspecting street.

"Oh, it's my friend. Well, listen, I've got to get going, but it's been nice to meet you. We'll have to talk about your crime program very soon."

"Well, I'd like to speak with your friend, if she has a moment."

Del joined us without throwing the old man so much as a glance. "Hey, Roxie wants to meet you."

The evening had plummeted into a death spiral. "Oh, well—"

But the man only politely beamed at Del. "Hello. I was just commenting to your friend, 'Kiki,' here, how odd it is for this neighborhood to see three ladies wandering around in the dark like this. And doing some awfully strange things!"

It was as if Del hadn't even heard him. "Come on!"

My partner had succeeded where I had failed: the old man's smile faded, his energy-sucking blocked. "So did you get the directions you were looking for, Miss?"

Del froze, her back to the man, yet her voice aimed directly at his throat. "Look. If you promise to go back to wherever the hell you came from right now, I promise not to beat the living shit out of you for harassing my friend. *Come on, Kiki.*"

She turned toward the Kravitz's; I didn't have to think long about what to do.

When we were out of earshot: "Thank god you came—"

"Listen, we don't have much time. Roxie is watching us out of her living room window, so act natural."

"Roxie?! I am acting naturally."

"No, you're not. You look like you just murdered your fucking grandmother."

"But you're not serious about me meeting her—"

"Don't worry. She's great. She really is. Like after only five seconds, we were talking as if we'd known each other forever!"

"But I *can't* meet her—"

"Look, you said you wanted to get inside her house, right?"

"Not me, her landlord!"

"Well, you're getting in. Deal with it."

"But I don't need to see her *living room*! And she can't meet *me*! Not yet!"

Del was actually chuckling. "Lady, you better learn pretty fast how to roll with the punches, because that's the only way you're going to survive around me."

"What?! What did you tell her? Why would you even mention me if you only saw a rat on her roof? Del?!"

But Mrs. Kravitz had opened the screen door, the sweat pants pooling around her bare, newly pedicured feet. I found myself staring at the particular shade of red there, dismayed at the fact that this should've been a color for the future, not the present. The sound of a television drifted out into the night from behind her.

"Hi!"

"Hey, Roxie, this is Yolanda."

"Hello."

"Come on in!"

So much of the Kravitz's living room was familiar to me: the yellow walls, the unattractive 1980s torchiere, the cluster of photographs standing on the table behind the sofa, the print of the Native American on horseback over the mantel. It was surreal, though, to see everything so naked, life-sized, distinct. Previously, they'd only been gentle grades of color far, far behind sheer curtains.

The two Schnauzers, who ordinarily barked whenever they sensed that I was anywhere near their house, now ran up to me, insanely wagging their stumps.

Mrs. Kravitz gasped. "Wow! Brownie and Doodles usually only act like that with people they know!"

I bent down to pet their quivering heads. "Oh, well, that's impossible." I realized that it was an odd thing to say only after it had left my mouth, but Mrs. Kravitz seemed not to notice.

"Yeah, unless you ever lived in Kankakee. That's where we just moved from."

"Is that right?" I rose. "Well, it was very nice to meet you, but—"

Del was like a large rock near the door, solid and denying, somehow. "Don't worry. I told her all about us."

A tingling in my scalp erupted and quickly spread down my skull, through my ears and across my face, starring my vision and tunneling my hearing. I was about to faint.

"Hey! Sit down here."

Mrs. Kravitz grabbed my shoulders and dropped me into the velveteen arm chair by the corner window that no one ever sat in. Even though I was passing in and out of consciousness, I noted the firm seat cushion and deduced that this had to be the special spot for guests, for strangers. In my muddle, I found myself about to reassure her that I could just sit on the couch, in the spot where Chelsea usually curled up, nearest the brass tiger on the side table, to read her teenage ghost romances.

But I merely leaned back: "I'm so sorry. Bad mahi mahi."

"Do you need to, you know, throw up or anything?"

I hadn't until Mrs. Kravitz had mentioned it. "Ummm."

Del was in emergency mode: "Where's your bathroom, Roxie?"

"It's upstairs! But I don't think she's going to want to walk up those stairs."(Little did she know.) "Maybe a plastic bag or something?"

"Okay. Where are they?"

"Under the sink in the kitchen. One of the white ones."

My eyes were closed now, an antimacassar at the back of my head.

"You're getting a little color back. Maybe you'll be all right."

I didn't trust myself to respond, so I merely smiled weakly. In actual fact, I didn't want to feel better, because that would mean that I'd have to confront the deteriorating situation. For instance, if Danny happened to wander into the room and discovered me in his house—the woman from the bus he'd left before finishing his story—my life would be cast into ruins. Or worse.

Del returned with the plastic bag, and when Roxie turned away from her, she shot me an extremely significant look. Unfortunately, I had no idea what it might signify. Recognizing that I wasn't grasping her meaning, she mouthed two very cryptic words: "Saint Fatima." I was even more lost, but it was clear to me that I had to take the reigns now. Perhaps she was finally accepting me as her maternal leader.

"I think I'm doing much better now, thank you, Mrs.—or Roxie." I sat up a little. "I suppose that Del told you all about Saint Fatima."

Del had not told Mrs. Kravitz all about Saint Fatima. "No."

Looming behind Mrs. Kravitz now, Del mouthed something I had no problem decrypting: "No."

But it was too late. "Oh, I thought she had."

Then the connection hit me: Saint Fatima! Danny! But how on God's green earth had Del known? I'd breathed a word to no one about my plan, about its origins! Had she rifled through my writings while supposedly "dropping a deuce" at my home? Apparently, I had an even greater need of a secret compartment than I'd originally believed.

But it wasn't the time for recriminations; it was the time for explanations, judging by the look on Mrs. Kravitz's face. And to make matters worse, the cruel smile Del was now offering me indicated that she'd decided to let me twist in the wind.

I would begin innocently, sparingly. It might be all that was needed. "Well, she's more commonly referred to as Our Lady of Fatima. Have you been to Portugal, Roxie?"

"I haven't been to New York, yet, let alone Portugal! Is it some sort of religious thing?"

"As a matter of fact, it is." Of course, this didn't satisfy her. "And Del and I are just planning our visit. To Fatima. In Portugal."

"Oh, wow! I guess I should know this one. So why is she a saint?"

I had to remain as vague as possible. "Oh, the Roman Catholic Church believes that something happened there."

"Oh. What?"

"Just a miracle."

"Wow! What miracle?"

She could easily look it up on the Internet. "The Virgin Mary said some things to some people."

"Oh, so it's an ancient miracle?"

"Well, no. The Twentieth Century."

"Really! So what did she say?"

"Some predictions for the future. To be honest, they were kind of vague. You'd really have to be Catholic to understand them."

"I am."

"Oh. So do you have a favorite saint, or—"

"And the Virgin Mary was seen by the whole town?"

"No, umm… Del, could you just hand me that bag? I think that maybe—"

I held the bag to my face for as long as I could, wishing now that I would vomit. Finally, I spoke: "I'm so sorry about this! I really think I should just get back home and out of your hair."

Del pushed me back down in the chair. "No way. Not in this condition. You still look like hell." She was actually enjoying this, another manifestation of overcompensating for her core desire to be submissive.

I had an idea. "But I'm so thirsty." With Mrs. Kravitz out of the room, Del could debrief me.

As expected, Mrs. Kravitz squeezed my arm. "I'm sorry! Why didn't I—"

But Del put her hand over the one Mrs. Kravitz had placed on my arm. The increase in pressure was pronounced. "No, no, you stay here and let Yolanda finish her story. I'll get her some water."

Del's emotional issues were becoming a severe disappointment.

"I really don't know what Del means, Mrs.—or, umm, Roxie. There isn't any more to the story, really."

"Remember, Yolanda? You were going to tell Roxie what happened when the Virgin Mary appeared to some people."

As Del left the room, I pretended that I needed to sneeze. I squeezed about ten seconds out of the bluff, the whole time wishing I really was devout so that I could fall back on prayer at this point. "Well, she appeared to three children. And that's the whole story."

"Really. Isn't that weird. Because my youngest says the same thing kind of happened to him. Danny."

Del had managed to catch this statement on her way back from stomping all over the ground floor of the Kravitz's home. "Really?!"

"Yeah! It's so weird that we would be talking about something like this! The whole 'kid with a vision' thing—"

I had to take control. "Oh, my goodness! We've got to go, Del! I just realized that I forgot to deliver my mother-in-law's dinner! Ida must be starving! She has low blood sugar, and the slightest deviation from her schedule—" I rose as quickly as I could.

"Oh. I thought Del said you just moved here."

"I have! So I can take care of my mother-in-law."

Roxie still shot a confused glance at Del, who attempted to plaster a serious look on her face and failed. "Yolanda, I told Roxie about why we *really* came."

"Yeah, and I'd be glad to let you wander around the house. Maybe tomorrow, when the kids are at school. But right now, they're sleeping, so…"

The look of devastation on my face must have been amusing because now Mrs. Kravitz was hiding a smile from me, too. She continued: "Listen, I drove by my old house in Cedar Rapids when I went back to visit, but I was too scared to knock on the door. Plus, I didn't have a lot of nice memories, so that was kind of another reason not to want to go in. But I still drove by."

I, on the other hand, had "a lot of nice memories of growing up in the Kravitz's house," according to Del's raised eyebrows and smirk. The last fifteen minutes had been too much on my nervous system; I was no longer able to determine whether these developments were a good thing or not.

Mrs. Kravitz herded us to the door. "But anyway, you've got to get to your mother-in-law. But it was nice to meet you guys! Finally, I know someone in Two Rivers besides my landlord."

Del paused at the door, rubbing her boots against the edge of the entry rug. For the first time since I'd known her, she was not completely self-possessed. "Yeah, it was great to meet you, too! Even under the—you know—sort of crazy circumstances." She jerked her head toward me in what was meant to represent a humorous observation.

My shock allowed me to ignore anything, and I merely shook Mrs. Kravitz's hand. "You've been very kind, Roxie. I look forward to dropping by in the near future. When the kids are at school."

"Absolutely! Oh, and I hope you feel better. I can imagine what an emotional shock it must have been to walk in here after so many years."

"Yes, well…"

When the front door closed behind us, Del began to titter: "Saint Fatima?!"

"Not here."

"What the fuck!"

"Ssshh! Not now!"

"You crazy bitch! I was saying, 'shut your fucking mouth,' not 'Saint Fatima!'" Now that the adrenaline was beginning to be reabsorbed by my body, I felt my anger rise, mostly toward myself. In the past, I'd known how vital preparation was to executing a plan; my carelessness was now its own bitter punishment.

As if to physically reinforce my guilt, the sound of pebbles hitting vinyl siding could be heard on the other side of the Kravitz house. And then the sound of a window shattering.

Pipe smoke near the Regency was enough to warn Del and me not to acknowledge the noise, but rather to calmly enter the car and drive away, into the night, into the roiling curtains of suspicion that were already beginning to envelop our enterprise.

5

I had a funny dream.

There was something very comforting to me about the smell of peroxide and styling products. It was always present when I closed my eyes and the tepid water ran through my hair. I could depend on a lifetime of scattered salons spread across the globe, each with its own particulars, but every one with these particular scents in common. In fact, the human race itself had decided that there was something right about this process; for a moment, I felt embraced by our universal culture, protected from anything too specific by the gentle blanketing of our shared life experience. In fact, our existence was simple, obvious to me for an instant: several things happen to us, and then we die. Everything was really *one* thing. And then it was even simpler: only the fingers stroking, massaging, so effortless, so direct. Even Two Rivers. Even here in Two Rivers.

Two Rivers! It all came crashing back to me, and I reemerged into the conscious world. No amount of philosophical relaxation could eradicate the previous night, and Monique must have sensed this because she stopped shampooing.

"Everything okay?" Her voice, though soothing, had the unmistakable nasality of the upper Midwest. Every syllable reverberated through the sinuses, bringing to mind the ill-borne kazoo.

"Oh, it's nothing. I just noticed the time; I'm starting my first day of a new job in an hour." And before she had a chance: "Food technician at Darby Hills Elementary School."

"Lunch lady? Neat! Remember, they're growing, so extra gravy!"

I wasn't at all sure of Monique's logic, so I merely smiled as she wrapped a thick towel around my head and sat me back up.

"I'm kidding. My mother used to think that gravy equaled strength. But really, when we talk about it now, it usually means extra stuff, you know? 'The rest is gravy.' But it's more like extra fat on your bodankadonk!"

An astute observation. "Have you ever been betrayed, Monique?"

"What do you mean, like my boyfriend?"

Two Rivers! "Not necessarily. Just betrayed."

"Umm, I guess so. Oh, you know what? I think Kari-Anne is ready for you."

I slipped her a ten dollar bill. "Exactly. Why should I feel so special?"

That truly was the question. I was nothing more than an atom in the workings of the universal experience; I needed to process what Del had done to me and simply focus on my first working day—and my new, lunch-lady hair style. (Claude had always insisted on looking the part, too. Each role was a chrysalis to him, an opportunity to develop, hidden. And afterward, when he emerged, his patterns were a little more complex, his palette of living widened forever.)

I thrilled as I described the ugliness of the cut to Kari-Anne. Her look of barely suppressed distaste was my first step, my first wiggle in the hard shell I was creating for myself.

"...and feathered bangs."

Feathered bangs happen to us! I felt electric, at one with the early autumn storm on the other side of the plate glass. Why was I allowing anything to worry me? Because life was really quite simple: feathered bangs happen.

Feathered bangs happen to us, and then we die.

I felt the truth of this last statement so intensely that I shared it with Kari-Anne, who never again looked me in the eye.

Universal truth could have that effect.

Lying back as she began in earnest on the travesty, I considered the previous night:

"Hey, I told you I like to fuck with people. And that definitely includes you."

Del was still chuckling about the evening's operation an hour after it had self-destructed. She'd bought a six-pack of "Old Milwaukee," shocked to hear that I didn't stock any, and was completing the third one at my kitchen table as she explained her particular philosophy to me. (For a reason I couldn't quite determine, Del would crush each can when she was through with it and throw it in my sink. She couldn't be a recycler—did she assume that everyone ground up their empties in their garbage disposals as she did? Or did she just need a mother's discipline!)

"Yes, you did say that."

"Saint Fatima! What the fuck is wrong with you!" She was still amused.

And I still wasn't. Del hadn't yet allowed herself to develop any respect for my authority, and it was beginning to jeopardize the entire mission. In fact, because of Del's caprice, my entire plan had to be completely redesigned. Even now, she acted as if I were a push-over, someone "with whom to fuck." So far, I'd given her leeway, I'd been supportive, encouraging her to find a path to her true self in her own time. But more than ever, it was becoming clear that she needed much more active guidance; all this acting-out was really a plea for an "alpha dog" to urinate on her.

And now, I was more than happy to oblige. It was just about time to release the hounds.

As I felt my rage crest, I glimpsed a reflection of myself in her eyes: a human hurricane. It was interesting to note that my fury also asserted itself in a counter-clockwise fashion. "Del—"

"No, you're not. Things have changed, and this is how it's going to work: we're doing things my way from now on. Because we've got a brand new mission on our hands."

"New mission? That's—"

"That's right. New mission. Operation Roxie." She cracked open a new can as she said this. The action was somehow profane, salacious, but she looked down as she said it. There was weakness somewhere in this that calmed me.

"Operation Roxie?"

"Yeah. I want to get with her, so that's the new mission."

"Get with her?"' But I knew. And she knew I knew.

"Or! Or. Or, you know, I blab your whole fucking crazy-ass business to anyone who'll listen. You know, I still have the *signed* blueprints for your secret-bookcase-compartment-closet. That alone is enough to get you locked up in some crazy bin."

"But you don't need a plan for Roxie! Just ask her—"

"I'm telling you! I need a plan." She was more uncomfortable than I was at this point, her words exposures, little private defeats, each of them.

My hounds all retreated back inside. No one was urinating on anyone else this evening. She was having a breakthrough, finally admitting her dependence on me.

"Okay."

Now Del did look up at me, surprised and distrustful. To cover the tell, she gulped down the entire high-boy, her throat constricting and relaxing in my face.

"That's fair, Del. You help me with my mission, and I'll help you with yours."

"Umm, not quite. You help me with my mission, or I tell the world about yours, and I help you with your mission whenever the fuck I feel like it. Or not."

She'd never knowingly sabotage things again. I knew her better than that because it would mean that she could never serve under my leadership again.

"Okay, Del. It's a deal."

"Actually, it's not even open for discussion, but anyways."

She had to feel the victor in this exchange. I understood. "I understand, Del."

"Do you understand that I will punch you in the face—even in your own kitchen—if you use that tone with me?"

I had unlocked her humanity. She was all bark and no bite. "Of course, I do, Del."

She rose as if to "assault" me, but the sudden appearance of a ghostly face among the moths at the screen door "distracted her from beating me up."

"Are you mad at me, Yolanda?" Of course, it was our vandal of the evening.

"I'm not mad at you, Mrs. Stefano. Why don't you come in?"

She remained on the stoop, safe with the moths. "I'm so sorry about the whole window thing. That big pebble was heavier than I thought. It didn't go as high."

I briefly wondered about her definition of "pebble," then dismissed it. "We know that. Come in, and we'll discuss our next move. Del has a mission now, too, for us to complete."

Mrs. Stefano looked at Del very uncertainly, the aimless flutter of innocent insects offering a visual representation of her emotional state: a furry, gray, nervous aura.

"Were you going to punch Yolanda just now?"

"Yes."

"Are *you* mad at me?"

"Just get your ass in here!"

It was all Mrs. Stefano needed. She joined us, keeping as much of the table between us as possible.

"So what happened after I threw the pebbles? Did they think it was a rat?"

Del returned her full attention to me. "Yeah. They thought a rat threw a rock through their window. Look, just forget about that, Heather. I was about to ask a very interesting question. Roxie said that her son had been visited by a saint or something, and as soon as she said that, Yolanda here looked like she'd just seen a ghost. Care to share, Yolanda?"

It was time. Neither of them was near ready, but it was time.

I took a deep breath, long, slow nods of my head indicating a sangfroid surrender to pragmatism. It was time to reveal the future of Two Rivers and the person at the heart of this revolution.

"Dorothy Hamill?"

"Yes."

"You know, I don't actually know what that means."

Kari-Anne's kind concern for my fashion sense pulled me from my reverie, although I wasn't at all sure about the frosted pouf on top of her head and what it might signify as to her particular sense of style.

As I did with every new environment I entered, I'd scanned the entire salon the moment I'd walked in for threats, for opportunities. There was a computer in one corner. "Why don't you Google surf for it? 'The Dorothy Hamill bob.' That might make the most sense, Kari-Anne, don't you think?"

She looked over at the computer, almost afraid. "Oh, yeah. That's a good idea."

With her absence, my mind wandered back to the previous night's unveiling...

"About three months ago, while on a Greyhound bus to Sheboygan–"

"What the fuck were you doing on a bus to Sheboygan?!"

I was merely still. Del's interruptions would be irritating only to herself.

"Christ! All right, you were on a bus to Sheboygan."

"About three months ago, while on a Greyhound bus to Sheboygan, I met Roxie's son, Danny."

"Oh, god! Is this a love story?" Mrs. Stefano wanted a love story.

"He's six."

She considered this a moment. "Well, you did say a bus."

I wasn't sure what this meant, but I let the comment pass. "And he—"

"Oh! So this is why you wanted to get a job as a teacher for his class! Because he lives right next to Darby Hills! And why you wanted your landlord to get into his house! Why did you want your landlord to get into his house?"

"Mrs. Stefano, I promise you I'll explain everything now."

She tittered. "Sorry! I've just been going crazy trying to figure out what we're doing, but you never tell me anything!"

"I'm trying to tell you now."

"So you're sure it's not a love affair—"

"Heather! Shut your frigging pie hole!" I was confident that after Del's request, I'd have no further interruptions from either of them.

I decided to take a different tack: "Look, what does Two Rivers mean to both of you?"

"What does it mean? It means small-town boring hick nowhere lame-ass dead zone where I was unfortunately born and raised and now can't get out of to save my fucking life."

"Okay, Del. Thank you. And how about you, Mrs. Stefano?"

"It's nice." Her face darkened. "But that's the wrong answer."

"Absolutely not! They're both the right answer. Don't you see?"

Del rose again as if to "strike" me, so I good-naturedly joined her in the pantomime and gestured that she should "calm down."

"Two Rivers is a bit provincial, it's true. But there is so much potential here, if the residents were only invited to think outside the box, as it were! To get off the Midwest treadmill and experience the rawness—the immediacy of the joy of life!"

Of course, they weren't following. But how could I make my case clearer?

"Look, when was the last time you really, truly experienced life? The adrenaline, the surprise, the visceral pleasure of our earthly plane of existence?"

"Give me five minutes with Roxie." Del followed up this inappropriate comment with an even more inappropriate snicker.

Mrs. Stefano only shrugged. "My niece's soccer games are pretty fun."

"All right. Now, what if we spearheaded a movement that would allow Two Riverians to experience something completely unique, utterly whimsical? Something that existed solely to add flourish to life, to help us really and truly 'be here, now?'"

"What, like Disney World?" Mrs. Stefano was feeling my enthusiasm.

"Similar, yes. Only unique to Two Rivers."

Del wasn't feeling my enthusiasm. "Roxie's kid told you to open an amusement park in Two Rivers on a Greyhound bus from Sheboygan?! That's your fucking plan?!"

"To Sheboygan."

"*To* fucking Sheboygan?!"

"No."

"Then what the fuck did he tell you?"

"...to cook the lima beans until they're mushy, next time."

I suddenly became aware that Kari-Anne had been giving me a blow-by-blow of her previous evening's meal for several minutes. My response was overdue. I obliged: "Oh, yes?"

"Carl's mother was German, and I guess she cooked everything until it fell apart."

She continued, moving onto the pork and allowing my mind to wander back to my final revelation of the previous evening:

"Not-tay why yay-yee?"

Del stared at Mrs. Stefano disrespectfully. "No, Heather. She said, 'Not A... Y... Period. A... E...' Sundae."

"Oh. Oh! Like the ice cream! 'Sundae school!' A school for making sundaes! *A school for making sundaes?*"

"Exactly." It was thrilling to hear it finally said out loud by another soul. "When Danny awoke (he was seated next to me on the bus), he shared with me that an angel had just appeared to him and told him that there should be a 'sundae school in Two Rivers.'"

"An angel? Is that where you got Saint Fatima from?" Del had quite quickly made the connection. I was impressed.

"I thought that's where *you* got it from!"

She continued, her frown increasing the number of already numerous shadows cast down her face by the overhead light. "An angel. Did he say he *saw* the angel? On the bus?"

"No, in his dream. But what's important is that it's a brilliant idea and—"

"Wait a minute. So you want to open an ice-cream school in Podunk, Nowhere, U.S.A., because some six-year-old had some goofy dream. You do realize that's even crazier than opening up Disney World in Two Rivers?"

"Not necessarily—"

"Because this is where the sundae was invented, right?" I positively basked in Mrs. Stefano's lack of resistance. "I get it now! But why did you want to check out Danny's room? And teach his class?"

"Because he and his family got off the bus before he could tell me all the particulars! I know no more than what I just told you! We need to know everything the angel told him: where to build the sundae school, how to construct it. Plus, Danny should be at the center of this! It's his vision, it's his crusade! I'm merely here to support him, to facilitate the process."

"And by 'process,' you mean 'fucking nuts.'"

"Del—"

"Wait. Hold on. Just let me see if I've got this right. So you were worried that it might look a little odd if some *fifty-year-old woman* who just suddenly showed up in town started hanging around with a first-grader she met on a bus. Is that right? But you feel that in order to start a school that teaches people how to make ice-cream sundaes, you need the details of a dream that's probably not going to make any sense, anyway. So you're having other people do the dirty work for you, like sneaking into his room, which somehow is going to tell us what he dreamed about."

"I dream journal could—"

"Oh, yeah. He'll have one of those. And meanwhile, you're going to be 'bumping into him' in the cafeteria every day so you can build up his trust in you or something. Is that about right?" Someday, Del's wit would work in our favor; presently, it wasn't. "Oh, that's great, Mrs. Sanity."

"Actually—" I caught myself just before correcting her use of the word "Mrs." Instead, I continued, undeterred: "Actually, to be honest, I also wanted to be sure of his situation before moving forward. And I'm *forty-eight.*"

"His *situation*?! He's six-years old! His 'situation' is fucking cartoons and Kool-Aid and footie pajamas!"

"Look, Del—"

"Look, Yolanda. I know that asking nut-jobs logical questions is like pissing in the wind, but here goes nothing. Why don't you just go over there tomorrow and ask him, '*what happened in your dream?*' Instead of getting a job just so you can stalk him and making up insane stories like rats on roofs and Saint mother-fucking Fatima?"

"I didn't make that up."

"Is this the only reason you moved here?"

"Don't tell me you've never been inspired by a serendipitous event to—"

"To what? Be fucking mentally unstable? I'm telling Roxie all about this tomorrow. You're certifiable."

"Tell her, and I will, too."

"She'll figure out what I'm after soon enough."

"Maybe not the way I tell it."

"How about I just put you into a coma?"

"How about I just wax a little around your eyebrows?"

Kari-Anne had finally noticed that I was going for a more natural, old-fashioned look, a vital aspect of my lunch-lady persona. I managed at last to focus on the mirror before me: the site was hideous. I looked just like a librarian from 1977.

"Oh, that's perfect! No, I'm going to leave my brows alone, thank you. Maybe even dye them, so they look fuller."

Kari-Anne pulled a very polite, very insincere smile across her face.

"Well, then, fuck you. There's no way I'm going to play any part in this crazy-ass scheme of yours." Del rose, being sure to grab her last can of beer. "Keep your money and your secret hiding places and your ice-cream angel dreams." She then proceeded to "get all up in my grille," to which, I believe, it's referred. "Now, *I'm* not going to say anything to Roxie, and *you're* not going to say anything to Roxie, and when they come to cart you away to the loony bin, I'm going to be there to shut the ambulance door on your ass. Okay?"

Her home life as a youngster must have been hell: the uncaring, weak mother who only ever wanted a "Wisconsin Barbie;" the years of subtle destruction. Del's extreme response merely confirmed that the process of transferring her subconscious mother-role to me was taking place—as predicted. It was a perfectly logical progression. In fact, it was clear that presently, we were reliving her teenage rebellion years. Soon, she'd progress into an adult relationship with me, her respect becoming deeply organic. So my next step would be to facilitate the process by providing a patient, empathetic, accepting presence. She wouldn't reject membership on Team Polanski for long.

I knew that now.

"I support your decision, Delilah."

"I'm going to fucking kill you!"

But before any "punch" connected, Mrs. Stefano rose and "restrained" Del. "Come on! I know it's a little weird, but it sounds like fun, too! Sundae school! If I help, do I get to take the classes for free?"

"I'll see to it, myself, Mrs. Stefano."

"I love whipped cream."

Del cackled suddenly, cruelly. "Fine! Buh-bye, folks!" She approached the screen door, her boots stomping out the existence of years of patent-leather pumps, of ballerina slippers. "I hope they give you both lots of great drugs in the nut house." And she was gone.

Mrs. Stefano grimaced. "Geez."

"Don't give it another thought! She's neck-deep in the process of coming to terms with her relationship with me right now. It'll be tough going for a while. But Del's a smart woman; she'll have a break-through any day, and then she'll return as an even more valuable member of the team because she'll welcome my authority, rather than fight it. Our Delilah just has to realize that the scissors she holds are only poised at her own hair."

"Uhhhmmm... Okay. Oh, I forgot! Remember I told you I had something for you?" Now Mrs. Stefano grew coy. She stood up, tearing at the edge of the paper bag she had in her hands. "I guessed about the size and all, but anyway. I'll see you tomorrow at work and you can let me know then and stuff."

She threw the bag across the table toward me and ran out the door, once again enveloped by the sultry night. I imagined the moths following their queen in the moonlight, finally a direction, a goal, a destination in their short, ecstatic lives.

The bag contained what appeared to be a full squirrel costume, complete with a bushy tail and fur-covered, papier mache head.

It had been a long night. I rose, now conscious of the fact that I would have to commit a bit more thought as to the precise composition of Mrs. Stefano's inner workings.

As I turned out the light, I glanced back, the squirrel head seemingly returning my regard.

Apparently, I was expected not only to wear it, but to look out its nostrils.

6

I have to know more!

"But they called it 'uncrustable' on the computer!"

"Well, to me, that would mean that it would be impossible to put *another* crust on the sandwich, rather than indicate one that's had its crust *removed*."

My lilac polyester pantsuit somehow managed to employ perspiration as a catalyst for a particularly cruel kind of burning itchiness, and considering my circumstances, I resisted with all my might the urge to scratch at my inside thighs.

The little girl stared up at me over the steam table, her brain carefully processing the information I'd just provided. Finally: "Okay."

With my plastic-mitten-sheathed hand, I carefully placed what passed as food in Wisconsin onto her plate, the whiteness of the bread glowing like a white-hot spotlight in the cabaret commotion of the Darby Hills Elementary School cafeteria. It was a bitterly regretful outcome for both of us.

Even more of a disappointment was the fact that Danny hadn't appeared in the cafeteria yet. The thought occurred to me that Mrs. Stefano might have broken more than just a window with her "pebble," so I visited the main office after the first lunch period to ask her if Danny was injured, or perhaps simply ill.

"Oh my god! Why are you dressed like that? And your hair! And those glasses are so big!" She was alone.

"I refuse ever to play a part half-way, Mrs. Stefano."

"But you look... kind of a little weird."

"Absolutely! Lunch ladies are a weird bunch."

As with most things, Mrs. Stefano quickly let go. "Okay. So what did you think? Did you like it?"

"Well, I'll never be able to look ravioli in the eye again."

"No! I mean the—you know."

"Oh, the squirrel suit?"

She shook her head violently, looking around the empty room. For some reason, the costume she'd made me was supposed to be a secret.

Actually, I wasn't sure of *any* of the reasons for the squirrel suit, but I appreciated that she'd spent a sizeable portion of her life creating it for me, so respect was in order.

"Oh, well, it's absolutely beautiful. The handicraft. Very lifelike, with the tail... and the nostrils—"

"But—you know."

"Do I?"

"Is it—you know—*right*?"

Mrs. Stefano stared up at me, her tension made even more naked by the fluorescent lighting, the edges of her mouth turned up in rapt expectation. If a woman's heart ever stopped beating from hope, this was it.

I stared at her blouse, today covered with Deputy Dawg in various action poses (where on earth did she find these fabrics?!), and I searched the images for something that might offer a clue as to how to respond to her question. There were only lassos and saguaro cacti.

Mr. Krimm's door opened, quickly shut, then opened again, his face now carefully drained of the shock at seeing my new image. I never thought I'd ever be so glad to see the man, but I'd managed years ago to be surprised at nothing—even my own reactions. In my universe, the gut was the alpha and the omega.

I threw my huge glasses off kilter. "Mr. Krimm! How are you?"

"Fine. Heather, I'm just heading out for lunch. I'll see you in a few." He'd barely slowed down his stride to deliver this information, but at the door, he struggled internally, paused. "*Ms.* Polanski, aren't you supposed to be in the cafeteria now?"

"I just needed to pick up a form from Mrs. Stefano."

"I don't see a form."

"She's was just about to make a copy for me."

"Which form?"

"Emergency contact information. It just changed."

"It just changed *since this morning*?"

"Funny, isn't it."

"Hilarious. What changed?"

"My aunt's cell-phone number."

"Oh, did she move, or—"

"Fascinating story! She actually dropped her old cell phone into a freshly squeezed pitcher of orange juice that she'd just prepared for her church choir. She'd placed the phone in her chest pocket for some reason, and it happened when she bent over to reach for the sheet music that had fallen under her piano bench. How often do you suppose I've begged her not to use those pockets! Her reading glasses, for instance. It's an absolute recipe for disaster."

"She put a pitcher of orange juice on her piano bench."

"It's a terrible thing to admit, but my aunt isn't the most—let's just say 'aware' person on the planet. At fifteen, there was a dressage accident."

"Is that a fact." I could almost see the cogs grinding against one another behind his hawk's glare, the quick-moving consideration of the raptor sizing up its prey. In this instance, I would *not* play the squirrel and merely smiled pleasantly back at him. For that moment, I believed my story completely; it was a technique that had never failed me, and it didn't fail me now.

Dissatisfied by his position of weakness, Mr. Krimm turned his keen gaze on Mrs. Stefano, who was too busy with something on her desk to meet his eyes.

"Bye."

The chance to delay my response to Mrs. Stefano's squirrel-suit question was walking out with Mr. Krimm. "Actually, I'll join you on the walk back to the cafeteria! I'll be on the lookout for that form, Mrs. Stefano. Thank you for your help."

In the cool corridor, Mr. Krimm managed somehow to walk forward and yet at the same time, remain turned away from me at his side. I found this aptitude for asymmetrical, negative body language quite admirable and stored the maneuver away for future use. No doubt the uneven nipples helped.

"You know, I probably can't fire you for making up some cock-and-bull story about your aunt, but I won't hesitate to terminate you if I find out you're lying about anything to do with this school."

The adrenaline rush of a worthy adversary! "I can assure you that I would never do anything to jeopardize my position at Darby Hills. It means far too much to me."

"Yeah. For instance, if you told a lie just like that one." He pushed open the door to the boy's bathroom, and I banished an image of his six-foot, five-inch frame at a two-foot, six-inch urinal. Over his shoulder: "And do me a favor: stay away from my office."

The door swung shut just as the bell rang. I was late.

As I began to modify my orange juice/aunt story to explain my tardiness at the lunch line to my manager, Kryst'l, Mrs. Stefano ran up to me. "Yolanda, Yolanda!"

The swirling torrent of children in the hallway was slowing my progress enough; I certainly didn't have time to stall on the question of the costume's "rightness."

But I turned to her, as always welcoming a challenge. (Claude had once been challenged. He'd gone two days without urinating in Moab, Utah simply because an imbecilic rancher had commented that he had a bladder the size of a pea. The medivac team had likened the water he'd eventually passed to molasses.)

"I forgot to tell you! Danny isn't here."

"Ahh! I thought not."

"No, I mean, he doesn't go to this school! I think his mother enrolled him at one of the parochials. St. Matthew's."

I closed my gaping mouth as soon as I became aware of it. By the reactions of many of the young students around me, the delay must have lasted several seconds. "St. Matthew's?"

"Well, I guess it makes sense. Catholics, you know, believe in miracles and stuff. Like *the angel*." She whispered her last words, an unnecessary act for so many reasons.

I was dumbstruck. After having worked so hard to position myself in precisely this situation and catalogued counter strategies for every possible scenario, I found it difficult to believe that fate had still managed to drop my plan right into the piano-bench juice.

"Sorry about that. I guess I could have checked the enrollment forms before."

It sunk in. Despite my urbane history, my world-class education, my native intelligence—despite it all, I was now serving 'uncrustables' to second graders in Two Rivers, Wisconsin while sporting bushy eyebrows, a purple torture device and a haircut that went out of style with disco. For nothing.

But I would consider all of that later; right now, I had to resume my post at the "whipped, reconstituted potatoes."

"Thank you, Mrs. Stefano—" Mr. Krimm emerged from the boy's room, rolling his eyes when he saw us, "—for the emergency contact form."

Mrs. Stefano quickly retreated, stricken with an air of pantomime guilt, as I turned back to my original course upstream.

Always upstream. But even when it makes an occasional, tactical error, the Chinook commands respect, admiration. In the final reckoning, what more could matter?

* * *

"Sassy by Sissy." The entire enterprise had been a mistake from the moment of its naming to the present. This was clear to me now. So why hadn't I sensed it before I'd walked in?

"Because you want to cover your toilet brush, right? And it has scent crystals built right in. Totally my idea." The woman, whom I assumed was the aforementioned Sissy, seemed very, very proud of this fact. She had the large eyes of a faun and the tight jeans of a Gloria Vanderbilt circa 1981. I told myself the look must have been on its way back "in" again, but the lie rang as hollow as Sissy's "Miss Piggy" cookie jars. There were eleven of them, at last count.

"My old boyfriend, Gerald, thought I could patent the process, but he tried to patent his mini-helicopter idea, and that went nowhere fast. Just like his mini-helicopter! But I loved the goof."

"Oh." It was very hot in the cramped, former Photomat. The homemade jewelry, clothing and household novelty items pushed in on me—each red-velvet bow, every sinister rhinestone, all the Christmas sweaters with their angry cross-stitching. It was all a manifestation of the crushing provinciality that had compacted this woman's life down to a small box stranded in the pitted parking lot of a dying mall. I wanted only to embrace her. She had spent a lifetime alone—dismissed by those she loved as a "goof" undoubtedly—her elemental need for expression, for originality choked off into some kind of Midwestern kitsch-fest, a capitulation to the world she'd been strapped to all her life. And now she was trying to sell it to the rest of us.

"Or maybe you're into zircons!"

"Sissy, have you ever wished you could transcend our mundane existence for an hour or two and just venture into the whimsy of life, participate in a creative activity that has absolutely no purpose but to be experienced as a joyous thing in itself?"

"No."

"Yes, I love zircons." I was squeezed by the store's dry, cinnamon-scented heat and was sure, now, that my pantsuit had been designed solely for the purpose of destroying its occupant, slowly, so slowly. "And I see you've glued them to cell phone covers!"

As Sissy spread before me her semi-precious misjudgments, I snuck a peek over her shoulder, across the street, into the Kravitz's backyard. St. Matthew's was on the other side of town; Mrs. Kravitz would have to pick her children up. It was nearly four p.m. She'd have to be home soon.

I managed to refocus on the woman before me, who had incorrectly determined that the sole purpose of communication was to string several words together, much like her faux Indian-bead necklaces. "—exactly like Lindsay Lohan, although I guess we're not supposed to like her, anymore. Of course, what do you expect, being raised like that. Oh, no! You're not from L.A., are you?"

"Hmm. I wonder why you'd ask me that?"

"Oh, well, I don't recognize you, and you've got that whole kind of retro thing going on. It's neat."

The extent of a community's naiveté was directly in proportion to the outlandish assumptions it made about the "neatness" of the outside world.

"No, no, I live here." Mrs. Kravitz pulled into her driveway. "Well, thank you so much for showing me all your creations, Sissy! I don't need anything just right now."

"Oh, well, you know where to find me!" But before I left her shop: "So what's so interesting about across the street?"

The populace of Two Rivers! My heart rejoiced, as it had so often since appearing in the town. These people might have been culture-starved, their horizon extending for a block, rather than spreading across a globe bursting with traditions and landscapes unknown, unfathomable. But they weren't without a certain sharp, natural perception. With some time and coaching, they would sense the genius of my Sundae School and the myriad ways it would benefit their community just as, somehow, Sissy had sensed on some primal level that I was concerned with the events at the Kravitz household.

"Because you've been staring over my shoulder for the past half an hour."

Brava! Ought I to recruit? I considered my next move. Con: a homemade tampon holder designed to look like a wallet—but truly didn't—in a steaming Photomat that was nothing more than a tragic symbol of a creative instinct perverted by backwater Wisconsin. Pro: an undeniable ingenuity that was undoubtedly burning to embrace other, less heartbreaking ways of expressing itself.

She had earned a commission in my army.

"Very astute of you, Sissy. Look, I am in the process of bringing the joy of now to Two Rivers. And that light green house across the street is at the core of this transformation."

"What do you mean?"

I couldn't help but smile. "In a few weeks, you'll know exactly what I mean. But right now, what our team needs is someone with a creative mind, someone who can create something out of virtually nothing." I glanced around the room, a punctuation. "And once I've been informed exactly how our plan must be carried out by the young man who originated the project, we're going to need to find a space, a building that can be converted into an educational facility here in Two Rivers. It's going to take a keen eye to find the right structure, someone who can take something perhaps a bit shabby and turn it into something magical, unique. Someone who may have been waiting a lifetime for permission to really let loose, to finally execute something profound and important on a grand scale."

Pausing, I allowed the opportunity to sink in.

"Oh. Well, good luck with that."

I'd been too subtle. Another visit to Sissy would be in order later, after the significance of my words had time to sink in.

Then slowly, her smile slipped. It became pained, tremulous. "But hey, you know what? I don't need 'permission' to do what I do. I've never asked for it. All this may not seem *important,* but, you know, it's what I love."

I'd hit a nerve, just as I knew I would. Sissy needed more time to process my offer, to revisit the foundations upon which her existence had been standing for so long. It was ridiculous to think that I could open her eyes with a few passionate sentences.

It was also disturbing to see how upset she'd become. "Of course, Sissy. You know, actually that toilet brush cover might be a nice gift for a friend."

"That's all right."

"Honestly, I'd like to buy it."

"Well, it's not for sale."

There was more fire in her belly than I'd thought.

"All right."

"Well, bye."

"Goodbye."

As I bowed a little to her, surrounded by all the detritus in the cramped space, the smell of glue gun and Charlie body spray following me out into the sunshine, I vowed that I would somehow enroll Sissy in sundae school and pay every cent of her tuition. If nothing else, she'd be my exemplar, proof that native creativity needn't always end up so misdirected, so in-grown.

I quickly crossed the street, the cool scent of fall in the air. Wisconsin in the winter might not have been the best time to launch a revolution, but perhaps it would be the best time of all! What else would the populace have to do?

For the first time, I allowed myself to visualize. I imagined a frosted window that framed snow-gear dropped anywhere, people of every age laughing and rejoicing in the warmth, each positioning a cherry on top at the exact moment their revered guru commanded. Rows and rows of kaleidoscopic ice-cream creations extended out, hazelnuts and lavender and peanut-butter marshmallow and cerulean and blackberry truffle and delicate cream and homemade banana-bread topping and caramel that hardened into a crunchy shell the moment it came in contact with fruit-studded, tangerine sherbet. There was the young girl with a stack of fluorescent spheres rising fifteen high with mango drizzle circling around and around to the sherbet summit, a remote mountain trail of golden Hawaii. There was the monster-truck driver with the traditional banana split before him, only the bananas were chocolate-covered and the ice cream was chocolate-covered and the dusting of almond slivers was chocolate-covered and the bowl was chocolate-covered and the spoon was chocolate-covered and the doily beneath it was chocolate-covered and the creation was itself a challenge, an invitation to figure out the best way to eat it without missing a molecule of its dark brown theme. Then there was a mint-chocolate-chip Parthenon devised by a woman too old and poor to ever see the original herself, and it was all hers now, to ingest no less wonderfully than would one who ascended the Acropolis and ingested the beauty there, chocolate chips arranging themselves into constellations, establishing the astrology of a private pantheon, the celestial tang of gods and goddesses in every spoonful. Of course, Sissy was there, too, crafting Miss Piggy out of cinnamon-apple swirl and perhaps disguising something inside, such as a lime-sorbet Kermit or a dream-catcher key ring.

And at the very heart of my sundae school, and just as primary, stood life's only and always twin choices: to gobble down or melt away.

Inspiring all this—because of all this—would be a spirit of wonder, of joy in the boundless bounty of the moment, a reminder that anything is *precisely* what should always be happening in one's life, anything and anything and anything at all, the plot not forever predicted, dreaded, demanded, regretted. This would be the gift given *by* Two Rivers *to* Two Rivers, to a community that had forgotten that there is only ever a *now*. And this would be the gift given by a young boy whose innocent words and divine prescience might someday be known and celebrated across the globe, with my humble support to gently guide him.

"Yolanda?!" Samuel immediately emerged from the shadows behind Mrs. Kravitz and the front door. His gaping smile quickly faded into a gaping frown as it neared the afternoon light, his good humor seemingly photosensitive.

"You guys know each other?" But already, Mrs. Kravitz turned to Samuel.

"She's another one of my tenants." He spoke to her, but he looked right at me. "Someone threw a rock through one of Roxie's windows, so I'm here to fix it. What are you doing here?"

And then, movement behind him. Chelsea? Shay?! *Or Danny.*

I managed to find my voice. "How are you, Sam? Mrs. Kra—Roxie? We seem to be running into each other quite a lot, lately, don't we." My peripheral vision burned inside my brain, so desperate was I to determine who was in the murkiness behind Sam. But choking smoke filled so many of the chambers of my mind; I was panicking—sober on the exterior, but blind and directionless as to my next move, my facial muscles twitching and squirming under the strain of my "casual grin." One "coincidence," I could gracefully finesse: I had already developed an intricate scenario if Danny should happen to mention to his mother that he recognized me before I had a chance to explain everything to him. (I'd simply give them the details of my doppelganger, a.k.a. Cherie Gustafson, who had been spotted around northeast Wisconsin for years, my Moby Dick in a way, and no less destructive. I'd go on to say that she'd bounced several checks in my name and had a documented interest in the dream lives of young boys. Then, only after pointing out that I'd very recently returned from helping to build a Congolese desalinization plant and deflecting any suspicion from myself, would I gently enquire into Danny's dream and finally extract the information I needed, à la Queequeg.)

Yes, a single "coincidence" I could quite easily smooth over, but three acts of supposed kismet would involve a narrative schematic even I couldn't concoct at this terrible juncture. At this sunny, autumn doorstep of my future.

But my luck had always sustained me! I felt the whispering tug of a long life of happy events trailing me, every one an amalgam of skill and fortune that had inspired a robust belief in my future. My luscious fantasy of a few moments before would not be a fantasy for long; it was still gloriously, glowingly in my grasp. I would save the day.

"You're not here to try to get into Danny's room, are you?"

"Danny's room? I thought you wanted to see the house because you used to live here."

"She's never lived here before! It's my grandfather's old house. Hey, you didn't have something to do with that rock through Danny's window, did you, Yolanda?"

"You're the lady who sat next to me on the bus!"

And then, an evil chuckle behind me: "I guess the cat's out of the bag, Yo-yo."

Del.

Everything was lead: my brain, my body, the air around me.

"Del."

I'd turned my back to the Kravitz front door, drawn to the sniggering behind me. I couldn't turn around again. My back was my only shield against their confusion. I looked out into the street, instead, imagining the breeze that might cool my shame as I ran away, envisioning the relief that might now, at least, come from the absence of hope's pressure in my life.

It was all over. I was all over.

Del, almost as if for the first time, seemed to look at me, to see me. She said, simply: "Shit."

Then she barreled forcefully past me and toward the others. I remained where I stood, huddled alone against them all.

"Hey, listen, guys, this is kind of all my fault."

I heard a definite querulousness in Samuel's tone. "I'm sorry. Who are you, now?"

"Del. I kind of talked Yolanda into doing all of this. It seemed to make sense at the time, but now—I don't know what the hell I was thinking! God!"

Now I did turn around. Del was the one under fire.

"What are you talking about?" Her normal graciousness having dried up, Mrs. Kravitz's sounded hoarse, tired.

"The whole thing. It was my fault. Even the window. I'll pay for it, whatever it costs. The person who threw it was supposed to hit the roof with a few pebbles, not heave a rock through a window. That's actually why I was coming."

"But why would you want to know what's in Danny's room?" Sam simply couldn't forget my subtle interrogation about Danny's room at the Piggly Wiggly, but at least the question was aimed at someone else.

"Well. It sounds kind of crazy. No. No, it doesn't sound 'kind of crazy.' It sounds totally insane. I know that." As Del rubbed her forehead with her large, shaking hand, it was clear she was having difficulty with what to say next. Only I knew she didn't *have* anything to say next.

But she surprised me: "Let's see. How am I going to put this? Well, I might as well just come out and say it. I figured that, you know, people like to talk about their kids and stuff. And it's the same with that whole story about Yolanda living here. I figured if she could see inside, she'd give me stuff to talk about. Or ask questions about. Or she'd find stuff out. About you, Roxie. You see? I told you it was crazy." Del dropped her head—I was sure for the first time in her life—in an attitude crushed, exposed.

The obvious question blared in the minds of everyone on the porch—even mine. I couldn't ask it, and Mrs. Kravitz looked too pained to ask it.

So that left Samuel: "Why do you need something to talk about with Roxie?"

"I'm sorry." And without a look toward any of us, Del fled the scene, the shame seemingly pushing down her shoulders, squeezing down her healthy frame to a much smaller, intensely humiliated object. And despite my predicament, despite the fact that all eyes would soon be trained on me again, I felt a shock of empathy for poor Del: she'd just pretended that our operation from the night before had taken place because of her feelings toward Mrs. Kravitz!

And it must have been immediately and painfully clear to her that Mrs. Kravitz returned none of these feelings. Through no actual fault of my own, I'd exposed Del yet again to the rejection she'd always faced in this cruel, supposedly "modern" world. I'd reminded her that in Two Rivers, her chances at love were about as promising as the opening of an art-house cinema, or a proper crêperie, or a day spa that could work the tension out of my shoulders from what seemed like a lifetime of awkward interactions with the natives.

But yet again, my heart was buoyed by my sundae school. Once its reputation was established, fame was bound to attract all sorts of free spirits to Two Rivers—people who'd seen the world, people who understood that love was as kaleidoscopic as every individual on the planet because it was fundamentally unique to each. People who could appreciate, could return Del's love because their hearts were open to joy.

So in addition to everything else, my transformation of Two Rivers would provide a fighting chance at a happy future for Del and everyone like her. I knew now that I owed her that much and much else besides, and I found myself more determined than ever to bring Danny's vision to life.

For Del's sake.

Such a rainbow of emotions in such a short time! But now that the exhilaration was greasing my synapses, I could handle anything: the questions, the suspicions, the temporary rejections. I would salvage the situation; I would again triumph!

Mrs. Kravitz was the first to speak. "Don't worry about it, Sammy."

Then their eyes were trained again on me, and I realized, just as Del had—just as Sam and Mrs. Kravitz were about to—that there were gaping holes in her explanation. It wouldn't be long before they were peering over the edge, shouting down to gauge the depths of these holes with echoes, unwilling or unable to throw me down a line.

"I'd better see if she's all right." And with that, I was gone, too. (I promised myself to work on untangling this even knottier wad of lies later, after a lapsang souchong and a calming dose of Proust.)

Instead, as I trotted away, I considered how I would communicate to Del my deep appreciation for what she'd just done for me. We'd had issues with communication in the past; I couldn't allow that to happen now that—finally—she'd acted in someone's interest beside her own. And to think, I'd actually begun to doubt my persuasive abilities because of her resistance to accept my maternal position! I could admit now that this resistance had led to quite a crisis for me—one of the most demoralizing ever—but the icy wind of doubt was no longer at my back. I'd broken through!

Del had finally become a Team Polanski Player.

I wasn't a hundred yards down the street when Del accosted me. She'd been standing behind a large tree trunk and was suddenly before me, titanic, brazen.

It was disconcerting to find that my first reaction was to be annoyed that she'd known I'd flee so quickly.

More annoying still was an absence of the humility she'd shown only a minute earlier. She was tittering behind her fist. "That look on your face was fucking priceless! I have never seen shit hit the fan so hard in my life! That was fucking awesome!"

I'd need some time to reconsider my self-image as a profoundly empathetic human being: my concern for Del evaporated as quickly and completely as hers had for me.

"And I just came in on that shit and *ironed it all out*, man! I was like the Terminator! Bam! Bam! Bam! I totally saved your ass."

"Although I think you might've made things quite a bit more difficult for me now, to be honest."

"What?! You know I saved your ass! But yeah, I made things more difficult for you, too." She giggled again. "Shit, you still have that look on your face! Honey, I'm really enjoying watching you squirm around in your own fucking insanity! It's way too much fun."

And then it made sense. Del was embarrassed that she'd just exposed her feelings so completely before all of us; she needed me to believe that she was too callous, too unencumbered to ever take someone else's needs into consideration.

But I knew better. She'd just sacrificed her own, faulty self-worth for the benefit of the mother she'd never had: the good one.

She'd done it all for me.

"Plus, I didn't want you blurting out your sick little plan for an ice-cream school, because some of that crazy would've rubbed off on me, and I can't be tainted by that shit now that I've put step one of my own plan into action."

I was impressed by her ability to so quickly rewrite her motivation. Clearly, she'd been doing this in regards to her birth mother her entire life.

Thankfully, my clear thinking had returned: "So you'd been planning to take responsibility for that night all along?"

"No! That's what I mean! I was totally on fire! While you were busy creating the biggest clusterfuck I've ever seen in my life, I realized that this was a perfect opportunity. I could play the love struck goober and build up some sympathy. Plus, it gives Roxie the chance to get used to the idea, rather than having to deal with everything right away. It's fucking perfect!"

"So you didn't do it to help me out."

"No! You're in worse shape than you were! And I cannot wait to hear how you plan on explaining why you already know that kid."

"Del."

"What."

"I know why you really did it."

Her fists balled. "I just told you why."

"And perhaps, in some way, your submission to my leadership will help you with the next step: learning to forgive your mother. For your name. And its identity as a stealer of strength. Because you've got strength to spare, young lady."

Once again, she pulled some bluster out of her worn, sad bag of tricks, apparently still feeling it necessary to exhibit the semblance of "rage." Considering all her terrible history, these coping mechanisms all made perfect sense.

But a second before she "attacked" me: "Excuse me, ladies, but may I ask just what it is you're doing on my lawn again?"

The older gentleman who had grilled us the previous evening was descending his porch. For some reason, his gray cardigan frightened me more than anything else; it was sepulchral, somehow, a denial of life amid the riot of fall color and sunshine surrounding it. It fed on light as he fed on energy.

I looked up, only now realizing that the tree Del had chosen to hide behind was the old oak that stood before his house.

But it was as if Del hadn't even heard him; her attention remained firmly on me. "You know, lady, you honestly need your ass kicked. I mean, it's almost my duty."

I backed onto the sidewalk as the man approached. The disturbing contortions his face was undergoing seemed to indicate that fury wasn't an emotion he had much experience with. "I'm sorry, but I really don't appreciate your language."

Del remained as firmly planted as the tree that rose above her, and in just the same way, did not in the slightest acknowledge the owner of that tree. "I'd actually be doing you and the world a huge fucking favor if I just totally creamed your ass right now."

"I think you should know that I've called the police."

Still without a look toward the man, she walked right at me, a freight train thrusting itself, relentless and fire-filled, down a long, straight stretch of track. I knew she wouldn't do anything to me; I stumbled backwards a few steps simply to reassure her of her "power," to avoid humiliating her at such a vulnerable moment in the heart-wrenching psychodrama that was her life.

Del grabbed my head and tilted my ear up to her mouth; I knew it must have looked worse than it felt because the old man actually winced.

I wasn't aware that a whisper could sound so fierce: "You are so lucky I can't afford to fuck up my parole."

And with that, she was gone. This left me standing in the street with the old man, both of us waiting for the police to arrive.

Realizing this wouldn't be the ideal outcome, I capitalized on what I hoped would be a remnant of pity for Del's treatment of me and quickly walked past him, my head down, "overcome," "ashamed."

"I'm sorry. Excuse me."

It seemed to work; he let me go, although I felt him continue to sap my energy for several yards. This no doubt caused the disorientation I exhibited over the next several minutes, and consequently, the slightly less than ideal circumstances that resulted.

For I'd realized that I'd just lost my grounds to return to the Kravitz's in the future. If everything I'd accomplished up to that point had supposedly been in aid of Del's mission, why would I ever darken that momentous doorstep again? The only logical reason left seemed to be to return immediately so that I could report on Del's emotional condition. In addition, I'd formulated a new tactic that I believed, at that moment, to be brilliant.

As I walked back to the Kravitz's, I marveled at the fact that I'd reformulated my strategy even more quickly than I'd expected of myself. All of these minor complications, these silly little issues seemed to be, in actuality, exercising my ingenuity. I seemed, in my befuddled condition, to be quite simply sparring with fate and winning!

Mrs. Kravitz was understandably more hesitant this time; she stood behind her screen door, one hand ready to shut me out at the slightest whiff of danger. Soon, Samuel appeared at her shoulder, uniting with her in a line of defense against their "common enemy."

I merely smiled back. I felt I was ready. "I just wanted to let you both know that there's nothing to worry about. Del's feeling much better now. And I'd also like to apologize for all her—well, let's just call it acting out. I know it's rather a circuitous route for such a simple destination, but Del… I know she seems very confident and strong, but underneath all of that is a little girl nursing the wounds of a lifetime of neglect at the hands of—to be honest, I'd really rather not get into it, if you don't mind. I have a great deal of training in psychology. Sometimes, it's a curse."

Samuel and Mrs. Kravitz looked at each other, drained of any expression.

"What the hell is going on." The sentence wasn't interrogative; it was declarative, as if Sam didn't expect an answer but was simply commenting on the whole sordid business, exhausted.

I had to play this carefully.

"Saint Fatima."

"I've evicted people before, Yolanda. I have grounds."

"Sam, I know we have a history—"

"We don't have a history."

"—but don't let that close your mind right now."

"We don't have a history."

"Let's try to keep what we have separate from this."

"There is no history. You really are disturbed."

At some point in the future, I had to determine the precise reason why Sam mistakenly identified me with his only previous love, little Brenda from Detroit, as our every encounter seemed to revivify the long-ago lunch room humiliation. Only through solving that puzzle could I overcome his resistance to the attraction he felt for me and help him to accept his true, reckless, impetuous nature (which was what I *truly* represented to him: a mirror, a partner in crime). To me, he would always remain a member of Team Polanski, even if he was no longer exactly key in the sundae school mission. And I still found him attractive; I knew enough not to deny that.

But that was for another time. Presently, I recklessly soldiered on: "Saint Fatima. Now, I realize it might be a bit difficult to imagine, but Del is a very religious person. Her Catholicism is at the heart of everything she does. In fact, at one time in her youth, she'd actually considered taking orders."

Their stares were heartless, dead. I rallied.

"I believe that on some level, she still considers herself a bride of Christ. Perhaps that's why she doesn't find men—well, now is clearly not the time to discuss it, but allow me just to say that there is a sound psychological basis for her 'situation.'" Why did it always pop up when I needed it least? Sam's humor possessed him suddenly, a demon, and he was forced to choke out a laugh. Almost immediately, his judge's frown returned, his flat-lipped rejection. I proceeded with my explanation, undaunted.

"A few weeks ago, I'd mentioned to her that I'd spoken with a little boy on the bus to Sheboygan about a dream he had. Now, I thought it was simply a wonderful story of a child's innocent imagination, angels and so forth, but Del immediately recognized the hallmarks of what—to her at least—represented a holy miracle. Quite quickly, she became fixated. Now, I don't really understand all that much about Catholic history—" I paused here to allow Mrs. Kravitz the opportunity to mention her own strong faith, but she merely watched me, a paroxysm of confusion distorting her normally firm, almost noble features. "But she seemed to recognize a few parallels with the miracle at Fatima and so became obsessed with meeting Danny. Believe me when I say that I have a great deal of empathy for those suffering from obsession—and especially an obsession for someone who represents an all-consuming hope." Here I threw Samuel a forgiving glance and received an exasperated sigh in return. "So, although maybe it was ill-advised, I agreed to help her meet Danny, who offers more than a simple anecdote for her, but in fact represents a last-ditch scramble to save her battered faith. And quite possibly her life."

"But you said her faith was strong." Any trace of Sam's humor was gone.

"Since Danny, it has been. In a single moment, it could be broken, destroyed."

"Why didn't she just explain that, then, rather than putting Roxie and her family through all this craziness?"

"Well. You saw her just now. She's very, very fragile."

Sam smirked.

"Samuel, I know you. And I know you're perceptive enough to recognize that Del's gruffness is just a front, a final, desperate wall." I was warming to my own story.

Mrs. Kravitz looked at Sam; I had her.

But Sam was the tough nut to crack: "This is what happens when you put two unstable people together. It's like the Keystone Cops meet Taxi Driver."

"Oh, so you're a classic movie buff, too!"

"Yolanda. Just don't." He returned his attention to Mrs. Kravitz. "What is she talking about? What dream?"

She shrugged. I could tell she was beginning to savor the idea that her child might be gifted in some way, chosen. And he had been—by me. "Well, he had this dream on the bus. An angel told him that there should be a school built in Two Rivers where people could learn how to make ice-cream desserts and stuff. A sundae school, as in ice-cream sundaes. It was just a dream." But to Mrs. Kravitz, it was no longer just a dream! She was thawing. "It was so vivid, I guess. He was really affected by it for a long time. But you know, he's six. He hasn't mentioned it in weeks."

I nodded, a sage, an oracle. "And you know, that's not really such an awful idea, now that I think about it. A 'sundae' school. That's actually kind of clever. Isn't Two Rivers the birthplace of the sundae?"

"Ithaca, New York." Samuel was still solid granite.

I remained pleasantly polite. "Is that right? Well, even so. A 'sundae' school. Hmmm."

Our silence was filled with village sounds, autumn murmurings. I knew when to let things sink in.

"I can't even believe I'm having this conversation. Roxie, I could talk to my friend, Bill; he could get a restraining order issued if you want—"

"No. No. I know all of this is a little weird, but nobody's trying to do anything wrong. We'll just forget about it."

She was sliding away again! "I completely understand, Mrs. Kra—I'm sorry—Roxie. And I agree: I really think that the best thing for Del at this point would be the right therapist. But you know, the more I think about it, the more I'm fascinated by this whole 'sundae school' idea. If I remember our conversation correctly, I believe Danny said the angel told him how to go about creating his 'sundae school'—you know, the details and such—but he never finished his story. Wouldn't it be interesting just to hear everything that she told him? Didn't I see him running around earlier? I wonder if Danny would want to speak with us—"

"Goodbye, Yolanda." And Sam summarily shut the door on me, on his undeniable emotions. It was actually quite loud, and I instinctively glanced down the street. Needless to say, the old man was watching me under his magnificent oak tree, his eyes beacons of malevolent mistrust, searching for a way into my soul.

I waved and walked away. Things could have been worse. Both Del and I had a foothold in the Kravitz home now, and while I understood she wouldn't be pleased about the details of the most recent cover story I'd created about her—even I had to admit that picturing her as a nun was a bit of a challenge—I would somehow get Del back on board with Team Polanski soon enough. Once her "temper" cooled. (Claude had always said that it was easier to ask for forgiveness than permission, although he made a point of never doing either.)

It was a brisk, clear day, and I found myself embracing Two Rivers as I walked across it, the humble homes girding already for winter, the citizens hale and straightforward. I even managed to accept a black Hummer that passed me as merely sculpted metal, decaying already in its secret folds and many cubbies, moving not just forward down the street, but through its life to the crusher, just like the Kias and Civics it presently growled by. In fact, it was as black as a nun's habit and just as inscrutable, and it would doubtlessly have shaved its head, too, if it had had one.

My next move was clear, and time was of the essence. But first, long-overdue recompense...

7

I don't really know you.

The accordionist was barefoot, his toes curling up and down to the beat, his nodding a dip, a swirl, a soar. Nineteenth-century Germans and Poles hovered in the shadowy corners, bristling with moustaches, putting off until the morning the laundering of their beer-stained petticoats in warm, sudsy tubs forever.

"You *do* know how to polka!" It was a statement I'd been dreading, but I'd known that Mrs. Stefano would have to say it, eventually.

"The world is a big place."

"Oh! Is it so popular in other countries?"

I was surprised she thought polka was popular in *this* country, but the real surprise was Mrs. Stefano herself. Even leading, she was quite an accomplished dancer. The pounds seemed to come to attention, to accentuate her movements, rather than drag her to earth, stricken.

She was a force on the dance floor, and it made me wonder if everyone was beautiful, a transcendence, when the right circumstances were stumbled upon. My heart went out to the millions of souls suffering that very instant under the impression that they would never rise above their mediocrity simply because they hadn't yet discovered their sport of cricket, or their art of haiku, or their craft of Egyptian bottle-carving. My heart went out to Mrs. Stefano, too, who instead of celebrating her life spinning across the polka dance floor, was merely spinning and spinning, caught up in the polka of life, of Two Rivers.

But soon enough, I reminded myself, life in Two Rivers would be transcending that very mediocrity, would be blossoming into a beauty of its very own.

"Can you smell me yet? I'm getting all sweaty!"

I could, in fact, smell Mrs. Stefano, but I merely smiled. She didn't care, and I didn't care, and we could both believe that at that very instant, nothing else was real at all but the risings, the heady crests of music.

And then the song was over.

"Gosh, I'm still a little rusty! Did I step on your toes?"

"Not one time, Mrs. Stefano. Not one, single time."

She shone. "Oh, that's good. Do you mind if we sit this next one out?"

"I'd welcome it. And I bet that you won't be hard-pressed to find other partners, now that they've seen you in action, as it were."

We found our table and our steins. I watched, a moment, the small movements of the seniors as they crossed and re-crossed the floor. The exaggerations of youth had been worn down to telegraphed gestures, almost representations of gestures—all that was needed or expected now, in their world. I looked forward to a time when I didn't have to operate on the grand scale that I did, when I might contemplate the past rather than rouse up the future.

"So your dress, Yolanda. Is that a ball gown or—?"

"Pollera Boliviana de los Caporales en la Carnaval de Oruro."

"Oh."

"Gracias for noticing."

"It's real neat. And your hair is different, too. Back to, well, sort of normal. So I guess that means you're planning on quitting your lunch-lady job?"

"It's served its purpose."

"And what's that in your hair?"

"Oh, this? It's red laver. I thought it might make a nice accent piece. Seaweed."

"You put seaweed in your... but I guess it's not my place to *you know*," Here she scrunched up her little, round nose, "about what people are wearing!"

Mrs. Stefano was also sporting a marine theme for our polka night. In her case, it was a loose dress with seahorses and starfish dancing their way across it—chasing? Being chased?

"Speaking of *stuff*, you never told me if I was right about *you-know-what*."

I knew *exactly* what she was talking about. I simply didn't know *what* she was talking about. I chose non-committal acquiescence. "Oh, absolutely right."

"Really?" She was overjoyed for some obscure reason, and once again, I plumbed the depths of Mrs. Stefano's psyche. Perhaps since her love never did displace her father's relationship with his dog, she attempted to turn her friends into pets, the only "real" connection she believed anyone could have with others. But why a squirrel?

"You know, I was flossing my teeth this morning when I realized that I hardly know anything about you, Yolanda! You're always so worried about other people; you don't let us be worried about you!"

"Isn't that a wonderful thing to say! Very Mrs. Stefano. The best nurturers are those who've had to learn to nurture themselves. A Corgi could never do that."

She looked at me uncertainly. "How do you do that?"

"Decades of empathetic observation—"

"No, I mean always change the subject back to me whenever I ask about you."

Mrs. Stefano! How she delighted. "All right. What would you like to know?"

"Why did you come to Two Rivers—really? And why do you want to build an ice-cream school? Really. Because, you know, it's kind of a little weird."

How could I communicate my belief that "weird" was precisely what the world needed without sounding even "weirder" to her? In short, I couldn't, so instead I acted upon one of my earlier observations. The youngest man in the room, probably in his late fifties, and sporting cowboy boots and Brylcreem, had been electrifying the female population of the Ashwaubenon V.F.W. Hall all night. As if a player in the animal kingdom, he'd been proudly displaying his suave moves, confident banter, and a hearty chuckle that brought to mind Santa Claus and/or Satan as the waves of polka carried his presence aloft along with—above, even—the spirits of all in attendance.

And with much significance, he'd been cutting his eyes at our table all night.

Mrs. Stefano seemed oblivious, focused solely on the dance. I felt this was unacceptable.

"Before we discuss all that, you must have noticed him."

She was pliant. "Noticed who?"

"That gentleman over there, the younger one."

She glanced over and turned back much too quickly. "You mean the guy *with the greasy hair*?" The patented Stefano silent whisper.

"No more than carefully groomed, I'd say, but yes. He's taken a shine to you."

Mrs. Stefano frank gaze almost seemed hurt by this. "Why would you say that?"

"Because it's true." I rose. "I'm going to bring him to our table."

"No!" She grabbed my arm, her entire body stiffening. "No, please. He's not looking at me! He's probably looking at you."

"Believe me, if there's one thing I know, it's affairs of the heart. He's smitten."

I fairly jerked my arm out of her grasp, intent on bringing a little "weirdness" to Mrs. Stefano's life. (Years earlier, Claude had challenged me to a footrace across Bali because I'd suggested we stay in a proper hotel for once. He'd jerked his arm out of my grasp, in much the same way as I just had, and disappeared into the Indonesian moonlight, glistening with the promise of cozy lagoons and coconuts.) (I won.)

When I approached, the man barely registered me. He was leaning proprietarily over a grouping of ladies in their sixties, their seventies, their eighties, ankles crossed under their table in a very certain manner.

"—but oil stains on taffeta are another kettle of fish, as they say."

"Excuse me, sir. I hate to trouble you, but my friend and I had a question about a particular oil stain, and we were hoping you might be able to offer some guidance."

He rose. Over his largish paunch, he was quite a tall, lanky individual with a lopsided smile over regular teeth. I immediately thought him highly suitable.

"Isn't that funny! We were just talking about oil stains. They're the worst, aren't they."

"It's really for my friend over there, Mrs. Stefano. Heather Stefano. She's a seamstress widow, and she's produced some of the most unique pieces of clothing I think I've ever seen. Especially rare materials. And one of them, unfortunately..."

He leaned in. "Burke Smollett." His hands were especially soft; I sensed emollient.

"Yolanda Polanski."

"Been to my shop?"

"You have a shop?"

"Dry cleaning. The best in Wisconsin. Well, *I* say, anyway."

He followed me over to our table. Mrs. Stefano had fixed an especially gruesome smile on her face as she pointedly watched the dancers bouncing past her toward the opposite side of the room. Strangely, she behaved surprised when I squeezed her arm.

"Burke Smollett, I'd like you to meet the very creative Heather Stefano."

"Yolanda's told me all about your work."

The smile remained doggedly fixed. "Pardon?"

"Your creations. I think I can help."

Slowly, steadily Mrs. Stefano's head pivoted toward me. Her dimples were pulled together into a mask of devastation.

"My creations?"

Burke could only speak to the back of her head, but he sensed something had gone wrong. "Absolutely. Honestly, you know, I'm an expert–"

And Mrs. Stefano was gone. I watched her push her way to the exit, the surefootedness I'd so recently witnessed replaced with her more usual harried stumbling.

"Burke, will you excuse me a moment?"

She might have sometimes been a bit clumsy in her motions, but Mrs. Stefano could move. Her lightly dented Korean car had already left the lot before I emerged into the chilly night.

Burke had followed me outside, and he stood behind me, watching the taillights recede into the spreading suburbia. "What did I say?"

Those taillights were my ride home. I wasn't even sure where we were, but I knew that it had taken Mrs. Stefano an hour to get there. "Where did you say your dry cleaning shop is, Burke?"

"Manitowoc."

Manitowoc, the stunted Eng to Two River's Chang. Once again, my unimaginable luck had kicked in.

"Well, isn't that funny!"

Of course, I'd have to make polite conversation on the ride home, but I looked forward to committing the majority of my brain power to solving the riddle of Mrs. Stefano's violent reaction to Burke. Had I been so perceptive that I'd stumbled upon a man who was the spitting image of her dismissive father? Or perhaps one of the husbands? Or was it even more irrational than that? Did lopsided smiles remind her of a dream she'd had when she was five, a dream in which a clown with a sideways grin lived in her mattress and tickled her whenever she tried to sleep?

The human brain was unendingly engrossing.

Burke's brain had been affected by extended exposure to perchloroethylene. This became clear to me on the way back to Two Rivers, as he spoke for a majority of the drive about his failed relationships and the many dating challenges that faced a man of his age. He seemed utterly unaware that I wasn't listening. But I was grateful, really, because it gave me a chance to determine my next step with Mrs. Stefano.

I couldn't lose her now; she was my first officer, my Friday, my mascot all rolled into one. She'd been the only person thus far who'd never wavered in the face of ignorant hesitation about the Sundae School, who'd stood fast, faithful, at my side, nearly as committed to our goal as I was. I wasn't too proud to admit that at times, I actually needed her.

Eventually, I decided that Burke's old-fashioned appearance must have been at the heart of the matter. He had stirred up Mrs. Stefano's struggle with the absence of paternal approval, and it was high time that she addressed this issue—that she overcame it. She'd be a much more integral individual, then, much happier. And although less important, it was still worth noting that once she'd dealt with this issue and no longer had an ancient trauma to constantly trip over, she'd be a less "error-prone" member of the Sundae School Task Force.

I thrilled to the image of a well-adjusted Mrs. Stefano dressed in smart business attire—perhaps a jaunty little hat and patent-leather pumps. Soon, she'd naturally outgrow the ill-fitting, synthetic, cartoon-themed materials that were better suited to a three-year-old's diaper-filled jammies. In fact, it was this professional, mature image of her that finally convinced me to take action.

I interrupted a story about Burke's last girlfriend, who'd apparently burned meatloaf on two occasions. "Burke, you should understand something about Mrs. Stefano."

"Who's that now? Oh, your friend."

"You have a striking resemblance to her father."

"But I'm not that old!"

"A resemblance not in age, but in aura, if that makes any sense."

"Oh."

"Her father didn't take much interest in her, and it's a wound that's never entirely healed. But it's a wound that could be healed, with the right approach."

As we neared the few, meager lights of Manitowoc, Burke's rather broad features were gradually illuminated. He was carefully considering my offer, my assignment.

And he accepted: "Boy, you're really a good friend to her, aren't you. That's nice. I guess people need people."

"People most certainly *do* need people. I knew you'd agree."

"It was a song or something." He sung a few bars. "*People… people need some people.*"

It was close enough for me.

At long last, we rolled up to my front door. And just as I'd predicted, Mrs. Stefano's car was hidden behind an SUV down the street. I knew she'd be worried about me, perhaps a little guilty. I intended to use this to my advantage.

"Burke, would you like to come in for a moment?"

There was a parody of concern about the time, a glance at his watch, and then we were in my repressive living room.

"This is real cute."

"Yes. Would you like some coffee? Or tea?"

"I hate to be a bother."

"Irish breakfast tea it is. Excuse me a moment. You might find that book on the coffee table interesting."

"Agrarian Themes in Pre-Columbian Peruvian Pottery. Hmm."

"Exactly."

I raced out of my kitchen door and up to Mrs. Stefano's car window. She was looking glum, but she didn't drive away.

The pane glided down to admit my presence. "So that guy gave you a ride?"

"He's quite a gentleman."

"I'm sorry about leaving you there like that. But I just couldn't believe what you did. You know how sensitive I am about that! And you know how I get kind of panicky, sometimes."

"Mrs. Stefano, I'm profoundly sorry. I do know how sensitive you are, and I can't believe how insensitive I was. I wholeheartedly apologize. Can you forgive me?"

She shrugged, then nodded in short, sharp jerks. "Yes."

"And I think you should know that Burke is still interested in getting to know you. The whole trip here, he spoke only of his desire to meet a woman just like you."

She squinted out her windshield, past Two Rivers, past Wisconsin, past a turbulent history to a pinpoint, the origin of something, a defining moment. Was she thinking about her family? An ordeal? A nightmare?!

"You know, Mrs. Stefano, clowns are almost never *entirely* evil."

She didn't seem to hear me: "He wants to meet me, still?"

"Absolutely."

"Even after you told him about me?"

"I think it's partially *why* he wants to meet you. You know, in my youth, a certain someone had once told me that I had a striking resemblance to Princess Diana." I paused to allow her to agree, but she was still too distracted. She'd comment later, after she'd had a chance to recognize the likeness. "I certainly didn't avoid the gentleman after that!"

Once again, the familiar defense mechanism: Mrs. Stefano glanced at me as if confused. Nonetheless, she was making progress on this front too, as these periods of "confusion" were progressively shrinking each time before she dismissed them.

"Of course, what I looked like on the outside was random, a gift from god, as it were. It bore no relation to who was inside. It's the same thing with Burke, Mrs. Stefano."

"Well, I guess *you've* been okay with it. With me. And my friends online, too."

She'd apparently made impressive strides with her Internet therapists. I was pleased. "Absolutely. Now, why don't you come in for some coffee. And just be *yourself.*"

Her hands tightened and loosened on the steering wheel, tightened and loosened.

"I figured he would drive you home." This was a huge step for her, coming face-to-face with the specter that had led to her "apparel infantilism." (I briefly considered writing a paper on this novel subject, then dismissed it. Of course it would be groundbreaking work, but presently I had a much more important calling.)

Her body spasmodically lifted from the little vinyl seat, and she squealed. "Okay. Okay! I'm going to do it. I'll be over in a minute! Just let me, you know, *get ready*."

"Oh, Mrs. Stefano. What a brave, brave woman you are!"

Her dimples were canyons whose depths reached her soul. She beamed.

"You're totally sure, right? About him?"

"I couldn't be more so!"

When I returned through my kitchen door, I found Burke leaning against the stove. "I was wondering what happened to you."

"Well, as a matter of fact—"

"You weren't planning on making tea."

"I'm going to do that right this very second."

"I should go."

"Absolutely not!"

Burke slumped. "Look, I know what's going on here. It's okay."

When I came closer to the cabinet next to the stove, he backed away toward the living room. "Honestly, you don't have to do that."

"You don't want tea?"

"It's because of the chemicals."

"But it's organic Darjeeling—"

"You know what I mean." Now he turned and quietly shuffled toward the front door.

"But Mrs. Stefano—"

"Well? What about her? I didn't drive *her* home."

"No, but you're the only person who can help her, right now. Only you can pull her through possibly the most serious crisis of her life."

"And how's that?"

"Do you have a dog?"

"What?!"

"I believe that if you simply ignore your dog in her presence and instead praise her as if she were a dog, perhaps little treats, some sort of ball—"

"Look, I'm not an idiot. I know why you just assumed I'm not good enough for you, why you think her and me 'belong together.' You know, I wasn't going to say anything, but that was kind of rude." Suddenly, with his hand on the door knob, he turned— "on me," as it were. "No, that wasn't kind of rude, that was *just plain rude*. In my case, I can't help it; it's just one of the hazards of the dry cleaning business, when you're around that stuff all day. I accept that. But your friend could certainly do something about it. I mean, see a doctor or something, because I know they have prescription-strength deodorant. If you were a real friend to her, you wouldn't ignore her problem, you'd tell her how bad she smells. It's much worse than me—"

Burke froze, his stare unblinking over my shoulder, and the freeze was absolute, almost frightening. It was a freeze that was longer and much more profound than was appropriate for the realization that Mrs. Stefano had come through the kitchen and was standing behind me. It was a freeze that should have been reserved for alien sightings, for the ghost of Milton Berle chomping a cigar in drag. I found myself unable to turn around.

Finally, he spoke: "What the hell is going on here?"

I couldn't avoid it any longer, and slowly I pivoted. Standing in the kitchen doorway was a human-sized rabbit. Or rather, Mrs. Stefano dressed in a white rabbit costume, including an oversized rabbit head.

This was a deviation from my diagnosis.

"Yolanda!" It was muffled but definitely my name. I searched the nostrils for any sign of Mrs. Stefano, but all was obscure.

She turned and ran back out the way she came, her pink ears slapping against the top of the doorway. I was left with Burke, whose open mouth was an accusation.

"Why was she wearing a rabbit costume?!"

"Well, that's an interesting question. Initially, I'd say that as a child, she'd gone hunting with her father and—"

"You know what? I don't really want to hear any more of your crazy explanations. As usual, I end up with screwballs—two, this time! She's dressed like a rabbit and you look like some kind of Mexican whore—"

"Actually, this is Bolivian—"

"Uh huh. And here I was, thinking *I* wasn't dating material! Oh, brother." He threw open my front door and paused, seemingly unsatisfied. It was to hurl a final, apparently terminal insult: "Peruvian pottery! What a crock!"

Burke left me furiously debating whether or not I should follow Mrs. Stefano. The major stumbling block was that I had no idea what to say to her. Why *was* she dressed in a rabbit costume?

The front door gaped, which allowed Tabby III to slip in. I immediately heard him gagging on something in my bedroom and was glad. In fact, he'd made up my mind: first, I'd deal with the vomit on my bedspread (he'd doubtlessly eaten the Ghiradelli wrapper by my bed), and then I'd devote the rest of the evening to carefully determining the right course of action to take with Mrs. Stefano.

One thing was immediately clear: she'd believed I knew why she was dressed as a giant white rabbit.

Perhaps it was time to face the fact that Mrs. Stefano might be even more delusional than I'd originally thought.

* * *

I'd almost become immune to the coarse cackling. Over the preceding months, it had gradually become necessary background noise, like a jackhammer helping build the Empire State Building, or the crack and crunch of our forefathers' westward-bound wagon wheels as they struck through the stinging Nevada desert. Hopefully, her harshness had made me taller, tougher, too.

Finally, Del gained enough control to speak, her sibilance abrupt even over the phone. "You know, it's actually kind of fun, being around total nut jobs. Keeps me on my toes."

"Del. Let's not judge her—"

"I'm not judging *her*, I'm judging *you*! I couldn't give a flying fuck what Heather does for kicks."

I took a breath. Challenges help us to grow as individuals.

"Do you have a better suggestion, Del?" This didn't sound as sarcastic as I was worried it might, and I was glad. Part of the process I'd designed for Del included building up her self-respect, and I knew that this was only really ever achieved by learning to respect others. It was important for her to believe that, as her "new mother," I thought her ideas weren't misguided and gratuitous.

"Are you kidding? No, I do not have a better suggestion! I think your plan is totally insane, and I love it! I'm totally on fucking board!"

"You really mean that? You truly feel that you're ready to accept my authority? You're not going to sabotage, or undermine, or—"

"My goodness, Yo-Yo! You make me sound rather like a fucking bitch."

"Del—"

"So, I'm thinking grizzly. Or wolf. Or no, maybe *wolverine*!"

I held back a groan as I reminded myself that sometimes, predictability was a useful element of interpersonal interaction, even if it could occasionally border on cliché. *Wolverine*! But at least Del seemed finally to be growing comfortable with my guidance. Progress was being made, thanks to my patience, my generosity.

"And now you're going to return the favor, fruitcake. Call Roxie and tell her I'm feeling really embarrassed about what happened and that you think she should come over and check on me. Give her my address. And yes, I do realize this isn't seventh grade, but you're turning me into some kind of zany broad who believes that crazy schemes just might work. I'm totally fucked. So thanks for that."

I'd neglected to mention the mistaken understanding Roxie now had of Del's identity, thanks to the confused state I'd recently suffered due to the gray-cardigan man's insatiable hunger. It had since become harder and harder to broach the subject, and the insults weren't making it any easier.

"All right. Oh, and speaking of Bram Stoker—"

"No, you're not going to change the subject. Things with her aren't about you, anymore, got it? They're about me. You had your chance and totally, spectacularly blew it. So no freaking Roxie out with your crazy-ass stories about saints and angels and ice cream. She doesn't need to be reminded that I hang around with some religious loon; she might think I'm just as fucking cracked. And leave that kid alone. I'm serious; I'll destroy you." (Claude had attempted to destroy me once, but all it had led to was his love of Japanese Samurai swords and a lifetime ban from any building owned by the Des Moines Public Library System.)

"I'm not religious." But I acquiesced as humbly as I possibly could to Del's demands, still placing our conversation in the success column: she was actually going to *support*, rather than *take over* my operation with Mrs. Stefano! No so-called online psychotherapist could've ever achieved results that quickly.

Yet soon after our conversation, I found myself back at the water's edge, considering my dilemma along with the gray sky and grayer lake.

The gulls were focused, businesslike; their dismissal of my presence was a comfort to me, a reminder that the world was filled with millions of crustaceans and fish and dramas that were just as important as my own. I couldn't help but wonder how a seagull would handle my situation, how those steel, workmen's eyes would view my options. As I watched their labors, I became aware of one thing—whatever their strategy, it would definitely involve mid-air defecation. From this, I grew only more downcast; even such a simple, freeing experience wasn't open to me.

Instead, I faced a strangling wad of issues. Mrs. Stefano was all but lost, and Del would be as soon as she discovered that I'd told Mrs. Kravitz she wanted to be a nun. I was no nearer my goal of creating the sundae school, but I *did* spend most of my day slopping "chili soup" on unsuspecting youngsters' trays. At least one person on Earth felt that I looked like a Central American prostitute (South American). If it weren't for my solid track record of overcoming each and every adversity thrown across my path, I might have been considering taking quite a long walk off the relatively short pier.

Del and I wouldn't be completing our healing visit to Mrs. Stefano until that evening. So what would I say to her beforehand at work? What could I do?

I was a little relieved when I attempted to slip past her office and found that she hadn't arrived yet. Initially relieved, I was very soon quite concerned. As I wrestled large pans of what had once been spaghetti but now appeared to be simply wheat paste floating in tomato paste, I realized that this was a very bad sign. Mrs. Stefano was never absent; it was school legend that she'd once worked through the pain not only of an infected appendix, but a half an hour into a burst one before fainting. Apparently, it was only once she was unconscious that people had been able to shift her from her little, gray, ergonomic chair. She'd attempted to file a report on the operating table, and the anesthesiologist reportedly had had to use an amount of drugs that would've taken down a rhino to keep her still. A disturbing, probably overblown story, but one with a certain ring of truth.

"I don't want that meatball. It's broken."

"That gives them a chance to breathe."

"They don't breathe! That's gross!"

The entire state of affairs in the cafeteria was "gross," but who was I to comment?

Instead, I fished out a "whole" meatball, which was about as beneficial as a "whole" nuclear warhead, and considered the subtleties of the evening's mission. I recognized that Mrs. Stefano's approval issues were a bit more complex than I'd initially diagnosed, and I was sure she'd interpreted my reaction—shock, mostly—of the night before as a rejection of some kind. (Of course, hearing Burke's comment about her odor couldn't have been too helpful, either.) It was all very upsetting—she'd had more than enough rejection in her life; I couldn't allow her to continue to believe that I was no better than her father!

So Del and I would visit Mrs. Stefano at her home—I dressed in my squirrel costume, Del as a wolverine or other, equally bloodthirsty beast (there were only ever winners and losers in her world). By embracing Mrs. Stefano's interest, showing her that both Del and I were perfectly comfortable in our animal suits, I hoped we could convince her to relax into her "bunny persona" and realize that in the scheme of things, this wasn't anything to be ashamed of, exactly. I also hoped she'd forgive me.

I took a deep, steadying breath and immediately regretted it, as I was now standing over a steam table that featured "garlic fingers." As I faced a little girl with something hanging out of her nose, I couldn't help but wonder what these foods were doing to the children. At least a few of them would go to their graves believing that garlic had hands, or perhaps even that garlic *was* hands. I imagined the little girl going home that afternoon and giving a command performance with her dollies to the imaginary sound of one garlic hand clapping.

But this line of thought was profitless, and I refocused on my sphere of influence. Honesty was at the heart of everything I accomplished. And if I were perfectly honest with myself, I had to admit that there was another issue I had to contend with: I was slightly surprised that Mrs. Stefano had chosen as my animal incarnation the squirrel. After all, what were squirrels but nervous, fluffy rats that seemed very busy with their individual tasks, yet ultimately only moved a few nuts around and spread rabies? Why not a swan? A lioness? A fir tree, if there were no restrictions on the kingdoms of living things?

I didn't like it. I didn't like it at all. Still, I had to remind myself that it was less a reflection on me, and more an illustration of Mrs. Stefano's inability to wholly understand me. So, yes, for her sake, I'd play the highly strung, neurotic creature chasing in every direction after the merest promise of an acorn. I'd been Desdemona off, off, off Broadway. I could stretch.

* * *

In the end, the best Del had managed to throw together was a cat costume involving an ear-tiara, glue-on whiskers and a flaccid tail that she tucked into her dungarees. She'd attempted to draw feline features on her face with what appeared to be a Sharpie. The final result was dismal at best, although it was a relief, in a way, to know exactly what I'd be having nightmares about that evening.

I, on the other hand, was pleasantly surprised to find how well my squirrel costume fit. Mrs. Stefano really knew what she was doing at her sewing machine. Even my nostril line of sight was perfect.

Del was a little more amused by the outcome of Mrs. Stefano's labor than impressed. "It's like I'm seeing the real you for the first time!"

Glad that my squirrel head hid my reaction to this, I cleansed my voice of all annoyance: "Didn't she do a wonderful job?"

"Yeah. She totally captured your essence. Heather fucking rocks, man!"

We were standing in my dusk-shrouded backyard with Tabby III sitting in judgment on a nearby trash can. His final ruling was clearly "guilty," but then it always was.

"So did you call Roxie?"

"I did. I left a message." If I called Mrs. Kravitz by the end of the day, this wouldn't be a lie, exactly.

But even through the black slashes marring her face, Del was clearly unconvinced. "If you didn't call her, you're going to be eating your fucking vichyssois through a feeding tube."

"It's vichyssoise. You pronounce the 's' at the end."

"Okay, then. You're going to be pronouncing your 's's through a fucking feeding tube. Does that meet with your approval?"

"I wonder if you've ever had a family member in a vegetative state before. How terribly painful that must've been, losing that maternal figure. A grandmother, maybe. Or a maiden aunt."

"And I wonder if *you've* had a family member in a vegetative state. Or any kind of state. Because you're really good at analyzing everyone else's family, but when it comes to your own, we don't really hear all that much. Maybe you're really pissed off about the squirrel suit because you had a maternal figure who looked like a squirrel. Or a maiden aunt who stored nuts in her cheeks."

She was the only one to find her comments riotously amusing; I simply sighed inside my squirrel skull.

When she died down: "All right, Yo-Yo. Let's do this thing. As Superman would say."

Another unnecessary comment, which for some strange reason made me aware of the fact that the interior of my costume was getting a little warm. I welcomed the time I'd be spending behind the wheel of the Oldsmobile, when I'd have to take off the head, and I didn't relish the thought of putting it back on. Still, I was prepared to do quite a lot for Mrs. Stefano. Quite an awful lot.

"Yes. Let's."

Things were worse than I'd expected at Mrs. Stefano's house. She was loading a box into the trunk of her Hyundai when she saw us approaching, and she immediately "turned tail" and ran back inside.

"It looks like she's moving! What the fuck!"

"Maybe not—"

"Yeah, she's moving! Jesus, you really screwed the pooch on this one. You've actually managed to drive someone out of town!"

The cool breeze from my open window was failing to reach the inside of my suit; I could feel my core body temperature rising. "Del. Comments like that aren't going to help anything."

"What, you mean comments like the truth? Christ! That poor woman. I should've known that she was too innocent to hang around with you. I should've said something. Now, the poor thing's running away. And I was just getting used to her."

"I'm sure she's not running away—"

"Look. You stay in the car. I'm going to talk to her. I'm sure the last person in the world she wants to see right now is your sorry ass."

Del looked at my costume disdainfully for a moment, her eyes brushing over the reddish, artificial fur. "In fact—" She removed her ears, whiskers and tail. Apparently, whatever was on her face wasn't indelible ink, because she managed to transfer most of it from her face to the front of her shirt. "This isn't funny, anymore."

"Del, you cannot just change our plan like this. I won't allow it, young lady. Now I know Mrs. Stefano much better than you do, and I understand her case—"

As if I hadn't said a thing, Del got out of the car, swooping menacingly back at me. "Stay in the car. Stay in the car. What did I say?"

"But Mrs. Stefano is—"

"What did I say?"

"You said, 'stay in the car,' but—"

"You really don't get it, Yolanda." This was delivered through an upturned mouth, a hideous parody of a smile. "This is serious, now. Heather is going to move away because of you. If she does that, it means you really, really screwed up her life. *You.* Not her daddy or her rabbit suit or her relationships. *You.* Now, what did I say?"

"Stay in the car."

"For her sake, please keep out of this."

And with that, Del slammed the door in my face and hurried up to "repair the damage that I had done."

But what Del didn't seem to understand was that birth was painful, both for the mother and the child. And since Mrs. Stefano was emerging from her own womb, it was twice as uncomfortable. She needed a midwife who understood the process, who could stand by, prepared for each and every eventuality. Who supported, rather than judged, or ridiculed, or bulldozed her way through everyone else's life, leaving killing boot-tracks wherever she blundered.

I could feel perspiration pooling throughout the suit, mixing with the fabric backing of the fur, producing noxious compounds that itched and burned and seeped into my skin to do more obscure damage, perhaps only revealed years later in a CT scan or routine X-ray. But by then, it would be too late because the disease would've spread throughout my body.

Del was screaming at Mrs. Stefano's front door. If Mrs. Stefano was planning on moving out of town with as little fanfare as possible, she was bound not to appreciate this. Finally, she opened her door and peeked over the chain. Their voices lowered, revealing only snippets of pained peaks and tortured valleys. Mrs. Stefano was probably saying something about how she'd believed that she'd been perfectly clear to me about her penchant to dress as a rabbit, how she'd even gone so far as to make a suit for me, and yet I still hadn't appreciated the extent to which she'd exposed her deepest, most cherished desires. And now that the "bunny was out of the bag," so to speak, she simply couldn't live in a town where everyone would throw carrots at her, perhaps singing "Peter Cottontail" under their breath the moment her back was turned. It was possible that some local jokester would even go so far as to leave a trail of Easter eggs wherever she went, cruelly crushing her already weak spirit.

Now Del began in earnest. She was undoubtedly telling Mrs. Stefano that we'd already forgotten about her fetish, that no one would ever mention it again and that life would continue on as normal if she would just stay in Two Rivers, just try to put the whole thing behind her.

Of course, by putting Mrs. Stefano back in the "anthropomorphic animal closet," Del was doing irreversible damage to Mrs. Stefano, who was—at this very moment—at the most critical, most vulnerable point on her path to a new, actualized lifestyle. Moreover, by stressing that we'd ignore her proclivity, what Del was truly communicating was that the rabbit suit was a behavior of which she should be ashamed, something appalling that demanded averted eyes and wordless pity.

Superheated, moist air from the suit was rising into my face now, bringing with it the stench of artificial dyes and the pulverized rat and roach droppings that the adolescent Chinese workers continually swept into the air of the factory where the material was produced. I wondered what heat stroke felt like.

And then it all became perfectly clear to me! I cursed myself for realizing the truth so late in the game: this was really all about Del! Her family, her friends, her community—possibly even a boyfriend (!)—they'd all done their level best to shove *her* back into the closet, reinforcing the idea that who she truly was represented nothing more than a shameful secret worthy only of cringes and slow, disgusted shakes of the head. So in response to what had been perpetrated against her for her entire life, Del was now returning the favor to the universe: she was unconsciously exacting her revenge on Mrs. Stefano—giving her a biblical haircut, so to speak!

By this point, Mrs. Stefano had opened her door up completely, and the two of them seemed to be having a calm, reasoned discussion. Del's attack, unconscious though it was, was beginning to do permanent damage. Mrs. Stefano was falling for it.

I jumped out of the Olds and quickly secured my squirrel head, which immediately filled up with the searing, dangerous gases. But the cool breeze of a Wisconsin autumn so close to my skin felt encouraging as I ran toward Del and Mrs. Stefano. Unfortunately, I found that although my sight was perfectly clear ahead of me, the nostrils restricted my peripheral vision a bit, and I tripped over curbs, sprinkler heads and low shrubbery as I raced to staunch the damage being committed ahead of me.

A man was walking a pair of basset hounds on the sidewalk across the street, and when the dogs saw me, they reacted violently, howling and baying incessantly. Rather than politely removing them from the scene they were creating, the man merely aped his dogs' behavior in his own fashion: he gawked at me as I gradually made my way across the street. The commotion attracted attention from the neighborhood, and I could hear people emerging from their homes, apparently having never heard a dog bark in their lives. Even Mrs. Stefano and Del were peering though the darkness at the dogs; neither one of them had noticed me yet.

"Over here, Mrs. Stefano! I'm a squirrel!" My voice only reverberated around the inside of the squirrel head, but I'd never consider taking it off, at this point.

Probably due to the shame Del was forcing Mrs. Stefano to feel, she appeared stricken with horror when she finally caught sight of me. I had to reverse this damage immediately.

"I'm a squirrel! And it's okay! It's okay to be whatever animal you want to be!"

I'd reached them by now, and neither one of them seemed especially glad to see me. But I was certain that my words were already beginning to take effect.

"You see? I'm embracing my inner animal! And Del could put on her cat ears and tail. They're just in the car!"

"You idiot! I told you to stay away!"

Mrs. Stefano looked out into the neighborhood that she'd inhabited for nine years and quickly pulled us both inside her house. She was crying now, her face red and shiny.

As I knew she would, she turned to Del first. "I thought she didn't tell you why I was leaving!"

Del's expression was initially twisted with rage as she pivoted toward me. But it quickly slackened; she'd been exposed to my rational influence for so long that she was actually learning how to control her anger. Despite the situation, it was edifying, and I felt safe enough finally to remove my squirrel head.

"Okay. Okay, you know what, Heather? You *should* go. It's probably in your own best interest. Not about the rabbit thing; that's no reason to leave Two Rivers. Fuck 'em if they can't take a joke. You'd actually be making the place more interesting. But Yolanda is going to end up destroying your life if you stay. Because I thought she was *good* crazy, but it's becoming clear to me now that she's *bad* crazy. She's got me lying to you and making up ridiculous stories to tell Roxie. She's got you moving out of town. God only knows what she's done to other people around here. So get out of here, Heather. I'm serious. She's not going to rest until she's completely fucked up the lives of everyone in Two Rivers. I'll take care of everything here."

Mrs. Stefano turned to me. "Is that true? I mean, why did you do that to me with that man?"

"I didn't exactly understand—about the—"

"But when you first talked to me in Arby's, you said you knew what I was doing."

"Actually, I misunderstood slightly. I thought you were having an affair. With Mr. Krimm."

"Mr. Krimm?! I thought you were telling me that it was okay to be me, that I should make my own costume, instead of just making costumes for people in other places! I thought that's why you were friends with me."

"Oh. And I thought you believed in the sundae school. And that was why you were friends with me."

"That *was* why! Because it was so important to you."

"But don't you see? I support you, too! What you're doing—who you are—that's wonderful—"

"No, it's not! It's horrible! After just now, seeing how stupid you looked running down the street. Dressed like that. I won't ever let anyone ever see me like that again. Never!"

And before I could do so much as respond, Mrs. Stefano bolted through the door and out to her car, and it was only at that point I became aware of her living room. Somehow, she'd managed to empty it of all her belongings in a day.

I started after Mrs. Stefano, but Del grabbed my shoulder. "Let her go."

"You don't understand what's going on. Her father clearly had a favorite rabbit that—"

"No, *you* don't understand! Because you're not right in the head! Oh, and speaking of which, Heather told me what you said to Roxie: that I was super-religious and only interested in her because of the angel miracle. And that I was a *nun*."

"That's not true! I said you *wanted* to be a nun—"

She chuckled, and the dead sound ricocheted ruthlessly around the room. "You know what? If this wasn't my fault, mostly, you'd be laying in a pool of your own blood right now. But it is my fault! I knew you were nuts the moment I met you, but it was kind of fun for a while, you know? My life has been so fucking boring lately, and the fucked-up stunts you pull kind of took my mind off that. So, if I'm really going to be honest with myself, I was kind of taking advantage of you. And I guess that wasn't really fair, especially since I know that you aren't actually trying to fuck with people; you've just got some major problems."

"Del, Mrs. Stefano just needs—"

"No, no, no. I can't, anymore."

And with that, she pushed me out the door and closed Mrs. Stefano's home to me.

Needless to say, the man across the street hadn't moved an inch, and I was forced to make my way back to the car with a hound-dog chorus. Most of Mrs. Stefano's neighbors immediately reappeared on their porches and at their windows; I only realized when I reached my car that this time, my squirrel head was under my arm and they could see who was wearing the costume. I'd yelled rather loudly that I was a squirrel, and now I was identifiable. I wasn't sure how I felt about that.

I also wasn't sure how I felt about driving home in the poisonous, suffocating suit. The air conditioning had never really worked in the Regency 98, although I was sure that it couldn't have penetrated the diabolical fake fur, anyway, so I paused outside my door and waited until the Bassett hounds were out of the vicinity. Then I entered the car and quickly wrestled off the suit, the cool air meeting my perspiration and producing the most exquisite chill. I realized only then that I wouldn't have made it another minute in my rodent prison; I would've fainted at the wheel and doubtlessly rammed through the parlor of some grandmother, considering my luck that day.

Revived, I pulled out into the street. No, I wouldn't allow myself to wallow in thoughts of "luck." *I* was responsible for everything that had gone wrong, and I had to face this fact, squarely and maturely.

I shouldn't have brought Del with me. Her family and community's reaction to her lifestyle had permanently scarred her. It was difficult to admit, cold even, but she was damaged goods, and there really wasn't anything even *I* could do to help her. I realized that now. The pain was too deep.

If I'd just visited Mrs. Stefano alone, she and I would have been laughing over a cup of cocoa in her kitchen, both dressed in our animal suits, both completely respecting each other's life decisions.

Everything would've still been okay.

Apparently, I'd been so absorbed in my thoughts that I'd failed to see the police officer who'd pulled up beside me. In fact, I seemed to have driven nearly a half a mile before realizing that his flashing lights were meant for me, and I pulled into the parking lot of a convenience store.

I didn't like to think of anyone as a cliché, but he even had the moustache.

"Ma'am, can I ask you what you're doing, driving around in your underwear?"

I took a deep, calming breath and began my story from the beginning.

After all, he was an officer of the law.

8

Why not take a chance?

"Aww. And you just missed Sputnikfest!"

Two Rivers, Wisconsin had the jolly sundae at the heart of its identity: a treat, an event, a celebration. This flavored everything at the heart of the town, and its inhabitants clung to it as butterscotch syrup clings to the roof of one's mouth. I even found myself matching ice cream flavors with people, after awhile, which had to be the town's main pastime. Mrs. Stefano was strawberry with little, colored marshmallows suspended among the chunks of fruit. Del was midnight chocolate with shards of crunchy, savory walnuts. Samuel was a sensuous coconut/mango concoction that aroused as it soothed. I could almost taste each of them.

And if I had to be honest with myself, I was champagne sorbet with twenty-four-carat gold flakes dusted throughout, to be served in fluted crystal, a cleansing and delighting of the palate, yet with a certain tart gravitas.

The people of Manitowoc, on the other hand, had at their core identity molten space junk flung at them by a repressive, Communist regime. It seems that in 1962, a section of Sputnik IV had landed in the center of town, and the residents had taken a great deal of misplaced pride in the accident ever since. (Claude had once been engaged to a Cosmonaut briefly in 1982, but the Russian authorities couldn't construct an acceptable narrative for his past and so dumped him, blindfolded and nude, in a village in Kamchatka. One of the nearby active volcanoes was still nicknamed Claudushka.)

"Yes. I understand it's a great deal of fun. 'Sputnikfest.'" I was beginning to understand the pity the good people of Two Rivers felt for their twin city. Desperation and self-delusion were never pretty, and I was now discovering that these were both clearly reflected in the faces of the Manitowockians. Their brows seemed heavy with the concerns of the Neanderthal, somehow; there was a slowness to the townspeople's reactions, an inability to reason out even the most basic of quandaries. It was easy to see why they'd clung to an event as random as a piece of metal falling from the sky. Rain and snow must have fascinated early Homo sapiens.

So with nothing in its history to compete with the birthplace of an American culinary institution, Manitowoc had apparently created Sputnikfest. I wanted to know nothing more about it, but the young man felt compelled to educate me on the town's self-inflicted mortification.

"We even have a great art competition at the museum. Space-themed. It's real fun. And all because of that totally weird coincidence from, like, fifty years ago. It still blows my mind."

"I'm sure. Especially if you're a religious man."

He found this impossible to process, and his eyebrows, almost too blond to see, squeezed together. "What do you mean?"

"Well, I can imagine how the citizens back then might have felt that the incident was an act of god, in more than one respect. Perhaps that the Supreme Being, or whatever one believes in, was in actuality warning Manitowoc that its residents might have become a little backward, or in some ways ignorant. A wake-up call that they might want to focus more on education and maybe less on interbreeding. That sort of thing."

He stared at me, his eyes clouded, slightly crossed. Then he tittered. "Totally! I never thought of it that way! This place is a total backwater, and I should know; I grew up here!"

"Well, let's just hope God doesn't have to bomb Manitowoc again."

He put up his arms in mock terror and yelled, "Aaaahhh!" It was nice to see someone in the town could joke about it. This was the first step in the healing process.

"So, anyway, is there something I can help you with?" The entire wall behind the young man was covered with "Beanie Babies," one of which he'd been fondling throughout our conversation. A pink Tyrannosaurus Rex. I felt that there was something I could help *him* with, but I declined commenting.

"Thank you. I'm actually here to see Roberta. I mentioned I'd be stopping by. Yolanda Polanski."

"Oh! Okay. Hold on a second." And he passed through the cards and crystal and ballerina figurines of his Hallmark store. There were Hallmark stores throughout the country, I told myself; it wasn't at all fair to consider the Manitowoc example somehow more ludicrous or banal. Digging my nails into my hands to feel the pinch of reality, I reminded myself that just because Two Rivers considered Manitowoc nothing more than an "ape farm," there was absolutely no reason for me to yield to these prejudices. Just because I called Two Rivers home, I didn't have to mindlessly accept its bad with its good—and one of its few, outright bad qualities at that. It wasn't logical, it wasn't sophisticated, and it wasn't kind.

Roberta looked like a pin-headed aberration from a Nineteenth-Century freak show. I wished desperately that it wasn't the case, but if I didn't respect reality, what would I be left with?

"Hi! Yolanda? I'm Roberta. We spoke on the phone."

Stating the painfully obvious wasn't necessarily a sign of mental subnormality. There were a whole host of other reasons.

I shook her hand, which featured fingers that were so short and conical that I wondered how she managed to feed herself or administer her home perms. From the looks of it, at the same time.

"It's so nice to meet you, Roberta. You've got a beautiful store here. It's very... pretty."

"Thank you! We've been here fifteen years now. I don't know where the time goes!"

I knew she couldn't possibly believe that time "went anywhere," so I immediately rejected my urge to explain Einstein's theory of relativity to her. It was a far too complex theory to break down into elements someone like her could understand, anyway.

"Isn't that true."

"So would you like to come back to my office?"

"That would be wonderful."

Roberta's purple Capri pants drew attention to her feet, which were as short and tapered as her hands. Hooves. Hooves! My baser thoughts were screaming at me now, but I was decent enough to push them carefully to one side. Promising myself that I would allow no further prejudice in my heart against the woman, I followed Roberta as she trotted to her office.

On the other side of the closed door, it smelled of cabbage and regret. This wasn't *good*, but it wasn't necessarily *bad.* It was just a fact.

"So, you're interested in Water Street."

"Very much so, yes."

"Well, that's just great."

"I would just need to go over a few particul—things."

"Ask away!"

"The suite is on the *third* floor of the building, correct?"

"Yes."

"And it faces the East Twin River?"

"Uhhhmm. Gosh, I never thought about it before. But yes, I guess it does."

"And is there a wood floor? And a closet with a door? And does it—or could it be made—to smell of citrus?"

Roberta frowned.

"You know: lemon, orange, fruit of that nature."

Her frown increased. I'd known a forty-one-year-old in Chattanooga who'd never had broccoli before in her entire life, so it wasn't as if it were completely unprecedented. Not having been exposed to some of the most important gastronomic ingredients known to man didn't necessarily reflect Roberta's mental capacity, or that of her parents and community.

"Tart, basically. Aromatic. In other words, it *smells nice.*"

* * *

At long last, I'd reached the first major goal in my quest—in a rather ingeniously simple way, if I were the kind of woman who congratulated herself. Earlier that week, I'd finally connected with Danny!

After so many months of planning—my scheme to infiltrate what I believed would be his new school, and my attempts to gain access to his home—in the end, it had been just as straightforward as quitting my lunch lady position; joining the Women of St. Matthew's Organization; posing as a pious widow named Bernadette McNair; volunteering ten hours a week for two months to clean all the bathrooms on the church grounds; waiting for a Holy Day of Obligation that Danny would attend with his brother and sister while their mother was at work; lingering until he was waiting alone for his siblings as they finished up their altar service duties; conveniently bumping into him outside of the sacristy; fabricating what appeared to be a sign from god in the day chapel; and explaining that I believed the sign was meant for him and that he should witness it immediately, at which point, I would finally have him alone and could quiz him on the specifics of the Sundae School that the angel had provided in his dream.

It was difficult to understand why I hadn't thought of this scheme the moment I'd moved to Two Rivers, but I had time to chastise myself later.

"Is that your real hair?" Danny was as candid as ever.

"Why don't we just focus on the sign from God."

"You're that lady from the bus who came to our house. My mom said I shouldn't talk to you."

"That was Yolanda, my sister. And your mother simply doesn't understand her; it's not that she's dangerous or wants to abduct you or corrupt you or anything of that nature. She's actually quite a brilliant human being."

He stared up at me, processing, weighing. "She's funny."

Inwardly, I cursed the ignorance of the parent and how it perpetuated itself in the ignorance of the child. I had to end this cycle of obtuseness before it progressed any further.

"But let me ask you: 'funny' or visionary? I should know; as her sister, Bernadette McNair, I understand her as no one else possibly can. And anyway, I'm reasonably certain that your mother has never told you that you can't speak to *me,* correct?"

"But you look like that other lady, only you're wearing different stuff."

Of course, Danny was gifted! I would've never risked so much for an ordinary child.

"It's true; my sister does have impeccable taste, even if she found it necessary to dress temporarily as a frump from 1977 recently. But as you can see, I have a completely different aesthetic. My Irish husband, Eamon, always encouraged me to embrace his proud heritage by wearing the tartan of his clan. Now that he's passed on, it's one of the ways I honor his memory. And of course, my hair is auburn, with soft curls."

"I have to go."

"Of course, you do. But before you go, you have to see the sign from god in the day chapel. It was pointing right at you a moment ago! I hope it's still there. I'm sure you'll know what it means."

My ploy was working; he was intrigued. Yet, he continued to resist. "My brother and sister are going to be out in a second, and we have to go home."

Yes, they were! I had to get him alone immediately—this was my only chance in this guise. Once he told his mother about the nice widow he met at church who had the vaguest of likenesses to the nice lady he met on the bus to Sheboygan, months of toilet-scrubbing would've been for naught because I'd never get near him again.

I attempted to relax and allow my increasing level of adrenaline do its work.

"Or aliens. It could be a sign from aliens, possibly. Do you like Star Wars?"

He just looked around the room, frowning. "I have to go."

"Chewbacca from the future? Or one of those robots, perhaps, the one shaped like a trash can. Whatever it is, it's going to disappear in a second, so this is really your last chance. Or maybe the ghost of Scooby-Doo! Or the Green Bay Packers?"

I was losing him.

"Did you hear that?" I cocked my ear to the door of the day chapel. "It just said, 'Danny.' Are you Danny?"

"I didn't hear anything."

I rushed to the door and put my ear up to it. "Yes, it's unmistakable: 'Danny.' If you're not Danny, I suppose the sign must be for someone else."

He remained rooted to the spot. "Is it an angel?"

Why did it take a six-year-old to reach the most obvious explanation for a celestial message?! Briefly, I predicted how furious I would be with myself in a few hours for not building my plan around his dream narrative, and then I took up the thread of his story. "Wait! The voice says it's the angel from your dream. The angel who told you that Two Rivers needs... an ice-cream sundae school! Well, that's it. I have to find out more."

And—appropriate to the setting—I took a leap of faith and hurried into the day chapel, trusting that Danny would follow.

He didn't.

Of course, my "miracle" didn't exactly jibe with the angel explanation, and on one level, I was glad he hadn't immediately followed me in.

The Sun is an endlessly fascinating presence in our lives, and the previous two months had allowed me to fully appreciate the spiritual resonance of Ra, Louis XIV, and the Raisin Bran two-scooped mascot. And all because I'd become more intimately familiar with the Sun's behavior than I'd ever dreamt I would. Needless to say, I was thrilled to add this knowledge to my already overflowing databank of useful facts, but at this point, I desperately needed results, not information.

After many, many attempts and between vigorous urinal wipe-downs, I had perfected my "sign from god" the previous week. By carefully placing two sticks at the correct angle on top of the truck belonging to the church's maintenance man, which was always parked outside the day chapel's south window, the Sun would cast a cross-shaped shadow that pointed directly at the word "Daniel" in a Bible quote I'd framed and quietly hung on the opposite wall. It read:

"And Daniel was visited by one of God's messengers in a dream, and the angel did tell Daniel to go forth and share his message of education and joy with the village. And lo! did the people of the town erect a temple of knowledge true to Daniel's vision. And it was good."—Ephesians xix, 35.

Strictly speaking, the quote hadn't been included in the King James edition, but it had been on the wall for two weeks, and no one had questioned it—not even Father Lansky. I felt this in itself could've been interpreted as a sign from God. In fact, a religious person would've believed it indicated that she was doing the work of the Lord, perhaps even that the Divine spirit wished this very quote to be included in the next version of the Bible. I made a mental note to investigate who made these editorial decisions the next time I was "online."

Rushing up to the picture, I attempted to move it slightly to the right so that the Sun's angle was perfect.

"Danny! A miraculous cross is pointing right at your name!"

But I'd spoken too soon: the window of opportunity had been missed, owing to the discussion of Star Wars' robots into which I'd allowed myself to be drawn. I could move the picture only far enough for the cross to point at "lo!" now—the only word in my quote whose meaning I wasn't one-hundred percent clear on. If asked, I decided I would explain that it was analogous to "yo."

I adjusted: "The angel's moving the cross, now! You've got to see this!"

But Carl, the janitor—for the first time in the two months of my observations—decided to get into his truck at this precise moment. Once he drove off with my little wooden cross and shadow, I'd look a fool, but I could still use the powerful quote to convince Danny that God wanted him to tell me exactly what the angel told him. I just had to hope that Carl wouldn't notice the cross on the back of his truck before it flew off, possibly injuring or killing another motorist or pedestrian.

"It's fading, Danny! Hurry!"

But Carl didn't move; he sat in his truck. Staring at me. At first, I thought I had yet another inappropriate suitor, but all too soon, I realized what was happening: Carl had seen my miracle. And he was amazed. But his amazement would end the moment he saw that someone had taped a popsicle-stick cross to his vehicle, and then it wouldn't be long until Danny learned that I'd engineered the whole phenomenon.

It was apparent to me now that a certain physical reaction to stress had recently grown stronger in me: I felt a wave of dizziness, and stars frosted my vision. However, in this instance, I was also nauseous and couldn't decide whether to run to Danny, to Carl, or to the bathroom I'd just polished to god-fearing perfection so that I might throw up.

I didn't have to choose: Danny entered the day chapel and Carl jumped out of his truck and headed to the nearest church entrance. At least there was divine intervention: it never occurred to Carl to glance back and determine just what was casting the shadow.

I didn't have time to vomit; I couldn't allow Carl and Danny to experience the miracle together, so I ran out of the room and toward the entrance opposite the one I knew Carl was running into. "Danny! I saw something out here! An angel in white!"

No child could resist a chase, and Danny raced after me into the parking lot. "Where?"

"You keep an eye out here; I'm just going to check around the corner!"

And with that, I sprinted toward Carl's truck. Peeking into the day chapel's window, I found him with his back to me, reading the "Bible quote."

I yelled around the corner and toward the door, "Carl," and he turned momentarily toward the interior of the church. This gave me a moment to snatch the cross, throw it under a car parked nearby, and without breaking my stride, return to where Danny had been standing.

"Did you find the ang—"

But he was gone.

If his brother and sister had collected him, all hope was probably lost. I knew that Roxie would forbid the poor child from speaking even to the sister of the "funny lady," and I'd have to start from scratch all over again. But I was in a house of the Lord; I couldn't lose faith that casually!

Running back to the day chapel, I paused outside.

Carl was speaking to someone: "Really? What was it about?"

I would be forever grateful to fate for the next second. Feeling the smooth plywood of the day chapel's door and the cheap Berber carpeting that adorned its floor, I was a millisecond away from entering it fully when I heard Danny's voice: "Oh, well, it was high up in this building with shiny wood on the floor, and there was a river outside that sparkled from the sun coming up, and it smelled like Pledge like my grandma's tables, and there were funny animals there that figured out how to open up their closet door, and so they came out and played with the angel who said it was an ice-cream sundae school."

Although the blood draining from my skull stilled my body, I barely managed to move back and out of their line of sight. Remaining erect would be a further challenge. But at long, long last, I had what I needed to forge ahead with my master plan!

"Oh my gosh! That's the same as this passage from the Bible! Look! You're Daniel, and an angel came to you about an educational thing, too! And that cross shadow was pointing right at it. I saw it with my own two eyes! I've got to tell Father Lansky about this. He's going to flip! You wait here, okay?"

I knew that Carl was headed straight for me. How could I explain my "miraculous" experience to the Father without drawing far too much attention to myself—or rather, "Bernadette?" Moreover, how would it seem when someone finally noticed that the Bible quote wasn't—*technically*—in the Bible?

I dove under a nearby table that was completely draped in purple velvet. Once again, the Father, Son and Holy Spirit were smiling down on me because Carl never noticed the swinging fabric. (His glasses were quite thick, and he did have a tendency to blink a few times at everything he scrutinized; I'd noticed that.)

Now that I'd gotten what I'd come for, I had to remove both the framed quote and Bernadette from the premises immediately and permanently. Under closer inspection by a clergyman, my miracle would not hold water, and I wished as soon as possible to cast it out into the darkness, where it would be lost forever, the Mary Celeste of Catholic revelations.

Carl's footfall disappeared down a corridor, and I quickly emerged from under the table. Only after becoming upright, however, did I realize that Danny's siblings had just emerged from the sacristy and were standing ten feet away from me. Apparently, my wig had taken on an unnatural angle because they were both staring at the top of my head.

To adjust it would be to admit defeat before the eyes of God. I stood firm.

"Oh, hello. Have you seen a, uhhh… Oh, there it is." Grabbing a hymnal from the back of the nearest pew, I smiled graciously at the children while my brain burned through the dwindling set of options left to me. Now that I knew the entire angel dream, I had to get rid of the three children, the Bible quote and Bernadette McNair before Father Lansky returned. Otherwise, the media might again distort the situation, somehow casting me in an unfavorable light and making things more difficult for the Sundae School.

"Danny! Danny!" I infused my voice with as much passion as I could, and sure enough, the young man quickly emerged from the day chapel and approached his siblings.

"Hey, you guys! The angel from my dream came back to me! And everybody saw it!"

Chelsea and Shay looked sharply at me; apparently, their mother had gotten to them, too. I had to shift blame, and fast.

"The *janitor* said he saw a 'miracle.'" I looked, full of "suspicion," in the direction Carl had just gone, screaming at my facial muscles to hide my nervousness. "But I'm sure he's nothing to worry about; I don't think he's necessarily *criminally* insane. Oh, by the way, do either of you know any martial arts to protect yourselves? Or perhaps you carry tasers or those oriental numchuks? How big would you say Carl is? About six-foot-four?"

That seemed to do the trick: the boy and girl each grabbed one of Danny's arms and pulled him out of the church. I could tell that the threat of a mad janitor had worked wonderfully because there was more than gratitude in the older children's eyes; when they looked back at me, there was sheer terror.

Danny resisted. "But she saw my angel, too! You guys!"

His brother and sister weren't about to let him go, and they dragged the squirming boy out into the safety of the ever-creeping, treacherous Sun. (I promised myself to move to an overcast country next, where I would never again be forced to rely on the capricious behavior of our Solar System's "star.")

But there wasn't a second to lose. Racing back into the day chapel, I snatched my quote off the wall at the exact moment I heard Carl and Father Lansky enter the main chapel. I couldn't get out of the building now without being seen by them, and there was nowhere to hide myself anywhere in the room. My adrenaline levels had reached an all-time high.

Then I reminded myself who I was, what I'd accomplished. I wasn't about to allow a priest, a rather slow custodian and a ball of flaming helium defeat me. Instead, they would inspire my next move!

Just as I'd predicted, Father Lansky was the most resistant, the most inhibited by "logic."As he approached, his voice echoed ecclesiastically everywhere: "I'm not aware of any story like that in the Bible."

"But it's there, right on the wall! And Bernadette saw it, too!"

The two men froze when they entered the day chapel and saw the fire.

I stood over the smoking frame on the floor and stared down at my Bible quote as if I'd just seen the face of Jesus himself. "It just spontaneously combusted."

While the two men raced to put out the flames and minimize the damage to the room, I quietly passed out the door. Never again would Mrs. Bernadette McNair wipe a Christian pubic hair off the toilets of St. Matthew's Catholic Church while humming her late husband's favorite tune, "The Hills of Connemara." She had been sacrificed at the altar of the greater good. *Amen.*

* * *

"Yes, I know what citrus means, Yolanda. I'm just a little confused, to be honest. Why do you care if the office space smells like citrus?"

I was so close to realizing my mission, yet before me lumbered the genial dead weight of a Manitowockian. How could I explain things so that they would make sense to someone like Roberta?

I looked around her room and noticed several rainbow picture frames encircling photographs of a small, red-haired girl who had been posed in front of the following backdrops: a cartoon schoolroom, Shamoo leaping into the air, and the Alps. Clearly images of Roberta's child, it seemed as if special care had been taken by the studio photographer to use vibrant, striking backgrounds, perhaps to draw attention away from the girl's features, or her posture.

"What a lovely little girl."

"Oh, thanks! That's Kayla. She's nine, now."

"Is that right? Well, it's the same thing as Kayla, really. Her photographer was very careful to find just the right environment, or *place*, for each of her pictures. We need to do the same thing."

"But why citrus? If you don't mind me asking."

"Oh, I don't mind at all."

I noticed that her mouth was wider than the width of the top of her head. Did extra chromosomes mean extra teeth?

"Do you mind telling me?"

"Of course not."

Her ears were lower down than most normal humans', and I wondered if this meant that her brain was lower, too. If that were the case, though, what was above it? Skull? Water?!

"Now?"

"Oh, I'm sorry. It's part of our vision."

"Part of your vision?" Her smile was truthful, pure—the kind of smile that could only come from truly innocent creatures who had never faced the dilemmas, the moral complexities of the lives of the fully developed. "You actually haven't told me what kind of business you'd like to operate there."

"Haven't I? A training academy."

"Really? Oh! Well, I have to say that's very exciting news to me. You know, before my store, I actually used to teach college. University of Wisconsin at Green Bay."

There was a tragically high level of lead in the public water supply of Green Bay.

"That's nice."

"So what sort of training would you be offering?"

"Culinar—well, we'd be *making food,* basically."

"Really! But you know, the space isn't set up for food preparation. No ovens, no walk-ins, and I couldn't really pay for those kinds of alterations—"

"No, no, no. Of course not. We'll just have a few freezers. We'll be training people how to make ice-cream confections."

I was sure she'd had ice cream before, but she still seemed confused. "Ice-cream confections? A *school* to make ice-cream confections? Well, I have to admit that sounds like a lot of fun, but I don't know if it would really work in this area. I mean, it's kind of specialized, and to be completely honest, I'm not really sure that too many people would be interested in that kind of education—"

"I'd pay the entire rent due for the year up front."

"You'd... pay the..." Roberta's voice trailed off into a mumbled confusion. (And Claude's voice rose, unbidden: never trust an idiot with money, but never pass them by. I could only pray I wasn't as cutthroat.)

"I'd pay you *the money*."

It was indescribably gratifying to see the woman suddenly understand what I was saying. Magically, comprehension dawned across her face, almost a kind of intelligence. Perhaps all Roberta needed was to be exposed to people outside of Manitowoc, to have her intellect occasionally challenged, and she would blossom.

"You're the lady who was arrested driving around in her underwear. And running around in a squirrel suit. In the paper."

"Oh, that! The charges were dropped."

"You know, I don't really think—"

"What if I were to pay you double."

"Eighteen-hundred dollars a month?"

"The entire twenty-four thousand dollars right now."

"Uhhmmm. Actually, I think it would be... twenty-one thousand, six-hundred—"

"Whatever you say, dear. But that's *less* than twenty-four thousand dollars. You should be bargaining for *more*."

"Well, that sounds very tempting, Yolanda. But I'm not sure you're entirely—"

I rose, not wanting to take advantage of her situation any more than I might already have.

"I'll have a cashier's check in your hand in an hour. Unless you'd prefer cash?"

Of course, she knew what "cash" meant. She must have manned her Hallmark cash register before. But yet again, I received only the glassy-eyed, addled Manitowoc stare in response.

"Cash?"

Once Two Rivers' Sundae School was a success, I would look into opening up a remedial educational institute in her sister city. Perhaps basket weaving, or landscape maintenance.

It just seemed like the humane thing to do.

* * *

That evening, I stared up at the future home of the Two Rivers Sundae School on Water Street and considered all I'd had to do to get to this point, marveling at all the eggs I'd had to break. A lot of the eggs were upset with me now; others thought me a little too *avant garde* for their community. But I knew that I'd develop a plan to win them back soon enough and that their yolks would pool in the heart of the town and harden, providing me with a solid foundation on which to stand as I realized the dream of an extraordinary little boy and transformed their village into a Mecca of *joie de vivre*.

A sophisticated radar system based on scent. It was the only explanation for Tabby III's uncanny ability to find me anywhere in Two Rivers. As he twisted through my legs, undoubtedly transferring to me his own odor and that of the feces in which he'd been rolling, I noticed that he carried something in his mouth.

There, at my feet, in the fast-falling dusk of a Wisconsin autumn, lay a petrified rodent of some kind that Tabby III offered up to me.

Instantly deciding that the eyeless, twisted corpse was an auspicious sign for the future, I carefully placed it at the front door of the building. I then turned for home and the next step in my plan.

It was comforting to know that at least one Two Riverian still believed in me.

9

An angel with no wings said there should be an ice-cream sundae school.

For Two Rivers, by Two Rivers. For Two Rivers, by Two Rivers.

Looking down a bleak, Green Bay street bled of all its promise decades earlier—a promise that seemed to have been replaced with only a certain embalming ennui—I reminded myself of the wisdom of my Sundae School mantra. *For Two Rivers, by Two Rivers.* But even stepping outside of my city's borders now felt as if I betrayed, I abandoned, I compromised. Shivering, I considered the gray slush that surrounded and threatened me as nothing less than a deserved retribution for this, my shameless transgression.

But Mrs. Stefano *was* Two Rivers to me: kind, innocent, pleasant. I would walk through the filthiest precipitation on the planet for her—even Green Bay slush, which really was saying something. I owed Mrs. Stefano so terribly much, and I could no longer allow her to be deaf to my apologies; she deserved nothing less—certainly not banishment to Green Bay, if she was, in fact, here! Plus, it was clear that I needed her, now more than ever. In its way, the details of young Danny's dream had been an astonishing revelation whose meaning I still struggled to process. Lemon Pledge? Shiny wooden floors?! But one thing about my enterprise had been perfectly clear from the start: I needed Mrs. Stefano.

I'd already attempted several times to get back into contact with Del, but she'd somehow always managed to see through my carefully orchestrated ruses. Our last exchange at Mrs. Stefano's had suggested two facts: one, that Del had not, as of yet, processed through her feelings for me, and two, that reconciliation with her was only possible if there were a reconciliation with Mrs. Stefano first. To begin the peace process, I'd hired an attractive young actress from Madison with a slight resemblance to me to play the part of a wealthy debutante. In the narrative, she, desperate to break out of the stifling role society had thrust upon her, had left her family to found her own golf store in Two Rivers. Unfortunately, not only did Del not accept her offer of a substantial payment for remodeling a storefront that I just happened to pass every day, but she also asked my actress to convey a very specific suggestion to me. The message involved several golf balls, a golf club, and a pair of golf shoes that sported especially lethal spikes.

Undaunted, I had come prepared for Green Bay. In an effort to avoid notice, I'd opted for the guise of the mid-century Soviet worker: brown, rough babushka, shapeless shoes, and a gray-flannel dress that screamed for pinking shears to put it out of its misery. My single note of hope—symbolic perhaps of the almost comatose echo of faith still faintly glowing within the heart of the innocents trapped in this wretched city—was an upliftingly intense dose of bright red rouge. It attested to the fact that I was downtrodden but optimistic; barren, yet as insistent of my vitality as a Socialist peasant. I had to blend in, as I simply could not afford to arouse any suspicion.

Green Bay was a place for the dying, the dead, and the dead at heart. Green Bay politely asked you to check your dreams at the door and then to suck on the icy despair flowing from its frigid, frigid teat. Green Bay held you close, not to warm you, but to drain you of all warmth, a leech of sorts that thrived not on human blood, but human faith, human dignity. Green Bay stole into your soul and laid its black eggs of poisoned nothingness.

"Oh, hello! I wasn't sure if I heard someone knocking. Gosh, you look completely frozen. Your cheeks are so... Why don't you come on in?"

April Stefano looked nothing like Heather Stefano, but why would she? She couldn't have been more than a relative of Mrs. Stefano's late husband—or a relative of a relative. She was young, short, very dark (possibly African-American), and wiry, inspiring visions of balance beams, pummel horses and glistening leotards. I couldn't help but wonder if the highest uneven bars in the world could help April vault herself out of Green Bay and into a place that wouldn't greedily starve her of her future. She, just as all the others here, deserved better.

"Josh! If you don't turn down that Guitar Hero right now, I'm going to come up there and tan your hide!" This exclamation had been quite loud and startled me severely. Presently, she addressed me: "I don't even know what 'tan your hide' means! What is that, like tan leather? Why am I even talking about tan leather? JOSH!!!"

I couldn't hear anything, upstairs or otherwise. In fact, the exterior of the house had appeared to be single-story.

"So anyway. Sorry about that! Arrgghh! Come and sit down *JOSH!! Turn that down!*"

My nerves were being affected by her interjections now. "Really, I don't mind."

"But he has to learn to respect me, you know? I mean, if not now, then when?"

I smiled, prepared for the shouting that I knew was about to come. But there was only silence. Awkward silence.

"So what can I do for you? You know, you look like maybe you got a little frostbite because you're really... or maybe not."

"Actually, I'm looking for a possible relative of yours: Heather Stefano? I was hoping you might know where I could find her. I thought that she might be in Green Bay now."

"*Heather* Stefano? Hmmm."

But this was all she said. Apparently, the ball was in my court.

"Heather was a close friend of mine, down in Two Rivers. She left rather abruptly, and I wanted to be sure she was all right."

"Why do you think she's a relative of mine?"

It was at this point I began to be a bit concerned about April's state of mind. "Your common last name. Stefano? I didn't know where else to turn."

"My last name's Brown."

"Oh. But in the phone—"

"JOSH! I'm coming up there!"

"—book."

"Well, yeah, it *used* to be Stefano."

Another uncomfortable pause. I was beginning to form a diagnosis, but I needed a little bit more information about April. "You were the only Stefano I could find in central Wisconsin. Come to think of it, I never did ask Mrs. Stefano about her husbands. Where they came from. I suppose that was insensitive of me, but I thought it might still be a painful subject for her. Actually, no, I didn't. I never thought that. She and I were both so focused on a certain project that we spoke of little else. Anyway, how can you apologize for the past, really?"

"JOSHI'MCOMINGUPTHERE!"

"Josh," a "second floor," her inexplicable evasiveness about her last name: it all made perfect sense now. April had been driven mad by Green Bay. She was simply living in a parallel universe where she had a son who haunted her from some phantom space hovering above, tormenting her day and night. She could hear the boy as plain as day, but she could never, ever find the stairs that led to his room, and this forced her to question everything about her life—especially the reality of her extended family and her own identity. In short, she was a paranoid schizophrenic. While I realized that lately, some of the psychological deductions I'd made had been slightly off target, this was another matter entirely. This was a textbook case. In fact, the supposed confession I'd just uttered was a test to prove my hypothesis, and she'd failed with flying colors. After all, if April *really* didn't know Mrs. Stefano, she wouldn't have paid such close attention to my comments. For her, clearly, Mrs. Stefano was simply a denizen of that other, dimly lit, evasive universe, the *real* one where April had a family with the last name Stefano, and she lived all alone in a ranch-style home mired squarely in the center of Green Bay, Wisconsin. But this was too much for her, so the stark truth was kept at bay by a rambunctious "upstairs child."

"But how can you apologize for anything else?"

"I'm sorry?"

"You asked how anybody could apologize for the past. What else can you apologize for?"

"It's so interesting that you'd say that, April."

"Why? It's true. You can't apologize for anything until it's already happened, right?"

"You have a very unique perspective on the world. I really respect that. So back to Heather."

"What was the project?"

The paranoid schizophrenic's desire to change the subject whenever it ventured too close to them! Two could play that game.

"Well, you wouldn't be interested unless you knew Heather."

"I'm just interested, is all. You said you guys were totally focused on it JOSH!! I'm going to whup you!"

I toyed with the idea of a type of Tourrette's Syndrome that involved indiscriminately shouting the names of imaginary family members. But perhaps "Josh" wasn't her son? Her lover, then? Or maybe something even less plausible? In her mind, was a giant turtle or demon engulfed in flames playing computer games in rooms of her house that didn't even exist? My heart went out to the poor girl, and I resolved to see what I could do to ease her suffering.

Taking advantage of the lull that seemed always to follow her outbursts, I inspected the room. New, cheap, dusty-rose furniture, Navajo rug knockoffs, a Green Bay Packers banner on the most prominent wall. It was clean, orderly—obviously too clean and orderly—and the obsession with the Green Bay Packers indicated a psychotic fixation. I had what I needed.

"You look so exotic, April. You must have Native American ancestry—or perhaps an Indian spirit guide?"

"What?"

"And the Green Bay Packers! What a wonderful team. But probably very filthy from all that rolling around in mud and whatnot. So, so filthy and disorganized. I hate when things aren't exactly right, don't you?"

"What are you doing here."

"Of course. We don't need to talk about all that now. You asked about the mission Mrs. Stefano and I have been working on. I'll tell you: we were establishing a new educational institute in Two Rivers, an ice-cream sundae school. How does that make you feel?"

"What an interesting idea. Where did you get it from?"

"A young boy's dream. An angel told him we should found the school in Two Rivers. Who was I to ignore a sign like that? Do you see signs, April?"

"So if your friend left, maybe she didn't want to help. Maybe she thought it was kind of a weird thing to do, and she changed her mind."

I was beginning to wonder if she were more delusional than I'd originally determined. It was becoming clear that I couldn't help her, so I decided to refocus on my original task.

"It sounds like you might know Heather, April."

"No, no. I don't think I've ever met her." She rose, the pink vinyl squeaking obscenely under her. "Anyway, I've got a whole lot of things to do, so—"

I stood, too. "Who's Josh, April?"

"He's my son." She herded me toward the door.

"When do you hear him, usually?"

"What do you mean, when do I hear him? When he makes noise."

"Maybe he knows Heather. Can you ask him? Or maybe your Navajo spirit guide knows her. Or the Packers. Can you hear them? Do they live upstairs, too?"

"Uhhmmm. I really need you to go." April opened up her front door, annoyed that in such a short time, I'd peeled back the complex, psychological layers her other doctors had never even realized were there.

I handed her my card. "I hope you'll call me if anyone remembers anything about Heather. I can't open the doors of the Sundae School without her. Or you can call me if you just need to talk, April. About escaping. I'd really like that."

She stared at me, some sort of furious conversation with her other personalities going on in her mind. Finally: "Josh!! Come down here. I baked peanut-butter cookies."

"That's all right, April. I don't have to meet 'Josh'—"

But suddenly, there was the sound of little footsteps banging down a staircase somewhere, and before I could process the event fully, a boy of about ten was standing before us wearing a baseball hat carefully placed at a strange angle on his head.

"Where are the cookies?"

"Don't worry. I'll bake some. But while you're here, why don't you say 'hi' to this lady."

Josh looked me up and down. "Hi."

The poor child inspired my maternal instincts, and I lowered myself to his level. "Hello, Josh. How are you doing? Are you holding up?"

"You've got lipstick on your cheeks."

Competing with the specters of his mother's twisted imagination must have been unbearable for him, so naturally he lashed out. And of course, Green Bay had no social services to rescue him! I barely restrained myself from embracing the poor devil.

"Mom! How come you said there was cookies?"

"Because I knew there was no other way I could get you down here! Now you can go back to your game, but keep it down. I'm serious, young man."

"You better make some!" And with that, he raced back to where he'd come from as quickly as his white-socked feet could take him.

"What a wonderful, brave little man."

"And he's real."

"It's nice to hear you say that."

She clucked a little and opened up her door.

"Remember, April: call me if you or anyone else remembers Heather, all right?"

"Bye."

But after she'd closed her storm door and I'd once again taken up battle with my sworn enemy, the city of Green Bay, Wisconsin, April stuck her head into the cold.

"Hey! I'm not the crazy one. I *do* know Heather, and you'd better stay away from her!"

I turned back to the little gray house, its dull aluminum siding absorbing what little light had somehow managed to survive in that city. On closer inspection, there *was* the possibility of a second floor.

"I knew who you were the second you showed up at the door, because I saw you on the Internet! I just wanted to see if you were really as much of a nut-case as they said. I mean, Heather said you were a little coo-coo, but you're a full-on whack-job! They called you the 'squirrelly nudist' in the paper, and now, you're dressed like some kind of depressed hobo in clown makeup! I don't know why she'd want to hang around with you, but you better leave her alone! You screwed up her life enough as it is!"

My strategy had worked! Not only had I gotten April to crack, but I'd extracted information that made my heart soar, even here, in the harrowing depths of Green Bay. Mrs. Stefano "wanted to hang around with me!"

I cheerily waved goodbye to April, verbally correcting her: "I believe it was actually 'nudist squirrel!" And then I silently wished her nothing but the best with the management of her illness. She had a long, difficult journey ahead of her, which was made a thousand times worse, thanks to the merciless city that had ensnared her. And then there was Josh, who could only play video games to drown out the pain and the deluded promises of cookies that would never, ever come.

When I returned to the Oldsmobile, I found that the fifty extra pounds of slush collected behind each wheel still hung there, steadily corroding the metal after which it lusted—nothing less than Green Bay etiquette. And although I'd originally been delighted that my trip to the city would kill two birds with one stone (doubtlessly a common occurrence here), I now wondered if I had the strength to face another moment surrounded by such insidious decay. Could I continue on to Ray's Old-Fashioned Ice Creamery, situated in the very blackest heart of downtown?

A lone raven cawed in the distance, a warning, a plea, a cry for help that would never come.

* * *

"Do you need anything else?" We could do something about the pimples later.

"This masterpiece!"

"It's just a sundae."

"It's much more than that! The proportions, the placement on the dish, the natural instinct of the whipped-cream patterns. Hasn't anyone ever told you that you are an artist, Darren?"

"No."

"Well, it's true. It takes a very special person to handle frozen confections."

Blushing for Darren meant only that his acne became angrier, but that wasn't important now. Now, I had to apply every ounce of my not inconsiderable charm. This moment was far too important to my mission to lose focus on a rather intense case of "zits," and I realized, as I studied the long line of soft whiskers across his neck he'd missed over what appeared to be a week or so of shaving, that I might never again have another instant that provided such a palpable connection between myself and the young virtuoso before me.

"So, Darren. You don't eat too much ice cream here, do you? Because all that fat and sugar... it just can't be good for your—for you."

"Uhhmmm. I've got to get back to work, so..."

Darren left my corner table and hurried back to his station behind the counter of Ray's Old Fashioned Ice Creamery. The place was almost a parody of itself, and I couldn't help but wonder if a cliché of a cliché negated its original triteness, or if this suddenly placed it in the zone of extreme irony the young people today found so "cool." Or if it just made things worse. (Claude had insisted on wearing a bowler hat the entire time he erected "Ejaculata," his largest piece to date, near Piccadilly Circus. Only after razing his work at the insistence of a few narrow-minded shopkeepers nearby did he remove the hat, the jigsaw cutting through the metal, the lemur bones, and finally the soft felt of the bowler. The resulting detritus was christened "Double-decker Cliché" and could still be seen in the National Gallery, if one asked politely.)

There were red-and-white-striped curtains at the windows of Ray's; tiny, hexagonal, white tiles on the floor; and twisted-wire café chairs huddled around twisted-wire café tables. The workers wore white paper hats and bright red bow ties. There was a calliope in the corner threatening patrons with its multifarious valves and whistles. There were doilies and the undeniable scent of a handlebar moustache.

I concluded that the victims trapped in Green Bay had invented this place to convince themselves that hell could be held at bay, one scoop at a time, but I feared even they knew that Ray's merely cast the agonizing despondency of their situation into higher contrast.

And despondent, it was. Not surprisingly, the "parlor" was nearly deserted on this frigid Wednesday afternoon. The only other customer was a large man desultorily eating a hamburger in the shadows of a far booth. Strangely, the scent of stale frying grease wafted from his direction, although the kitchen was on the other side of the establishment.

The silence provided me with a moment of reflection. Since my moment of notoriety a few weeks earlier, I'd actually received a steady flow of applications to teach at the Sundae School, mostly through strange emails from men with addresses like "hungpapa69" and "grizzlethwaite@tonguepierce.com." I didn't like it.

I'd also received a few postal letters, mostly from prison inmates who only seemed interested in seeing video of me smashing balls of ice cream with my bare feet. My heart went out to them, but my shoes remained on. Then there were the phone calls. A woman in Modesto, California swore that she'd been visited by the ice-cream angel, too, who had instructed her to build a new Mount Rushmore entirely out of "Cherry Garcia." It would consist of four busts of Gerald Ford, each with a different expression, which she'd designated as "happy," "sleepy," "bashful," and oddly, "doc." While I supposed it was possible that she'd been in contact with a celestial being, I could only consider her for a place as a student and told her so.

Oddly, no actual soda jerks or ice-cream artists had been in contact. This was perfectly fine with me, though, as I preferred to do my own footwork. And my feet had worked their way right up to Green Bay and Ray's Old-fashioned Ice Creamery, widely considered the best spot for frozen confections north of Lake Butte des Morts. Their menu included the classics, such as the banana split and the tin roof, but it also dove into more experimental, daring concoctions. For instance, there was a tropical extravaganza that involved coconut shells, a calypso soundtrack, and a sparkler. (My mind floated back to Martinique and Claude, clad only in a palm frond, asking a little old lady for a dime so that he could call his bookie. Claude! There are no "dimes" in Martinique! I could still taste the salt water and frustration, and looking back, I wondered if a sparkler wouldn't have defused the entire situation.)

"Is everything okay with your sundae?"

"You know, it's funny, Darren, but for some reason, I was just thinking about Martinique. The orgiastic abandon of a Caribbean luau. I lived there for a while, not so long ago. Have you ever been?"

"That's so weird, because I used to live there, too! Let me see if I can remember: *De quel côté de l'île avez-vous habité?*"

"Isn't that charming! I'll let you know if I need anything else."

While Darren wandered back to his cleaning duties, I began to doubt my original assessment of his work. Clearly, the school required an instructor for the introductory classes who was strong in the fundamentals, yet who felt comfortable expanding the boundaries of the modern-day frozen dessert. Darren understood the hot-fudge sundae, but did he *live* the hot-fudge sundae and *breathe* the hot-fudge sundae? It was impossible to say, and subtle clues as to a certain, supercilious attitude might've been surfacing. Ultimately, the answer lay in the next test: could he tackle more elaborate fare?

Darren had been peering at me for the previous few minutes over his cleaning rag and swaths of nickel-plated hardware. I waved him over.

"That was a pure mitzvah, Darren."

"Sorry?"

"And that's the last time you are ever to apologize to me. After this." I indicated my empty dish. "Now, this 'Very Berry Volcano.' I have a choice of lava?"

"Uh-huh."

"Wonderful. Make it strawberry."

"You want me to *make* you one? Because it's real big. It's for, like, seven people or eight people or something. It's like this." He spread out his hands to indicate that the dessert was approximately two and a half feet in length.

"That's fine. Whatever I don't eat we'll consider a sacred offering to the gods. You'll be further blessed."

"Uhhh—"

"And Death by Chocolate. Kill me, Darren."

"But that's for a whole bunch of people, too. Like, a lot of people."

"Then I'll savor it with the ghosts of dinner companions past."

"Plus, it's, like, forty dollars."

"Think of the tip."

He did. And he continued to think, his pimples all pointed at my cheap, little table. Darren's hair was dry and shaggy, and it reminded me of those male mannequins from the 1970s who sported cheap wigs perched unnaturally on their heads. I had flashbacks of plaid, polyester blazers and vowed we'd put that to rights—along with his complexion—before classes began. If he could pull this next assignment off.

"Okay." This came out quite shyly, a timbre to his voice that I'd not been exposed to, as of yet. Somehow, it revealed a certain kind of eagerness that, for Darren, was clearly inspired by ice cream. "You wait here."

I wasn't at all sure where else I would want to go in that god-forsaken city, so I merely smiled and nodded. Who was I to deny it? I had a good feeling about Darren.

What hadn't felt so good was all the press coverage over the previous weeks. Somehow, the dash-cam footage of me being pulled over while driving in my underwear had made its way into the "U Tube," and my court appearance had subsequently been closely followed by the local press. I couldn't explain the underwear without explaining the squirrel suit, and I couldn't explain the squirrel suit without explaining the Sundae School, so I'd started at the beginning and led the judge through the entire saga, holding back little. She had been polite enough never to interrupt.

However, the media seemed to find it all quite noteworthy, and I'd spent a few days as the darling of the Internet, an admittedly premature celebrity. While I was well aware that any PR is good PR, I was disappointed to find that local response to my master plan for Two Rivers was lukewarm at best, and I'd failed to build the alliances I'd so hoped would result from it all. In fact, the town itself seemed unhappy with the brief notoriety, and although no one was ever as tactless as to confront me, my presence at the very heart of Two Rivers seemed to be an irritant, of all things. Of course, the analogy of the oyster immediately came to mind, and I recognized my role as the lustrous, precious pearl, just as I knew the townspeople would, soon enough.

At this point, my mind slipped further into reverie. Toying momentarily with the CB handle of "Wisconsin Pearl," I envisioned my eighteen-wheeler, with a paint job producing a rainbow burst with each and every sunbeam, hauling ore one mile ahead of the county sheriff and two miles behind the trucker of my heart, Jimmy Dean and his Green Machine from Moline.

"Ma'am?"

At some point, the desserts had arrived. They barely fit on my table, and running my eyes over their chilled contours and melting, sugared valleys, I could barely express my awe. The young man *was* a genius; I wished I had a sparkler I could hand him.

"Darren! These are… I don't know what to say. Epic. Profound. Lush. Important. Joyful. Bravissimo!"

All I got was the shag on top of his head. He'd grown coyer the closer we'd approached the bearing of his soul, and here, packed on top of the little disc of plywood before me, was Darren's very essence. He'd waited his whole life for someone to recognize all he held inside, and I was that someone. I vowed to myself that instant, as he stared at the retro, Gibson Girl flooring, that I would never, ever let him falter in his onward journey into history and ice-cream legend. This young man needed a champion, and he'd just found her.

"I just follow the steps in this book they gave us—"

"Darren, I'd like you to sit down with me for a moment."

He turned sharply toward the grease-man in the corner. "I'm not really supposed to sit down when I'm working, so…"

"Darren, it'll be worth your while."

I received the merest flash of a look from somewhere deep among his bangs, and then he shot off toward the man in the corner. They discussed some serious matter for a moment, both glancing in my direction, and then Darren returned and dropped onto the uncomfortable chair across from me.

"Kenny said it would be okay for a second. He's cool."

"Is he? Well, he should be more than 'cool' on you, as far as I'm concerned."

Darren giggled a bit at this. I'd have to gently break him of the habit before he made his debut before a sea of students.

"So, I just turned eighteen and everything. You know."

"An adult! I can see it in your work."

"Yeah, I'm a senior and stuff, you know, so…"

"So you're ready for some adventure."

His grin expanded a moment, but he suppressed it. "Yeah. That's cool. Hey, I like your look and stuff. Did you just get out of prison?"

"Darren, I think you know why I'm here. Your expertise shouldn't be left to rot away, here in this desperate clawing at a time machine. It's time you did what you were born to do."

Another giggle. "Okay."

His eyes had yet to rise farther north than the front of my dress. The poor boy would need a great deal of coaching to overcome his fatal shyness, but I was confident I could wring it out of him in a week or so.

"What do you make here, if you don't mind my asking?"

"Huh?" Now, he did look me in the eye.

"I'll double it."

"Double it?"

"Don't you think you're worth it?"

He didn't seem to know how to respond to this, and instead picked at a scab on his thumb for a moment. His voice became thin, as if the restaurant was running out of air, and his blemishes took on a slightly purple tone. "God! That's kind of a freaky question."

"Darren. Promise me that you'll never underestimate your talent. False modesty is a silly waste of breath, and we both know what you're capable of."

"Uhmmm."

"And you've got transportation?"

"Uhh, well, my truck isn't really running right now. And I have to work until seven tonight, but maybe after that..."

"Transportation is key, of course." I rose. Darren would be ideal, and I had to get back to Two Rivers to oversee the installation of the hot-topping equipment at the school. I handed him my new business card, "Yolanda Polanski, Chancellor, Two Rivers Sundae School," which featured the coat of arms I'd designed months earlier.

"I'll have one of these made for you before classes start."

"Classes?"

"First, though, I'll need you to do a bit of surveillance work here, in Green Bay. On a Miss April Stefano, or rather, Brown. Just write your number and address on the back of this, and I'll forward the full dossier."

He did as he was told, but seemed even more perturbed than earlier. "Dossier? I'm not totally—"

"Will a hundred dollars cover your work today?"

"Uhhmm, I'd have to ring it all up first—"

"Then here's two hundred."

"No, that's way—"

"Consider it an advance."

He handed me his contact information. "But wait a minute. I don't—"

"Darren, I've got a caramel warmer on the way. But of course, *you* understand." I shook his hand warmly, an encouraging, welcoming gesture that expressed so many more emotions than I could verbally at that moment: my appreciation, my respect, my unwavering support of his advancement. He responded with a bashful smile, but there was a certain candor behind it; already his confidence was firming up. It must have been the thought of his ice-cream future. My heartbeat quickened: I was having a positive effect on him, and I'd only been in Ray's for half an hour!

I hurried toward the door; it was later than I'd realized.

"A caramel warmer on the way?" He looked at the mountains melting in front of him, then over at the large man in the corner, who appeared to be leering at me.

As I passed into the foyer of the restaurant, I heard Kenny mumble something about Darren's Cougar and titter in a manner that was frankly distasteful. He must have overheard what Darren and I were discussing, and was preparing to talk Darren out of the most propitious opportunity that would probably ever present itself. Of course, I understood perfectly why Kenny would do this; who'd want to lose the work of such a craftsman? But I wasn't worried—I'd seen the look in Darren's eye a moment earlier: conspiratorial, candid, a passionate affirmation. The raw desire was undeniable: the almost erotic lure of ice cream had set Darren's soul alight.

I emerged into the gray street and found myself once again swallowed up whole by the gaping, gluttonous maw of Green Bay. I was almost positive that "Cougar" was the name of a car, rather than a truck, but if

I'd learned one thing in my short, dynamic life, it was never to be one-hundred-percent certain of anything.

In fact, the only thing I was one-hundred-percent sure of was that Darren was stimulated by the thought of a new career as an ice-cream instructor—the eagerness fairly leapt from his eyes. At long last, someone had taken the time to recognize and validate his unique talent, and I knew he'd be eternally grateful, going the extra mile to give me his all and then some. The boundless drive of youth!

As I sidestepped the salt-encrusted mounds of ice on the sidewalk that appeared in such a regular rhythm that one couldn't be blamed for assuming they were deliberately placed hazards, I grew philosophical. When all was summed up, did human beings simply represent a collection of feelings to one another? Was Darren nothing more than an amalgam of my elation, my respect, my goodwill? And if the emotions his friends and family felt for him were added up, too, would that sum represent Darren's very soul?

By this point, I'd reached the Oldsmobile. It seemed to sag under the resentful atmosphere of the parking lot, and as I pitied the poor thing, I wondered if the car had developed a soul of its own, thanks to all the emotions I felt toward it. Briefly, I considered investigating the history of car baptisms when I noticed Darren running toward me.

"Excuse me, ma'am?"

"Yes, Darren."

"Uhhmm, I don't want to, uhhmm. I guess I kind of know that you weren't trying to get with me just now, and that's cool and everything or whatever. But I think you might be thinking that you just hired me to do something, and I don't want you to, you know, like, get the wrong idea, either. Because that would not be cool. For you, I mean."

There were too many extraneous words in this statement for me to be absolutely sure what he meant, so I simply allowed him to continue.

He appeared to take this as agreement on my part: "Because I'm still in high school, and I'm going to college in the fall and everything, and I'm, like, sure that there isn't anything I could do that would, like, require a business card, anyway! I mean, that's, like, hardcore or whatever. And I didn't want you going and thinking that about me. Because, you know, you seem, like, kind of nice or whatever, too, so…" The "too" in this last statement briefly puzzled me, but I tucked it away in my memory bank, promising myself that I would ask Darren to elucidate once we'd developed a communication model that functioned a bit more effectively.

"Darren, you are worthy of a *gilded* business card. A platinum engraving! Truly. This is coming from a woman who has seen enough of humanity to know of what she speaks."

"Okay. Well, anyway. Here you go. Bye."

Before I could process what was happening, he'd placed something in my hands and run back into Ray's. Looking down, I found one-hundred and fourteen dollars and sixty-eight cents, along with a receipt.

He hadn't even taken out his tip.

Anyone who knew me knew that I relished a challenge. Over the course of years, I'd developed a reputation as a scrapper, willing to go to any lengths to get what I needed from others—as long as my actions were ethically acceptable. This was simply who I was.

But as I got into the car and listened to the engine laboriously work its way up to ignition, I felt a fatigue in my bones that I'd very seldom experienced in my life. Wisconsin was wearing me down, and if I were completely honest with myself, I had to admit that I wasn't exactly relishing the thought of the work it would take to convince Darren to join the team. The hour commute each way, the foul Kenny sniggering in the corner, Green Bay. I could almost feel the slush hanging down from my heart, slowly corroding my fortitude.

And then, of course, there were all my other commitments, which deserved no less of my consideration: tracking down Mrs. Stefano and convincing her to rejoin the effort for the school, persuading Del to build a secret closet in the Water Street facility, having the school up and running before the new year, communicating the necessity of my mission to Two Rivers so that the city council would no longer stand in my way. (The President of the council, a Mr. Bruce Fontaine, was especially resistant, using such unnecessary terms as "demented crusade," "embarrassing tomfoolery," and "dingbat screwball." Clearly, his printed tirades about me and my mission revealed a young, headstrong man with a particularly intense, psychosexual response to my prowess. It was obvious that I could easily convert him to Team Polanski's way of thinking by simply flattering his wavy, leonine mane and occasionally, almost accidentally stroking his inner thigh during an especially heated "information-gathering." I looked forward to the challenge.)

There was even a second-tier goal to achieve: convincing Mrs. Kravitz to allow Danny to be featured as the poster child for the Sundae School.

So as Midwesterners would say, "my plate was full," and I was beginning to have a vague suspicion of how Job must have felt at a few, key moments in his life.

But Satan had lost that bet, too. My next move was to develop a plan that would accomplish all these goals at once, even as it helped promote the new school to prospective students in Two Rivers, and then Wisconsin—and then the world!

As a few options occurred to me, I found my grip on the steering wheel loosen, despite the quest of Green Bay's potholes to tear the wheels off of my car and throw me through the windshield, another sacrifice to the city's ravenous, macabre appetites. I was sure the solution to all my challenges was quite simple, but the start of classes was only two weeks away. I had to be even more brilliant—and judicious—than usual.

Pondering my next move, I passed a couple of children building a gray, dirt-and-grass-encrusted, irregular snow man, and my heart nearly broke. This Frosty would never come to life for them; he'd merely harden into ice, and once transformed into the undead—just as so much of the city—he'd wait patiently for an innocent child to attempt to climb him, at which point he'd chip a tooth or break an ankle before being reabsorbed into the feculent earth that had spawned him.

I briefly considered stopping my car and taking a hammer to the monstrosity, but I felt there was a possibility the children might misinterpret my actions.

After all, sooner or later they would have to face their hometown's intrinsic malevolence. It might as well start with the vices of youth.

10

Why on earth did she do that?

"So the curling iron was floating a foot off the floor. That's pretty impressive."

I reclined a bit farther on my bed, halfway now between sitting and lying, halfway between lying and honesty. My satin lounging pajamas shimmered in the dingy, petty room's harsh bulb, and for a moment, I did feel ashamed of wielding my sexual power over Sam like this. It wasn't a fair fight, but it was for the right reason, I reminded myself, and it wasn't as if I were twisting his arm...not yet, anyway. The only real challenge to me would be surviving his one—though considerable—flaw: the tiresome, defensive sarcasm.

"Sam, let's not argue the fine points. I didn't see how it started. Right now, I just need you to help me." Décolletage backed up my plea, but he merely smirked.

"Look, Yolanda. It's pretty obvious that a curling iron did not start this fire. It was started—*somehow*—by a heat source held to the curtain a foot off the ground."

"But the smoke damage—"

"Is not my problem. You're clearly responsible for starting the fire. Read your lease." He took a deep breath, his eyes running over my body. I could practically feel his gaze, velvet, steel, exploring what I offered up. I knew I was responsible for one fire: the inflagration burning in his very marrow.

Yet, he resisted. "Ahhhhhh!!! I've got to stop this."

"Sam, don't try to fight—"

"Sammy! It's Sammy! It may sound juvenile, but my whole life, everyone's called me Sammy! I'm not the person you seem to want me to be or think I am or whatever the hell is going on in your mind, and you know what? For some bizarre reason, that bugs me! Why would I want to be the person *you* think I am? Because that really *is* insane."

"Maybe I see the adventurous audacity no one else has ever been able to recognize before."

"But when have you ever seen me do anything even slightly adventurous or audacious?"

"I see with my heart, Sam. With my guts. We're two of a kind, like that. We sail with our souls into the wind!"

He chuckled at this. "God! There really is no off switch, is there. I'm sorry, but there's no soul in the wind over here. There's no adventure. This is it! Just regular, old Sammy! It's all I've got going on." He studied the gray haze that coated the ceiling, shaking his head, and I couldn't help but notice how manly his Adam's apple was, bold and prickly. "You know, I was telling myself that I let all this go on because you're so funny, you know? And you are hilarious, although I know that's not what you want to hear. But that's not all of it. Not if I'm being totally honest with myself. And someone has to be."

There was that juvenile coping mechanism of twisting everything into a tight, choking knot of humor. But it didn't matter; I knew what he was working his way up to. Consummation neared. My extremities tingled.

"For whatever reason—and I take total responsibility for this—I kind of like living in your world, at least for a few minutes at a time. It's like being in a movie or something. Like being an extra, like I become part of the entertainment. I don't know. That doesn't sound very nice, does it. I'm sorry."

I couldn't imagine why he was apologizing. As far as I was concerned, he was my side-kick super star. But perhaps Sam was another Catholic, and this was his way of dealing with the guilt he knew he'd feel after our upcoming cinematic, climactic intimacies. I suppressed my judgment reflex and merely smiled, encouraging, self-possessed.

"I was actually excited when you were in the paper and on the Internet and everything. Can you believe that?! And I know that must have been tough for you. See? I'm not the guy you wish I was! All I thought was, 'that's my tenant!' Stuff like that just plain doesn't happen in Two Rivers, so when it did, I kind of liked being a part of it, if only indirectly."

"And that's completely natural, Sam, feeling a familiar, almost harmonic resonance at the very core of your—"

"Please, for the love of god, don't. And you know, the funny thing is that I wouldn't have figured all this out, except Del—"

"Del?"

Sam pulled a short gasp of air through his teeth, then folded his arms across his chest—defensive, yes, but also an admirable way of displaying his upper-body physique. Why didn't people turn around and flex their glutei maximi when they realized they'd said too much? I wished he would.

"It doesn't matter. Look, if I allow this to continue, something really serious is going to happen, and I'll be partly responsible. So I'm going to have to ask you to move someplace else. I'm sorry, Yolanda, but you're going to burn down my house at this rate. Or something worse. And I've got other, more important things to worry about."

I held my facial muscles perfectly still; I always could do a wonderful job of that. At the same time, my mind went into overdrive. How had he taken the natural, pyromaniac tendencies that I'd already determined were simmering just below his consciousness and somehow twisted them into being in any way applicable to me? The human mind was an astoundingly many-coursed feast. But more importantly, why were Sam and Del in contact with each other? And why had Del told Sam that the best way to seduce me was to threaten me with eviction? Clearly, her obsession with false dominance had something to do with it, but didn't Sam know that games of any kind were unnecessary at this point? That I was his just as he was mine?

Clearly, I had no choice but to accept this game. If I were honest with myself, I had to admit that he really was the one with power at this point—or at least the one who had to *believe* he held the power. Victory so often was predicated on an unflinching view of reality; years of complex relationships had taught me that.

I pulled my kimono closer around my midriff, my eyes averted now, timid. I had no choice but to embrace the dynamic of the scene and accept my position—no, *revel* in my position! I was the consummate player; let the play begin!

"Sam. What... what do you want from me?"

And then the tittering began; the harder he fought to control it, the more it squealed forth. He looked at me, then at the cindered curtain and giggled, desperate to deny the hunger, the need. Although it was peevish resentment I felt, I arranged my whole body to appear stricken, humiliated.

"Please don't, Sam. It's so demeaning. I'll do whatever I have to. You're in charge."

His frantic laughter only increased. "*I'm* in charge? If I was in charge, you would've been out of here six months ago! I'm not in charge, I can tell you that much! I wish I was."

"Please, Sam, just tell me what I have to do to keep my home. Del was right."

"Del was right about what?" At least this choked off the laughter.

"About you. About me. You have me 'over a barrel,' Sam. I admit it, all right?"

"What? Del never talked 'about you/about me.' She just told me that she was in the same position as me. We call it—" Here he broke up again. "No, I'm not going to do that. God! What is wrong with me?"

"Please, Sam. Now is not the time to get coy with me. Not now. Does Del still need my guiding presence in her life as much as that? I have to know: what am I to the both of you?"

He took a shallow, uneven breath and attempted to collect himself. It took longer than was necessary, and I found myself with nothing better to do than grow increasingly annoyed. My strategy was mutating; perhaps he wouldn't be reaping my spoils that night after all.

"Look. I just think it's better if you moved out. I'll give you until the end of the month, as long as you promise not to pull any more stunts. Because next time, I'm going to have to go to the cops. I just can't take any more chances. I'm sorry."

"Sam, what do you and Del call me?"

"Not *you*. We don't call *you* anything. Well, Del calls you 'Yo-Yo.' But it's not you; it's the effect you have on us."

"Please. I've been caught in the middle of two gang wars, including a certain triad that will go unnamed. I've had to butcher my own meat. *Yak*, Sam. I've been caught in an anonymous media battle with Jack LaLanne. I've faced much more challenging situations than you two could ever throw my way. Now, what do you call the effect I have on you?"

He chuckled, but it was without humor, just nervous energy being expelled from his body. "'The Vortex.' And once, Del called it the 'Yolanda Pull-in-ski.'" I sat back, nodding with a vague rumor of a smile at my lips. "The Vortex." "The Yolanda Pull-in-ski." Clever. So it seemed that no one was denying my magnetism, but somehow, the two of them had managed to make it sound almost negative.

Now I pulled my kimono completely over my body. It had grown so cold in the room—paltry, rheumy radiators! If Sam were such an exemplary landlord, the heating system wouldn't have functioned so intermittently, as if begrudging my presence.

But what an edifying revelation! From the first, I'd recognized Sam's attraction; it had been as plain as could be. Del's feelings, however, had been more of a studied deduction. She'd kept them so well hidden under that layer of coarse irritability! I found my mind going back now over each and every roughness, re-examining them all in a completely different light. I'd always known that her gruff, vulgar treatment of me had been used to hide much more complex, challenging emotions. It was there even in the insistence on physicality: she'd constantly threatened me with a "beat-down," a "whupping," a "slap upside the head." Clearly, she'd been shielding some deeper truth, but I had to admit that at some of the more difficult times, I'd actually told myself that I might have misunderstood. But now, I knew: the only thing stronger than a mother's love for her child was that child's love for her mother.

I was deeply touched, and my heart went out both to Del and the man who stood before me now, so closely, so gingerly. Of course, in a few, superficial angles, they both could define this undeniable attraction as negative. Nonetheless, I had to focus all my attention on the situation at hand. Surprise and tenderness had softened my head, but it was clear now that Sam had been thrown into a precarious emotional state because of all of this. My immediate tasks were to extricate and ameliorate. In that order.

"Sam, I don't know how to make you believe this, but you really have no reason to be jealous of Del." I had to speak above the latest round of sniggering. "I love her as an ally, my faithful sergeant, but that's all. Honestly, Sam, I wish you'd learn how to confront your pain with something other than giggling. It can be quite unattractive."

He paused to consider this, then: "No. No! I'm not going to blame myself. I mean, this is just too perfect—"

"It could be much more than perfect, Sam—"

"Stop! Please. Do I have to evict you, or will you just move out? I'm sorry, Yolanda. I just can't take the chance anymore, and you're not some kind of circus freak. You don't deserve this."

One thing I could never grow used to was the terrific jealousy that drove men to such extreme actions: the mistakes made; the words best left unsaid that were instead thrown in the face of the innocent party; the mirthless, cruel tittering. Poor Sam was writhing in his own, seething misconceptions, and it was clear that I could do nothing to help him at this point. Instead, I'd have to convince Del to ease his mind—which I now realized would be an even more intricate dance, thanks to her confirmed adoration of me and the fact that she'd taken out that restraining order.

So now there was nothing left to do but introduce the real purpose of Sam's summons. I felt I was at a distinct disadvantage without our erotic encounter under my belt, but there was no helping that now.

"It's so funny that you'd mention circuses. Big tops and such."

"Oh, my god."

"Sam, you know that large parcel of land next to the Kravitz's house?"

He turned and walked toward the door, then walked back to the foot of my bed, then back to the door, then back again. "You see? This is the exact point when I should go, but I can't! It's like an addiction!" He no longer even seemed to be addressing me, but rather his own, ruthless demons. "But it doesn't mean I have to do anything. If I just listen and then go, I'm not actually doing anything wrong, really. Not making anything worse, really. It'll just be an extra couple of seconds from my life. That's all. What about circuses and that vacant lot, Yolanda."

"Well, it's just another example of how we seem to be always on the same wavelength. Some sort of psychic connection that transcends ordinary logic. It's actually eerie."

"Just tell me."

"You know, Manitowoc has that whole, unfortunate Sputnikfest thing."

"Oh, Jesus."

"Needless to say, if those poor people can manage to put on *any* kind of a festival in their 'state of affairs...'"

"What do you mean, 'state of affairs?'"

"...then it should be a positive breeze for Two Rivers."

"We have lots of festivals."

"So I thought, what better way both to introduce the festival concept to Two Rivers and to show my community that, although a few of them may have misinterpreted my media coverage a bit, I bear absolutely no ill will to anyone in town?"

"You want to have a festival on a vacant lot in the middle of a residential district."

"And then it came to me: The First Annual Two Rivers Winterfest. We could have all sorts of activities."

"Manitowoc already has a Winterfest."

"All sorts of unique activities."

"What sorts of activities."

"Oh, just all sorts."

Sam balled up his fists and stared through the wall above my bed. I wouldn't have been surprised if he could see Two Rivers' twin ferry port, Ludington, Michigan, right through the plaster, his focus was so excessive, relentless.

"Please answer my question."

"Well, first, I thought it would really appeal to the residents if we gave them an opportunity to dress up as their favorite animals, sort of a variant on the traditional costume party."

"So you want people to dress up like animals in what will probably be sub-zero-degree temperatures."

"They could wear their jackets on the inside, couldn't they?"

"Does this have something to do with that squirrel suit of yours?"

"Oh, that's true! I've already got my costume! You see, you're already helping me think this through. And then I thought that for the ladies, we might hold a carpentry competition."

"For the ladies."

"Hmm. Just a little harmless fun."

"A carpentry competition."

"That's right."

Again, he seemed to peer into the soul of Ludington. He was intrigued.

"And of course, what winter festival would be complete without a service?"

"A service."

"You know, high Roman."

"A church service."

"I don't want to alienate the more religious members of our community, Sam! It's vital to embrace their faith. And perhaps the service would be specifically for the children. Yes, that's interesting. Children. Only. And of course, sundaes. And polka."

"Jesus. H. Christ." A smile seemed to pain Sam momentarily, and then the conflict returned to his face, tensing his lips one moment, furrowing his brow the next. "But you seem to have a limitless supply of money, Yolanda. Why don't you just pay people who *want* to work for you, instead of trying to lure—"

"Samuel. And abandon those who have sacrificed for me, stood firm by my side until very recently? Surely you know me better than that."

"But..." His attention returned to the fire-ravaged curtain, and he studied it, the gleam in his eye almost fascinated. "Jesus Christ. A Winterfest." A moment of reflective teeth-gnashing, and then, to himself: "This place can't be worth more than forty grand. And it's completely insured. If it doesn't happen here, it'll happen somewhere else. To someone else. I guess that's not right, either." His gaze flew up at me. "You can stay until you finish your Winterfest, but then you have to go. Son of a bitch."

The honest truth at last! "Sam. Now do you see that I understand you even better than you understand yourself? I told you we were two peas in a pod, destined always to throw caution to the wind and risk it all on escapades that—"

"Oh, I'm not having anything else to do with this. I just want to see how badly it goes wrong. Yolanda, I need you to understand something right now. Can you do that for me?"

"I think I already do—"

"No. No, you don't. Are you paying attention?"

"Always."

"Then this is what I need you to understand: I'm sane."

I crushed my head deeper into my soft pillow and imagined how my hair must have caught the light as it framed my face, a halo.

"All right, Sam."

"Aaaahhh!!!"

And with this, he left my bedroom.

Once Sam's dynamic, masculine presence had retreated from my most private of spaces, I found I could finally allow the muscles in my rigid body to soften, relaxing their vigilance. This had all been quite a bit more combative than I'd been prepared for, although I did find myself disappointed by the absence of the extreme physicality that had so nearly come to pass. In fact, at that very moment, the sensual hunger in my very pith was still delicious, the savor still ravenous. My soul screamed that a liaison between Sam and myself was entirely overdue, so when would we stop punishing each other? And ourselves?

But I had to rein in my roiling responses, and I did, gradually. Sam would come later; presently, I had to face the disappointing fact that another trip to Green Bay was in order. (If anything could squelch the fires of passion, it was the thought of a visit to Green Bay, Wisconsin. I was certain its residents were so utterly robbed of their libidos that they considered their pudenda some sort of vestigial growth that needed de-lousing from time to time and nothing more. Procreation must have been accidental there and involved toilet seats.)

* * *

The foot well was surprisingly clean—even the heating duct was free of dust and appeared to have been glossed up with some sort of protectant. Obviously, when Alexis had said they'd detailed the interior thoroughly, she hadn't been whistling Dixie, although I couldn't imagine a resident of Two Rivers ever whistling Dixie. Neighborly honesty was at the core of the town's simple value system.

Still, the position I'd had to wrench my body into while under the dashboard was quite uncomfortable, and I wished that Darren would return soon. Moreover, the interior of the car had also grown very cold over the previous ten minutes, which seemed to make the fact that I had to use the ladies' room more urgent still.

Finally, I could hear Darren step away from April Stefano-Brown's doorstep. But instead of returning to the car, the crunch of his shoes echoed down the desolate street and up to the porch of one of April's neighbors, which was followed by a bang on their storm door. The following conversation was audible from my position:

"Yes?"

"Hello. I'm just handing out these flyers for the Two Rivers Winterfest on Saturday, so if you're, like, interested…"

"Two River?" The man's voice had a distinct accent, and my imagination soared. It would be a positive delight to have some Asian representation at my event, and I quickly reviewed some last-minute finger foods I might offer: Laotian smoked squid, or perhaps some North Korean braised beef tendons.

"Yeah, I guess it's a town down south somewhere. It should be, like, fun."

"Okay. Two River Winterfest. Sound nice."

"Yeah, so... Anyway, bye."

Now Darren did approach the Firebird. I waved at him to enter the car when he stopped to stare down at me through the window. Of course, he instantly got the message and took his place behind the wheel as if there weren't a fully grown woman crouched down next to him.

"Did she see you?" He said this without moving his lips.

"I don't think so. Just drive off."

"Sorry, but she was watching me, so I had to go next door and, like, make it look like I was passing out the flyers to more than one house here. I think she might still be watching me from behind her curtains."

"Just drive off, Darren. This position is putting quite a bit of pressure on my bladder."

"She *is* watching. Should I hand out more flyers?"

"Darren, if you don't get me to a restroom soon, your new car is going to lose that nice coconut smell. Surely, you'd like to be reminded of a tropical cruise whenever you get behind the wheel, rather than some Croatian pissoir."

"God! She's coming out. She's coming this way!"

"For god's sake, leave, Darren, leave!"

"It's too late! She's walking down the center of the street!"

"Then back out!"

"All the way down the street? But there's all that ice, and I don't back up too good, and it would look weird if I did that, anyway, wouldn't it? She's almost here!"

I could always count on my inventiveness when the chips were down, and this was no exception. Without hesitation, I removed my coat and draped it over my body.

"Shit, shit, shit."

"Put something on top of me, Darren. The flyers. Something!"

I could feel an object being placed on top of me at the exact moment I heard Darren roll down his window.

"Hey. Sorry to bother you, but it doesn't say on this how much it costs to go."

"Oh! Oh."

"So, how much does it cost?"

"Oh, it costs about, uhhmm. I think it's free. It's free."

"Okay. Would you be able to get in touch with someone to make totally sure?"

"Yeah. But no. Yeah, not now. Because it's, they're busy."

"Is she handing out flyers, too?"

"Huh?"

"The purse on the coat next to you."

Of all things, Darren felt that my handbag would best help camouflage my presence.

"Oh, no. That's my mom's. This is her car."

"Oh, okay. You might want to tell her not to leave her purse in her car like that. Anyway, there's no contact information on this, and it doesn't say who's putting this whole thing on. I mean, it is a little unusual, isn't it? Ice cream and a ladies' carpentry contest and a church service? I guess I'm just having a hard time understanding what any of that has to do with winter."

Darren laughed, but it came out like the dying scream of some animal. "Well, that's the whole thing! It's supposed to, like, take your mind off of winter, so that's why."

"But those are some crazy things to have at a festival, aren't they?"

"I know, right?"

"Are you raising money for your church?"

"Yeah, and anyway, my mom needs her car back now, so bye."

Darren was still getting used to the car's power, and he squealed the tires a few seconds before managing to pull away from April.

"Fuck!"

"Roll up your window, Darren."

"Fuck!"

When he had done so, and I felt the car lurch sufficiently to the left and right to indicate that we were off of April's street, I extricated myself from the foot well. The urge to pass water had grown unbearable.

"I'm sorry about that, but I never figured she'd come up like that to the car and stuff!"

"Is there a convenience store around here?"

"She knew what was going on, man. I could tell! Dude, she was messing with my head! Asking me all those questions! I'm sorry, but you didn't tell me what to do if she figured out what was going on!"

"Do you live nearby?"

"No. Do you think she knew you were in the car?"

"It's very possible. Why don't we pull into that restaurant up there."

Running up the slippery, cracked pavement that led to "Geoffrey's Cabin" was inadvisable, although the instinct was strong. I remained as poised as one could be who was suffering from the knowledge that a slight amount of moisture had passed into one's undergarments and immediately made a beeline for the back of the establishment.

"Order whatever you'd like, Darren."

"Cool."

When I returned, I was unfortunate enough to get a closer look at the dining room. It had been decorated as "mock colonial pub" in the 1960s, but was now "genuine grease hole." Still, it gave the city's cursed inhabitants a change of bleak scenery, if nothing else.

"They've got onion rings!"

"Do they."

"So I'm sorry about that. I just didn't know what else to say. She, like, totally caught me off guard, you know?" Darren leaned back on his bench, which was mostly duct tape at this point in its career.

I'd given the matter a great deal of thought while in the other room. "Darren, everything you did was absolutely perfect."

"Really?"

"Really. Now that I think of it, April would've probably worked the whole thing out at one point or another, anyway. Polka. Animal suits. Two Rivers. But now, after asking those questions of you—and possibly recognizing that I was hiding under my coat and purse—she's bound to mention the whole thing to Mrs. Stefano. And after all, that was the purpose of the entire operation today."

"Cool. So did you want onion rings, too, or, like..."

"Mrs. Stefano is bound to come, now."

"Or wait! They've got tater tots! That's awesome! In a regular restaurant!"

The poor unfortunate believed that this was in any way a "regular restaurant." The sooner I tore him from the clutches of Green Bay, the better.

"So you're not, like, mad at me or anything."

"Not at all."

"So I still get the car and everything?"

"I'm a lady of my word, Darren. And the 'tater tots' are my treat."

"Really? Cool." He pointed his smile down into his lap, eager, as always, to conceal his excitement at his recent change of fortune.

It was all very gratifying. Darren was still in the first stages of wonder, like a Calcutta beggar snatched from the black jaws of death by Mother Theresa a moment before succumbing to leprosy, or a Van Gogh who never had to self-mutilate because a highly perceptive, visionary art expert had noticed his sunflowers in a dirty corner of the Champs Elysees.

Darren was one of the few, lucky ones, and he knew it.

"This has been totally awesome. In, like, so many ways it's unreal. Doing all this stuff together and everything. Having me dress up like a Mormon and stuff—"

"Homeowners trust Mormons, Darren. Never forget that."

"Totally. Yeah. You are totally awesome, Yolanda. Just totally."

His youthful exuberance for the future was contagious: in five short days, he would be serving up his signature ice-cream art for festival-goers—and not long after that, teaching them the fine art, themselves!

"And you'll even have marrons glacés at your disposal! They came in yesterday. Now, how's that for continental?"

There was a flash of confusion on his face, then the more familiar gratitude. "You rock."

"Darren, you're the person who's doing all the rocking at this table. I'm simply a facilitator, your support staff. I'm here to make sure you get whatever you need."

His level of appreciation was so intense that it was almost palpable across the table. His acne flashed ardently. "Cool."

After the bartender took our order, Darren put his arm over the top of the booth and assumed a serious air. "So, like, I even get the title and everything?"

"Of course: Director of Confectionary Education."

"No, I mean, for the car."

"Of course. It's yours now."

"Yeah, don't get me wrong or anything, it's the most awesome car ever and everything, but it doesn't really seem all that fair to you."

"Can we make a deal right now, Darren? Why don't you worry about what's fair to you, and I'll worry about what's fair to me."

He unslouched slightly. "Well, that's the whole thing, because it's, like, *too* fair to me. I mean, what if I'm not a good teacher and stuff? And you want to fire me after a week or whatever? Or maybe some other stuff happens between us? You know. I'd want to give you your car back."

"First of all, that's not going to happen, because I know you're going to be an outstanding educator. Second of all, I don't need another car, so I wouldn't accept the Firebird. And finally, it might just be time for you to begin to develop an ability to accept the good things that come into your life, just as you have been forced to accept all your misfortunes here."

"What misfortunes?"

"Green Bay. You know. And after all, you have to have reliable transportation to get to work—it's your job. Your Midwest work ethic is at stake!"

"I guess so." He seemed to relax. I must have divined the right counter-argument. "You're so awesome."

"You're the 'awesome' one, Darren. Don't forget it."

"Whatever."And again, the pimples shone. "But how are you going to get home if you drove the Firebird up here?"

"I was hoping you might be able to drive me back to Two Rivers this evening."

"Gosh, I've got to work tonight—"

"Well. Perhaps it's time you handed in your notice?"

"Oh." He grabbed a napkin out of the nearby dispenser and began to torture it. "Quit my job."

"Quit your dead-end past."

"Hmmm." This hesitation didn't upset me; rather it cheered my heart. As I predicted, there was quite a bit of Midwest work ethic stored up in the young man opposite me, another admirable trait that further supported my belief that I'd made the best decision I could have for my sundae school trainer. "Without any notice or anything?"

"Why don't you test the waters with your manager. We'll see how he reacts. If he's a good person," (I was extremely unconvinced of this statement), "he'll want to see you do what's best for your career."

"I guess so."

At which point the food arrived, precluding any further sensible conversation. Ms. Yolanda Polanski did not compete with "tater tots."

* * *

I saw the entire scene play out through the large plate-glass window of Ray's Old-fashioned Ice Creamery and over the cherry-red-and-white-striped hood that spread out before me in the deepening dusk.

At first, Kenny had stared out at the Firebird and me, his mouth actually agape; then there was the odd, male ritual of the "high-five;" then a series of guffaws hidden behind his hand as he swiveled on his soda-fountain stool like a six-year-old, listening to Darren. I wanted to believe that the man was happy to hear of his ex-employee's good fortune, but it was clear that his intent was to mock Darren, to ridicule him in an attempt to shame him into remaining mired in the fouled fly-paper that was Green Bay.

But I knew Darren better than that; I knew, as he peeked tentatively out at his new car and me—a secret smile of encouragement playing on his lips—that he would never waver in his resolve. That smile was a promise to me that he was prepared to assume the yoke of success, that he'd accepted his course for a better future with dignity, humility and strength.

When he returned to the Firebird (with Kenny hanging out the restaurant's door, leering salaciously at everything he would never have, an idiot's grin plastered across his bland features), Darren downplayed the trauma admirably.

"Kenny's such an ass-wad."

I remained silent. How better could one sum up with such finality the ill-fated, fetid product, the wallowing discharge of an unclean mother? I could only wish that some other angel, somehow, somewhere, would swoop down, too, and rescue Kenny before Green Bay swallowed him up entirely, re-digesting the human leavings it had so unceremoniously eructated fifty years earlier.

11

For fun.

Looking back, I told myself that things would've been quite a lot less dramatic if I'd only gotten more sleep. Founding an educational institution was enough of a challenge (ordering equipment and supplies; developing, producing and distributing marketing products throughout Two Rivers and the world; working with central Wisconsin's brightest architects and interior designers on the most utilitarian, yet most aesthetic design). Add to this the management of a winter festival that would be held within a few days, and I'd managed to sleep approximately four hours over the course of the entire week.

Add to this the fact that it was snowing quite heavily on the morning of the First Annual Two Rivers Winterfest. Meteorologists blithely referred to it as "Snowmageddon," the third such "Snowmageddon" of the season. Still, this one was a "doozy," as they say. I'd managed to drag myself out of bed at seven a.m. to inspect the grounds, and the situation was not good. The tents had been erected the day before, but now they visibly sagged under the weight of at least ten inches of snow. The parking area was identifiable only by a few carefully placed, wooden stakes with red plastic at the ends of them, and even though Wisconsinites were a hardy, resourceful lot, I wasn't sure how anyone would be able to park there in anything less than a snowmobile.

I was also unclear as to how festival-goers would be able to receive their tickets, as the ticket booth hadn't been fully erected the night before, was buried under an especially significant snowdrift, and was without an attendant. The young woman I'd hired for the position had called earlier that morning to say that she couldn't dig her car out, and that I ought to "just let people in."

In fact, several workers had phoned in their apologies by the time I'd returned home. The polka band felt that they might be able to make it later in the day, but the trip was taking them much longer than usual from their small town in the Dells. Apparently, they'd gone five miles in the past hour. In the north, Darren's mother wouldn't allow him to leave the house in his new Firebird until the road to Two Rivers was fully plowed and salted—in other words, the following day. My troupe of "animals" coming up from Milwaukee, "Love and the Cuddles," had flatly cancelled; their leader, Shana, was scared to drive in snow after having been "T-boned" and "flipped" in a storm the year prior. I thought she'd been sexually assaulted until she'd explained otherwise.

Only the priest from Manitowoc's Our Lady of Sorrow had arrived—quite early, in fact—and was sitting in my living room, looking through my coffee-table book of phallic images from ancient Assyrian decorative art and drinking the last of my Fortnum & Mason's Royal Blend Loose Leaf.

The morning hadn't started out quite as encouragingly as I'd hoped.

As I joined Father Carol at eight a.m., he positively jolted when he looked up, managing to spill tea all over a depiction of an especially considerable membrum virile belonging to the god Baal. My first reaction was to assume that he'd been shocked by my physical appearance; I knew the craggy effects of sleep deprivation were especially arresting in the morning light. However, the direction of his gaze immediately corrected my misapprehension.

"Oh, no! I'm so sorry! I just didn't expect that you would..."

"Be wearing a squirrel costume? Nor did I, but the animal people have to be represented at the festival."

"The animal—what was that now?"

"Don't try to—you can just give me the book, Father. I'm sure I can salvage... well, at least the last few pages. Now, for your children's mass, do you need anything that I might have here? Any wine, or perhaps some crackers—"

"Oh. So, you're thinking that we should go ahead with everything? Because it's gotten quite a bit heavier in the past few minutes. The snow. I can't even see my car across the street."

Father Carol was shaping up to be a very special kind of Manotiwockian, so it seemed. On the surface, he didn't appear to have many of the issues surrounding basic comprehension that his fellow townsfolk had, and he clearly couldn't have had any epistemological issues with a faith in god's existence. But he seemed unwilling—or unable—to believe in anything else that he couldn't personally see, hear, taste, smell or touch. A very interesting case.

"I'm sure it's still there, Father. And I was thinking that your sermon could be on miraculous visitations. You know, angels, the solemn obligation to heed their decrees—that sort of thing."

Perhaps he was drawn to my phallus book for more than its representations of outsized, provocative organs; perhaps he found himself mysteriously drawn to a primitive culture that shared his overdependence on sensory input to make sense of and interact with the environment. I couldn't help but wonder how high in the ranks of ancient Assyrian idolaters Father Carol would have risen, if he'd only been fortunate enough to have been born three-thousand years earlier. (Although it wouldn't have been possible anyway because of "Bernadette," I was still glad that I hadn't asked Father Lansky to lead the Winterfest Children's Mass. Baal would have never allowed him to rise above the position of toe-oiler in pre-Christian Assyria.)

"But you think people are going to come? In this kind of weather?"

"Several people are already on their way, Father, and I fully expect our neighbors to join us. In fact, I have it on good authority that the house right next door to the festival is home to several Catholic children—two of whom serve as local acolytes! They're bound to attend your service."

Father Carol's skepticism remained, but he said merely, "Oh. Okay."

Peering out into the blank whiteness again, he twitched his nose in consternation, and I was suddenly struck by the fact that Father Carol looked quite a bit like a hamster. He had prominent front teeth; round, full cheeks; and eyes that might've have been referred to as "beady" by someone less charitable than I.

This led me to wonder if his hamster features would be the envy of the animal/people at the Winterfest whom Mrs. Stefano was bound to bring along. (I'd imagined she'd undoubtedly blossomed against all odds in Green Bay and had reached out to fellow travelers.) Would they gather around Father Carol, sniffing and rubbing up against him, immediately accepting him as one of their own?

"Yolanda?"

"Yes, I'm sorry, Father?"

"I was just asking if you felt that you would be able to see in all this weather to even drive across town."

Now the image of Father Carol as an Assyrian/hamster high priest sacrificing goats at the foot of a giant phallus flooded my mind, and I realized with alarm that my lack of sleep was having a significant impact on my ability to reason. Glad that I recognized this before my guest suspected I was in any way compromised, I took immediate steps to counteract any concerns: "Just because one can't *see* the road doesn't mean it isn't *there*."

"Uhhh..."

"I know this town like the back of my hand." I raised my hand so that he might comprehend the concept. "See?"

If anything, he seemed more confused. Manitowoc had definitely dulled whatever natural sense he'd been born with. "Can we back up to your costume, for a moment? Did you say something about 'animal people?'"

"Naturally. We should really get going. I know it's a little optimistic to think that the polka band has already arrived, but you never know!"

"Polka band? But there'll be snowboarding and cross-country skiing and ice sculptures and things like that, too, right? Activities like Manitowoc's Winterfest?"

"Good lord, no."

"Okay. So what exactly is the theme?"

"Hmmm. What an interesting question. 'Reconciliation,' I think."

"Reconciliation? For whom, may I ask?"

"Father, your natural curiosity is a wonderful asset, and I'm sure it explains how you've managed to remain as lucid as long as you have in your situation, but we really have to get going."

"Yolanda, why don't you sit down for just a minute."

"Father—"

"Please. For me."

Why did I feel that his collar somehow gave him an edge in our relationship? As I found myself next to him on the couch, I tucked into the back of my mind the thought that a collar of my own would open so many doors that were presently closed to me.

"Now, Yolanda, why is 'reconciliation' the theme of your Winterfest? I'm really very interested."

His eyes were small and rodent-like, yes, but they were also a soft brown; there was no resistance in them, only a gentle steadiness. They doubtless would have been used to calm sacrificial lambs on ancient Assyrian altars, even the relentless, pelting sand somehow becoming reassuring in his presence.

"Well, the residents of Two Rivers have been a little uncomfortable with my ice-cream Sundae School, and since its first classes are in a few days, I thought that a Winterfest might be an ideal way to show my neighbors a little of my appreciation."

"How nice! And so you're the lady with the Sundae School! What a fun idea. So, about these animal people?"

"Well, there are some residents—*specifically*—whom I would like to thank. With some particular interests."

"Oh, I see. So a friend of yours enjoys people in animal costumes. That sounds like a hoot."

"Do you think so?"

"Absolutely. And my service must be for one of the more devout on your list. Is that right?"

"A young boy. Danny. He's been absolutely instrumental in transforming my life."

"Really! Is he the boy—"

"Who had the vision of the angel. That's right. So they have some sort of newspaper in Manitowoc, too? That must be nice for those of you who read. And of course, surely *you* can appreciate Danny's situation."

"God's certainly performed more mysterious miracles than that! But why the Winterfest? Couldn't you just show each person your appreciation individually, somehow?"

I hadn't held still this long in a week, and my mind was swimming. Had Father Carol moved closer to me? Or were his eyes growing, enveloping me as molten chocolate cradles a virginal strawberry, perfectly ripe and sweet?

"Well, the thing is. The thing is. Maybe 'mongoose' is better than 'hamster.'"

"I'm afraid I don't follow, Yolanda. Mongoose?"

"I'm a squirrel, you're a mongoose. It's not me, it's Mrs. Stefano. You can talk about it with her in confession."

"Okay. You know, you seem like you might be a little overtired, Yolanda. Maybe you'd like to lie down, and I can make a few calls. We can just have Winterfest on another weekend, when the weather cooperates more."

My vision began to tunnel, and my voice raced ahead of me.

"Another? No, Father, for I have sinned. Mrs. Stefano and Danny and Del and Darren. And Sam. I need them for my mission and everything's gone wrong and they're all mad at me and they have to know that I'm sorry and need them back on Team Polanski. That's why. I have nothing else. Can I wear your collar, Father? It would make things so much easier."

His chuckle seemed far off, and I remembered in a very vague way that what I was saying might be regretted later. Or I remembered that I remembered.

"Why don't you just lie down, and I'll make a few calls."

There were soft, soft pillows in his eyes—no! I stood up, and although swaying a little, collected myself. I would work the slur out of my voice as soon as I could. "Thank you for your concern, Father. You're really, well, a kind man. But I have to do this."

A beatific smile remained on his lips as he studied me. "Hamster" was correct; a mongoose had schemes behind his eyes, extreme motives and silent stalkings. Hamsters merely noted things mildly.

"You *have* to, Yolanda?"

From somewhere, tears had worked their way onto my cheeks. "Yes."

Then there was a long moment, although I couldn't have said whether it was ten seconds or ten minutes. Father Carol's head, inclined slightly to the left, was pointed at the floor next to my feet, the same smile that Jesus wears—that Mary wears!—on his lips. He became an icon in that moment, frozen in a belief system that had frozen people so far back in time into their smiles and their good deeds and their suffering, frozen saints for the future faith of millions, even though the freezing led to a brittle coldness in the hearts of so many of its faithful who were unwilling to warm or bend, mistaken clergymen, for little innocent girls who desperately needed the charity from god that had been promised them since the first time they were told to sit still on a cold, hard pew.

At some point, Father Carol's face had become level with mine. I could almost get him in focus. "All right, then! Let's get this show on the road. But I drive, Yolanda. My car has got to be worth less than yours."

"If it still even exists!"

But who was I to question a man of the cloth?

* * *

"You look like hell, Yolanda."

Although the hard wind and harder temperature had done a great deal to wake me up, my reflexes still weren't quite up to their usual standard: "Sam?! I love you... Being here."

From what little had been visible to Father Carol and I as we'd worked our way to the chapel tent, things had gotten worse at the Winterfest site. The large polka edifice was leaning away from an especially menacing snow drift, and a few of the lighter structures seemed to have disappeared entirely. Now, the chapel tent creaked in the wind around us, flaps periodically snapping in one direction or the other, most of its folding chairs sparkling with ice crystals.

I was surprised to see Sam there, even though he'd expressed an interest in the festival at our last meeting. My hope rose at the thought that he might finally be throwing caution to the wind and joining me in this adventure, but something about his eyes spoke otherwise.

I was even more intrigued to find a large Asian family standing behind him who appeared to represent the sum total of my Winterfest attendance.

"Where is everyone?"

"Yolanda." Sam passed me and shook Father Carol's hand. "Hello, I'm Sammy Ziewick."

"How nice to meet you, Sammy. I'm Father Carol Stanislaus."

"Father, I'm sorry about this."

The Arctic fury of the weather was now having the opposite effect on me, having in some way partnered with Sam's funereal manner. Suddenly, I wanted just to sleep, along with my fingertips and toes. I wanted all my bouncing atoms to be stilled by the temperature, all their hard work and all my hard work to simply cease, the frenzy calmed to a flat, empty horizon of snow-covered peace. The color and movement and heat of regular living couldn't possibly have been as important as it made itself out to be.

"Please. No need to apologize. We figured that there might not be too many people here."

I heard words come out of my mouth, bubbling up from the molten core of my memory, as I found a hoary, plastic seat under me. "But where is Danny? He's so close."

Sam was next to me. "I'm sorry, Yolanda, but Roxie just didn't feel comfortable sending him over here."

I knew the cracking feeling I felt somewhere in my stomach wasn't a positive thing. "But he's so Catholic. *Nobody* came?"

"Well, the Nguyens came all the way from Green Bay, Yolanda. They're a little disappointed."

Sam's movement helped to bring me back to the present, slightly. He turned to look up at Father Carol, who had joined us. Significance crackled between them, although I could no longer remember what made significance so significant. Penitence infused every one of Sam's words: "Father, this is my fault. I knew something like this would happen."

But there was something in focus in the tent: it was the priest's smile. It was like the cold because it accepted. "Well, Sammy, I think what's important right now is that we get Yolanda to bed. She's pretty tired."

Yolanda said something to this, but it was unintelligible, merely hot air around the lips that turned colder after the moisture chilled on them.

Then there was movement on the body, touching shoulders, pulling limbs, and then movement across the tent, at the door flap, brightness working its way around dark figures, and a ceasing of movement, only the tension of potential movement remaining, building and building in the vicinity.

"That's her right there."

The sound was a voice, and the voice was familiar, inhuman. I swam up toward consciousness, a defensive reflex that worked on different rules, prehistoric, animal. I realized first that I was shivering.

A man approached me. I could recognize again: it was a police officer with a brushy moustache, coppery and indignant.

"I know who it is, Mr. Fontaine."

In fact, I could recognize more fully—it was the police officer who had arrested me for indecent exposure, Officer Nast.

He was now quite close. "Miss Polanski, it's against the law to hold a public event in a residential district like this. You need permits; it has to be approved. I'm afraid I have to shut this down."

But I was focused over his shoulder, past the trouble in front of me and across to the greater threat that fumed at the flap, his breath steaming off and whipping itself into the blizzard with just as much antagonistic force.

It was the energy-sucking old man from down the street with the oak tree! *He* was Bruce Fontaine! And next to him stood the woman from the Photomat tchotchke shop in the abandoned mall's parking lot, Sissy! Somewhere in the recesses of my mind, I sensed that there was a term for what was happening—*danger*—and that I should react in a certain way. But all I could seem to feel was worry that the disgust distorting Mr. Fontaine and Sissy's faces would offend the Nguyens—until I realized that it was aimed squarely at me.

I wanted to be fully aware; it was probably important now. But I was still numb at the edges, my tongue a little slow. "Why do you hate me so much?"

Mr. Fontaine shifted his vehemence toward Officer Nast. "Jack—"

"Miss Polanski—"

"It's... Well, it's not 'Miss,' anyway. It's something else."

"*Ms.* Polanski, nobody hates anyone else here. You're breaking the law. Are you all right?"

"But *he's* the one who's making everything so hard for me in the city council! He hates me. And he wants to drain me of my desire to make things better for Two Rivers, to improve life here for the natives so that they can learn to have some fun for once! But all I get is resistance from everyone! The people who like to dress as animals, the lesbians, the cat population—"

Officer Nast had asked Sam something while I was talking; I got only Sam's reply: "No, she's just exhausted. She's been working so hard on all of this."

"Ms. Polanski? Why don't you just go on home with your friends, and worry about this later? I think we need to get out of here. This tent doesn't look too stable."

I looked around at the fifty chairs, the delicate flower arrangements I'd done myself at either end of the altar, the stained plastic-wrap windows of the Last Supper I'd worked on the entire night before. And then there was the polka tent next door, with all the sound equipment and the dance floor and the hundred pounds of kielbasa, and the other tents, and the parking lot, and the ticket booth with the kerosene heater to keep the young lady, Mariel, warm—who never even bothered to dig her car out and help me!

I looked around at the shivering, confused Vietnamese, and Sam and Father Carol, all of whom stared back with nothing left but pity, and Officer Nast, who'd seen the cut and color of my underclothes and yet still didn't seem interested in seeing me as anything more than a silly, pathetic perp. But this was backwards; I comprehended that much. There was something not right with these interpersonal dynamics, because *I* was supposed to be the one pitying *them*.

And then there was Mr. Fontaine and Sissy, who both utterly, utterly hated me.

At this point, Frank and his polka band entered the listing tent, looking around from person to person, red-eyed and accordion-burdened.

Frank smiled thinly at the strangers ranged before him, aware only that something momentous was happening: "Oh, golly."

If he wanted something momentous to happen, I was only too glad to oblige. My mind instantaneously crystallized just as the water vapor did around me: since moving to Two Rivers, I'd been applying my psychological acuity to everyone I met, when all along, I should have recognized that this was utterly hopeless! I considered Manitiwoc, with its stunted populace, and Green Bay, with its pitiless oppression, and I realized that Two Rivers was just another, unfathomable enigma. I'd been wasting my time in trying to analyze these people, to befriend them, when the laws of psychology simply didn't exist in north-eastern Wisconsin. It was logic's no-man's-land; it was Chinatown. How unhinged were they to believe that they ought to pity *me*?!

And to think that lately, I'd actually been questioning my abilities, wondering why I hadn't predicted an outcome in which everyone I'd helped would pull away from me like this. How funny that it was only right here and right now that I finally recognized normal standards of practice succeeded only with normal human beings! After all, one can't play the game if there were no rules, and there simply were no rules east of Osh Kosh. The thought was galling: I'd actually allowed myself to consider that it might have been *me* that had been the problem, when all along, it had been *them*!

This realization was a crystal that broke the surface of my consciousness and rose, rose into the blizzard sky, the thrust as proud and pure as a monument to cold, cold reason. But the force of it dragged my energy with it. And just like a fog that steals imperceptibly into a private vacuum, a thought presented itself: over the last few hours, I hadn't been quite as effective a communicator as I normally was. However, I could allow the others to be confused no longer; what I was about to say had to be just as sharp, just as singular as the epiphany that had inspired it.

All eyes were on me.

"No, my tent is not stable! It's falling down all around me because my poles don't want to hold it up. Because they let a little wind and snow bend them rather than standing up with me. Who knows why, but they did. And I accept that now. So I have to evacuate! We all do! All the way back to Sheboygan so you can have your town back, and do the same things and say the same things and push the ground down walking the same pathway over and over and deeper and deeper until it becomes your own graves."

Now it was time to make a graceful exit. I pushed against the wind that was blowing into my face and making my eyes tear up. I pushed past Officer Nast and Frank's Hot Polka Nights Band. I pushed past Mr. Fontaine and Sissy, who had won.

A sneer twisted her face: "You really need help."

"That's all I've ever asked for!"

And Mr. Fontaine: "She means mental help. Nothing you do or say makes any kind of sense whatsoever."

"You've got your oak tree and your scary cardigan. Why do you want to rob me of everything?"

He looked at Sissy, the life-force he'd extracted from me causing him to look almost pink, like a human. "You see what I mean? We should just thank god I'm on the city council."

I was almost beyond the stares, the defeat, the pity. The flap and the blizzard it shielded were directly before me. I had to get away before I lost everything to Mr. Fontaine and his minions.

But at my back, I heard a question carried above the wind. One of the Nguyen's children, probably a girl, asked, "How are we going to get home from here?"

As the fury enveloped me, I couldn't help but ask a question of my own: *after all is said and done, how would any of us really ever get home from here?*

* * *

In my case, it was in Father Carol's car, with Sam sitting in the back seat.

I'd been revived slightly by the effort it had taken to generate such melodrama and so was able to recognize that I'd just said several things that might wither in the glare of retrospect.

As if to confirm this realization, Sam leaned forward, his deep, caressing voice a few inches from the tender curving of my ear. "Yolanda, you said that you were going back to Sheboygan. Is that where you're from? You know, none of us knows anything about you."

Father Carol was driving so, so slowly, the tires crunching on the fluffy surface of the road in such a regular rhythm that Chinese water torture immediately came to mind. Although I was almost one-hundred-percent sure that this wasn't the man's intention, I nonetheless noted that my blood pressure was rising.

"You heard the Fontaines, Sam. Nothing I say or do makes any sense whatsoever." Sam had explained to me that Sissy was Bruce Fontaine's daughter (unfortunately for both of them).

"They're a couple of small-minded, petty, disappointed assholes. He's wanted to run the city council and Two Rivers for years, but his personality always stood in the way until a couple of months ago. They finally just let him be in charge to shut him up. And how could Sissy not turn into a bitter, old spinster, living her entire life with that old S.O.B.? I'm kind of surprised they haven't killed each other. Or bored each other to death." Sam put his hand on Father Carol's shoulder. "Sorry, Father. That's not very nice of me."

Father Carol turned his wince momentarily into a smile. "Is this an intersection?"

"I think so. And there's something else I don't quite understand, Yolanda. You seem to have so much money, but you were on a bus when you sat next to Danny. Why would you take a *bus*?"

It would have actually taken half the time to get home if I just got out of Father Carol's car and walked. It was only because I was a little unclear as to exactly where the sidewalk was that I didn't do precisely that.

"Sam, I'll be gone tomorrow. Then you, and Del, and Hamster Carol, and Mrs. Stefano—all your lives will all go completely back to normal."

He looked at the roof of the car for a moment, shaking his head. Then: "Yolanda, I did try to help you."

"Did you, Sam? Did you really?"

"Yes! Father, isn't helping someone a good thing, no matter what the reason?"

"Well—I—can't—see the road, anymore. The river isn't around here, somewhere, is it?"

The leather seat squeaked as Sam moved even closer to me. "Yolanda, all you've done since you got here was to try and use people. I would never help you with that."

"And now, you won't have to worry about me, anymore. And my affect on you. So you have your resolution, Sam."

He sat violently back into his seat, mumbling something that I was glad Father Carol wouldn't understand: "The Vortex."

The term had grown no more palatable since the first time I'd heard it applied to me. What was doubly galling, though, was the knowledge that so much of this trouble—and the most recent, shameful, Winterfest scene!—might have been avoided if I'd simply solved the riddle of Sam's desire to sublimate his attraction to me. It was clear to me now that if I had, I would have also solved the even more baffling riddle that confronted me that blustery morning: why had none of my friends even bothered to come to a festival that had been created expressly for them? After all, Sam's attraction was wholly analogous to everyone else's—and analogous to the town's interest in me, too, albeit on a lesser level. Everyone obviously felt a pull of one intensity or other. So how had I allowed the narrative to go from "attraction" to "fatal attraction?"

It was shaping up to be a eureka morning, and all at once, everything became clear. Things had ended up the way they had because I'd lost my clinical distance—and with everyone, in one way or another. My sense of equilibrium had flown, replaced with an irrepressible enthusiasm for my mission—for my team!—and I'd failed to react in a manner that was wholly considered and professional for each situation I'd encountered. Now, I had to accept that the die had been cast and come up snake-eyes. I simply hadn't been up to the task of cracking the "Two Rivers code."

However, I refused to be anything but gracious in defeat.

"I wish you nothing but the best in all your future real-estate endeavors, Sam, and I thank you again for allowing me to remain in Frick Street until now."

He stifled a cry in the back seat, and the little car reverberated with the frustration of a man depriving himself of his own sensuality. It was haunting.

"Say, do either of you know if we're on that house's lawn?"

"What's so wrong with living a normal life, Yolanda?! You make it seem like it's something to be ashamed of. But where has all your wackiness gotten you?"

The steady crunching of the snow, the heater blasting moist, hot air into my face, the hypnotic horizontal trajectories of millions and millions of snowflakes simply doing what they must to reach the end of their gravitational pull to earth. Too much was happening for me to keep track of, and before I knew it, I gave in to my exhaustion and slept.

* * *

I was later told that I'd managed to sleep through the tow truck pulling Father Carol's car out of the ditch, but I did have vivid dreams of trying to eat a pineapple "Sno-cone" that continually jumped out of my hand each time my tongue neared it until finally, it simply ceased to exist.

12

Isn't that odd!

Tabby III had clearly never used a litter box in his life. He wasn't prepared to begin now.

I was finally awakened in the afternoon of the following day not by the blinding light blaring in from every window in my little house, nor by the fact that the temperature seemed to be hovering around thirty-five degrees in my bedroom. Instead, it was the particularly upsetting scent of feline feces somewhere close by.

As it turned out, it was very close indeed: the cat had freshly defecated on the pillow next to mine. If there had ever been a clearer sign from man or beast, I had never witnessed it.

Tabby III had then wisely retired to the other end of the house and could now be heard ripping something to shreds in the kitchen. I knew I should be glad that he felt so comfortable expressing himself in my home, but all I could muster was a mild urge to vomit.

After all, it wasn't his fault that I'd decided to offer him shelter from the blizzard, just as it wasn't Two Rivers' fault that the snow storm had developed into something so substantial. It had barreled through so many states and caused so much untold devastation to those who had been unlucky enough simply to be Midwestern that now the weather people referred to the system as "Snowmageddon of the Century." I took issue with the moniker's logic, but its heart was in the right place.

So why did the blizzard feel like just another stab in the back by my adopted hometown? Why did it appear that the drifts in my yard were so much higher than in anyone else's? Or that my furnace had decided to pick that very moment to give up the ghost? Or that the buried roads made it impossible for me to make a quiet, dignified escape? It was now clear to me that since I'd moved to Two Rivers, the town had done its level best to expel me; yet as soon as I'd resigned myself to its victory over me, it refused to unlock its icy, desperate grip. Tabby III and I were equally prisoners, pacing the halls fitfully and marking our dissatisfaction in whatever fashion we felt might be open to us. The cat's arsenal was regrettably limited; mine stretched out and out, thousands of things a woman could do to express her dismay, and nothing but time in which to accomplish this.

Deciding to address my kitty protest after it had a bit of time to solidify, I entered the poky kitchen for any kind of warm sustenance. Tabby III ran past me and away from my shredded seat cushions, giving me time to accept the fact that it wasn't just my furnace that wasn't working—it was everything. The power was out. A quick look out the window explained it all: the electrical lines that swooped out of the trees and to my back door hung down almost to the top of the snow cover. (I only very briefly considered giving Tabby III his wish and opening up the kitchen door so that he could decide for himself whether he preferred a torturous, resentful life to an instantaneous death.) (And, of course, the option was now open to me, as well.)

In any other circumstance, I would've immediately been on the phone to my landlord, but after our last exchange, I knew that Sam wouldn't welcome a call from me. And to be truthful, I wasn't in the least interested in speaking with him, either. A clean break was necessary, and if this was the case, then it would evidently have to be a very clean, very cold break.

The steam emanating from my nose seemed such an alien, uncanny phenomenon in the vicinity of my toaster that I actually considered putting the appliance into a cabinet. The juxtaposition was almost too upsetting, but I merely turned my back on the whole ordeal, both figuratively and literally, and headed for my bathroom. A warm shower was the goal until I remembered that my water heater was electric, too.

Snowmaggedon of the Century. As I sat on my icy toilet and stared out at the soulless, graceful drifts visible behind an old, vinyl blind, I considered my situation. It was perfectly understandable that as a warm-blooded mammal, I'd been resisting the blizzard and everything it had done to me. It did represent death in the abstract—and in my case, the concrete, too, potentially. But was it just that? After all, I'd been resisting everything thrown in my path since I'd moved to Two Rivers. At what point in my life had I become so contrary?

Then I glanced between my legs to find a crust forming. On the surface of the water below me, eloquent crystals were asserting themselves, heedless of their humble location. It was actually quite beautiful. There was a peacefulness to their calm, steady progress in the face of their unseemly situation that I admired, and as I pondered the profound power they exerted by merely existing, I was suddenly struck by yet another epiphany. I was facing a choice as to how I would manage my relationship with my environment from this moment on: I could be the crystals, or I could be the toilet.

I made my choice.

Hurriedly gathering my warmest clothing, I was on my front lawn within a minute. Up and down the street, neighbors were digging out their sidewalks, driveways and vehicles, but my single-mindedness prevented me from even acknowledging their presence. I had much more important work to do.

How to convince all that my presence would be gone from Two Rivers soon—just as the snow, just as the winter? My urge to join Tabby III in offering an expression of my displeasure was understandable, but it wasn't admirable because it wasn't *Zen.* Now, instead of once again offering Resistance, I would Accept and Embrace. I would sweep and dip with the snow; I would Flow along as one with the Arctic air, a cheerful zephyr. Yolanda Polanski would register a protest as the Mahatma Gandhi of Wisconsin, the toilet ice of Two Rivers!

It was all so simple: I needed snow rocks, and I needed snow sand. Retrieving a rake from the service porch, I gently experimented, learning the limits of the twenty inches of snow, testing its malleability, its unique properties. There was also the issue of the large holes left by my footprints; these had either to be assimilated or corrected. I took a deep breath of the frigid air, my lungs burning but alive. I would let Fate decide.

My "pebbles" offered up more of a challenge, as it was a bit too cold for the snow to adhere to itself and allow me to fabricate what I needed. But I was a Windchime; I was a Leaf carried along a Secret Brook. With my new philosophy, I quickly realized that forming rocks out of the snow would never be accomplished by forcing snow powder together. Instead, one had to respectfully break down the hard crust until one was left with a pebble-like object. I simply found the faux pebbles that had been there all along, resting in the snow, waiting patiently for me to uncover them and put them to their preordained Use.

My core body temperature might have been dropping, but I'd never felt more Conscious, more Still. As I worked on my project with Focus and Grace, it was inevitable that some of my neighbors would be attracted to the event. The day before, I might have suggested to them that they return to their own Paths, but now, I opened my Heart fully and allowed it to be led by their interested, innocent Questions.

"So, you know you're never going to get dug out if you use a rake. You're not from Florida or something, are you?"

"No, sir. But I'm not looking to 'get dug out.' I'm Accepting what Nature has bestowed on me."

"Is that right? So you're accepting the snow with a rake. That's interesting."

"That's right, ma'am, I am! I'm Accepting it, and I'm also working with its natural grain and surface to heighten my Experience of it, while at the same time, allowing the resulting art to express its fleeting Uniqueness."

"Hmm. That's sounds pretty artistic. And what about those chunks of snow you've got squirreled away behind that tree trunk?"

"Well, 'squirreled.' I'd say 'placed' behind the tree trunk, but yes, let's say 'squirreled.' What's 'squirreled' away back there and out of the sun are my pebbles and rocks."

"But you're not going to use them in a snowball fight or anything, right? Because when snowballs have rocks in them, they can take out a person's eye."

"No, sir, I'm not going to be using them as weapons. There are no *real* pebbles or rocks inside; those are my *snow* pebbles and rocks."

"Oh, I get it! You're doing a Zen rock garden, only out of snow!"

"That's absolutely right, ma'am! Before it melts away, as do All Things, I'd like it to signify my complete Acceptance to Two Rivers of everything that's happened to me while I've lived here. This is just my Way of expressing my inner Peace with the Path that Life has chosen for me."

"Oh, you mean that whole hub-bub about the ice-cream school? So what, that's not working out?"

"Look at the lines that swirl out from my rake, around and through, waxing and waning. Do they 'work out?' Or do they simply Exist, soon to

No Longer Exist, but to be carried back up into the atmosphere to delight us as snow again next year?"

"Oh. That's real neat. Totally Zen."

"Yes."

"Too bad about your sundae school."

At this point, the elderly lady who lived next to me fired up her snow blower. We'd never had much to say to each other, although Mrs. Dietrich had always been pleasant enough.

Now, however, the scream of her power tool was testing my ability to remain Placid; it reminded me that my fingers were numb, that there was a steady ache in my shins from the snow that was pressed up against them. The machine's belching fumes assaulted my senses, eloquently illustrating humankind's Desire to bulldoze Nature whenever it was inconvenient, and I suddenly became aware that my nose must have been running for quite a while. It was a detail that couldn't have appeared in the slightest "Zen" to the small crowd that had come to watch me meditate.

But what was the point of being one with Nature and Fate if one folded at the slightest Challenge? Wasn't this the Cosmos' greatest Gift to me, yet? So I inhaled deeply and listened, attempting to discern a note of lilac in Mrs. Dietrich's exhaust, a strain of Beethoven in the raucous decibels that shook the neighborhood. Although it might have made for a saccharine song, it was still a core Truth of the Universe: *Everything is Beautiful, in its own Way.* And now, in spite of Everything, I was bestowing Something Beautiful on the inhabitants of Two Rivers to ponder, if only for a few hours. The Zen Snow Garden was an Opportunity to expand their Horizons while finding a little Peace in their small patch of town, and I genuinely hoped they would.

It took her quite a while, but eventually, Mrs. Dietrich noticed her neighbors gathered around my work, and she pointed her blower in our direction. Interpreting everyone's waving as an invitation, rather than as a warning to stay away, she came closer and closer, shouting "What?"—even though it was physically impossible to hear anything we were shouting over her roaring blower. Finally, she managed to cross the Gulf and obliterate my entire Zen Snow Garden with her Eliminations, smiling all the while.

"Say what now?" This after she'd turned off her machine and lifted an ear muff.

I felt everyone's eyes swivel upon me; some hoping for a gentle chiding of the woman for her considerable lack of Awareness, a few of the less enlightened breathless for a fight.

I looked into the least lazy of Mrs. Dietrich's glassy eyes, aware of the excess skin that drooped and waddled across her exposed flesh. Her Ignorance was expressed by a heavy, spittle-covered lower lip that had formed from years of gaping, her sharp beak of a nose pressed into place by decades of scowling at things that didn't fit into her debilitating, pre-digested, Betty Crocker Existence.

In short, Time had kneaded her fat face into a revolting mess that undoubtedly reflected the Revolting Mess that had been her Life.

"How are you, Mrs. Dietrich?" But what a wonderful Opportunity to share my newfound Gift of Inner Peace! There couldn't be a person who needed it more.

"What's all this about, now? Something happen?"

"Everything and nothing."

"What's that supposed to mean? Did somebody die?"

"Something died, and out of it, something was reborn."

"Somebody's dog give birth and pass on in a snow hole?"

"No, Mrs. Dietrich. I guess I was just referring to the Circle of Life."

"Well, I'm sure I don't know what you mean. I thought something was wrong, what with everybody waving me over like that. Henry, what's going on?"

"You wrecked her Zen snow garden."

"Why, I haven't been near a garden of any kind. In this weather? Are you people pulling my leg or something?"

"Jesus Christ!" It was a cry of urgent, excruciating frustration, and the group parted, swiveling to its source: Sam, who stood on its edge.

He rushed up to Mrs. Dietrich and herded her back in the direction of her home. "Thank you so much for letting me know about that downed cable, Millie. Never mind about all this; you just get back to your work. If you need any help, you let me know, okay?"

"Oh, fine. Glad to help out, Sammy. Honestly, I don't mean to be dumb or anything, but I just can't figure out what everyone was waving at me for!"

"They were just saying 'hi' is all."

Here, she used a stage whisper. "And I can't make heads nor tails of that whole 'circle of life,' dying and living and who knows what else. I'm just an old lady."

"I'll have that cable fixed by the power company just as soon as I can."

"Good, because someone could really get hurt."

"I know."And Sam pushed the snow blower back to its own driveway, Mrs. Dietrich toddling behind him in the narrow canyon the machine had ripped open.

Some of my neighbors giggled, some seemed sad while they looked at my yard. Some were pained by the situation. I merely Accepted. It would seem that the Zen Snow Garden had been destroyed before it could come into full bloom and offer its Beauty up to everyone's Benefit. Parallels might be drawn to my Sundae School!

It would seem to be a Thing That Was.

After the crowd dispersed, mumbling it way back to its origins, I took the huge, slow steps required to traverse my front lawn and return to the house. Before I'd made it very far, Sam had returned.

"Yolanda. Why didn't you call me about the power line?"

"Calling is Doing, Sam. I'm Being."

"Oh, I see. So building a Zen garden out of snow isn't doing?"

"Sometimes Doing is Being." I was almost to the door.

"So what, you're not even going to flirt with me?"

"Goodbye, Sam."

"Does your new attitude have something to do with Sheboygan?"

Periodically, the old storm door would stick. It was sticking now. I deliberately slowed my movements, as there was something about harried jerking that didn't seem at all Accepting of the Flow of the Universe.

"Look, Yolanda, I'm not trying to harass you. I'm worried about you. We all are. What happened in Sheboygan? And where did you get all this money? You didn't do anything illegal down there, did you?"

He was right behind me now. I stopped my attempts to force the door open, which should have been replaced thirty years before I moved into the resentful little shack. Forcing wasn't deferring to the Will of the Cosmos.

"Would you open this for me, please?" The storm door immediately yielded to him. "Oh."

"Are you really abandoning the Sundae School? And Two Rivers?"

Now the front door was sticking. "Sam, did I 'abandon' my snow garden?"

"So is part of being Zen responding to everything with a question?"

"What is Life but a Question?"

"All right." He opened the front door, too. "All right. I'll have somebody out here right away to fix—did it cut your power?"

"Sam, if my power hadn't been cut, I never would have had Toilet Crystals."

He paused, his expression seeming to fight a far-off battle. Finally: "Okay. But you can't stay here. It's freezing."

"I'm leaving as soon as the plows come through. I'll send for my things later."

"Send for your things? What is this, the Nineteenth Century?"

"Sam. You Exist. I Exist. We don't have to Exist together, if it's just going to upset you."

"What's that smell? Is the plumbing backing up, too?"

"No, it's the response to my good deed of the day, which I have Accepted as another Gift of Fate and Two Rivers. You said 'all.'"

"I said 'all.'"

"'We're *all* worried about you.'"

"Roxie and me."

"That doesn't constitute an 'all,' Sam."

He squinted into the gloom of the living room, rubbing a sharp edge of the storm door with his elbow. "That smells like cat shit."

"Sam."

"Well, you *are* going with the flow now, so I guess it won't bother you. I've kind of become friendly with Roxie, thanks to your shenanigans, and so has Del. And Del tracked Heather down, so we kind of all hang out."

I discovered that shock was an easy emotion to Accept because it prevented one's ability to process the information that had shocked one in the first place.

Even my voice sounded calm. "Oh, that's nice. I'm genuinely happy that I've provided you all with some entertainment over the past few months."

"That you have." Here, he chuckled. "But we're friends, now, too. That's a good thing, right? And it's thanks to you."

"You're right. It's just a little ironic that the people I chose to be my friends are friends with each other, yet can't tolerate the thought of coming to my Winterfest. So does your group have a name? The Vortex Club?"

"Careful, Yolanda. You don't sound Zen."

He was right, of course. I took a deep breath, my exhalation carrying out with itself the tension in my shoulders, in my neck. Existing was a Process, not an Accomplishment. "I have stated a Fact. Nothing more, nothing less. I'd like to start packing now, Sam."

He took a deep breath of his own, the now all-too-familiar Inner Conflict pulling an eyebrow one way, yanking the edge of his mouth another.

"So you've given up on your mission."

"Are the salmon 'giving up' when they swim downstream to mate?"

"They swim upstream, Yolanda."

"The point is that they don't fight their Nature: they Accept What Must Be."

"You're right! The Sundae School was a crazy idea that made absolutely no rational sense. I'm sure it would've failed in a month and completely destroyed you in the process. You're right!" Yet he seemed sad on the stoop.

"I'm not sure about that, but I do agree that it simply seems Not Meant To Be. Two Rivers has made that very clear."

"Whatever, but Two Rivers is *not* that little fucker Fontaine and his uptight daughter, making Valentine's Day candles that nobody buys and witches with dried apples for heads and whatever the hell else she does in that Photomat all day long. God, they're a couple of freaks."

"I don't think that Two Rivers is just the two of them!"

"Yolanda—"

"It's you, and it's Del, and Mrs. Stefano, and Roxie and Danny and Tabby III and pretty much everyone I've met here. Absolutely none of you want to have anything to do with the Sundae School. Or me. You just said yourself that it wouldn't last a month. Well, I'm finally hearing all of you. I've Evolved. I know When To Let Go. Yolanda 'Pull-in-ski' has pulled in her last innocent bystander. Unfortunately, what might've been your last Opportunity for Adventure leaves with me. I think on some level, you sense that, and I'm sorry for you."

Sam's head tilted forward, and he shook it from time to time in rhythm with some intense, internal dialogue. I felt a certain amount of

Empathy for him as he struggled, but it was a Struggle that he had to resolve Alone. I would no longer interfere with the Way of Things.

At last he spoke, balling up his fists and failing to look at me. "Just don't go out near that cable until I can have it fixed."

And with that, he was gone.

It had all gone absolutely perfectly! I marveled for a moment at the fact that my most recent Realization had actually provided me with *two* Tools for Success: an ancient Philosophy with which to Accept—rather than Conquer—Two Rivers, and a cover story that allowed me to complete my Mission unmolested by those who had once been Comrades but who were rapidly proving to be Hindrances to my cause, if not quite Adversaries.

I would Accomplish the Sundae School Alone. And in Secret.

With a feigned air of defeat, I closed the door behind me, even though there was no reason—the yard was warmer than my living room at this point. Tabby III sat in a corner, observing me maliciously, his tail twitching up against a two-hundred-year-old porcelain figurine next to the fireplace screen. I'd been threatened before, and I'd be threatened again. It was the Eternal Curse of the Visionary.

I pushed against the door and into my home with renewed vigor. (In fact, the temperature in my house was energizing!) My heart really did go out to Sam, because what he didn't seem to understand was that Acceptance didn't always necessitate Surrender. He'd failed utterly to grasp that simply because I'd admitted to the fact that Two Rivers didn't want me or my Sundae School, this didn't mean I had to "go with the flow" and flee. Sometimes, the "flow" was directed by the Strongest, the Fittest.

And the Vortex was one of Nature's strongest forces.

If I'd just given Sam and my neighbors the impression that I'd folded in the face of a little Opposition, they would eventually just have to do a little Accepting of the Truth, themselves. In actuality, Sam's sudden appearance had been serendipitous; now, he would pass the news of my surrender on to the entire Vortex Club. And since everyone believed that I'd be leaving Two Rivers with my tail between my legs—a newfound, Eastern philosophy my only balm—I was free to put my final strategies into place with no fear of interference. The city council, the Fontaines, those who had helped me rise to this Position of Strength—now none of them would be prepared to stop the opening of the Two Rivers Sundae School in three, short days.

In a way, I was almost disappointed that those who knew me thought that I could've been that weak, but then I had to remind myself of my natural acting abilities. A Farewell Zen Snow Garden! Abandoning my mission! If I were completely objective, I'd have to admit that everything important I'd gotten done in Two Rivers, I'd gotten done on my own. Accomplices were for the Weak, the Unenlightened. I could see that now. Toilet Crystals were a Solo Performance.

I leaned against the door, wondering how I would manage to perform normal, household tasks with my mittens on. There was another Zen lesson on Acceptance in there somewhere, a "wax on, wax off," and for a brief moment, I even entertained the thought of washing my car in the driveway, a deliberate hardening of my Tolerance for the cold. I imagined the living room would seem positively cozy after my winter wear had become ice-caked and the Arctic wind had dried the water spray on my exposed flesh.

But moving to a motel wouldn't be Surrender, it would be a Tactical Necessity, and I briefly reviewed the admittedly limited choices in town before selecting the least mediocre: the Sand Duner, which the locals referred to as "The Sand Downer," or simply, "The Downer."

As we both knew he would, Tabby III smashed my priceless figurine against the bricks of the hearth and ran into another part of the house to inflict some new form of damage. Naturally, my mind searched for metaphoric Meaning, and I was awestruck by the result: Tabby III no longer represented Two Rivers and the porcelain sculpture, my goals! Now, *I* was directing the Flow of Meaning! Now, *I* was Tabby III, and the figurine was the Fate of the town's Opposition. Now, *I* conducted Reality, Accepting the Existence of Antagonists but not yielding to them. Now, *I* was the black-belt standing alone, embracing the Teachings of Zen, yet able to cut down any villain who stood in my way.

Even the reek of Tabby III's second bowel movement in an hour (the linen closet?) couldn't weaken my elation, because everything had changed: now, it was my Adversaries who had to smell my Wrath and eventually clean it up!

The tables had turned, and Two Rivers was in for the fight of its life.

13

I think it's time to go now.

"I'm pretty sure that's illegal, ma'am."

"Pretty sure, or absolutely sure."

"Well, I wouldn't take a chance."

"But you're not. I am. Please ring it up."

One of the more unfortunate conditions of my new, covert operation was that I had to conduct all my business within the leaden stupor of Manitowoc and away from the prying eyes of Two Rivers. I would've gladly gone farther afield, but the plows were still digging out Wisconsin's network of highways.

The young clerk stared back at me in his green, polyester vest with a vaguely rabbit-like twitch, and I couldn't help but imagine how easy it would be to rob the store: simply make a large bang, and the employees would scamper to their warrens, cash registers agape.

"Okay..." He said this as a warning, probably the only concept to which the workers in the store responded.

"How much is the total? *The money I owe*?"

"Eight-hundred and seventy-six dollars and sixty-eight cents."

"Here you are."

"Cash?"

"That's right; this *is* cash. Do you want me to count it for you?"

"No, it's just... No, I got it." He screwed up his face as he counted the money. Twice. "And so now, you'll just have to wait forty-eight hours for the background check."

"When exactly does the forty-eight-hour countdown begin? What time should I return? *Come back?*"

"Oh, like, two days from right now, basically."

"Because I've really got quite a tight schedule."

"For a semi-automatic rifle?"

"Well, rifles can't actually have schedules, but yes, let's say it's the rifle's schedule, if that makes it any easier for you. What time will the rifle be expecting me?"

This didn't seem to make it any easier for him, and he just stared at me and then at a clock on a nearby wall. "Uhhmm. Let's say four o'clock."

"Goodness, that's cutting it close. But I suppose it is the law."

"So, you going for white-tail?"

"Absolutely."

"But isn't the season over?"

"Oh, I thought you were talking about white-tailed deer."

"I was."

"Then no."

"So you're not going for white-tailed deer?"

"White-tailed rabbit."

"White-tailed rabbit? I never heard of them before."

"They're from Minnesota. White-tailed rabbit."

"White-tailed rabbit."

"White-tailed rabbit." Apparently, he could grasp concepts better if there was some repetition involved, but I really didn't have the time.

"Huh. Because I *have* heard of cotton-tail rabbits."

"Exactly. In Minnesota, they're called white-tailed."

"Wow. I never knew that before." But I could see he wasn't processing the information. In his world, things had only one name, like "pizza" and "remedial."

The clerk eventually decided to dismiss me: "Well, good luck."

"And you, too."

"With what?"

"Oh, well. What do you need luck with?"

"I don't know."

"Well, we'll start with that, then."

Emerging from the sports store, I looked around the town, amazed that even the cars were slower here. Of course on the surface, Manitowoc seemed like any other, normally abled, Midwestern town, but if one looked closely, there were a multitude of signs to the contrary. And quite literally at that moment, for I stood across the street from a restaurant with an image of an Antarctic bird next to the words "Penquin Drive-In." In a place like Manitowoc, success meant simply getting most of the letters right.

I turned away from the town's shame and headed for my Oldsmobile, straddled by parallel hills of snow. Forty-eight hours was cutting it pretty closely, but it still gave me three hours to finish things up before class began.

I assumed it wouldn't take long to find a farm store in a place like Manitowoc, but I didn't even need my car: a few hundred feet away from the sporting goods shop was Merle's Farm Supply. The older gentleman cleaning up some sort of dry-food spill had to be Merle. He was wearing overalls.

"Hello there. Just give me a second to clean all this up, and I'll be right with you."

"Merle, I need fertilizer. *Crop food.*"

He chuckled as he swept the feed into a dustpan. "Oh, I'm not Merle. There hasn't been a Merle for twenty years, but we kept the name. Everybody knew it, so—"

"Of course." The image briefly crossed my mind of Manitowockians wandering their streets, looking in vain for Merle's like an army of zombies, passing the newly named Cletus's Farm Supply again and again and again, cows and pigs and chickens all over Manitowoc County dying slowly of starvation.

Eventually, he was finished. "Now, what can I help you with? Fertilizer, you said?"

"That's right."

"In this weather? Are you stocking up or something?"

"It's for my greenhouse."

"Greenhouse? Well, that's fine. Isn't it funny that I've never seen you here before, with a greenhouse and all."

Did all the salespeople in this town feel it necessary to baldly pry after every innocuous statement I made? But I paused, reminding myself that mental development relied heavily on inquisitiveness. I couldn't deprive the man of whatever little hope he might've had left of increasing his capacity to reason, so I attained Zen Balance, smiling. "It's a new greenhouse."

"Is that right." But he seemed to look at me strangely as he walked me into the bowels of the building. Or it could have just been his eyes. "What type of crops?"

"Lettuce, cabbage and silverbeet."

"Lettuce, cabbage and silverbeet?"

I was worried I'd be forced to repeat everything with this gentleman too, and I still had quite a lot to do that afternoon. "Lettuce, cabbage and silverbeet."

"Hmm. And that's all you're growing."

"Just a little hobby of mine."

"Lettuce, cabbage and silverbeet are a hobby. You know, I'll be honest: I don't even know what silverbeet is."

There had to be another farm store in Manitowoc. "Oh, it's delicious. It's silver. I love salads."

"So, you're not growing anything else. You know, people sometimes grow marijuana in greenhouses, and no offense, but I just don't want to get mixed up with—"

"Marijuana?! Do I look like I would want to grow marijuana?"

"Well, it's just that I've never seen you before, and you have a new greenhouse, and you know, most people around here don't usually wear ponchos—"

"Sir, I don't know why you seem to think that I'm somehow suspect, just because I've got a new greenhouse. It's true; I'm not from Manitowoc, and I have an internationally influenced sense of style. But has that become a crime in this town?"

"Okay. You're right. I apologize."

We stood among rows and rows of fertilizers, whose bags were covered with confusing groups of numbers and technical-sounding names. "All right. Now lettuce, cabbage and silverbeet need quite a bit of nitrogen, so I suppose I'll need a large bag of ammonium nitrate. And do you happen to carry fuel oil? Kerosene or naphtha—"

"Are you kidding?"

"Why would you ask that?"

"Because if you are, you could get into a lot of trouble. And if you're not, you could get into even more trouble."

He almost seemed furious with me—and in such a short period of time! Of course, sudden, careening shifts in temper must have been quite common in people who were able to process only meager amounts of information and therefore didn't have to waste much time considering the full panorama of facts.

I was milliseconds away from responding when we both jumped at a new voice: "She's not kidding. She's checking. And you passed with flying colors, sir." The voice behind me was unmistakable. Del! I turned, but she was wholly focused on keeping the man's attention. "I know this all seems like a strange way to check your training, but we can't be too careful nowadays. Even in Wisconsin."

He had no reply for her; his eyes just slashed from her to me and back again, his arms crossed in front of him.

Del put her hand on my shoulder, and a little more heavily than was necessary. "All right, Ms. Polans—skiwitz. Let's get back to the office."

"This lady's not checking my training! She's serious."

Del moved her center of gravity quite close to the man; it had to be pulling at his viscera. "Sir, do you honestly think that we'd use agents who couldn't convince you that they were serious?" And she laughed derisively. "Now look, we're under what we call 'deep cover,' so it would be great if you could keep this under your hat until we've checked out all the fertilizer retailers in the area."

"Can I see some identification, then?"

She moved even closer. "I guess I should've explained what deep cover is. No identification. No nothing."

"Don't I know you? Don't you work over at Menard's?"

Del lifted her lip in the approximation of a sly grin. "Exactly."

"So Menard's is..."

I was standing several feet away from the pair, but it did appear that she actually winked in response. Realizing, as we all did, that she had gone too far, Del froze. As we all did.

Then before I knew it, she'd grabbed me by the poncho and was dragging me out of the store.

The man followed us. "Hey, I'm calling the cops!"

But we were already several aisles away.

"Come on, Yolanda! You didn't do anything illegal, exactly. Shit! Why did I have to wink?!"

"But I *want* him to call the police."

"What?! Jesus, you're just getting battier and battier every minute, aren't you."

She pulled me out into the sun and down one of the nearby residential streets, glaring behind us until she was sure we weren't being followed.

"Damn it! I almost had him, but what the fuck! Spies don't fucking wink! Who fucking winks? Cartoons and clowns wink!" In spite of the self-flagellation, she seemed to be enjoying herself.

I wasn't. I had Learned to Accept that my Path was to be walked Alone. It had clearly been much harder for her. "Del. Please just let me go."

Grasping my arm even more tightly, she looked around the neighborhood, and when she spotted the main street nearby, she dragged me toward it. "Come on. Let's go to my truck."

I wasn't sure how I felt about the situation. I was glad that Del didn't seem angry with me, anymore, and that she'd come to accept her true feelings. But she'd also just managed to sabotage a vital step in my latest, top-secret plan, and with the opening of the Sundae School only two days away, I couldn't afford even the slightest deviation. It was very possible that Del had just destroyed my last chance to realize my Vision for Two Rivers.

When we finally made it to her truck, I was livid. However, I recognized that Rage wasn't an element in the Zen Master's Existence, so I searched the dashboard for something to steady me, to remind me of the Insignificance of Everything I did, including this. The speedometer was the most calming, so I imagined the speed going from one-hundred and twenty to one-hundred to seventy, all the way down to about thirty miles an hour. Even in this weather, that was a safe, placid speed.

"Del, I'm glad to see you, but I'm very concerned about what just happened."

"Concerned?' 'Concerned?!!' You were a second away from being thrown in jail for trying to buy bomb supplies! You *should* be a little 'concerned!'"

"Of course, I wasn't going to be thrown into jail! That man just thought I wanted to grow marijuana."

"He thought you wanted to blow something up! A fourth-grader would think you wanted to blow something up. Why the fuck do you want to blow something up?"

Good air in, bad air out. In through the nose, out through the mouth. "Del, there was a time when I really needed your help with the Sundae School, and I tried everything I could to inspire you—"

"Like throwing a "Winterfest" in the middle of a blizzard with an all-girl carpentry contest? *That* was supposed to convince me that you have your shit together, now?"

A Wind-chime needed Wind to Sing. Del was simply Blowing. "I tried everything in my Power to change your Mind, but you didn't want to have anything to do with me. And I Respect that. So I've moved on. And you need to, as well, I'm afraid. What you're feeling for me—"

Hideous cackling.

I continued, undaunted. "Someday, you'll be able to Accept your Love, your Respect for me as I do. And anyway, as I'm sure you've already heard, I've moved out of Two Rivers and have given up on my dream to open a school for ice-cream creations."

"Oh, is that right?"

"Yes."

"Then why did you want that man to think you're a terrorist and call the police? Just for shits and giggles?"

I'd already forgotten about that heated confession. But in the Way of the Dao, there is no Self-Recrimination; there is simply Endurance. "I didn't want him to think I'm a terrorist. Just that I want to build a bomb."

"Shit, you really are getting dangerous, on top of everything else, aren't you." She looked at her sun visor, almost in an attitude of prayer. "Okay. So I know that the answer you're about to give me is going to fucking piss me off, but why did you want him to think you're building a bomb?"

"I Accept your Question and ask you to Accept the Fact that in Life, Questions don't always have Answers."

"And should I also just accept that you purchased a semi-automatic rifle a few minutes ago?"

"You *were* following me! Why were you following me?"

"I accept your question, Yo-yo. Now why don't *you* bite off a nice piece of Acceptance and Suck on it a while."

"You were following me! But it's more than just what you feel for me, isn't it, Del. This kind of operation takes planning. Organization! It's all of you, isn't it! Do you all hate me so much now that you're actually trying to sabotage my life?"

"You all' as in the 'Vortex Club?' Oh, yeah, Sammy told me about that one. I'm not supposed to say it, but—"

"You *are* trying to destroy me! But why? I mean, I know you all believe that I've made a few mistakes—" Here, she snorted, "but I've never been malicious! You know that."

"Oh, please. Nobody hates you. We were just 'concerned.' I mean, you didn't honestly believe that any of us would buy that 'leaving Two Rivers' and 'giving up on your mission' shit, did you? Give us a little fucking credit."

"But I *am* giving it all up. I've found a new Path."

"Yeah, Sam told us about that. What a pile of horseshit. You'd sooner give up a kidney than give up on that loony Sundae School. I mean, you moved to The Sand Downer, for Christ's sake, which is smack dab in the middle of town, and you drive a 1986 Oldsmobile! Did you honestly think anyone in Two Rivers wouldn't see you're obviously still in town?"

"It's the Sand *Duner.*"

"Yolanda, we could tell you're planning something, we just didn't figure it would involve mass murder."

"So you've been following me everywhere, then."

She shrugged. "I just happened to run into you a couple of times."

"But what were you doing in a farm supply store?"

"That's where I get my udder balm."

"Udder balm? Del, I realize we're in Manitowoc. But simply *being* in Manitowoc doesn't mean that I've suddenly *become* Manitowockian."

"*Manitowockian*?! What the hell is that supposed to mean?"

"Mongolia: Mongoloid. Manitowoc:..."

"Are you saying that people from here are retarded?"

"Well, that's such an antiquated word."

"Yeah, and 'mongoloid' isn't from 1937."

"*You're* from Two Rivers. I'm not imagining things."

She rapidly beat her steering wheel, frustrated that I'd so quickly cut to the heart of her hometown's prejudices (accurate though they were).

Finally, she choked out her apology. "I guess it would be wrong to make you any nuttier than you already are. People might get killed. So yes, Yolanda, I've been following you. And not just me. Roxie and Heather, too. We've been taking turns. Frankly, I'm shocked that you didn't notice any of us. Heather practically ran her car into you a few times."

I wanted to say something, but instead, I imagined myself hiking a quiet, sun-dappled path next to the Yellow River, my peasant shoes Worn, but Sturdy. Built To Overcome the jagged, lethal rocks that fouled my way at every turn.

I was the Way.

I remained Silent.

"Now, the mailman costume you rented yesterday has got us the most confused. Heather thinks you want to become a postal carrier, so you wanted to see how you'd look in the outfit." She paused to gauge my reaction. There was none. "But Roxie and I both think you're planning on delivering something to someone that you didn't want to go through the real mail. It isn't a bomb, is it?"

"No, it's not a bomb—" I hadn't wanted to reveal this. But it was a Reality. I Embraced it. "Why isn't Sam following me?"

Here, she actually looked away. "Because he's an adult and not a fucking fruitloop, maybe?" But Del knew she had to answer the Question; she felt my Mastery over her even more emphatically now that I'd learned to Channel my Energies so effectively. "He's taking a breather from the Vortex Club is all. I guess he felt that his work was kind of done, after he convinced the rest of us that we might've let you run a little wilder than we should have. And anyway, he's focusing on going back to school to be an accountant."

It was like a Num-chuk into my Heart. "An accountant?"

"Yeah, well, all's I know is I'm surrounded by whack-jobs. Speaking of which, Yolanda, how about telling me what the fuck's going on?"

I averted my eyes, the lightest trace of a beatific smile on my lips.

"Ah. So you're really planning on acting like the fucking Dalai Lama with me. Sammy told us about your 'Zen snow garden.'"

"It was a Thing That Was."

"Is that right. You don't know the first fucking thing about Zen Buddhism, do you."

I pushed open my creaky door; clearly, there would be no Understanding reached during this meeting.

"Yolanda! We're going to watch your every move! Don't make us go to the cops. I fucking hate cops."

I had to find my car in the maze of Manitowoc's ill-designed streets.

"But I know you're not really planning on doing something dangerous, right?—" I shut the door firmly but quietly, eager to communicate the fact that she wasn't upsetting my Equilibrium with her ignorant comments.

Del rolled down her window as I walked away. "Because there's no way you can open up your school in a couple of days. Even if you somehow convince Fontaine and the city council to go along with it—and Fontaine fucking hates your guts—getting those permits through will take at least a month! Remember? I'm a contractor?"

How little Del thought of my Abilities. Even after everything she'd seen me Accomplish.

"Hey, maybe we could help you! But we need to know what's going on!"

Apparently, she believed I'd vomit up my entire, secret plan based on such a vague—and clearly insincere—suggestion. Or was it?

I turned back to her and her huge-tired vehicle. "And if I told you 'what's going on,' you'd do exactly as I say? You wouldn't commandeer the entire mission?"

"Sure. I'll blow up a few people up for you."

I marched swiftly away. "I'm sorry, Del, but I just can't be your mother, anymore."

Of course, there was cackling. "Hey, Yo-yo. Your car is just across the street. Remember? I was following you?"

Disappointingly, the Olds was just opposite Del's truck.

"And try to keep your speed down, Mom. I'd hate to lose you, now that I know you're planning on blowing up Two Rivers dressed as a postal worker."

* * *

Building a fire wasn't as easy as I'd expected. Even with the artificial log, there was smoke, there were dangerous, floating embers that sizzled through my couch's velour. I vaguely recalled hearing people talk of "flues," but it took the pierce of the smoke alarm to motivate me to search the fireplace for some sort of apparatus. Finally, I found a lever, and once pulled, things improved.

Of course, the damage had been done: the smoke alarm had had an unfortunate effect on Tabby III, and he'd somehow managed to climb to the top of the living room drapes. Any attempts at getting him down were met with ripped skin and foul-smelling hisses. As I cleaned up my wounds, I wondered if there were any truth to "cat-scratch fever," because if there were, I was certain Tabby III was a carrier and I was about to die.

I'd been returning to the house in the evening to feed the cat and assess his damage for the day. Since it had become clear that no one believed I'd left Two Rivers—and in fact, I was being "tailed" there was no reason to conceal my presence by the darkness. Yet I still arrived at night, like a Whispering Breeze through the Bamboo that flutters the Leaves sensually and is Gone. And of course, it didn't matter if "The Club" knew I was here; this activity wasn't mission-vital.

The cat had taken to voiding in my bonsai trees. As I was on my hands and knees in the thick of my Zen forest, flashlight in the crook of my neck, trying to determine which delicately exquisite form had been fouled with his putrid feces and had to be disposed of this time, a knock echoed from the living room. It was too gentle to be the police, or at least my stereotype of police behavior, but as I approached the front door, I nonetheless reviewed the range of emotions I'd prepared for the authorities. I would begin with surprise, move onto horror, and end up at calm and guilty—but not so guilty that the police had anything to actually act upon, simply enough for them to put me at the top of their list of the suspicious. After all, Del had been right—I hadn't done anything *illegal*, exactly.

The woman from whom I'd eventually purchased my ammonium nitrate and kerosene must have contacted the authorities—I'd been careful to give her all my contact information, ostensibly for a "Mary Kay makeover," whatever that might've meant. Apparently, I was an "autumn." Dread gripped me then; what if it were the same woman at my door, and I was about to be "made over" to look like this Mary Kay person?

Passing through the living room, I was amazed to find that the soft, ever-shifting firelight cast a glow that actually made the house appear as something other than insipid—probably for the first and last time in its history. As Buddha taught, there were benefits to the un-electrified house.

It was Mrs. Stefano.

"Hi, Yolanda."

"Mrs. Stefano! Please, please come in."

"I'm not really supposed to."

She seemed extremely uncomfortable, shifting from one Keds to another, the fire catching stray hairs in its radiance. But she looked sadder, so much sadder than I'd ever seen her before.

While it was true that I had Sloughed off my Earthly Ties to Humankind in a Solitary Quest to Achieve my Goal, I couldn't ignore the Pain now before me.

"No one's tailing you, are they?"

Mrs. Stefano looked furtively out into the dark. "I don't think so."

"Then I promise I won't tell anyone that you came inside for a little while."

She peered past me and into the jumping shadows and flickering, orange glow. "Maybe just for a second."

Mrs. Stefano could no longer deny her need to reconcile! I was positively joyous until: "So does your restroom still work?"

The biology I'd been cursing only a few moments earlier while on my hands and knees, I now silently thanked, even though I was disappointed that she still wasn't comfortable being completely forthright with her feelings.

With the suspicion that the slightest jarring movement could send her skittering away, I gestured slowly. "Of course. You remember where it is."

While she was gone, I took a brief moment to Meditate and prepare myself for the conversation that was about to take place. I Focused on my Chakra and Imagined that it was a Peaceful Dove nesting in a cave, that it was one of the dove's Feathers drifting left and right in the Wind, Happy to be blown to wherever it was meant to Alight. As I sunk deeper into my Trance, I allowed my Chakra to Consider the Situation: Mrs. Stefano might still be unhappy with the way things had turned out for her in Two Rivers, and she might still be holding me responsible. While I resented her interference—the interference of the entire "Club!"—I couldn't allow her to sense this. Instead, I needed to fabricate a cover story for my recent activities that she could disseminate to the others, so that they would stop surveilling me and I could return my full attention to the real task at hand. After all, I had less than two days left.

I also needed to uncover why she'd become so unhappy.

A flush. I brought myself back into the World, back into my Conscious State. I would allow Mrs. Stefano to accuse me, to question me, and I would remain perfectly Still, as unresponsive as a reclining

Buddha, festooned with jade and a mysterious Smile. Words were Dust; they were Shadow.

And then, skillfully, I would uncover her Truth.

"I always have to pee when it's cold!"

I was still in the Lotus Position.

"I'm sorry I'm following you around, Yolanda. Del told us you were kind of mad about it. And for me totally disappearing."

I maintained the Equilibrium of Mount Fuji.

"Anyway, I'm kind of glad that I left Two Rivers like I did, because it was a good thing for me to go live in Green Bay. I found a great guy there, a counselor, who's helping me get over my whole thing. You know, about dressing like a rabbit and everything. And I would've never gone up there if it hadn't have been for, you know, you. I just wanted you to know that, so maybe you won't be so mad."

So *that* was the source of her anguish! How could I not have immediately realized it?

Green Bay!

What else could that city do but rip what little joy an inhabitant clung to and replace it with naked desolation—in this case, some quack's erroneous diagnosis that occasionally costuming oneself as an animal was a behavior to be stamped out! I was reminded that celebration was nothing more than a cancer to Green Bay, and its residents a mindless, enslaved immune system.

"And April told me that you came looking for me and everything. And your whole winter fair thing. You wanted people to come in animal costumes and dance the polka so that I would come, didn't you. Because I really did kind of want to come, but everybody..." Here, she shrugged the shrug of the damned. "Anyway."

I remained Still, the Response of the Godhead. I knew I needed to remain Above, to never attempt to change the Course of the Stream. Mrs. Stefano had her Path now; it wasn't my place to Influence.

"So can I see the Sundae School?"

"Absolutely!"

* * *

There were a few things that hadn't been completed—half-painted corners, missing fixtures, a coat of drywall dust on everything. But for the most part, my school was ready for classes.

"Oh my gosh! This is great! It must have cost you a ton of money!"

"You've always known how committed I was."

"Yeah. And look at all that ice-cream! How many flavors?"

"Ironically, thirty-one."

"And all the toppings, and look at all those cherries!"

"I was very careful to locate and build the facility exactly as the angel dictated. There's even a closet over there from which—well, we don't need to talk about that. Let's just say that it was part of Danny's vision, too. It's just a shame that none of this will ever benefit anyone now."

Mrs. Stefano sat at one of the desks and drew a sad face in the chalky substance on its surface. "Sammy and Del don't believe that you're really giving up. That's why we're all following you and stuff. And now that you're buying bombs and guns, everybody is kind of worried."

On the car ride over, I'd been careful to keep Mrs. Stefano talking about her life in Green Bay: she was now a receptionist at a cat-food canning plant, was living in a single-wide mobile home built in 1978, and had taken up quilting (clearly a substitute proposed by her "therapist" to distract her from her normal, animal-based seamstress activities). Consequently, her monologue made it quite easy to devote my entire intellectual energy to developing a foolproof cover story for my recent activities.

I was as Prepared as the Panda poised in a Eucalyptus Tree.

"Mrs. Stefano, I suppose that Sam and Del have mentioned that I've embraced the Teachings of Buddha since my life started to unravel. Well, it's truly helped me to Achieve Balance. It has helped me to Accept what must be Accepted. My Old Dream has Ended. And that is a Thing that Is."

"Walter Cronkite used to say that."

This comment was a single Drop of Dew that slid down the stem of a Chrysanthemum and deep, deep into the Good Earth.

"So instead, I've decided to open a farm orphanage for Burmese refugee children."

"Oh! So that's why you need the fertilizer."

"You can't have a Burmese farm orphanage without ammonium nitrate. That's simply a fact."

Mrs. Stefano nodded her head, but her eyes belied comprehension. "So how come you bought that big gun?"

"Have you been to Burma, Mrs. Stefano?"

"No."

"Well, quite frankly, that's the only language they speak. I need to maintain discipline among the children, don't I?"

"But what if it went off by accident?"

I sat down on the edge of the desk at which she was seated, adopting the most benign, professorial attitude I could muster. "Mrs. Stefano, Del saw me buy a semi-automatic rifle, correct?"

"I guess so."

"Did she also see me buy any ammunition?"

"Oh! But won't the kids figure out that it's not loaded?"

"Well, I'm confident that with the proper amount of meditation and organized play, that won't ever be necessary."

"Uh huh. And what about the kerosene?"

I exuded Quiet Confidence, Tranquility.

"That's what I'm going to clean the gun with."

"And the mailman costume?"

I commanded my Body to be Relaxed, to radiate Honesty.

"I've got to train the Burmese refugees in some kind of trade, don't I?"

"They're *all* going to be mailmen?"

"And women."

"So why the farm?"

"We'll be self-sustaining."

"But then how will you—"

"*Would you stop*—worrying about it, Mrs. Stefano?" My voice had somehow managed to sound squeaky, of all things. I reminded myself that the Majestic Crane squeaked, too, so it couldn't possibly have been as unenlightened as it sounded. "Remember what the Buddha said: 'All in Good Time.'"

"Oh, is that where that came from?"

She may have just interpreted my Forthrightness as a lack of Patience, so I took a moment to Realign my Equilibrium. "And many things besides. Accept, as I do."

"Okay." But her tone was anything but "okay," and she shifted uncomfortably, her eyes falling sightlessly on one object in the room after another. At last: "Yolanda, Sammy kind of checked up on you a little. Just because he's worried a little. We're all kind of worried because we know how important the Sundae School is to you. I probably wasn't supposed to say anything."

Had I remembered to extinguish the fire back at the house?

"I appreciate your concern about my welfare, Mrs. Stefano, but we really should be getting back to your car. You've got work tomorrow, don't you?"

"And he kind of, you know, found out about Sheboygan. And where all your money came from."

The more I thought about it, the more worried I was about Tabby III. Would he try to attack the fire? Or worse—defecate on it? I'd never forgive myself if he burned alive.

"Actually, I may have left my fireplace on, and there were embers flying everywhere." Walking purposefully to the main entrance, I tightened my winter wear, ready once again to brave a Two Rivers December.

"I'm so sorry, Yolanda. Sammy told us about... That's why we started all following you and everything. Because we're all sorry. We really do just want to help you, if you let us."

"I appreciate that, Mrs. Stefano, but I'd really like to get back to the house now."

Finally, she rose. "Do you want to, you know, talk about it?"

"What I'd love to talk about is that new mobile home of yours. When did you say it was built again?"

"1978."

"And it's a single-wide. It sounds charming."

Mrs. Stefano glanced toward the closet door as she joined me. "You know, I asked Danny about his angel dream, and he told about me the animals in the closet that come out and play."

I found that my Chi was so out of Balance, thanks to the thought of a cat in flames, that I was barely able to process the fact that Danny had casually blurted out to Mrs. Stefano in a few seconds the same sacred information that had taken me six, difficult months to extract.

"And you wanted me to be one of the animals?"

"Yes. Imagine how the pupils would have loved you—especially the younger ones."

"Yeah, but that's not healthy for me, so anyway." Mrs. Stefano tore her eyes from the closet door. "I'm fifty-three."

"In Green Bay years."

"But how can you be so sure? That people would've loved me? And how are you so sure about everything else you do?"

"What would I get done if I were to question everything I did? Now, my house is probably on fire. We should go."

I thought I detected a note of wistfulness as she took one last look at the classroom, but I'd probably just forgotten the depth of her many dimples. Still, I joined her, assessing how much clean-up work I faced that night. (Since learning that I was the focus of a coordinated surveillance program—and not for the first time!—I'd taken to getting all my work done at the Sundae School at three o'clock in the morning, when I was sure no one was "tailing" me.)

"I would've never been my bunny in public, anyway. Even when I wanted to be my bunny."

After hearing this, for some perverse reason, I considered actually confessing my entire, true plan to Mrs. Stefano and begging her to make her debut along with the Sundae School in less than forty-eight hours. But battling Green Bay for her soul would've taken up my all my energies and exposed my operation to the others. And *they* would've doubtlessly tried to stop me.

I had to abandon her to her Fate.

"Yolanda?"

"We really do have to go, Mrs. Stefano—"

"I know, but... Can you promise me just one thing?"

Did dimples in some way contribute to one's ability to cause one's eyes to twinkle? "What's that."

"If, you know, you really *are* trying to start your Sundae School and everything, can you please try everything you can to not blow people up? You know, a peaceful solution? For me?"

I was Still, a Lakeside Monastery.

Her eyes unfocused then, as if reading her own reflection on the surface of an ice pond. They refocused over my shoulder, on the closet door. "I wonder what that's like: living out a real, actual dream."

Although Mrs. Stefano had no idea, I would be able to answer this question very, very soon, indeed.

* * *

Mrs. Kravitz had put forth even less effort to conceal herself than Del and Mrs. Stefano had. She'd sat in the fourth row back, as clear as day in her Cleveland Indians sweatshirt, and with a small video camera and an extremely broad smile that wasn't at all appropriate for the situation.

Afterwards, I approached her as she reviewed her video.

"Yolanda, that was awesome! Wait, let me show you where—"

"Mrs. Kravitz, I'm going to leave now, and I'd appreciate it if you wouldn't follow me." My Voice was the Snow atop Mount Fuji: Serene, Distant.

"Oh, I didn't follow you."

"Am I expected to believe that this is a coincidence?"

"Oh, no. We just knew you'd be here. It was on the Two Rivers web site."

Instantly, I regretted my recent P.R. savvy. Of course, I'd already dismissed Mrs. Stefano's advice of the night before about "not blowing people up" because Team Polanski was now a Force of One and in no way depended on anyone else's input. But after our conversation, I'd come to the *independent* conclusion that one final, "legal" effort was in order, so I'd conducted a whirlwind media blitz to attract the press—and public interest—to my appearance at this evening's city council meeting.

Unfortunately, only a handful of townspeople had attended—and no press!—so in the end, I'd managed only to attract the group I was least interested in attracting: The Vortex Club.

"Wow. So you really are pretty mad at us."

The Snow on Mount Fuji Rested.

"I know. I'm sorry, but those guys would've killed me if I didn't get all this on tape. And I'm also going to have to follow you now. But if it makes a difference, I've never had so much fun in my life! All this spying and running around. It's like a game for regular adults, with all the strategy and stuff."

Nothing made a difference to Mount Fuji, because all Differences became Similarities over relentless Time. I turned to go.

"Wait, wait! Here it is—" she paused her machine, waving it at me.

"I was here five minutes ago, Mrs. Kravitz. I—" Sensing a note of impatience in my tone, I straightened my spine, carefully aligning my Chi, one by one. "—I really have a lot to do."

"No! This isn't from the meeting just now. This is from when you were following that lady earlier today. You were so busy trying not to be seen that I was practically right behind you with my camera, and you never even noticed me! Wait, here you are getting your hair dyed by the same lady that—"

"Frosted."

"Look at this! I've got a camera pointed right at you through the window, and you're totally oblivious—"

"Goodbye, Mrs. Kravitz."

She put her camera down and gazed up at me, the smile having never left her lips. "You know, you don't see it, but I get you. I'm the only one! I've tried to explain you to everybody else, but they've all got their own theories, I guess. Maybe it's because you haven't messed around all that much with my life. But I really do hope you open up the Sundae School and mix things up a little around here. I get it!"

"Then you'll let Danny help me to—"

"No, no, no. I said *I* get you. My *six-year-old son* doesn't get you. At all. I'm sorry, but I've got to draw the line somewhere."

"Then you don't 'get me' at all."

Astonishingly, she rolled her eyes. "You see! I *knew* you were going to say that! I *totally* get you!"

Apparently, "getting" someone was far more satisfying than "being gotten." With the Grace and Eloquence of a Palm Tree caught in a Sea Breeze, I passed out of the meeting hall. Sure enough, she shouted down the corridor at me a moment later: "Wait up! Where are we going now?"

I continued toward the main entrance, Unassailable. In the parking lot, Mrs. Kravitz ran up to me. "Wait! So why don't you just tell me what you're going to do with the bomb and rifle and stuff? You know we're going to figure it out, one way or the other."

"Mrs. Kravitz. I'm sorry to say it, but this miraculous understanding of other people's minds that you're so convinced you have—well, you don't. Because anyone who truly "got me" would never ask a question like that."

She immediately held up a piece of paper on which had been written: *No one who really gets me would ask me what I'm going to do with the bomb, etc.* And following this was a "smiley face."

I realized at that moment why absolutely no Japanese art from the Shogun period featured anyone smirking. There couldn't have been a less Zen expression on earth.

I turned away from it and got into the Regency 98 just as she wished me, "Good luck! I'm rooting for you." She held up her video camera. "And those guys are going to love this!"

"This" was the recently concluded Two Rivers City Council meeting, a test of my Inner Peace if ever there had been one. I was still digesting the details in my mind. Pondering. Accepting.

Although the Two Rivers City Hall was a very gracious, comfortable building, and the room in which the city council meeting was held a cool, relaxing space, one could almost have applied the term "flop sweat" to my biological reaction as I stood before the members. I could've literally wrung out my handkerchief before them for dramatic effect.

But the Body was merely a Vessel for the Soul, and my Vessel was simply a little more expressive of my Soul than most.

After having engaged in a brief discussion about the Sundae School with the members, I affixed a beatific, inscrutable Smile on my face and was Still for what I knew was about to come next. As predicted, President Fontaine rose, and taking advantage of his position, verbally assaulted me and my plan for several minutes, during which time, he was variously illogical, histrionic, and unkind. Of course, I was able to prevent most of his vitriol from penetrating my Dharma by employing a subliminal Mantra. ("He Exists. I Exist. It is only through the Abrasions of Existence that we achieve Nirvana.")

Eventually, his increasing wheeziness must have acted as a trigger for me to resurface from my State of Meditation.

"...as well as the laughing stock of the entire State of Wisconsin." And it was over.

Silently thanking Buddha for the Abrasions of Existence, I chose to ignore Mr. Fontaine's unenlightened, petty words and simply, humbly presented my final argument. "The work is almost complete and will be within thirty-six hours. An inspector has, if you'll note on Document 84/AD, stated that we should pass all coding requirements with flying colors. If there are any overtime charges for the city inspector, I'd be glad to pay—"

"*Ms.* Polanski, that almost sounds like a bribe." While Mr. Fontaine wasn't wearing his funereal cardigan, he'd somehow obtained a tie that concentrated the color and texture of unspeakable grief into a few, broad, ochre stripes. While I Accepted this abomination, as I did him, it was as one Accepts the knowledge that rapacious organisms will someday feed on one's flesh as it molders in the grave.

I beamed, despite his attempts to sap my Strength. "Not at all, President Fontaine. I'd simply like to address any factors that could still be standing in the way of receiving permits on an expedited basis."

"But I'm afraid that wanting to open your school in two days just isn't enough of a reason for us to tell the building inspector to completely change his schedule." This from the sole female member of the City Council, Sherry Metz.

Her rather distant tone was somewhat to be expected, due to a slight tactical error on my part. I'd decided earlier in the week that Ms. Metz was my best chance to win over the council. So in an effort to encourage a sympathetic reaction from her, I'd taken the time to do extensive research on her style of clothing, hair, and makeup so that I might present myself in a "coordinated" fashion. (This research had been apparently thoroughly and distastefully documented by Mrs. Kravitz.) I'd also hoped my change of appearance, along with a rented car for my trip to the city council meeting, would throw anyone in "The Vortex Club" off my trail.

Of course, Mrs. Kravitz had since proven that unnecessary. But more disturbing was the fact that I'd done my job only too well—the curse of the extraordinary woman. When I'd arrived at the meeting, I'd been dismayed to find that I didn't appear *similar* to Sherry Metz, I appeared *identical*: the same tan suit, the same swept-up, lightly frosted hair, the same peach nails, the same starburst broach.

At first, the effect was a bit uncomfortable to everyone in the room. But reminding myself that the Enlightened supplied their own Comfort from Within, I simply refused to acknowledge the faux pas, and soon, my minor misstep was utterly expunged from everyone's Awareness.

"But I've already publicized the first day of classes in my marketing campaign, Ms. Metz."

Mr. Fontaine snorted. "I propose we take a vote on this issue immediately."

Ms. Metz: "Seconded. And it's *Miss* Metz."

If I couldn't get the permits to open the Sundae School, I'd either have to turn away hundreds of passionate students the evening after next or risk jail time. A single, treacherous droplet of perspiration slid down the small of my back, reminding me that I had about as much Control over my Physical Universe as I did the Unmovable Obstacles lined up before me. After all, they'd already made themselves perfectly clear as to how they would vote.

But I did have control over my Physical Universe! The Shaolin Monks spent months at a time remaining perfectly Still—why not employ their Sacred Techniques? In the blink of an eye, I reduced my heartbeat to near sleeping levels, opening up my Chakra to the Truth: Reality was Illusion, and Illusion Reality. Through this Knowledge, the Way of Zen was made Clear: I had to threaten the Two Rivers City Council.

"Well, if we can't work something out, then I'll be forced to found the Sundae School somewhere else."

This didn't have quite the impact on the members I'd hoped for. One of them actually yawned, and I began to weigh the pros and cons of a few weeks in a Wisconsin state prison.

But President Fontaine, in his relentless quest to draw the life force from me and consolidate his power, went one too far: "Really. Because I think we all can agree that it's even nuttier to open an ice-cream sundae school somewhere that isn't even the birthplace of the ice-cream sundae!"

One or two of the council members chuckled, but little did they know that I was about to earn my black belt! This was because they'd failed to recognize that their leader had just exposed his Weakness as the Cedar Tree exposes its Roots—by Accident. In fact, I noticed a flash of regret in President Fontaine's eyes a moment after he'd spoken and found myself almost pitying him.

Almost. But knowing that the best Ninjas only Pitied *after* Victory was Assured, I merely sighed. "Yes, well, Ithaca, New York has actually *invited* me..."

At this, Joel Matthews, the eldest council member, rose out of his seat, pink-faced and trembling. "But Ithaca is *not* the birthplace of the ice-cream sundae."

"Oh, it isn't?" I'd also done a bit of research on Mr. Matthews.

He swiveled at President Fontaine. "Bruce! Ithaca is *not* the birthplace of the ice-cream sundae!"

I could feel President Fontaine's glare turn on me, icy and enraged. "And no one's even going to so much as acknowledge that we're being asked to disregard our own rules by someone who, for some unknown reason, is dressed *exactly* like Sherry Metz? Am I the only person here in their right mind?!"

The Futile Squawkings of the Vanquished.

In the end, the meeting had been an energetic reminder to me that "Karma" was just another word for "Survival of the Fittest." And although President Fontaine had still somehow managed to throw a final wrench in my plans (I *would* receive the expedited building inspection, but a business license would not be awarded for several weeks), I nonetheless felt I'd won an important victory. After all, I was one step nearer my goal—and all while following the Glorious Path of Non-Violence.

It was a Path I hoped I could continue to follow, but certain doubts began to plague me now as I watched Mrs. Kravitz's headlights doggedly following me in my rental car's rearview mirror.

So just as the Shaolin Warrior Monk, I Recommitted to my Original Mission, which depended on nothing more than a fertilizer bomb, a Ruger Mini 14, and a custom-made mail carrier uniform.

And me. Absolutely no one but me.

14

But none of this makes any sense.

What would Buddha do? It was fast becoming my Mantra.

"But it's, like, after midnight!"

"Is it, really? After midnight?" I quickly decided that Buddha wouldn't flee the scene, as this would only make it appear as if he were guilty of breaking several federal laws.

Instead, Buddha would determine the Weakness of the young man before him and turn it to his Advantage: a Central Precept of the Martial Arts.

"So this is weird." He'd apparently returned from a bar somewhere, as he smelled strongly of alcohol. Beer, to be precise (or as the locals undoubtedly called it, "Wisconsin water"). I could tell that as he gradually became more aware of the situation, more questions would arise, so I decided to act quickly and use his disadvantage in my attack.

I swayed, almost imperceptibly, but enough to disturb his sense of balance and quickly cause nausea.

"Are you drunk, too, ma'am?"

Undaunted, I moved on to my next strategy: "No, but I just finished a terribly greasy pizza. I think something was wrong with the cheese, because it smelled a little like the corpse of a rotting skunk. I don't know how on earth I managed to eat it all—it was a large—because the anchovies were a lot slimier than they should have been, too. Have you ever noticed the smell of a public restroom that hasn't been cleaned in months? Well, imagine that smell being a taste."

"Hmm." He absorbed my description for a significant amount of time, clearly building up to a delayed response. I backed up in case this response was copious and far-reaching.

"So what are you doing delivering mail at nearly two a.m.?"

But perhaps his Weakness was his Strength. I'd heard tales of people surviving ten-story falls while heavily intoxicated. (In fact, at this moment, I wished he were standing at the edge of a ten-story balcony.)

But this desire wasn't of the Way, so just as the ancient Junk navigates the Yang-tse, I Changed Course. Obviously, he held his liquor better than most, as he'd probably been raised on the stuff. But this didn't worry me. I'd anticipated that I might be unfortunate enough to run into someone while on my mail route who'd ask similar questions and so was thoroughly prepared with a "sober" response, too.

"Well, the information in these brochures is time-sensitive, so I felt it was my duty to deliver them as soon as possible."

"But why isn't our regular guy doing it?"

"It wasn't his oversight, it was mine."

"Whose."

"Your 'regular guy.'"

"What's his name again?"

"Ron."

"No, it's not."

"How many fingers am I holding up?"

"Two."

"Actually, it's just one. You should really get to bed. Now."

He glanced down at the brochure. "You're that lady."

"How many fingers am I holding up?"

"The lady with the ice-cream sundae thing! Cool. But you know, you could get into a lot of trouble delivering mail without postage. And dressed up like a mail lady. I should know. I just took the bar. Woo! That was a real mother-fucker." The young man leaned in closer to me. "You know what, ice-cream-sundae-school lady? I don't think I passed. You're fucking hot."

"Well, goodbye."

"Wait! I have to make a citizen's arrest!"

"We'll just do that tomorrow, all right?" There was more ice on his driveway than most I'd walked down that night, so I had to flee much more slowly than I would've liked. It was the slow-motion escape from a shadow monster in a bad dream.

"Okay, but I'm really going to have to throw the book at you then. It's going to sting real bad."

He tittered at his comment, it was true, but he was joined by another snickering, somewhere out in the deep, cold night. I looked up and down the street in vain to locate the culprit, so it was a significant shock to feel someone's hand suddenly on my shoulder.

Of course, it was Del.

"Leave it to you to get caught breaking the law by a fucking lawyer!"

"How did you—But this is impossible! I changed rental cars three times on the way here!"

"Yeah, and all three times, you were the only person on the road! Hello? Two Rivers, Wisconsin at two a.m.?!"

I quickly dismissed my Annoyance; Nothing really Mattered, because no *Thing* really Mattered.

I turned toward my next mailbox, expressionless. "He didn't pass the bar."

Confucian doctrine held that there were times to be drawn into Battle, and times to Rise Above. I still had several hundred brochures to deliver, and only a few hours before people would be joining me in the streets. A choice now confronted me: reveal my displeasure in discovering that Del had somehow managed to successfully "tail" me again, or continue my work, Dispassionate and Empty of Base Triviality.

"Yo-yo, you are incredible! It's like everything you do turns to shit. No offense or anything."

"No 'offense' taken. 'Offense' requires Human Frailty."

"Boy, it sure does." She plodded a few boot falls behind me. "So you won't be 'offended' if I ask about the tilaka."

"Asking is its own Reward. Tilaka?"

"Jesus. That red dot on your forehead? You might want to stick with *one* religion—"

"As you can see, I'm really too busy to speak with you right now, Del."

"So your brochures, are they for that Burmese Farm Orphanage for Postal Workers? Oh, but wait! I remember now: they're for the Sundae School! I actually had a chance to look at one when you first started out on your 'route' tonight. So I guess that whole thing's back on now, eh?

But of course I knew that, too, because I saw your city council performance on video. And posted it online."

For the Enlightened, Wounds were Given, never Received. I merely breathed in, and out.

"Hey, how much did you pay for those brochures? It looks like they cost a fucking fortune."

"Stealing mail is a federal offense, Del." Another, ice-slicked driveway. "I say that only because of my Concern for your Wellbeing."

"Oh, thanks! And I guess what you're doing isn't a federal offense?"

Of course, the whole "Vortex Club" now knew about my plans to continue with the Sundae School opening. It was intensely annoying, but I reminded myself of the well-known fact that the Chinese character for "rage" was the same as for "opportunity."

I refocused my Energy on the Task ahead of me. In fact, the most dangerous aspect of my work that night was getting the mailboxes open and shut without them squealing or creaking—or in one case, breaking. The mailbox with which I was presently grappling croaked terribly, but I squeezed any Frustration out of my Consciousness; I was Master of my Body.

"So now that you've gotten all Zen on us, Yo-Yo, I know that you're going to just totally Accept what I'm about to tell you."

Buddhist monks were able to completely tune out their environment-usually just before they set themselves on fire. And I wasn't even on fire yet! Del's teasing was words and words were sounds and sounds were vibrations and vibrations were movement. Movement like the graceful kelp that moved back and forth in the tossing sea. Back and forth. Back and forth.

"…Burmese Farm Orphanage! Even Heather didn't fall for that one!"

I concentrated harder on the kelp, swaying, dancing, fluttering.

"…Yo-Yo! You didn't put a brochure in that last mailbox. You just opened it and closed it."

I tried looking at the kelp from a new angle: this time, from directly underneath. The sunbeams were laser-like as they shot through the ever-shifting organisms and murky water, pulsing and ceasing, pulsing and ceasing.

"...the only problem is, she's Fontaine's other daughter."

"What?"

"You put a brochure in Cheryl Wozniak's mailbox. Who used to be Cheryl Fontaine. So even if you're not delivering your little brochures to all the people on the City Council and all the police and the city manager and everyone else whose address you looked up online, they're still going to find out about your class. Yolanda, in case you haven't noticed, Two Rivers is a fucking Podunk town. Did you honestly think that you'd keep all the bad people from finding out?"

The kelp died a sudden, violent death, and I found myself tangled in the material world again—Del's material world, in particular. The Shaolin monks stayed away from regular people for exactly this reason.

"So I'll simply retrace my steps and remove the brochure from Cheryl Wozniak's mailbox—"

"Yolanda, you may get your permits now, but you still don't have a license. If you try to open a school, they're going to close it right down!"

The Arrogance of the Unenlightened! "Don't be too sure of that, Del."

"Okay."

I continued my route, my step lightened. She could follow me all night long, as far as I was concerned; nothing she could do or say would weaken my Serenity, my Communion with the Infinite.

"Okay, so let me take a crack at what you're planning on doing. I don't really think you're going to blow anything up—you're not that kind of crazy—and Heather told me that you don't have any ammo for that gun of yours. So I think you're planning on planting that stuff somewhere else in Two Rivers—probably as far away as possible from your little school, so that everybody will be distracted by it, and you can hold your class without the police noticing."

My mailbag only nearly missed her face. "I'm going to kill you!"

She backed away from each strike, giggling uncontrollably. "What happened to Zen Master Polanski? All I'm getting is the little girl from Sheboygan!"

"Why can't you leave me alone?!"

"But can't you see that bombs and guns and a school for making ice-cream desserts doesn't exactly fit in with Zen Buddhism?!"

If anything, my attack was becoming sloppier the more frenzied I became. I stopped. "Why are you being so horrible to me? Why?"

"Yolanda, your plan is insane! You'll only be able to have one class, unless you're planning on planting weapons and explosives someplace new every time you want the police to ignore you. And it doesn't matter, anyway, because the next day, you're going to end up in jail! Who's going to run your Sundae School then?"

I couldn't believe that I'd been pushed to the point of attempting to "beat up" another human being. Even if it was Del, who seemed disposed to that sort of thing.

"The only thing I can't figure out is why you want the police to know that you're the one who planted that shit."

"I would appreciate it if you could go now, Del. Please! Why can't you leave me in peace?"

"Why can't I leave you in peace?! Are you kidding?! *You're* the reason I can't leave you in peace! I'm a grown woman following another grown woman around the streets of Two Rivers, Wisconsin at two o'clock in the morning! *You* did this to me! I used to be normal!"

And so the blaming would begin. I turned back to the mailbox, only to find that the lights were on in the majority of the houses in the immediate area, and several residents were staring from behind curtains at Del and me. Knowing the good citizens of Two Rivers, it was only a matter of time before the police would make an appearance—or at least a pack of howling Bassett hounds.

"Look what you did, now, Delilah." I would have to return to this street later, so I hurried toward the next block.

"For fuck sake, my name is *Delfina!*" She unleashed a hoarse screech, waking up any of the neighbors left who might've managed to sleep through her tirade thus far. "You're still not getting it, are you?! You. Get. *Everything.* Wrong! Yolanda! I can't let you go through with this!" A pause here just lent more contrast to her other noises. "Look, we know about everything with your mother, but that's no reason for you to end up in jail, right?"

Of course, when the police found no one arguing where we'd been standing, they'd doubtlessly prowl around the area, so I decided at this point to return to my car and start on a completely different sector of the town. Luckily, the Olds was close by.

"Hey, I'm putting my foot down. We're not going to help you anymore if you don't do what I say." She still stood near the last mailbox I'd visited, her hands thrust in the tight pockets of her jeans. She must have been freezing the whole time.

"If you get into that car, I'm telling Fontaine about your whole plan. I swear it."

I was almost to my car. It had been a little fussy lately, and I was concerned that it might not start, stranding me in my technically illegal mail-carrier uniform with a bevy of police cruisers combing the streets for me.

"You've turned us into fucking fruitcakes, Yolanda! You owe us!"

But the 98 did start, and in no time, I was onto the next zone on my map. There were two houses I had to avoid here: the home of the chief of police, and the home of the owner of the town's seasonal ice-cream parlor. With years of experience under my belt, I knew that professional jealousy could quickly become ugly.

As I navigated the slick, empty streets, I found myself praying that neither were light sleepers.

* * *

It had been a definite relief to no longer be checking my rearview mirror every ten seconds for a "tail." Although I suspected that Del, Sam, Mrs. Kravitz and Mrs. Stefano had meant well, nothing else they could have done to me would have been quite as galling.

As I pulled out of the Sand Duner's parking lot, I couldn't help but share in the boundless peace that Lake Michigan seemed to have achieved. It raced off before me, *toward* the horizon yet also *of* the horizon: gray, ancient, transcendent. At the same time, it was liquid and formless, never the same body of water it was a millisecond earlier. Winter, spring, summer, autumn—it was a meditation on the only thing permanent in life: impermanence.

Yet humankind had been placed in a *physical* world in part to benefit from *physical* pleasures. This was the very lesson I had been chosen to teach the inhabitants of Two Rivers, who had been toiling, reproducing, and dying in a joyless cycle for generations. And it was also perhaps a concept that I was now beginning to realize might not completely align with the self-effacement of Eastern philosophy.

Rather, what I needed to do was *embrace* my worldly desires at this critical juncture, to channel them, just as I hoped my students would embrace theirs through butter pecan and chartreuse sprinkles and chocolate sauce that solidified the moment it came into contact with its frozen partner in a veritable gastronomic tango, thrusting into a crevice, yielding to a soft roundness. How could I be expected to shepherd my pupils down such a "rocky road" if I were myself in total control of my emotions? I needed to *listen* to what my body and world was telling me, not *transcend* it.

And what I was feeling was anger. Anger at an ungrateful town that was too ignorant for its own good; anger at a few petty locals who seemed especially bent on preventing their neighbors from celebrating life; anger at myself for allowing certain acquaintances to become too involved in my activities, thereby compromising everything and fostering the arrogant, mistaken belief that they somehow understood what was best for me better than I did.

It was maddening, and a thought instantaneously crossed my mind, then dissipated, unwelcome: perhaps I *should* invest in some ammunition, just to prove Del and the rest of her cohorts wrong about me. I had teeth, too.

Yet, a strange calm filled me as I reflected on the fact that in a little more than twenty-four hours, Two Rivers would be taking its first steps toward finally learning to enjoy the whimsy of life, the pleasure that has no purpose but itself. Anger yielded to a moment of well-deserved pride: my work was nearly complete, and because of my foresight, I knew that Mr. Fontaine would be powerless to destroy my school even if Del did, in fact, follow through on her threat of playing informant. And perhaps more importantly still, "my terrorist attack" could, in the end, save countless lives.

It had all been so simple that I'd formulated my strategy in a matter of moments, all the pieces immediately falling into place: Badger Night, eleven p.m., an armor fashion show, and Two Rivers' Exalted Ruler. In fact, it had all been so blaringly obvious that I couldn't help but feel dismayed that Del hadn't immediately deduced my entire plan from these four, commonly known elements.

But she hadn't. It was painful to realize that she'd not benefited as much as I'd hoped from her extended proximity to my compassion and wisdom, but obviously it wasn't the case, because Del believed the primary reason for my "bomb plot" was a selfish one—to save my Sundae School. Nonetheless, that was all behind me now. I experienced the pain and then let it quickly melt away, refocusing instead on the task at hand, which was to case the Two Rivers Elks Lodge on the northeast edge of town.

I pulled up, exhilarated by what I found. As Elks Lodges went, this one underwhelmed more than most: prefab, blue metal siding; a slightly sinister absence of windows; the requisite, plastic deer on the scrubby front lawn. As I studied the inadequate escape routes from the building, I couldn't help but think of Mrs. Stefano and her desire to become a rabbit. Was the binding force for this group of mostly elderly men their ardent wish to rut and feed, stampede and gallop? Did they secretly long to graze upon distant uplands, far, far from Denny's, colostomy bills and hedge trimmers? Did they fantasize about comparing magnificent racks with the other males in their herd? It all seemed to make perfect sense, but as far as the population of north-eastern Wisconsin was concerned, I was out of the psychoanalysis business. They'd have to take their insecurities elsewhere now.

I noted with pleasure that there were enough vents on top of the building to allow for the proper amount of oxygen to fuel a massive explosion. That would be the first thing the authorities would consider. Moreover, the lodge was surrounded by trees and a potentially catastrophic forest fire. It was all so perfect that I almost felt gratitude toward Mr. Fontaine and his ravenous appetite for innocent souls, because in addition to his dominance over the Two Rivers' City Council, Mr. Fontaine held the title of Exalted Ruler of Elks Lodge #4332.

In nature, the principal male was in a state of constant battle to retain his position. I was pleased to think that this struggle would now play right into my hands, because with one fell swoop, my "massacre" would be stopping a no less horrific massacre about to be perpetrated by my worthy adversary.

You see, the opening night of the Two Rivers Sundae School was also the Elks' much-anticipated Badger Night, a ceremony for awarding prizes, scholarships and the like to locals. This year, one of the scholarship competitions was based on a metal-working project, a challenge for area high-schoolers to build a suit of armor that they were then required to model, parading up and down the lodge's stage—just as the amorous bull elk was known to parade back and forth before his rivals in order to gage strength and resolve. Of course, it was clear that this pathetic pantomime of Nature's urges had been forced on these young men and women by none other than Exalted Ruler Fontaine. (In fact, I wouldn't have been surprised if he didn't require the competitors to then urinate into a hole they'd just dug and roll around in it, ultimately basing the awards process on two mere qualities, "depth and aroma," just as natural elk did.)

Of course, the true reasons for this contest were crystal clear to me. As a high-schooler himself, Exalted Ruler Fontaine had first hungered for the "mojo" of his metal-shop teacher and had been cursed to repeat this tragic dynamic with everyone he'd encountered since. Now, he'd finally determined a way to exact his cosmic revenge: the young people unfortunate enough to take metal-shop class at Two Rivers High School were to offer up their vital energies as they paraded before the world's first—and hopefully only—vampire Elk. Only after Exalted Ruler Fontaine was sated, and the young people retained about as much will to live as their empty armor, would the prizes be awarded. Of course, this all had to happen before eleven o'clock: the Elks' witching hour ("elking hour?").

In a cruel twist of fate, however, this was also the exact instant that the Inaugural Two Rivers Sundae School Ceremony for Ice-Cream Excellence was scheduled to begin. If Exalted Ruler Fontaine, gluttonous from his high-school ingurgitation, were able to sneak into class before our own rite was complete, the devastation he could inflict on my innocent—and mouthwateringly vitalized—students would be incisive.

I could not, in all good conscience, allow this to happen. So, in an effort to save the high-school armorists and, at the same time, keep my antagonist from my succulent pupils, I would provide him with a bit of a distraction. After parking my Oldsmobile "terror car" in the Elks parking lot during Badger Night, I would report its suspicious nature to the police. The ensuing chaos would take hours, emptying the Lodge, dominating the Exalted Ruler's energies and ensuring the safety of all.

Of course, if the authorities somehow did manage to descend on my little classroom before its safe conclusion, I wasn't worried. Once things had a chance to get started and the police witnessed the unencumbered, unrelenting creativity exploding from so many of their friends and neighbors, they were naturally bound to allow it to continue. Perhaps a few officers would actually sit down and explore the universe of joy, themselves—and even Exalted Ruler Fontaine would never attempt to suck the life force from a two-hundred-forty-pound, Two Rivers deputy! The image of unrestrained festivity sent a wave of warmth washing over my heart.

So Del had been dead wrong about my motive, and she was dead wrong about the future of my school: you didn't need a business license for the business of life! (Her accuracy regarding the bomb decoy had merely been what crypto-psychologists refer to as a "lucky guess.")

At this point, the Oldsmobile shuddered and died. In fact, my Regency 98 had been doing this quite a bit lately—stalling whenever we idled for an extended period of time—and I knew that I would be forced to wait a few minutes before I could restart it. (An excellent reason to *really* detonate a car bomb.)

Yet I caught my breath at this thought. Maudlin was a rare emotion for me, and I found myself less equipped to deal with it than most others. However, things would have to be different from now on: I had to refuse my first, Zen response to tame my feelings and instead force myself to experience them, to mine them for their best use. There might very well have been much more subconscious wisdom in my emotions than I'd ever given them credit for. Indeed, they might have been the key to my success all along!

So some questions had to be asked. Why on earth *was* I feeling teary and depressed when I was so close to realizing my mission? Why *was* I suddenly entertaining thoughts of buying ammunition and blowing up a third of Two Rivers? Why *did* Mrs. Stefano feel that I was the human version of a squirrel? Squirrels were industrious; they were intelligent and quick-witted. They had attractive, bushy tails and never menaced anyone or anything (unless, of course, they were rabid). They were fun. So why did I have the most overwhelming urge to blow up the squirrel suit in my fantasy car bomb? After all, Mrs. Stefano had put so much work into it, and even after her recent betrayals, I knew that the wound she'd suffer from this would be deeper than simply the destruction of some cheap, carcinogenous, fake fur. In a very real way, I would be destroying myself in her eyes.

The thought only made me more desolate.

What little ambient light was provided by such a stingy winter's day was ending. I would feel my feelings and welcome their wisdom whenever it became clear to me, but at this point, I had to press on. That evening I had to drop one of my rental cars off near the Elks Lodge and take another home. The next afternoon, I would return to Manitowoc to take possession of my rifle, carefully position it on the front seat of the 98 so that it would be visible but not obvious, and arrange the bags of ammonium nitrate on my back seat. Nearby, I would place the bottles of kerosene (which I'd emptied and refilled with water), drive my "Oldsmobile bomb" to "the target's" parking lot, and use the rental car to get to my first class. At some point, I would "cell-phone" the police and, using the inflection I'd perfected for Strindberg's Miss Julie, mention that there might be an unwelcome visitor at Badger Night. It was as brilliantly simple as that.

And Del was wrong about something else, too. Absolutely no law existed against placing a properly registered gun on the front seat of a car, nor one that prohibited the transport of fertilizer and bottles of water. There was no detonator of any kind. I knew that sooner or later, the authorities would trace the purchases back to me, so why attempt to hide anything? I'd been law-abiding, and anyway, the wisdom of the Sundae School would be apparent to everyone in Two Rivers by that point. The thought of prosecuting me would never occur to anyone ever again.

Brilliant though the plan might've been, I was still feeling dejected. My eyes were drawn to the deep forest near the Elks Lodge that had all of its leaves ripped off by time and nature, and stood now, barren, empty, absolutely dead in all but actuality. As I restarted the Oldsmobile, I had to remind myself that in a few short months, these very same woods would be teeming with green and animate life, just as Two Rivers would be reborn, thanks to its residents' newfound appreciation of simple pleasures for their own sake. And all thanks to me. This was a moment to rejoice!

Why, then, did my soul sag when I noticed how many of the trees in the forest truly were dead and needed to be cleared before they spread their fatal diseases? Why did I suddenly wish I were in my squirrel suit, protected from something threatening me, unknowable, within the heartless depths of the woodland, even though in the wild, squirrels were prey? When did my emotions pass over from simple, unconscious reflex into the shadowy realm of intuition?

The 98 backfired, throwing me back onto the concrete of reality. Although it would've come as no surprise to me to discover that I had the gift of clairvoyance, my premonition that I was now leaving the site of a future tragedy could not stand in the way of my mission.

It was too late for all that now.

15

Bye-bye.

Proof that I was, in fact, unerringly clairvoyant appeared just after I'd positioned the "bombed-up" 98 in the Elks' parking lot at precisely five-forty-five p.m. on the night of the Sundae School grand opening. Not a second later, my nightmare began, and as I watched the catastrophic events unfold, I cursed the moment twenty-five hours earlier when I'd deliberately, regrettably chosen to dismiss my gift of foreknowledge. Our modern culture, which trained humans—and women in particular—to ignore our natural gifts of intuition, had a lot to answer for.

The day before, I'd been at the school finishing up a few last-minute issues. Realizing that I'd completely overlooked the rights of pupils to work in the carbonated-beverage medium, I'd asked my general contractor to install at least one seltzer line for those who wished to create ice-cream-soda-based pieces.

His name was Harold, and he seemed to do a lot of lopsided squinting, rather like Sammy Davis, Jr. I'd had a premonition that he'd be difficult to work with when we'd started on the project. Unfortunately, I'd ignored this, and it had also come true.

"Seltzer line? I don't know what that is."

"Carbonated water. For ice-cream sodas and whatnot."

"Now."

"Well. Before class tomorrow."

"No."

"Then where will the students get their seltzer from?"

"They could check up their asses."

Harold was from Green Bay.

"I understand that you're—"

"Do *not* say anything about Green Bay. I'm serious. Look, I'm sorry that I said your students could check up their asses, but it's not because I'm from Green Bay, it's because we've got the last inspector showing up in an hour, and we still have a day's worth of work to finish, and now you're telling me to run a water line for pop. Go buy some bottles of club soda and please, *please* just let us do our jobs."

In a flash, my ESP revealed to me that all of Harold's squinting was actually a physical symptom of his adulation of Sammy Davis, Jr. After all, except for his height, weight, color and religion, he was the spitting image of the rat-packer. He even combed his hair in the same style, and his wedding ring was much more noticeable than was common for the men of Wisconsin. The more I observed, the more obvious it became!

So perhaps the key to lifting Harold's ever darkening attitude toward life might've involved more than simply rescuing him from the putrefaction of Green Bay. My intuition had been telling me to help this man for days; it was time I obeyed. After all, the deed was for much more than just his benefit: his well-being could mean the difference between a successful inspection and a cranky, disastrous interaction with the imminent officials.

"Harold."

"Awwww. Please don't." He was swiftly following the directions of his clipboard, stopping at this light switch, jiggling that fixture.

"I'm certain you have a beautiful singing voice."

"Not really."

"Have you ever entertained?"

"Entertained? Please, Yolanda, I really have to get this finished. You're paying me a lot of money to do this!"

"The stage, Harold, the stage! I know you've thought about it."

"No."

"Well, I have a feeling that you're destined for greatness, and my feelings are never wrong. Las Vegas is calling."

"Las Vegas."

"'Separate the sorrow,' Harold, 'and collect up all the cream!'"

"I'll get right on that." Of course, he was resistant at first, perhaps even flippant, but I knew this defense mechanism would fail sooner or later. And I'd be there for him when it did.

But then he stopped and wheeled around at me. "That's from that song—are you making fun of my glass eye?!"

"You know what? I'll just pop out for that bottle of seltzer."

And it was precisely at that moment, as I backed toward the entrance of my Sundae School and marveled at all the activity there, that I experienced my most profound premonition yet: *this room would never, ever contain a single class nor host a single student.*

Yet I'd chosen to ignore this message! I'd hurried out of the building as if pursued, and I had been—by the specter of doubt, that stinging friction between belief and malicious evidence that rends one's faith in two. And why? Because my "gut" had very clearly told me that Harold's deepest desire was to be Sammy Davis, Jr., yet this revelation had appeared dead wrong.

Of course in hindsight, I realized that my clairvoyance had been absolutely correct, just misinterpreted. It had been telling me all along that Harold was *physically* like the famous singer, in terms of the whole eye business, rather than *spiritually* like him. But this realization had come too late to save me.

Now, as I sat in my stalled car across from the huge shed that was Lodge #4332 on this black, black night, I could plainly see that my very definition of Yolanda Polanski had tilted and crashed into a million pieces since those I'd once considered friends had completely abandoned—most would even say betrayed—me. Finally, I realized that this rejection had done much more grievous damage to my psyche than I'd been aware of, so much so that I'd actually begun to question my gifts! After all, I'd always been nothing if not almost cruelly self-aware, and this ability had teamed up with the realization that my teammates had abandoned me to convince me that it was in the Sundae School's best interest to ignore any further bouts of extrasensory clarity.

So a day earlier, as I'd emerged into the gray, bitter day that had so accurately represented the Wisconsin winter, I'd pledged to dismiss the feeling that my school would never be a school, just as I'd promised myself to take no notice of the premonition that the Elks Lodge would be the location of some ruinous event.

Strangely, at that very moment, the sun had nearly burned through the low cloud cover, as if trying to touch my skin. It had felt as if, for an instant, the truth had been trying to reach me. But then it had died, a victim of the brutality of a Two Rivers December.

And the dark forest into which I presently stared was just as much a victim of this cruelty. What an apt visual metaphor to consider at the instant my life fell apart! In fact, I was stunned beyond action. *Exactly* as I'd predicted, the Two Rivers' Elks Lodge had become the site of my Little Big Horn.

"Bureau of Alcohol, Tobacco, and Firearms." The flash of a badge meant nothing to me. "Now, if you'd like to get out of the car and walk this way, Ms. Polanski."

I did what I was told, mechanically, hollowly. "But I've done nothing illegal. Why don't you arrest me later? In just a couple of hours—"

"Ma'am, I'm afraid I can't do that. Now, please come this way. And I'll need the keys to your car."

The man, Agent Gonzalez, was terrifying—heavy, frowning, and equipped with mirrored sunglasses and possibly the cheapest suit I'd ever had the displeasure to come into contact with.

"You don't understand, Agent Gonzalez. I've got something very important that I must—"

"Ma'am, I'm going to have to ask you again to get into the vehicle. Now." He had a slight speech impediment and was flinging icy spittle in my direction. As I got into the back seat of his sedan, my extrasensory perception revealed to me that this job was glorious for him: to be able to finally take complete control of something—in this case, me! Because no one would question the authority exerted by a federal agent, even if he sounded vaguely like Daffy Duck. (In fact, if I hadn't been so despondent, I would have probed him gently for his views on the connection between small, physical abnormalities and the choice of a law enforcement career.)

But as it was, I was entirely too horrified: my dream—just as I had accurately foretold!—was dying right before my eyes. I couldn't bring myself to look into the black, gloating depths of the woodland as we passed it by, but I pledged to respect each and every supernatural message that came through to me from that moment on. To ignore the natural gift with which I'd been blessed was akin to blasphemy.

"Agent Gonzalez, you look like quite a creative person. Imagine if you had at your disposal a palette of edible—"

"Ma'am, I'd appreciate it if you could remain silent. Anything you say can and will be used against you."

"But if we just made a slight detour for a couple of hours, your first lesson would be free—"

"Ma'am."

"But there are dozens—possibly hundreds—of students waiting for me! I can't let them down!"

"Ma'am!"

"I've already called the police! Terrorists don't call the police on themselves! And if you'd smelled it, you'd know that was water, not kerosene in the back seat."

"When did you call the police?"

"Just before you arrived."

"Shit." He jerked open a cell phone, the tires suddenly squealing in protest to our sudden increase in velocity.

"Red Devil, this is Blue Angel. The fuzz has been alerted. Repeat, the locals have been alerted."

Headlights suddenly illuminated on a side street, and Agent Gonzalez swerved to pull up next to them. As my eyes adjusted, I was shocked to see that the vehicle was my car! Or not exactly my car, but a very reasonable facsimile. Someone wearing a black ski mask was at the wheel.

Wordlessly, Agent Gonzalez rolled down his window and threw my car keys to the other driver, a very hoarse male who said, "I'll need back-up," and then raced off into the night.

Abruptly, our car spun around in a wild u-turn, and we followed the other car back to the lodge.

"What on earth is going on?!"

"Ma'am, we're also investigating the Two Rivers Police Department for possible corruption."

"But why is that person driving a car that looks just like mine?"

"Decoy. We'll be able to explain it all to you when we get back to headquarters."

Upon reaching the Elk's parking lot, we came upon the two Oldsmobiles parked side-by-side and the masked agent in the process of unscrewing my license plate.

Agent Gonzalez pulled up directly behind him and turned menacingly back at me. "Ms. Polanski, it is a federal offense to leave this car. If you do attempt to do so, I will have no choice but to use force to stop you, possibly lethal. Do you understand what I just said?"

"Yes, but of course—" and I was cut off by his slamming door. He ran up to the masked agent, took my license plate, and began to screw it onto the decoy car just as the distant sound of police sirens split the night.

The other agent looked around wildly, jumped into my car and drove it down a nearby street. The headlights suddenly pointed up in the air, and I realized that he'd just jumped the curb and was bouncing over the vacant land and toward the woods. My car was then swallowed up by craggy trees at the moment that flashing lights began to pick out the vertical elements before me: lodge, curb, car, lodge, curb, car.

Agent Gonzalez then proceeded to run back toward the glare of his car's lights, the harsh shadows of his girth bounding in several directions.

He threw himself back behind the wheel, and I was flung against the door as he raced away from Badger Night. Fully expecting him to leave the area, I was surprised when he turned down the street that the other agent had just taken. Suddenly, he pulled our car to the side of the road and turned off the lights. His face was alternately white and red as he watched the police cars fly down the Elks' driveway over his shoulder.

"Jesus." There was a trace of humor in his voice. It was too much.

"Agent Gonzalez, this is—"

The passenger door of the sedan was flung open then, and the masked agent jumped into the car. The two men exchanged an odd glance, and Agent Gonzalez calmly pulled out into the street, slowing down to look at the police activity and the Badger Night attendees sniffing around outside. Once we were finally clear of the crime scene, he sped up and headed back into town. Hopefully the high schoolers' souls, at least, were now safe.

But I was then incensed to notice that Agent Gonzalez was hiding a smile, and although I could truthfully tell nothing of what was happening on the masked agent's face, somehow he seemed quite pleased with himself, too.

"This isn't a good thing, Agent Gonzalez. While you're having your little fun, you're also destroying something I've put six months of blood, sweat and tears into!"

He grew solemn. "Ma'am, we put six months of blood, sweat and tears into the operation you just witnessed, too."

"What are you talking about?"

"The decoy is a trap. If the Two Rivers Police fail to report all the evidence they find hidden in the car—including fifty-thousand dollars and a kilo of high-grade cocaine—then we've finally got what we need to clean up this town."

"Fifty-thousand dollars? *Cocaine?!* But they'll think it belongs to me!"

"Ma'am, this is an ATF operation. You have nothing to be worried about."

But I was. Extremely worried.

Agent Gonzalez hit a few buttons on his cell phone. "White Knight? Any activity at Alpha-Bravo-Charlie?... Copy that." Throwing his cell phone on the dashboard, he turned to his partner. "Negative, but..." The agents seemed to size each other up then, some sort of wordless communication. Agent Gonzalez returned his attention to the road, his knuckles paling under intense cogitation.

"Ma'am, we're also investigating corruption in the Two Rivers Elks Organization. Apparently, a Bruce Fontaine is at the heart of a major drug-smuggling operation. We're going to have to make a momentary detour to monitor his activity."

"But before we go back, couldn't you just drop me off at 815 Water Street?"

"Ms. Polanski, I'll have to ask you to sit back and relax."

I had nothing more to say to either one of my captors at this point anyway, because once again, my extrasensory perception was furiously at work: I was being set up by the Bureau of Alcohol, Tobacco and Firearms! All at once, as if watching a film mercilessly play out before me, I saw my future. I would be the fall guy in some sting operation designed to prove to the nation that the war on terrorism was being won, and I was the terrorist! Harold the general contractor must have been in on the scheme, too, because the next scene suddenly appeared: Harold planting drugs and weapons all over the school, using my generosity and trust to condemn me. So my initial instinct that he would be trouble had been right all along! How could I have fallen for his cover story, knowing full well that illegal activities, such as planting drugs and denying seltzer lines, were commonplace in Green Bay? How could I have ever doubted myself?

It probably wasn't even a real glass eye.

I had to take immediate action to change my fate, and, like a faithful friend, my clairvoyance told me just what to do: a counter sting!

"Agent Gonzalez, you've uncovered my plot. But what you obviously don't know is that there is a bomb at 815 Water Street, and if you do not take me there immediately, it will destroy a majority of Two Rivers. Would you like that blood on your hands?"

He coughed a few times, while his partner wriggled in his seat. They were both clearly distressed at their blunder.

Finally: "Ms. Polanski, that's where we're headed."

"What? Exalted Ruler Fontaine can't—but Badger Night!"

"I'm afraid I can't answer any questions, ma'am."

And Agent Gonzalez didn't need to; my ESP answered every question that swirled around in the car—and more.

I now foresaw new images, and Mr. Fontaine was now the antagonist of my "movie." A montage of events: his instant, unmotivated dislike of me the first time we'd met in front of his house; the hateful, false things he'd said about me and my Sundae School in the paper and on the Internet; then finally an image of him, working late into the night—probably with his daughter—designing a scheme that would not only discredit me in the eyes of Two Rivers, but would put me behind bars forever. It wasn't the Bureau of Alcohol, Tobacco and Firearms that was after me, it was my arch nemesis! He had to be stopped.

Although I was almost physically wounded by the fact that Del had clearly followed through on her threat to rat me out to Mr. Fontaine—and surprised that he would actually forgo an opportunity to suck the energy out of several vital, young bodies (did the armor somehow block his ability?)—I had more important things to deal with at that moment. Carefully concentrating, I listened for the voice I knew would lead me out of this predicament, and it wasn't long in coming. A counter-counter sting!

"Exalted Ruler Fontaine has been blackmailing me to smuggle drugs for his syndicate ever since he uncovered my very brief affair with a certain celebrity. Now, if you'd just allow me to operate my school tonight, I can prove that—"

"Who was the celebrity, ma'am?"

"I don't really think—"

"Ma'am, it could affect our investigation."

"Hunter S. Thompson."

"I thought you said 'a celebrity.'"

"He had a Jacuzzi, and after making love, we'd read our gonzo poetry to one another—"

But my voice trailed off when I beheld the latest development. Pulling up in front of the Sundae School's building, the sedan's headlights found Mr. Fontaine pacing, enraged, at the main entrance. I hadn't expected that. I also hadn't expected the group of people who were congregated around him—in all probability, my students being dissuaded from their joyous futures!

"Ma'am, I'd appreciate it if you could remain in the car while we handle this matter."

The agents traded another meaningful glance, then Agent Gonzalez exited the car and approached Mr. Fontaine.

While they exchanged words, the masked agent passed quietly into the night, and holding to the shadows, went around to the back of the building.

I may have been unable to unlock the back doors of the car, but with both men occupied, there was no one stopping me from climbing into the front seat and freedom.

At first, I'd planned on sneaking into the side entrance to the building and then upstairs to the school, but I remembered that the ATF agents had my keys. This triggered a thought, and I looked around: no Firebird. Darren hadn't arrived! Had *he* let me down, too?

Then my ESP took over. Wedging myself between the front seats and then out Agent Gonzalez's door, I approached the group of people, who almost seemed to groan when they saw me.

Agent Gonzalez was especially upset when I neared. "Ma'am! Go back to the car!"

"Gee, I'm sorry, *Ms.* Polanski." Mr. Fontaine's voice was saturated with bilious anger, but he affected a light tone as he smiled, flaring, at me. "I heard everything on the police radio, and deliberately misleading the police is a felony. And even if they're not here, *we're* not going anywhere."

The "we" wasn't a group of potential sundae schoolers after all. In addition to the cheerless Sissy, they included ten or so other, frowning people, including Mr. Krimm and Father Lansky, the priest from St. Matthews. So *they'd* been in on the operation the entire time, too! Everything made perfect, disappointing sense now, but I simply couldn't allow these people to set me up as the patsy for their smuggling operation. It was no-holds-barred time.

A car pulled into the parking lot at this point, and although I hoped it would be Darren, who had another set of keys, it was just a little, red-haired woman wearing a parka with artificial fur at its edges.

I wasn't sure why Mr. Fontaine hadn't accused me yet of smuggling drugs, but I had the advantage of knowing what the ATF now knew. Or thought they knew.

While I mentally perfected my trap for Mr. Fontaine before things got any further out of hand, I sensed Agent Gonzalez's agitation as he watched the red-haired woman. Mr. Fontaine and his mob had their backs toward her, and it appeared that they weren't yet aware of her presence. Clearly, she was an ATF operative, possibly a double agent who'd infiltrated Mr. Fontaine's cabal.

I had to distract them. "Agent Gonzalez knows all about us."

Mr. Fontaine frowned towards his gang members. "*Everyone* knows all about you."

"I mean *us*. I've already told him everything, Mr. Fontaine. Anything you say can and will be used against you in a court of law."

"How dare you read me my rights! You really are disturbed. And if you think this is going to get me to move, you've got another think coming."

I surreptitiously watched over Mr. Fontaine's shoulder as the red-haired woman approached the main entrance to the building. "But the metal shop students! And the elking hour..."

Oddly, someone hidden in the lobby extended a sign into the middle of the glass door, and the woman read it and turned back toward her car. The sign then immediately vanished.

"The *elking* hour?!"

Before I'd had an opportunity to process what I was witnessing, Agent Gonzalez grabbed my arm and pulled me away from Mr. Fontaine.

"Agent Gonzalez, I have to stay here! It's the only way I can prove my innocence!"

"I'm sorry, but this is getting too dangerous. I've got to bring you into headquarters."

"But the bomb!" My threat didn't even slow him down, possibly because it was several cover stories back, at this point. I could feel my pulse under his firm grip and knew a physical altercation would be hopeless.

Mr. Fontaine only followed us so far, but his voice continued to claw at us as we approached the sedan. "What you're doing is entirely illegal, and I'm going to see to it that this whole thing is shut down permanently and you get the mental help you obviously need!"

I couldn't resist getting one final, damning statement out: "They already know about your involvement, Mr. Fontaine! I'd suggest you turn yourself in before things get any worse!"

But I knew he wouldn't. I had a blinding vision of the court case—Mr. Fontaine on the witness stand, snarling at me across the courtroom; my lawyer, the best and brightest from Madison, shaking her head slowly as the case against him continued to mount, thanks alone to his outpouring of vitriol. Harold was there, too, one eye fixed demonically on me, the other glazed and staring directly at an elderly juror, a native Sicilian quietly and continually making a gesture to stave off the evil eye under his coat. And then my exoneration came to me in a flash: the reporters asking about my harrowing time in prison; I, a media darling now, lightening the mood by offering wry comments about cafeteria mystery meat and awkward moments in the showers.

When I finally returned from my precognition and back to my fully conscious state, I realized that the car was moving again, the masked agent having returned to the passenger seat.

"Please don't ask me how, agents, but I know that this will all work out for the best."

But 815 Water Street was now far behind us. My premonition had come true: my Sundae School would never be.

None of it had worked out for the best. None of it.

The impact of the window on the bottom of my boots had a very particular vibration, almost as if my feet were ringing. Although it seemed like a very ordinary, gray midsized sedan, the Department of Alcohol, Tobacco and Firearms had clearly installed bulletproof glass in their back doors.

"What the hell are you doing?!" The masked agent reached for my shoulders, and I backed up into the rear seat, continuing my barrage on the window. "Yolanda!"

"Let me out!" My voice wailed out of me in an anguished desperation that must have embarrassed everyone in the car.

"Yolanda!" My name was muffled as he pulled off his ski mask.

Sam!

This stopped my legs, although they continued to vibrate.

He was actually smiling at me! "You're kidding, right? A government agent wearing a ski mask?! You can't really believe—"

"Sam! How could you do this to me?"

"Please, Yolanda. Just calm down."

Believing all the while that I'd been a master orchestrator, when in fact I'd been played as a pawn by everyone from the moment I'd set foot on Two Rivers soil!

Of course, if anyone was capable of finessing me, Sam was.

"So you and the ATF have been manipulating me all along."

"Yolanda! I'm not from the ATF—"

"So domestic terrorism, then. Sam, whatever you believe, that we should all live in fallout shelters and recycle our urine—"

"You actually think I could be a terrorist?!"

"So it's organized crime? Sam, I'm no Pollyanna. If you just let me get back to the school, then we'll set something up, some protection money on a weekly basis—"

"Jesus, only *you* would jump to every insane explanation except the truth!"

It was only then that all the pieces fell into place. "You've been working with Bruce Fontaine and the rest of them all along! That's why you didn't arrest him! And that's why you've wanted to destroy my—"

"Hey, hey, hey. Let's calm down a little, okay? Why don't you let me explain what's going on."

"Whatever he's paying you, I can pay you more—"

"I know that, but no one's paying me anything because I'm not working for anyone. Except for you, in a kind of crazy way."

"Sam, I find you attractive, but if I've ever given you the impression that I have an erotic fantasy about being abducted—"

"Yolanda! Take a break! Just take a break, okay?"

What story would he hand me now? But I had to listen. If nothing else, it would be a fascinating glimpse into the workings of an apparently warped, possibly criminal mind.

"Okay. So your plan was completely wacko, about the explosives and tricking the cops and everything. You would've ended up in jail. And you still might, but I think maybe we've got everything figured out."

"Who is *we*, Sam?"

"The Vortex Club."

"But I thought you weren't a member, anymore."

"Well, I just couldn't let you screw things up to that extent! None of us could. So we came up with a plan of our own. Which was almost as crazy as yours, only not quite."

Agent Gonzalez piped in here: "Uhhmm, I'm thinking crazier."

"Don't make things worse, Frank. She practically put her foot through the rear window. Do you want to pay Avis for that?"

I still hadn't quite determined why Sam had involved an ATF agent.

"So we kind of developed a plan of our own. We came up with this whole ATF thing to keep you away from your school, but since you called the police before we 'arrested' you, we had to go with our back-up plan. I found a car just like yours down in Chicago and had it painted to match your car. And we put stuff in it that looked a little like bombs and a rifle, but weren't, so that the police would just think that the "anonymous caller" was just mistaken about what it was, rather than deliberately misleading them. But now that frigging Fontaine figured it all out, you might still be in trouble, I don't know."

I was finding it extremely difficult to process anything I'd been told.

"And you would agree to cooperate with something like this, Agent Gonzalez?"

"Yes, ma'am." But he snorted derisively after this, effectively negating his statement.

"Yolanda! There are no agents! This is my friend Frank, who runs a bakery in Manitowoc! This was all fake, at least until Fontaine got involved. We were prepared for him, too, but he's a nasty son of a bitch. There's no telling what he'll do."

"Then let me get back to the school, Sam, so I can—"

"No one's at your school."

We'd pulled up to a small, nondescript office building. Agent Gonzalez turned off the car and looked expectantly at Sam, who looked expectantly at me.

"What do you mean? You sabotaged that, too?"

"Yolanda, you don't have a license to operate a business over there."

"But once everyone sees—"

"No! Not 'once everyone sees.' There's not going to be a 'once everyone sees.' That's not how things work! Look, just come with us."

There were lights on at the second story of the building, and sure enough, this was precisely where Sam led us.

He stopped before a door at the end of a hallway, the sign on it recently removed. "I own this building, too."

And Sam opened the door to reveal a fully functional ice-cream classroom.

Del was checking gallons of ice-cream in a large freezer. Darren was reading through some of his notes at the podium. Danny and his brother and sister were stacking the many types of sundae bowls and banana-split plates and fluted glasses for ice-cream sodas, and the long, long spoons that were used to ensure every particle of hot fudge could be reached if need be. There were my paper napkins and ice-cream scoops and a long, varied row of cold and hot toppings set up on a portable table in a corner. There were several rows of chairs at long tables, each with their own set of instruments, condiments, and decorations. In fact, the basic layout of my school room was mirrored here; it even had a wooden floor and smelled like lemon pledge, although how they'd done that, I couldn't say. And I knew that if I looked out the window, a river would be flowing nearby, there to catch the sunrise predicted in Danny's dream.

Everyone froze as they realized I had entered the office, their expressions electric yet neutral. No one knew how I would react.

And then I noticed the door. It stood in a corner, clearly the entry to a newly constructed storage space of some kind that protruded into the room a few feet. Del's handiwork.

Before I knew it, I found it growing nearer and nearer—my legs, still numb, functioned under their own power, moving as they had for years, only without any need of the rest of me. My brain, certainly, was otherwise occupied.

The silence seemed amplified by each person in the room, amplified and directed toward me, only it wasn't silence, it was something else, something palpable, a currency. I would've fainted at that moment, but I had to know what was behind that door, even though I already knew.

And I did: a human-sized rabbit. Mrs. Stefano, the final element of the prophecy, fulfilled. She hopped into the light and made real what had been only a hope for so, so long.

From inside her rabbit-head: "I don't want to go back to Green Bay."

"I know, Mrs. Stefano. You never will."

A cell-phone ring joined a wave of relief as it surged through the room. I could hear breathing now, and other noises of the world.

"Roxie?"

It didn't take much to redirect people's attention. I too, swiveled toward Sam; something serious was being discussed.

"When?... All right, come on back. Thanks." He turned to the rest of us. "We're not out of the woods, yet. Fontaine saw the sign."

"How many people did she get?" This from Del, who was sporting several, very theatrical sweat stains. I could only imagine how much work she'd directed and tackled, moving most everything from my school to this, real one.

Sam gave me a preliminary grimace. "That's why we had to go to Water Street just now. Roxie had been standing outside the front door to redirect people over here, but when Fontaine and his goons showed up, we had to get her your key so that she could get inside and still let people know to come over here without Fontaine noticing. But he noticed."

Del was still a little out of breath. "So how many people are coming?"

Again, the frown. "One."

"I mean, besides Fontaine."

"One."

"One?"

I knew who it was: "The lady with the red hair."

"It must be."

Everyone had stopped moving again. All eyes were fixed on me.

The truth of everything that had happened so overwhelmed me that I initially and briefly resented the assumption that I'd be able to respond to the situation quickly and with any amount of self-assurance.

But that was exactly what I did.

"Then our pupil will be here any minute. Darren, are you ready to begin class?" The nod was all I needed. "Sam, you make sure everything is in place here. Danny, Chelsea and Shay, clear away all of the items on these desks; just leave places for our student and for the rest of us. Mrs. Stefano, be ready in your warren for my sign."

Del's presence, rusty iron, stood by on my right.

"Del, you're coming with me."

The freezer door was slammed a little harder than it needed to be. "Are we going to bust some Fontaine ass?"

"In a manner of speaking."

"Well, I'm ready to bust some Fontaine ass in whatever manner you speak."

16

But where do we go from here?

Sam's building had been erected in the 1960s, when all commercial construction seemed to have been done on a seven-eighths scale. Consequently, the office doors we passed for dentists and doctors were a little narrower, the hallway a little tighter. It put me on edge.

So, instead, I simply focused on the musky scent that trailed Del, another tribute to her recent, Herculean efforts. I pictured all her grunting and straining, and was honored.

"So he's probably going to have the police with him, the little fucker."

"I'm sure."

"Why don't you let me handle it, Yo-yo? If you show up, they're probably going to arrest you."

The elevator seemed as if it were built for one and three-quarter persons.

"No. I think I've got the perfect way of dealing with Mr. Fontaine."

"Cool. So what's the plan? How are we going to get the redhead to class while getting him off our ass?"

"We're not."

"But I was thinking that we would—" And here, she sucked in air, blew it out. "Okay. Just tell me what to do."

Just tell me what to do. At long, long last, Del had learned to accept reality, humility—and me as her maternal authority! I was blessed with yet another flashing image of the future: Del, at a grocery store, relentlessly in search of a cantaloupe, digging through melons here, demanding satisfaction from skinny stock boys there. Suddenly, she's reminded of our time together, and her rough, capable hands close around a honeydew, satisfied, peaceful.

"But I still get to fuck him up at some point, don't I?"

I'd had a vision of the future. There was no telling exactly how far into the future it would be—twenty, thirty years, perhaps.

"All of this was your doing, wasn't it, Del. The whole plan to help me. No one else could have carried it off."

"Actually, it was all Sam's idea."

The elevator dinged at us to indicate that we were nearly at ground level.

"Sam? But he said he'd never—"

"He'd never what? Just like Roxie 'would never'—with me? Well, she probably never will, but you know what Buddha always says: Asking is its own Reward."

I, however, was having difficulty putting the words together to ask anything.

"Come on, Yolanda! We're almost there! What do you want me to do?"

I refocused: "Just follow my lead. The red-headed lady *and* Mr. Fontaine are going to take our class."

"What?"

And the elevator doors slid open to reveal Mr. Fontaine, his daughter, and three police officers standing in the tight lobby of the building.

"It's the only way." I summoned up my most winning smile for my adversaries. "Mr. and Ms. Fontaine! Officers! Welcome."

"That's her." Mr. Fontaine didn't even bother to look me in the eye.

The lead officer approached, her hands on her multifarious utility belt. "Ma'am, this gentleman seems to think you deliberately called in a false 911 report and are operating an illegal business here."

A distinct advantage: the officer didn't appear to like Mr. Fontaine much. This would definitely come in handy during the first phase of my plan, which included dismissing any possibility of criminal charges against me.

"Mr. Fontaine is a very civically minded individual."

"Ma'am?"

"There is no business in operation here. We're just a group of friends getting together to make some ice-cream sundaes. No money is changing hands, I assure you."

"Then she should be arrested for false advertising."

"As soon as I became aware that what I was doing might've been against the law, I stopped."

"You've known that for weeks."

"I've known what *you* told me, Mr. Fontaine."

"Oh, for gosh sake, just arrest her!"

His face had years earlier frozen into a sneer that he could modify into any one of an array of sneers, each based on a particular situation. I could see that now. Mr. Fontaine had his groveling sneer, and his enraged sneer, and his mocking sneer, and his threatening sneer. It was all quite pathetic.

But something I think I'd known all along became clear to me in that instant, as he provided me with the most ominous sneer in his arsenal. I understood precisely why I'd just told Del that Mr. Fontaine would be constructing frozen concoctions with the rest of us in a few moments: because he was exactly what I'd set out to change about Two Rivers all those months earlier! *He* was the eye turned away from progress and beauty and the unknown. *He* was the heart closed up by fear to simple joy, taking, taking and never giving. *He* was the mind that dropped itself onto a sharp, unrelenting track and followed it and followed it and followed it, never to pause or coast or acknowledge the other tracks stretching out in every direction, twisting and looping and soaring into infinity. My ultimate duty lay in curing the little old man before me of his sad, burning sneer at life, his voracious desire to consume, heedless of the destruction left in his wake.

Moreover, by offering Mr. Fontaine the secret of celebrating the present, rather than resenting it, I would be accomplishing everything I'd initially set out to do when I'd embraced a young boy's prophecy so many months earlier. That was because once he learned how to participate fully in the now, his influence and prestige in our small community would spread the word in a general blossoming, an awakening for each and every citizen. Soon, everyone in Two Rivers—and eventually anyone else with an open heart—would hear of the miraculous transformation within Mr. Fontaine. They would have no choice, then, but to embrace the opportunity to live a sneer-free lifestyle themselves, thanks to a few gallons of cherry walnut brownie and a little experimentation.

Perhaps Danny's angel had been aware of this all along! After all, "Saint Fatima" was very similar to "St. Fontaine." I found myself wondering if before me were standing a future beatific soul, a soon-to-be revered convert of the holiest order. (Perhaps there was just a little corner, well into the shadows, where an artist could include my image on St. Fontaine's icon, the rumored wise crone of the legend.)

"Ma'am. Ma'am? That still leaves the report of an Oldsmobile with a bomb in it. Did you call that in?"

I would tackle this one, too. "Yes. I thought it was a bomb. You see, I own what's fast becoming a rather rare car, so when I saw one that looked so similar to mine—here in Two Rivers, of all places!—I stopped to take a quick look. And when I did, I thought I saw some suspicious articles in it. So they weren't really dangerous?"

"No, ma'am. It was just a sack of oats and a pink water gun. But the car's registered to you."

I'd forgotten that Sam has switched the license plates. Why did he have to be so efficient and brilliant?! "Yes."

"Do you know why?"

"Well, you know, it's a funny story." But it wasn't a funny story. In fact, there was no story, funny or otherwise, forming in my mind. If I mentioned the real reason Sam had swapped the tags, I would implicate him in the whole affair, as well as incriminate myself. But who else would have done such a thing?

So I responded the only way I could: "I put the license plate from my car on the other one."

"Ma'am, that *is* against the law."

"Is it?"

Mr. Fontaine snorted. "For the love of Pete, arrest her! She's dangerous, and she's disturbed! What do I have to do in this town to get someone to arrest her?!"

"Sir, please."And the officer returned her full attention, stern, inscrutable, upon me. "Ma'am, why did you put your license plate on the car in question?"

At this point, I giggled. I actually giggled. It was something I hadn't done in years—decades! Yolanda Polanski's emotional palette was wide and rich, but it most certainly did not include "the giggle."

Yet I continued to giggle. If I were arrested now, everything would come out. My purchase of bomb materials and the semi-automatic rifle, Sam's involvement—and everyone else's—all would become public knowledge, and any hope for the Sundae School would be destroyed. And yet, the best I could manage to do was giggle, and it was getting shriller by the second.

Everyone in the lobby was frowning at me now, horrified by my lack of control. Still, I giggled, tears coming to my eyes, the blood pulsing in my neck and cheeks. I was even drooling, and my nose had begun to run. The worst part of it all was the look in Del's eyes: her mother/heroine was failing her.

"Yo-yo, you crazy nut! Sorry, but Yolanda's been so busy lately that sometimes, she just has to have a good laugh over everything, or she'd totally crack up!" Del put her hand on my back, patting more gently than I thought she ever could. "It's so silly, this whole license plate thing."

Although I was profoundly incapacitated, I could still recognize a car's lights flash in the parking lot. My red-haired, lone pupil!

"And what's so silly about it, ma'am?"

"Look at her! She's insane! Why are we even discussing this! Just take her down to the station!" This was from Mr. Fontaine's daughter, who was rapidly developing a set of sneer-exclusive expressions, herself.

"Please, ma'am! I'm not going to do that unless I have sufficient cause." It was a relief that the police officer was focused on Del now, but it was a guilty relief. "Now, why were license plates taken off of one car and put on another? If I don't get an answer, we *will* all be going down to the station."

The red-head was approaching the door.

Del shook her head, good-naturedly. "We don't need to do that, officer! She did it because the car she thought had a bomb in it didn't have license plates, and she was worried that the police wouldn't be able to identify it unless it did. So she put hers on there for you guys. Look, I know it's not the brightest move, but she thought there were terrorists in Two Rivers. She was just doing what she honestly believed was best for her country. How can you blame her for that?"

I'd immediately stopped giggling the moment Del began her speech. I'd managed to dry my face of all its fluids and now grinned meekly at my potential arresting officer, who skeptically processed what Del had just offered her.

The student had become the master.

"What?! Officer Heidelmann, don't tell me that you're going to fall for that, are you? Something else is going on here!"

The red-head now stood outside the door and peered in, confused at the scene.

Officer Heidelmann squinted at me, reviewing laws and procedures, weighing the bad with the good, the lawless with the mistaken.

"Officer—"

It was all Mr. Fontaine had to say. I saw something change in Officer Heidelmann's eye, a stone that finally rolled down its German Alp. "Ma'am, I'm going to issue a citation for failing to display proof of current registration. If you'd like to hold on here, I'll be back in a moment."

She and her officers turned toward the door.

"You've got to be kidding—"

"Sir!"

"But you can't just—"

"Sir, if you say anything else, I may still make an arrest."

Mr. Fontaine shoved past the officers and opened the door. "I'm calling Mueller right now."

"That is your right under the law, sir."

After Mr. Fontaine and his daughter pushed out into the empty night, I heard one of the male officers mumble something under his breath that sounded quite like "douche-wad" just before he and his cohorts passed the redhead and strolled toward their cruisers. I had failed Mr. Fontaine—and ultimately Two Rivers—but there was no time to process this. I had a student approaching me with needs of her own.

I leaned into Del. "You get her upstairs no matter what. Tell her anything you need to." I smiled at the woman as I passed her. "Who could have imagined what a fuss would be made for not properly displaying a car registration!"

The redhead smiled uncertainly, then much more certainly. "Oh, hey! I know you!"

But there was still time to rectify the situation with Mr. Fontaine. I couldn't allow him to get away and so didn't break my stride toward the door. "Absolutely! Del, will show you this young lady up to the classroom?"

And with that, I joined the police and my adversaries in the floodlit parking lot, perhaps the greatest challenge of my life directly ahead of me now, sneering.

He drove an Oldsmobile, too, and as I approached, I attempted to use this commonality to inspire a flush of camaraderie with the man. But the Oldsmobile he was unlocking was much newer than mine; I couldn't see much of anything in common with what was familiar to me.

As the salt crunched under my feet, I called upon my powers of prophecy once again for inspiration and guidance. I felt only the harsh, bony-fingered wind reach up my skirt.

"Oh, for Pete's sake." Mr. Fontaine had finally become aware of my presence, prompting a disgusted sneer—one of his most effective—as he stood at his door. "You know, I actually think it's a great idea, this whole Sundae School thing. Honestly. It could get Two Rivers a nice bit of really positive publicity. Aww, you didn't see that coming, did you?"

I felt him already attempting to bleed me of my resolve. "Well, that's certainly—"

"The problem I have is that it's being run by some pathetic, ridiculous nut-job who'd destroy any kind of positive media coverage the moment she opens her mouth in an interview and the world finds out that she actually, really believes that she's 'saving Two Rivers from itself with ice cream.' Oh, the nut-job I'm referring to would be you, dear."

The daughter had paused her car twenty feet away, and she watched us, the eerie glow of her instrument panel accentuating her nostrils and budding jowls. At that instant, I didn't mind if I never saw her again.

"Mr. Fontaine—"

"You know, I just can't figure out how you haven't already been locked up. Some of the things you've done! And the craziest thing about you is that you think *you* could ever help *us*! When you're the one that needs help so desperately! I mean, that's really rich. It really is."

"You could help me, Mr. Fontaine."

"Of course I could." He opened up his door, revealing a heartless, gray interior without a velvet pillow in sight. "But I never would."

Hanging off of his rearview mirror were dog tags. Judging by his age, he'd probably fought in Vietnam.

I was momentarily mesmerized by his memento, which seemed to mirror perfectly the desolate atmosphere of the car's cabin. Just as Mr. Fontaine had shown no pity to the Viet Cong, his Oldsmobile's interior showed not an atom of compassion for its occupants, all hard, cold leather and stiff, heedless edges. Graciousness had been ripped away and lay bleeding in the snow, denied and left to be ashamed of its own existence.

I had found the key to the only language Mr. Fontaine would understand.

"Go fuck yourself off, Fontaine."

A derisive sneer. "Excuse me?"

With every ounce of energy, I forced a low, sharp self-assurance into my voice. "Why don't you go and kiss my ass. Hole."

He dropped heavily into the driver's seat. "Well, at least I didn't see that coming."

"How would you like it if you just, just, if I just shat in your hair."

"Shat?! Anyone who knows the past tense of that word probably shouldn't make it common knowledge."

"Does that piss you off? Does it fuck you up?"

"I think those have two, separate meanings—"

"What are you going to do about it? Go fuck yourself over?"

"Once again, I don't think you quite understand—"

"You're not going home, Fontaine. You're staying right *fucking* here."

"Actually, the emphasis should be on 'here,' rather than—"

"This isn't up for assing debate. You're marching back into that building and taking the class with the rest of us, penis-features."

"Oh, my goodness."

"Look, I know the only thing that gets through to butt-pirates like you, and that's butt-pirates higher up on the food chain. Well, ass-personality, this butt-pirate is giving you a direct order. Get off your keester-cheeks and back in there, pronto!"

He chuckled and slapped his thigh. "I don't believe it. I actually want to stay and hear this! You've gotten so insane it's actually entertaining!"

"Just do it, *douche-wad*!"

"No." Mr. Fontaine's eyes remained fixed on his view of the quiet street out of his windshield. "Are you getting all of this, Officer Heidelmann? Did you hear what she just called me?"

I turned to find that Officer Heidelmann was standing a few feet behind me, her lips pulled down in a pantomime of suppressed laughter. She simply handed me a ticket and walked back to her police car, her shoulders shuddering in spasms of amusement.

"You see? That's how crazy you are."

I dropped down next to Mr. Fontaine, immediately shedding my Vietnam-drill-sergeant persona, which didn't appear to be having its intended effect, anyway. "Mr. Fontaine, what do I have to do to convince you to join us? Because without your support, we'll never be able to keep the Sundae School going. I know that."

"That's absolutely right."

"So what do you want?"

"I want to run it."

Somehow, I'd always known that this was what was in his deepest heart, another of my premonitions that had come true. "You want to run it."

"And I want you out. Permanently."

It was at this moment I became aware that Mr. Fontaine had never once bothered to look me in the eye that evening. What had his daughter's life been like, those decades and decades of mornings at the breakfast table, dreading such effortless invalidations?

"Vietnam must have been hell."

"For the love of God! Those dog tags are my son's. He was killed in Iraq. So I'm afraid I don't respond to army captains hurling abuse at me because I've never even been in the military. I just want your Sundae School. Now."

How did either Fontaine survive those endless, haunted mornings, choking down dry toast and each other?

"But my team-members—"

"—will all be replaced. Look, I know this town, and I know everyone who runs it. If you really want to improve Two Rivers, you'll remove yourself from the equation. Because you're the problem right now. You can never make it work. And even if you could, I promise you I'd personally see to it that you never do."

"Mr. Fontaine—"

"No. The only two choices you have right now are 'yes' or 'no.' This is not up for 'assing debate.'"

The most surprising thing about Mozambique was how cold it got in the mornings, in the highlands. There were banana plants scattered around that seemed to draw the eye, flapping and waving against their smaller-leaved, muted neighbors. In the mornings, the first thing I would always notice was the chill in the air, and then the small banana plant near the hut with a rolling fist of fruit that looked far too small and fat to ever eat. I never did get a chance to try them.

On that last morning, I'd awoken to find a man with a machete standing outside my door, right next to my banana plant. I didn't understand what he was saying, but it was clear he wanted me to make a decision. A mountain wind swooped down at that very moment, and the banana plant turned away from the scene before it, an African, too.

My decision had been to run away—from my hut, from Mozambique, from Africa. Machetes were very sharp. (Claude had once attempted to remove the cork from a magnum of champagne with a machete. The Belgian ambassador to New Zealand doubtlessly still awoke in the middle of the night drenched in sweat since witnessing *that* party trick gone awry.)

The classroom was quiet when I returned, and all the windows had been opened, so the room was freezing. Once again, all eyes were on me—including Father Carol, who'd managed to sneak in during my absence and had set up his work area next to Sam's.

No one else had snuck in.

Del was the first to move. "Yolanda, it would have totally sucked if that guy had been here. Forget about Fontaine. Let's just get started."

Ten people. My first and last Sundae School. Only ten people.

I felt tears coming to my eyes. It was almost too much to bear.

But there were innocent children; there was a five-foot-tall rabbit in the closet. I rallied for the last time.

"Mr. Darren, would you care to start the lesson?"

There were cheers then; there were broad smiles that reminded me of ice cream, somehow, perhaps because they were summer smiles, sprinkler smiles. The winter had been so long in Two Rivers, and it wasn't even half over. But here, now, it was warm.

My place was next to the originator of all that surrounded me. I had to keep up a strong front for a little while longer. "So, is this just like your dream, Danny?"

"Not really." He depressed the release button on his ice-cream scoop over and over, entranced. "But it's better because it's real."

I wished I could've believed that.

Then Darren began his instruction, and he was nervous at first, his voice soft, almost afraid of itself. But the goodwill in the room buoyed him; in a few minutes, his demonstration became confident, his art effortless. There were perfect spheres of vanilla to begin with—vanilla, that flavor that was almost something other than ice cream. A canvas. A foundation. And soon, there were fruit flavors and dense, designer blends. There were handy tips and traps to avoid.

The chilly air kept our work poised in a state of eternal grace, and I couldn't help but wonder if our angel hadn't passed into the room with the winter, helping pause the cruelties of time just for her short evening, just to revel in this devout submission to her will. Perhaps she swept over Del, steadying the pyramid of marshmallow-themed bricks, guiding her work-worn hands to craft such a rising, such a benediction. And I could almost hear the angel, accompanied by a calliope of all things, whispering in Sam's ear instruction more perfect than words, a language of sweetness that led him to exactly the right amount of pineapple sauce over precisely the right flavor of sherbet in a faultlessly immaculate draping.

And were there downy wings gathered around Father Carol, who built long and miscellaneous rows of ice cream, each scoop somehow complementing each of its neighbors, an inspired patchwork of contrast and harmony. Did a divine hand steady those of the children, whose work might have been more haphazard than most but was also more visceral, laying bare connections between coconut and strawberry, cookie dough and crushed peanuts that had been there since mankind had first tasted but which simply needed a night like this and souls like theirs to arise into glorious being?

Roxie seemed almost to be in a state of prayer. Each flourish she made was an exaltation: the whipped cream a light, crowning sacrament, the chocolate shavings a dusting of faith, every maraschino its own, sweet concentration of praise. Agent Gonzalez's work was masculine, unapologetic, with ninety-degree angles and razor-straight walls of pistachio that could only have been modeled on the ancient plan for Jericho. Even the strange, redheaded pupil had been touched by the celestial. Her creation was perhaps the most inspired of all: a house of worship, with candy-cane doorframes and biscotti windows and a pitched roof that glinted in the light—golden sprinkles that, rather than repelling the elements, invited contact instead, a tongue, a finger, a wish that all gables could be so happy. And the happiest blessing for me: a delicate, crystal flute filled with champagne sorbet shot through with gold leaf and layered with an ephemeral elixir of passion fruit. My teacher, my Darren, had not forgotten his redeemer.

And through it all wove our mascot, our faithful idol: a rabbit who hopped from one delight to the other, transforming into motion and sight the undercurrent that enjoined us all, a praising of the present and of the joy of joy.

There had been so much laughter, and promises and exclamations and murmurings of hope, but the room once again grew silent as we each neared completion, the frozen monuments absorbing the revelry surrounding them, the potential energy somehow stored within, ready to burst forth with the impending consummation.

But denying ourselves for a moment longer, we inspected our own work, the creations of the others. Each was so unique, so expressive of the artist who had created it that we were cowed into silence by the enormity of truth before us. If anything was said, it was to confirm our suspicions that this creator had focused on fresh fruit, that one on the depths of fudge and chocolate and cocoa. And if the happiest part of our souls could've been expressed through sugar and cream, we were all witnesses to this inflorescence.

It was surprising at first, then so clearly appropriate, to find that Mrs. Stefano had made her rabbit mouth functional and that she should be the first to taste of our imaginations. She took up one of the longest spoons in the room and dipped it into this soaring minaret, that lava pool of hot fudge. The act was a holy sacrament: we were obliged to make an offering to the individual present who most closely represented our Savior of the Classroom. In fact, if there were no angel who'd swept into that room borne on the December night, Mrs. Stefano was that and more, a manifestation of grace and preternatural love, a carrier of good wishes and supplier of affirmation unbound.

Then it was time for the general tasting. Our work had been created for the ecstasy of destruction, and so we did, our spoons clinking against metal dishes and glass tulips, against rum-raisin-covered teeth. There was a moment—so brief!—when the confections seemed to subsume our other senses, so that all our contact with the world was ice cream, and our entire universe became a crunchy, raspberry, melting, golden lip-smack of a place. It was just a moment, but it had undeniably risen into our lives, always there to be called forth throughout the string of scenes and stories that stretched ahead of each of us into further Decembers, further quarters.

I was inconsolable. Although I laughed and sampled with the rest, the whole exercise only made more real the monumental extent of my failure. I'd failed Mr. Fontaine, I'd failed Two Rivers, I'd failed my friends, I'd failed in achieving the one goal that had consumed me for the better part of a year. How had I ever grown so sure that I'd make anyone's life a more joyful affair, that I could ever really make a difference? Whatever slight wound that might have been created by my departure would immediately heal over, the town glad to have the irritating, foreign object removed. There wouldn't be even so much as a scar here to commemorate my efforts. I was ineffectual. I was silly.

The spoon in my mouth was so cold, and I tried to focus on that—the temperature of nothing, the temperature of stillness. Why had I not taken Mr. Fontaine's offer? My mission would have at least been accomplished had I done so. The short night was already nearly over, and now all that the team—for whom I'd sacrificed everything—would have to show for it would be a few brown stains on their sleeves, a sugar coma and a gnawing unease whenever my name was mentioned.

"So why a cathedral, Clara?" This as Sam licked a flying buttress off of his spoon.

For some reason, the red-headed woman looked at me. "I don't know. I guess you can't take the Catholic out of the girl, right?"

I just wanted to slip away, at this point. Nothing could be said or done. (Claude considered the social escape just as challenging as Houdini's underwater thrashings, and he approached it in much the same way. At a formal dinner in Lausanne once, I'd actually smuggled a small ordnance in my purse, which he'd proceeded to detonate between courses, providing a puzzling distraction that had allowed him to avoid brandy with an especially lecherous jade importer.)

"You still don't recognize me, do you?" The woman was continuing to speak to me. "I was on the bus? To Sheboygan?"

(But Claude hadn't managed to avoid that importer, in the end. In fact, he'd become so involved in the trade that Time Magazine had actually declared Claude the "Jade King" of 1994, and he'd coasted on his fame until the Russian Jade Mafia tracked him down to a certain brothel in Biarritz.)

"I read all about you online—you and Danny. I was in the seat just ahead of you. That's probably why you don't recognize me. But I definitely recognize you!"

The others had grown quiet now, almost fearful. Why? Did they honestly think I'd let them avoid the clean-up work? "I can't imagine how you people managed to get all this ice-cream over here so quickly from the previous location! It truly is impressive. But the mess!"

Yet it was the red-headed lady who responded. "I was telling everybody else while you were downstairs. It was you."

I started in on my own mess. At some point, I'd managed to spill some cherry juice, which had hardened into flat, gelatinous O's scattered across the desk. I rubbed and rubbed, but it just seemed to spread the stickiness. (Claude had been able not only to tie a cherry stem with his tongue, but he could fashion them into letters. He'd spelled out little messages to me across cocktail tables in the more colorful bars of lower Manhattan that summer, slowly, drink by drink, just as we'd spent our nights together there, sultry and electric.)

"You were talking in your sleep on the bus that night—and pretty loudly. You kept saying 'Sunday school' and something about 'Father Day' or 'Father Shay?' So *you're* the reason Danny had his dream! Isn't that funny?"

If anything, the sticky mess before me was just growing larger.

"Anyway, it's no big deal. I just figured you'd want to know is all."

"Is there another roll of paper towel, by any chance? Because it's getting late, and I don't know how much longer I'm going to last."

Sam sat down in the chair next to mine, and he turned to everyone who surrounded us, absorbing something from each one as he slowly inhaled, the worst part of a troubled sigh. It almost seemed to be a raising of the guillotine.

"I kind of did a little snooping around in Sheboygan, Yolanda, after we found out about the fertilizer and rifle and everything. I know it was kind of sneaky that I went behind your back, but we were all really worried about you." Another sigh. "So we know why you were going there on the bus that night: your mom's funeral and everything. And that the money you've been spending on the Sundae School was what she left you."

The paper towels were disintegrating in my hands.

"I also found out you were working in Terre Haute as a paralegal before you took the bus to Wisconsin."

I'd stopped rubbing the desk at some point. My fingers were turning pinker in the cherry juice. Did blood stain your fingers pink, or did it just wash away?

"Of course, we've been kind of wondering why you came here instead of your mother's funeral, but now that we heard about Father Shay from Clara... look, we know he was the priest at your mother's funeral because I talked with him. And he told me that he was one of your Sunday school teachers. Is that why, I mean, did he ever—"

"Not to change the subject, but this, I'm afraid, is it for tonight. An awards ceremony would be redundant because everyone's creations were equally perfect." I pushed a pained smile forward here. "Unfortunately, and just as my premonition warned, The Two Rivers Sundae School just didn't work out. But I am learning to trust my gift, so don't worry. I'll know better next time; I'll never put a step wrong again. And even though I appreciate everyone's hard work, I am going to have to leave now. I'm just exhausted."

"And go where?" Del's voice was scratchy and soft at the same time.

"To bed!" But this sounded entirely too brittle; the sentiment immediately pulverized under its own weight. "To somewhere else."

And then it came to me in a flash: The Virgin Islands! St. John, St. John. There was an old fort there, overlooking the sea, vined and nearly crumbled into dust, the fingerprints of slaves and pirates and hurricanes covering every inch of stone. At that very moment, in Sam's office building, in Two Rivers, on the cold side of winter, that fort seemed a million miles away. But in a day, I knew everything could change as completely and freshly as St. John. (Claude had attempted to sell a fake doubloon to a local there and had ended up being named the godfather of the man's infant son.)

I rose quickly, firmly, although my legs burned up at me. "Winter in Wisconsin is really too much, so I'm setting off for St. John tomorrow. It's about time I felt the ghost of Bluebeard blowing through me again."

Sam placed his hand on my wrist. How did he manage to remain so warm in that cold, cold room? "Yolanda, I was a week away from becoming an *accountant,* for Christ's sake—"

But he was interrupted by a muffled cry of "No, no, no!" And Mrs. Stefano removed her rabbit head, her hair matted across her red, moist face. "You didn't *make up* the angel! It's you! Don't you see? *You're* the angel!" Her voice was a bit strident, so she said this again, more quietly. "*You're* the angel, Yolanda. Our angel."

My eyes passed over the piles and piles of plates, dripping and tipped over and flecked with little diamonds of walnut; the doilies, never adequate against the lines of caramel that crisscrossed them; even the floor, sticky with runaway clots and slick with whipped cream. It all made me realize just how much work had to be done to the room—and just how much work moving to St. John would be. The mess, the chaos that seemed always to challenge me!

"Mrs. Stefano, why don't we just clean all this up. Please." And so as we began our work in earnest, I turned back to my spilled juices, which would certainly and permanently stain the beige Formica of my desk, forever making real what might otherwise have passed into a kind of dreamland again: the first and last class of the Two Rivers Sundae School. Wordlessly, Del handed me a bottle of spray cleaner, and I wasn't sure if I was smiling because she knew just what I needed or because I could already feel the St. John sun in my hair. (It was even possible that I'd yet again run into Claude there—a reoccurring phenomenon in my life if there ever was one.) And then the other students joined in, quietly working together at removing what they could of any traces my presence might have left in the room, on the town. The Vortex Club was proving to be quite a capable team, after all.

But it was strange: for some reason, my gift of premonition had grown oddly silent about the future, as though upcoming events were cloaked in dove gray silk, offering only a glimpse of silhouette here, a distorted, provocative shadow there. I couldn't be sure whether the sweetness drifting across my mind was the exquisite perfume of jungle blossoms, or simply the fleeting echoes of Chunky Monkey.

Perhaps I would remain the following day in Two Rivers, simply to recover from my recent exertions and clarify my intuition. Or a few days longer—maybe even the next week—just to tie up the few, loose ends that still fluttered in the polar winds of the Midwest: a gun, a cat, a *real* Regency 98.

And plan my next move.

www.ingramcontent.com/pod-product-compliance
Lightning Source LLC
Chambersburg PA
CBHW031119030726
47496CB00002BA/598

* 9 7 8 0 9 8 5 1 6 3 6 3 1 *